PLAYING THE PART

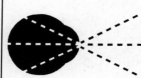

This Large Print Book carries the
Seal of Approval of N.A.V.H.

PLAYING THE PART

JEN TURANO

THORNDIKE PRESS
A part of Gale, Cengage Learning

GALE
CENGAGE Learning·

Farmington Hills, Mich • San Francisco • New York • Waterville, Maine
Meriden, Conn • Mason, Ohio • Chicago

LIBRARY OF CONGRESS CATALOGING-IN-PUBLICATION DATA

Names: Turano, Jen, author.
Title: Playing the part / by Jen Turano.
Description: Large print edition. | Waterville, Maine : Thorndike Press, a part of Gale, Cengage Learning, 2017. | Series: Thorndike Press large print Christian historical fiction
Identifiers: LCCN 2016041619| ISBN 9781410495686 (hardcover) | ISBN 141049568X (hardcover)
Subjects: LCSH: Actresses—Fiction. | Fans (Persons)—Fiction. | Stalkers—Fiction. | New York (State)—Fiction. | Large type books. | BISAC: FICTION / Christian / Historical. | FICTION / Christian / Romance. | GSAFD: Love stories. | Christian fiction. | Historical fiction.
Classification: LCC PS3620.U7455 P63 2017 | DDC 813/.6—dc23
LC record available at https://lccn.loc.gov/2016041619

Published in 2017 by arrangement with Bethany House Publishers, a division of Baker Publishing Group

Printed in Mexico
1 2 3 4 5 6 7 21 20 19 18 17

For Gretchen

1

October 1882 — New York City

"Forgive me, Miss Plum, but there's a gentleman outside demanding to speak with you. He claims to be your father."

Miss Lucetta Plum paused in the act of removing her stage makeup and turned, finding Mr. Skukman, an intimidating gentleman she employed to manage her overzealous admirers, standing in the doorway of her dressing room. "How fascinating, Mr. Skukman, especially considering my father died years ago."

Mr. Skukman arched a single dark brow her way. "Fascinating indeed." With that, he withdrew, pulling the door firmly shut behind him. Seconds later, the sound of what was surely some type of a scuffle drifted into the dressing room.

"This is an outrage," a man bellowed. "I demand you unhand me at once, sir."

Recognition of the voice was immediate.

7

Rising ever so slowly from a vanity stool upholstered in red velvet, Lucetta navigated her way across the cluttered dressing room. Stepping over a pair of high-heeled shoes she'd slipped off her feet the moment after she'd taken her last curtsy, she drew in a steadying breath and yanked open the door.

Exasperation mixed with a large dollop of annoyance coursed through her when her gaze settled on the gentleman Mr. Skukman was now muscling down the narrow hallway.

Knowing there would be little benefit in putting off what was certain to be a most disagreeable meeting, Lucetta lifted her chin. "You may release him, Mr. Skukman."

Mr. Skukman stopped in his tracks, glanced over his shoulder, and let out a grunt that sounded exactly how it had been intended to sound — menacing.

Lucetta barely batted an eye. While she'd hired Mr. Skukman because of his frightening demeanor and ability to make grown men shake in their boots, she was well aware there was a charming man behind the menace — a man who possessed an endearingly tender heart. That man enjoyed reading poems of a slightly romantic nature, and reciting those poems out loud in a soft yet dramatic tone of voice, when he thought no one was listening.

"Forgive me, Miss Plum, but I don't think it would benefit you in the least for me to release this particular man," Mr. Skukman argued. "He's obviously a most unpleasant sort, and I know you have little to no tolerance for unpleasant gentlemen."

"He is indeed unpleasant, Mr. Skukman, but —"

"I'm your father," the man yelled.

"You are *not* my father, Nigel," Lucetta said, holding up her hand when Nigel opened his mouth to obviously argue that point. "Officially, you're my stepfather, but ever since I was sixteen and you tried to force me to assist you with one of your nefarious schemes, I don't consider you part of my family. You're merely an unpleasant man my mother foolishly chose to marry."

Mr. Nigel Wolfe shook himself out of Mr. Skukman's hold and pulled his jacket over a stomach that was less than trim. While he'd once possessed boyish good looks, late nights with too much liquor and rich foods were beginning to take their toll on him. Nigel's jowls were heavy, and his complexion was pasty. Given the dark bags under his eyes, it was clear he hadn't slept well in days. His brown hair, now liberally streaked with gray, was mussed, and his general air

9

of neglect meant only one thing. . . .

He'd been gambling again.

"I need to speak with you privately regarding a matter of great urgency," Nigel said.

Lucetta refused a sigh. "Of course you do." Sending Mr. Skukman a nod even as she pretended not to notice the incredulous look her guard was sending back to her, she turned on a bare heel and headed through the dressing room again. Retaking her seat on the vanity stool, she watched Nigel from the reflection in the mirror as Mr. Skukman pulled her door almost closed before he took up his position directly outside it again.

Distaste settled on her tongue as Nigel strolled across the room and dropped into a deep-seated fainting couch, squishing the wig she'd recently taken off her head. He immediately took to scrutinizing his surroundings.

"The matter of great urgency . . . ?" she was finally forced to ask when Nigel seemed to have forgotten the business at hand as he continued perusing the room.

"Are those real diamonds?" He nodded to a necklace dangling from her mirror.

Picking up a jar of cream, she dipped a finger in it and then dabbed the cream underneath a blue eye with far more force than necessary, wincing when she unintentionally poked herself. "I'm sure they are, but since Mr. Skukman will be returning the necklace to a Mr. Dover later on this evening, it doesn't matter one way or the other."

"You're *giving* the necklace back?"

"Since I have no intention of paying the price Mr. Dover will surely expect if I keep his token of affection, of course I am." Lucetta snatched up a handkerchief and began blotting an eye that had taken to watering.

"That's incredibly foolish of you, my dear. You're neglecting a prime opportunity to secure yourself a tidy fortune."

Setting aside the handkerchief, Lucetta swiveled around and caught Nigel's eye. "While I would love nothing more than to continue discussing my admirers and their completely inappropriate gifts and expectations, tell me, what exactly are you doing in New York. And where is Mother?"

"She's back in Virginia at Plum Hill, preparing for a luncheon she's hosting to-morrow."

"Does she know you're here?"

"Who do you think insisted I seek you out after discovering I've landed myself in a bit of a pickle?"

A hint of something that felt remarkably

11

like hurt stole over Lucetta, taking her by surprise. She'd never shared a close relationship with her mother, having had more in common with her father, but . . .

"So if you'll just kindly fetch the deed to Plum Hill for me, I'll leave you in peace."

All sense of hurt evaporated in a split second.

"Forgive me, Nigel, but surely you didn't just ask me for the deed to Plum Hill."

"While it pains me no small amount to have to ask for a deed that should be in my name in the first place . . . yes, I did ask for the deed, and . . . I need it tonight."

"Do not tell me you tried to gamble away the plantation again."

"I didn't merely try, my dear, unfortunately, this time I succeeded."

"If I need remind you, Plum Hill isn't yours to gamble away."

"I'm well aware of that, but when I threw the promise of the deed into the game of cards, I wasn't planning on losing. I was certain I held a winning hand, but . . ."

Nigel shuddered ever so slightly before pulling out a pocket watch, took note of the time, and then shuddered again. "I'm under a bit of a time constraint, so if you'd just fetch that deed for me, I'll be ever so grateful — as will your mother who, again, *en-*

couraged me to seek you out."

Lucetta narrowed her eyes. "If Mother was so keen to encourage you to leave her without a roof over her head, why didn't she make the trip to New York with you?"

Nigel began inspecting his pocket watch. "I told you, she's hosting a luncheon tomorrow. Besides, you know full well that Susannah doesn't like to face the reality of having a daughter who treads the boards for a living."

"Mother's also not the sort of lady who'd want to face the reality of not being able to host luncheons in her very own home, which makes me question whether or not she really did encourage you to seek me out."

Nigel's head shot up. "Are you going to give me the deed or not?"

"Not — which I think you probably realized all along, but . . . even if I completely lost my sanity and wanted to hand you the deed, I couldn't because I no longer have the deed in my possession."

"You *sold* Plum Hill without seeking my counsel first?"

"Don't be ridiculous. Do you really believe you'd still be permitted to live at Plum Hill if I'd sold it to someone else? If you recall, I promised my father on his deathbed that I would always look after Mother. Selling Plum Hill out from under her would hardly be honoring my promise.

"For your information, Mr. Everett Mulberry has possession of the deed, but he's merely holding it for me to keep it safe, strictly as a precaution against situations like the one I currently find myself in. Furthermore, I've given him explicit instructions regarding the release of that deed — those instructions being that someone will need to present him with my very cold, very dead body."

Nigel smiled a smile that was less than pleasant. "That could be arranged."

It took a great deal of restraint to keep her temper in check. "I'm sure you do find the notion of my death vastly appealing at times, Nigel. Nevertheless, even though you're a remarkably disagreeable man, I don't believe you have the stomach for murder."

Nigel settled back against the fainting couch. "Probably not, but . . ." He suddenly brightened. "This Mr. Mulberry — he wouldn't happen to be one of the New York Mulberrys, would he?"

"He would, but before you continue on with what I know you're about to say — insulting me in the process, no doubt —

14

he's simply a friend of mine, married to one of my best friends, the former Miss Millie Longfellow. He's holding the deed for me because he owes me a favor."

"Would that favor be big enough that he'd consider making your stepfather a rather large loan?"

"No."

Folding his hands over his stomach, Nigel eyed her for a long moment. "That's too bad, but fortunately for us, we have another option available, and one that will keep me out of jail for not honoring a debt, or beaten to a bloody pulp, which might, indeed, be worse than a stint in jail." He drew in a deep breath, released it, and then drew in another as perspiration began to bead his pasty forehead.

Trepidation settled in the pit of Lucetta's stomach. "I'm not certain I like the sound of *we* having another option available. I had nothing to do with you losing something in a game of cards that wasn't yours to lose in the first place."

"We're family, and as such, our problems are shared." Nigel wiped his forehead with the back of his hand. "While I truly wish I *didn't* have to broach this particular option — because you're hardly going to like what I have to say — as you recently mentioned, you *did* promise your father you'd look after your mother. Because of that, and because you must know Susannah would be horribly distressed if I got hauled off to jail or harmed in any way, broach it I shall." He cleared his throat. "Do know that if I'd had the slightest inkling how events were going to play out, I would have never sat down to that particular game of cards."

"You've never turned down a game of cards with your friends," Lucetta pointed out.

Nigel's face, oddly enough, took on a tinge of green. "Oh, these weren't friends of mine," he began. "In fact, I'd never met any of the gentlemen before, but since they made a point of telling me how they'd heard about my reputation at the table, I certainly wouldn't have been comfortable refusing their kind offer of a friendly game."

Wrinkling her nose, Lucetta leaned forward. "Why in the world would you sit down to play cards with gentlemen who freely admitted they'd heard about your reputation for losing at the table?"

Nigel wrinkled his nose right back at her. "They heard I was remarkably skilled at cards."

"When you're not drowning yourself in a bottle of brandy, which, I hate to say, is something I'm afraid everyone knows you make a habit of doing most nights."

"I was *delighted* to accept the invitation after their flattering words," Nigel continued as if Lucetta had not spoken. "And was doing quite well, but then . . . I'm afraid I got overly ambitious and lost everything on a single turn of the cards. To my relief, Mr. Silas Ruff was incredibly gracious. When he discovered I might not actually have the deed to Plum Hill readily available, he offered me another way to honor my debt to him."

Lucetta suddenly found it rather difficult to breathe. "You sat down to cards with Mr. *Silas Ruff*?"

"Ah, wonderful, so you *do* know him." Nigel smiled. "He spoke most highly of you, my dear, and learning you're acquainted with him makes this so much easier to say."

"Makes what easier to say?"

"That Mr. Ruff is perfectly willing to take something in lieu of the deed to Plum Hill — something he seems very anxious to acquire. . . . That something being . . . well . . . you."

2

For the briefest of seconds, Lucetta thought she'd misheard him — until Nigel's bloodshot gaze began darting around the room, as if he didn't have the nerve to look at her. That's when she realized she hadn't misheard him at all.

The despicable man lounging on her fainting couch — a man who was unfortunately married to her mother — seemingly believed it was perfectly acceptable to offer up his very own stepdaughter as a means to honor a gambling debt, or more importantly, to save his own skin.

Tamping down the urge to throttle the man, Lucetta rose to her feet and pointed to the door. "Get out."

Nigel folded his arms over his chest and shook his head. "You're being unreasonable, Lucetta. Silas Ruff is a wealthy and influential man. Just think of everything he's capable of giving you, and . . . this is your way out of the Lower East Side." He nodded in a knowing fashion. "If you ask me, I'm doing you a favor."

The desire to throttle the man immediately returned. "While I'm sure you truly believe just that, I'm afraid I have no desire to abandon my principles in order to escape the Lower East Side."

"Principles don't guarantee a nice, cozy apartment, well away from the criminals I know operate in the neighborhood you currently live in."

Lucetta opened her mouth to argue the point but snapped it shut because the argument she'd been about to voice was rather pointless considering she no longer lived in the Lower East Side, not that her new address was common knowledge.

She now lived, thanks to the generosity of Mrs. Abigail Hart, in a completely respectable brownstone located in the heart of Washington Square, a brownstone she shared with Abigail and the members of Abigail's staff.

Abigail Hart was an influential lady, in her own right — one of the matrons of New York society — who had for some mysterious reason decided her deepest aspiration in her later years was to help young ladies living under difficult circumstances better

19

their lots in life. She'd recently invited Lucetta, along with Lucetta's best friends, Harriet Peabody and Millie Longfellow, to live with her in a most respectable, although not as fashionable as it used to be, neighborhood. Because Abigail's invitation had come at a time when Harriet Peabody's well-being had been in jeopardy, the invitation had been gratefully accepted, and though Harriet and Millie had found husbands along the way, Lucetta had continued living with her in Washington Square.

That Abigail had a distinct liking for meddling — and matchmaking, if the truth were known — was somewhat of a complication for Lucetta at times. But since Abigail had been successful with getting Harriet and Millie well settled, Lucetta hoped the lady's matchmaking tendencies would be appeased for the foreseeable future, which would allow Lucetta a bit of a reprieve from any and all matchmaking nonsense.

During that reprieve, Lucetta intended to convince Abigail that there was absolutely no reason to put any effort into introducing her to eligible gentlemen because Lucetta had no use for gentlemen at the moment. She was quite capable of taking care of herself and was fully content to continue doing just that for the time being, especially since she had yet to meet a man who saw through the unusualness of her face, or the curvaceous nature of her form, and . . .

". . . while I don't mean to rush you, my dear, do know that Silas is waiting for us in the lobby right this very moment. As I'm sure you're aware, gentlemen of his prominence really don't care to be kept cooling their heels for long."

Snapping out of her thoughts and back to the conversation at hand, Lucetta set her sights on Nigel again. He'd risen to his feet and was actually trying to smile at her — the smile causing her teeth to clink together. Lifting her chin, she marched to the door, pulled it open, and caught Mr. Skukman's eye. In return, her guard sent her a grim smile, cracked his knuckles, and immediately took to stalking Nigel's way.

Ignoring her stepfather's protests, Mr. Skukman grabbed hold of the man's arm and propelled him rapidly out of the room.

"What am I going to tell Silas Ruff?" Nigel demanded over his shoulder as he tried to wrestle his way out of Mr. Skukman's hold.

"I'm sure I have no idea." Shutting the door, Lucetta dusted her hands together and headed across the room again. Scooping up her shoes, she sat down on the vanity stool and stuffed her feet into the high heels, ignoring the large hole she'd acquired in her left stocking, one that allowed her big toe to stick through. Picking up a midnight-blue hat lying on her vanity table, one that complemented the blue-striped walking dress she'd slipped on after her dresser had gotten her out of her theatrical costume, she plopped it on her head. Before she could stick pins into it, though, her dressing room door opened, revealing Mr. Skukman again.

"We need to get you away from here post-haste."

Lucetta tilted her head. "Why do I have the feeling I'm not going to like what you're about to say?"

Mr. Skukman moved to her side, helped her to her feet, and hustled her to the door. "Silas Ruff is causing a scene in the lobby, claiming he's not leaving until he collects his winnings, which, as we both know, he believes to be you."

"So Nigel told him I wasn't being co-operative?"

"Indeed, right before he bolted out the theater door, which speaks volumes regarding the true nature of your stepfather." Mr. Skukman stuck his head out into the hallway, looked both ways, and proceeded to pull her from the room. "Miss Edna Hickley offered to distract Silas while I get you on your way."

"That was kind of her," Lucetta said as she teetered unsteadily down the hallway, the teetering a direct result of Mr. Skukman pulling her along at a rather fast clip.

"I don't know how kind it was since she is your understudy and has surely concluded that you might need to leave town for a while, what with the ruckus Silas is currently making."

Lucetta came to an abrupt halt, forcing Mr. Skukman to do the same. "Leave . . . town? Really, Mr. Skukman, that might be taking matters a bit far. Why, the social season has just begun, and ticket sales have been quite brisk. Besides that, everyone knows that Mr. Grimstone, that oh-so-mysterious playwright of *The Lady in the Tower,* specifically requested that I play the part of the lead heroine. He's certainly not going to be pleased if I abandon the role before the season gets into full swing. Why, he, as well as the theater, could suffer extensive losses."

"Losses or not, Mr. Grimstone will have no say in this, Miss Plum. Quite honestly, given his obvious esteem for you and your acting abilities, I have to imagine he'd prefer to find out you've gone missing over finding out you've stopped breathing."

"Silas doesn't want to kill me, Mr. Skukman. He wants to acquire me."

"You and I both know you'd never allow him to acquire you, and from what I just saw down in the lobby, the man seems to be on the verge of losing his sanity. There's a look in his eyes I don't care for at all, which is why we're going to get you into a hansom cab and on your way to Mrs. Hart's brownstone. Once you're there, I need you to pack as quickly as possible. I'll be around to fetch you just as soon as I'm able."

"You want me to hire a cab instead of traveling to Abigail's in my own carriage?"

"Indeed. It's not a complete secret that you now live with Mrs. Hart, which means it won't be too difficult for Silas to discover your direction after he learns you no longer reside in the Lower East Side. I'm going to try and feed him a false trail that will hopefully allow us precious time to get away."

Before Lucetta had an opportunity to voice another protest, she found herself sitting in a musty smelling hansom cab, barreling down Broadway at a high rate of speed, the speed brought about from the extra money she'd seen Mr. Skukman hand the driver.

Feeling a little queasy because the cab

seemed to be hitting every rut in the road, she tried to distract herself by looking out the window into the dark night, but with the buildings flying by so quickly, she settled for staring at her lap and breathed a sigh of relief a short time later when the hansom slowed.

Not waiting for the driver to assist her out of the cab once it came to a complete stop, she stepped to the ground, shaking her head when she realized Mr. Skukman had given the driver directions to let her off a good block from Mrs. Hart's brownstone, a clear mark of how determined he was to keep her safe, even from a driver she'd most likely never see again.

Stepping back from the cab after assuring the driver she did not need him to walk her to her door, she watched as the man flicked the reins over the horse and drove away, turning his head every other minute to look back at her.

Waiting until the cab disappeared from sight, Lucetta began walking through Washington Square, turning and striding down a narrow path once she reached Abigail's brownstone. Slipping around to the back of the house, she went in through a door normally reserved for the staff that led to the kitchen and practically jumped out of

her heels when a shadowy figure material-
ized right in front of her — a shadowy figure
that seemed to be holding a bat.

Reflexes born from living in the shady part
of the city for far too many years had her
hands balling into fists. But, before she
could take a single swing, a familiar voice
had her freezing on the spot.

"Miss Lucetta, what in the world are you
doing skulking into the house like a common burglar? I was just about to knock you
over the head with this bat."

Her hands immediately relaxed as a gas
lamp flared to life, bathing the kitchen in
soft yellow light. "Good heavens, Mr. Kenton, you scared me half to death."

Mr. Kenton, Abigail Hart's loyal butler,
stepped closer to her. "A situation that
could have been avoided if you'd used the
expected route of entering the house — that
being the front door." He cocked a white
brow her way. "May I assume there's a
reasonable explanation behind your peculiar
behavior?"

"I'm not exactly certain how reasonable
my explanation is, but . . . I've somehow —
through no fault of my own, I must add —
managed to land myself in a bit of a dastardly situation."

"Oh dear." Setting aside the bat, Mr. Kenton moved to her side and took hold of her hand, giving it a good pat. "And here I was just telling Mrs. Hart this evening that things seemed to be a bit too quiet of late, what with Miss Harriet and Miss Millie out of the house now."

"As circumstances would have it, I'm going to have to leave as well, at least until my dastardly situation gets resolved. I've only come back to say good-bye to Abigail and pack a bag."

Mr. Kenton squeezed Lucetta's hand and then tucked it into the crook of his arm as he steered her out of the kitchen. "I'm sure Mrs. Hart will have a few things to say about you disappearing into the night — none of them approving, I fear."

"I'm hoping she'll be groggy when I wake her up, so her disapproval will be kept at a minimum."

"Oh, she hasn't yet retired for the night."

Lucetta came to a stop directly beside one of the ancestral portraits that lined the hallway, a portrait that seemed to be watching Lucetta with a rather stern look in its painted eye.

"Why would Abigail still be up? It must be after eleven."

"Mr. Archibald Addleshaw returned from England only a few hours ago, and he and

Mrs. Hart have apparently lost track of the time as they've been catching up and . . . er . . ."

Alarm was immediate when Mr. Kenton abruptly stopped speaking.

"And . . . what?" she prodded.

"And . . . I just recalled that tea is very good for soothing the nerves. And because of your dastardly situation, your nerves must need soothing, so . . ." With that, Mr. Kenton released his hold on her and headed toward the kitchen again, his gait remarkably spry for a gentleman of his advanced age.

"I wasn't aware Archibald was expected home from England just yet," Lucetta called after him.

Slowing to a stop, Mr. Kenton heaved a fairly dramatic sigh before he turned. "Mr. Addleshaw wasn't planning on returning from England quite so soon, dear. But you can't be too surprised by this turn of events, especially since the blame for his early return can be laid squarely at your feet."

"Laid at *my* feet?" Lucetta repeated slowly.

"Certainly."

"I'm afraid you have me at a disadvantage."

Mr. Kenton heaved another sigh. "You've

not been cooperating with any of Mrs. Hart's ideas in regard to your future, so . . . she's summoned the troops."

"I haven't cooperated with any of her ideas because they've all revolved around getting me well settled with one eligible gentleman after another. I was hoping that if I ignored her outlandish suggestions, she'd lose interest in me and move on to another cause — one that actually needs her assistance."

"If you would have consulted me about that tactic, I would have told you that by ignoring Mrs. Hart's suggestions, you've simply managed to become a challenge to her." Mr. Kenton smiled as he shook his head. "She does so enjoy a challenge."

Having absolutely nothing of worth to reply to that, Lucetta watched as Mr. Kenton got on his way again before she turned and headed for the drawing room, Abigail's room of choice when she was in the midst of plotting. Reaching that room a moment later, she stepped over the threshold and considered the two people sitting on a small green settee with their heads bent closely together, a fire crackling merrily in the hearth in front of them.

Clearing her throat when her presence remained undetected for quite some time,

Lucetta smiled when the two heads shot straight up, right before two pairs of eyes blinked innocently back at her.

"Ah, Lucetta. I didn't hear you come in," Abigail Hart said, rising to her feet and hurrying to Lucetta's side. She kissed Lucetta's cheek and stepped back as Archibald Addleshaw, a distinguished-looking older gentleman with a full head of white hair, took her place.

"You're looking lovelier than ever, my dear," Archibald said, taking Lucetta's hand and placing a kiss on her knuckles. "Did you have a good evening at the theater?"

Lucetta smiled. "The performance went off without a single hiccup, but . . ." Her smile faded. "I'm afraid that after the show something concerning happened."

"Overenthusiastic admirers annoying you again?" Abigail asked.

"Silas Ruff is back in town."

Before Lucetta could so much as blink, she found herself sitting on the very settee Archibald and Abigail had recently abandoned, with Abigail sitting next to her, holding her hand, while Archibald sat in a chair he'd pulled up directly beside her.

She opened her mouth to assure them she was not overly distressed by the situation, but before she could get a single assurance out, Mr. Kenton returned with the tea. A moment later she found herself holding a cup of steaming liquid while Abigail, Archibald, and Mr. Kenton considered her with very worried expressions on their faces.

"Perhaps you were mistaken and Silas Ruff isn't truly back in town," Abigail finally said. "Why, after the embarrassment he suffered when he tried to ruin Oliver — in the midst of my ball, I might add — I would have thought he'd never show his face in New York again."

Lucetta nodded. "I would have thought the same, but he's definitely in New York — showed up at the theater tonight, and . . . I'm afraid that the unwanted infatuation Silas used to hold for me has evidently turned into more of an obsession."

Archibald sat forward. "Why would you believe that?"

"Because Silas has gone to extreme measures to get close to me. He somehow managed to locate my stepfather — which could not have been an easy task — and then invited him to join him in a game of cards."

Abigail sat forward as well. "You never once mentioned to me that you have a stepfather."

"Considering Nigel, my stepfather, just tried to serve me up as a means of honoring

31

his gambling debt to Silas, I'm sure you'll forgive my lack of acknowledgment."

"Your stepfather wagered you away in a game of cards?" Abigail asked.

"He tried." Lucetta summoned up a smile when a look of pure dismay flickered across Abigail's face. "Nigel has never been an overly intelligent sort, though, which is why I'm sure he didn't think matters through properly. He has no authority over me, so he can't offer me up as a means to honor his gambling debt. But by allowing himself to be drawn into a game with Silas, he's given that reprehensible man an excuse to pursue me again. That is why I'm being forced out of town until Mr. Skukman and I can figure out a way to deal with Silas once and for all."

Abigail shook her head. "You'll do no such thing, my dear. I'll hire guards to protect the house, and you know your Mr. Skukman will be more than diligent about watching over you at the theater."

"I'm not willing to put you in danger, Abigail," Lucetta began. "Silas Ruff is not a man to trifle with. He has the means to get his way in the end, and I wouldn't put it past him to threaten those I hold dear in order to get what he apparently desires at the moment — that being . . . me."

32

"But . . . where will you go?" Abigail asked.

"I considered making a trip to Boston to stay with Millie and Everett, but since I did mention Everett to Nigel, I decided that's not really a viable option. I have no doubt that Nigel will turn over any and all information he knows about me to Silas in order to save that less than honorable neck of his." Lucetta forced a smile. "I believe the only available solution is for me to board a random train and head for parts unknown, a solution that should make it next to impossible for Silas to follow me."

Abigail lifted her chin. "Absolutely not. It would hardly be acceptable for you, a young lady, to travel the country on your own. And don't tell me you'll disguise yourself. Heaven only knows what trouble that could cause in the end." She crossed her arms over her chest. "We need to think of somewhere else to hide you, somewhere Silas would never discover, and . . ." She stopped talking, her eyes began to gleam, and then she beamed a bright smile Archibald's way. "We'll take her to Ravenwood."

Archibald immediately began smiling as well. "That's an excellent idea."

Looking from one smiling face to the other, Lucetta frowned. "Where, pray tell, is

Ravenwood, or more importantly . . . what is Ravenwood, and who owns it?"

If anything, Abigail's smile turned brighter. "Ravenwood is a castle, located in Tarrytown, along the Hudson River, which means it's not far from the city. The castle is well guarded, comes with its very own moat, and . . . the owner of this castle can be counted on to be discreet, especially since he just happens to be my . . . grand-son."

3

Lucetta was coming to the conclusion that she was more flustered by Silas Ruff slithering his way back into her life than she'd let on because . . . why else would she have agreed to travel in the middle of the night to a castle, of all places, and one owned by Abigail's grandson, no less.

That Abigail was hoping Lucetta would find more than a safe haven at Ravenwood, there could be little doubt. But even knowing that, Lucetta couldn't deny she was feeling less anxious the farther they traveled from the city.

She was, much to her annoyance, terrified of Silas Ruff.

Silas Ruff, even though he'd recently been accepted in all the finest homes in New York, was one of the most reprehensible gentlemen Lucetta had ever had the misfortune of knowing. He was egotistical, wealthy, and belligerent, and he did not understand the meaning of the word *no*. He was also turning out to be a formidable adversary, apparently determined to possess her no matter the means required to do just that, simply because she'd tried to dissuade him from pursuing her.

He'd started stalking her at the theater months before, sending her roses numerous times per week, as well as invitations to dine with him. She'd refused every invitation, and had Mr. Skukman refuse delivery of his roses. Instead of discontinuing his campaign to win her over, though, Silas had increased his presence in the audience, leaving her unsettled and actually fearing for her safety.

When Silas had been released from his position working for Oliver Addleshaw, Archibald's grandson and husband to her very good friend, Harriet Peabody, Lucetta had finally been able to breathe a sigh of relief. His subsequent attempt to ruin Oliver had not worked in his favor, and feeling the displeasure of New York society, Silas had left the city for places unknown.

Now, however, he was back, and this time Lucetta had the unpleasant feeling he was not going to go away until he got exactly what he'd returned to New York for — her.

That notion was what terrified her the most. Admitting that terror was vastly uncomfortable and, quite honestly, set her teeth on edge.

She was a lady who prided herself on being utterly independent, but learning that Silas was determined to acquire her had left her feeling somewhat fragile, an emotion she didn't care for in the least.

The very term *fragile* brought up an image of a sweet and delicate young miss, something Lucetta hadn't been for a very long time, not since her father had died unexpectedly when she'd been barely thirteen years old, his death leaving her in charge of . . . well, everything. That circumstance had forced her to set aside her delicate ways, as well as the future she'd always been told was hers for the taking, and —

"I do hope you're not too put out with me for arguing with you about the best route to take to Tarrytown," Abigail suddenly said. "Especially since my route had us taking a tour of Sleepy Hollow."

Taking a firm grip on reins that had gone slack while she'd been lost in thought, Lucetta smiled at Abigail, who was sitting beside her on the small seat of their brougham carriage. "There's no need for you to continue apologizing, Abigail. I've always longed to travel to Sleepy Hollow ever since I read Washington Irving's *The Legend of Sleepy Hollow,* and now I can say I have. Besides, our detour only took us a few miles out of our way, and . . . how many people can say they've visited the Sleepy Hollow Cemetery in the wee hours of the morning?"

Abigail shuddered. "Probably none who possess an ounce of common sense." She shuddered again. "I really should have insisted Mr. Kenton accompany us on this madcap adventure. He would have sided with me on the whole stopping the carriage in the midst of the gravestones."

Smiling, Lucetta shook her head. "I'm not so certain about that. Mr. Kenton possesses a keen sense of adventure, and I'm sure he would have been pulled by the lure of reading a few grave markers in the moonlight, just as I was pulled. But you know he couldn't have accompanied us this evening, not with his being needed as an essential decoy in order to pull off Mr. Skukman's distraction plan."

"I, for one, am shocked that Mr. Ruff was so determined to find you that a distraction plan was even necessary," Abigail said with a huff. "Honestly, I think Mr. Skukman has the right of it and Silas has misplaced a bit, if not all, of his sanity."

"Which makes him more dangerous than I originally thought."

Abigail nodded. "Indeed it does, and makes me worry all the more for the safety of Archibald, Mr. Kenton, and Mr. Skukman." She crossed her arms over her chest. "I'm still not convinced Mr. Skukman's plan was a sound one, because you must know that it's highly unlikely Mr. Kenton will pass for me upon close inspection, even wearing one of my favorite traveling dresses and matching hat."

"Nor will Archibald pass for me, but trying to lure Silas away from where he'd taken up position in front of my old boarding-house was the best plan we came up with on such short notice." Lucetta released a breath. "It was only a matter of time until Silas discovered I no longer lived there, and given the questionable people wandering around the Lower East Side, well, I'm sure a few dollars would have earned Silas my new direction, and remarkably quickly at that."

"But there are a million things that could go wrong with Mr. Skukman's plan," Abigail said, clear worry marking her tone.

"Which is why you should take comfort in the idea that Mr. Skukman is a gentleman of many talents, one of those talents being incredibly proficient with a pistol." She opened up the greatcoat she'd borrowed from Abigail's coachman, a coachman she was currently impersonating, revealing a pistol of her own. "You should be relieved to learn that Mr. Skukman taught me how to shoot a few years back, and while I'm not as proficient as he is, I should be able to fend off anyone who gets too close to us, if we feel they're a distinct threat, that is."

Abigail narrowed her eyes. "You'd be comfortable shooting someone?"

"Well, no, probably not, but I wouldn't be opposed to giving them a good scare if I felt we were in danger. But thankfully, since we've reached Tarrytown, we're almost to our destination, and that means we should be out of any danger shortly." She reached up a hand and scratched at whiskers that were beginning to irritate her skin. "I won't be sorry to get out of this coachman costume — that's for certain. I forget that gluing whiskers on my face always has me breaking out into a bit of a rash."

"That you glue whiskers on your face often enough to know that is slightly disturbing," Abigail countered before she nodded to the river that they could now see through the trees. "There's the Hudson, so we must be close, but . . ." She suddenly

looked a little worried. "I've never approached the castle by carriage before."

Abigail leaned forward and peered toward
the river. "I've always taken a steamboat up
the Hudson to get to it. . . . Although I
should probably mention that I've never
actually docked at my grandson's private
dock, nor have I ever stepped foot inside
the castle."

Lucetta's mouth went a little slack. "And
yet you believe we'll be well received, even
though we're descending on Ravenwood unannounced?"

Abigail sent her a weak smile. "I'm almost
certain Bram will welcome us with open
arms, dear. Never you fear. Granted, I don't
share an especially close relationship with
my grandson given the acrimonious nature
of the relationship I share with his mother,
my daughter . . . but . . ."

She reached over and gave Lucetta's arm
a good pat. "Bram and I have corresponded
on a regular basis, and because of that, I
believe he'll be more than willing to offer us
refuge."

"What if your daughter's visiting him?"

"Iris is always in Cuba this time of the
year, so we don't need to worry about that.
What we do need to worry about, though,
is finding the castle from this vantage point

41

instead of from the river. I suppose we can hope Bram has some type of a marker leading guests to his home."

Finding that idea less than reassuring, but sending Abigail a smile of agreement nevertheless, Lucetta kept the horse traveling down the road, slowing its pace every time they neared a lane so they could read the small markers posted by those lanes.

"I think there's something right up ahead, and . . . oh . . . my," Abigail said, her voice trailing right away.

Bringing the horse to a stop, Lucetta leaned forward and looked down a well-maintained lane that led directly to what seemed to be some type of a gatehouse, but a gatehouse built to look exactly like a mausoleum, complete with stained-glass windows, stone sculptures on either side of it — not of the expected angels, but of . . . ravens. Turning to Abigail, Lucetta arched a brow.

"Should we drive closer?"

"I don't think this could possibly be the lane leading to Bram's castle," Abigail said. "I mean, why would anyone build a mausoleum to mark the entrance to their home?"

"I have numerous answers to that, but none I'm going to voice until we discover whether or not your grandson resides here.

Which, I'm sorry to say, could be a distinct possibility, since the castle's name is Ravenwood and there are two ravens guarding that building, and . . . if you look over the door, *Ravenwood* is etched into the stone."

"Oh . . . dear." Abigail pulled a pair of spectacles out of her pocket, shoved them on, and then looked closely at the building in front of them before immediately pulling the spectacles off again and repocketing them, shuddering ever so slightly as she did so.

"Would it be safe to say that your grandson possesses a slightly morbid nature?" Lucetta asked.

"Of course not. Bram's charming, and . . . the ladies find him to be completely delightful, from what I've been told — as I do believe I've mentioned to you a few times."

Before Lucetta could reply to that, the door to the mausoleum opened with an ominous creak. Abigail grabbed hold of Lucetta's hand and squeezed it, the squeezing becoming more pronounced as a man stepped through the door — a man who just happened to be carrying a rifle. He immediately headed their way, walking down the middle of the road until he came to a stop directly in front of the horse.

"Can I help you with something?" he

demanded in a rather intimidating tone of voice.

Not one to appreciate intimidation, Lucetta lifted her chin. "We're here to see Mr. Bram Haverstein."

"Mr. Haverstein didn't tell me he was expecting guests this morning," the man said before he turned and nodded to another man, who was just now moseying out from the dark depths of the mausoleum. "He tell you he's expecting anyone, Ernie?"

The man named Ernie shook his head. "Can't say that Mr. Haverstein mentioned a thing about any guests, Stanley, and he's not one to forget something like guests."

"We're not expected," Lucetta began as she nodded Abigail's way. "This lady is Bram Haverstein's grandmother, and she's here to surprise him, which is why you wouldn't have been apprised of our expected time of arrival."

Stanley stepped closer and scratched his head as he peered up at Abigail. "Begging your pardon, but I know Mrs. Haverstein, the grandmother Mrs. Haverstein, and . . ." He nodded to Abigail. "You're not Mrs. Haverstein."

"Of course I'm not, dear," Abigail said. "I'm the other grandmother, Mrs. Hart."

"I've never heard of another grandmother,

and I've certainly never heard of a Mrs. Hart." Stanley puffed out his chest. "Me and Mr. Haverstein are close, and I'm sure he would have mentioned another grandmother to me, if he did, indeed, have one."

Abigail beamed a bright smile Stanley's way. "How delightful to learn that my grandson maintains such a close relationship with members of his staff."

"If you were really his grandmother, you'd know that," Stanley pointed out.

Abigail's smile dimmed, the action causing what little remained of Lucetta's patience to run out.

"Now, see here, Stanley," Lucetta began. "Mrs. Hart and I have been driving all night in order to get to Ravenwood, and that is exactly why I'm going to insist that you step aside and allow us to proceed forward."

To Lucetta's concern, Stanley's only response to that was to cock the rifle, right before he sent what she could only hope was a warning shot into the air, the sound of the rifle blast sending their horse bolting down the road as fast as it could gallop.

4

"Excuse me for interrupting what appears to be a most delicious breakfast, sir, but I'm afraid we've had another incident."

Bram Haverstein lowered the coffee cup that had almost made it to his lips, releasing just a smidgen of a sigh when he caught sight of Stanley hovering in the doorway of the breakfast room. He would have loved to have been able to say that he rarely saw Stanley while he was attempting to eat a meal, but unfortunately, that wasn't the case these days. Ever since the ladies of Tarrytown had begun descending on his castle in droves — although why they'd taken to doing so, no one seemed to know — he'd spent many a meal with Stanley, listening to that man bring him up to date on all types of peculiar incidents that were transpiring in and around Ravenwood.

"What's happened now?"

"More unusual antics of the concerning

type, sir, but this time I'm not sure what the purpose of the interlopers truly was." Stanley stepped farther into the room and looked longingly at the silver pot resting on the sideboard.

"Perhaps you should pour yourself a cup of coffee and join me so you'll be more comfortable as you give me all the pertinent details of this latest fiasco."

"Don't mind if I do — thank you very much." Stanley moved to the sideboard, helping himself to a cup of coffee, along with a pastry and a plate filled with toast. He was soon sitting at the table, happily slurping his drink as he filled Bram in on the latest shenanigans.

"As calm as you please, they drove right up to the drive leading to Ravenwood, and didn't so much as stutter when they requested entrance." Stanley took another gulp of his coffee.

"But there were no young ladies present in the carriage?" Bram asked.

Stanley set down his cup. "See, that's the problem, sir. I'm afraid I might have startled their horse before Ernie and I were able to scout out the interior of their carriage. There very well could have been a young lady stashed in there. If that was, indeed, the case, well . . . it would explain the reason that elderly woman made the claim she was your grandmother."

Bram frowned. "While I'm not certain I understand the logic behind that statement, tell me this. . . . Should I inquire as to how you happened to startle the horse?"

"It would probably be in your best interest to avoid asking questions like that, sir."

Stifling a grin, Bram considered the man sitting across from him, a man who'd not been qualified in the least for a job at Ravenwood working on the grounds — or pressed into service inside the castle when the situation warranted it.

When he'd first run across Stanley, the man had been selling items of a questionable nature in the midst of the Lower East Side, an occupation that many a man down on his luck had resorted to in that dismal part of the city. Bram hadn't paid Stanley much mind, even though he had given the man a few coins out of his pocket, but Stanley had proven himself to be much more than a mere seller of questionable goods when Bram had been attacked by some unsavory characters looking for a bit of sport.

The two men had been together ever since, and once word had gotten out that Bram was more than willing to hire people from the tenements, others from the Lower East Side had joined their odd household.

Each of these members of Bram's staff possessed unique talents, but they were not talents of a domestic nature. Nevertheless, given Bram's unusual profession, he'd found some of these unique talents remarkably handy at times — especially since one never knew when skills such as pickpocketing or having far too much experience running confidence schemes would come in handy.

"If you'll forgive my impertinence, sir, the rest of the staff and I have decided that something must be done about all these unusual happenings here at Ravenwood, and . . . we've come up with a few solutions." Stanley stuck his hand in his jacket pocket, pulling out a handful of crumpled bits of paper that he took to smoothing out against the table.

"What do you have there?" Bram forced himself to ask.

Stanley didn't look up from his task. "Our solutions to restore order at the castle." He pulled one of the strips closer and bent his head over it. "This one suggests that you leave Ravenwood and buy a nice house on Park Avenue."

"That would only transfer the lady problem I'm experiencing at the moment because . . . Do you have any idea of how many unmarried ladies live in and around Park Avenue?"

Stanley crumpled up that particular strip of paper, tossed it over his shoulder, and moved on to another one. "Ah, here's a good one. Find a lovely young lady and get married, and . . . there are three suggestions — Miss Winters, Miss . . . I can't read the writing, and . . . *hmmm* . . . Tilda, the new scullery maid."

Stanley didn't even bother to ask Bram's opinion about that, but tossed the strip straight over his shoulder as he pulled another strip toward him. "Ah, another mention of marriage for you — this one recommending a lady by the name of Miss Buttermore." Stanley nodded. "I'm beginning to notice a trend, one that has you seeking out a wife, although . . ." He looked at the slip of paper again. "I do think Miss Buttermore might be the niece of Mrs. Buttermore, your cook, so . . ." That piece of paper went over his shoulder as well.

"I don't really see the need to continue with this, Stanley, given the somewhat problematic nature of the suggestions you've read so far, although do tell everyone on staff that I appreciate their concern."

Stanley heaved a sigh. "Begging your pardon, sir, but finding a wife might be exactly what you need. Why, even though I've never married, I understand that wives can be a great source of affection and companionship, and if you were to settle your affections on a single lady — such as . . ." He pulled another strip to him, tossed it aside, pulled another, read it, and smiled. ". . . a Miss Cooper, who, it is noted, is quite pretty — why, I have to imagine Ravenwood would no longer be inundated with ladies on a daily basis." He smiled. "A wife would also put an end to the rumors swirling around the countryside that you're the mysterious rider galloping around on a black steed at all hours of the night because you're up to something . . . interesting."

"I'm not getting rid of Storm, even if I do eventually settle down and get married. Although . . . calling him a galloping steed is somewhat amusing, especially since he almost never travels faster than a plod."

Stanley abandoned the strips of paper to pick up his coffee cup. "I don't recall mentioning a need to get rid of your horse. If you'll recall, I suggested you acquire a wife."

"And you believe that will put an end to

the rumors as well as put an end to all the shenanigans currently happening at Ravenwood?"

"If you're married, people will assume you prefer to spend the nights curled next to your ladylove, not gallivanting around the Hudson Valley. And, unmarried ladies, along with their matchmaking mothers, will no longer have a reason to descend on Ravenwood in droves if you settle your affections on a particular woman."

Bram took a sip of now tepid coffee and caught Stanley's eye. "Would it surprise you to learn that I've already settled my affections on a specific lady?"

Stanley blinked. "I have yet to witness you paying any of the ladies who've visited Ravenwood any special attention."

"That's because this lady has never been to Ravenwood. Truth be told, I've not actually been formally introduced to her."

Stanley abandoned his toast. "That seems a bit curious, sir."

"Indeed, but you see, the reason I have yet to be properly introduced to her is because she's a delicate sort, possessed of fragile and tender sensibilities."

Stanley's brows drew together. "You believe a lady with tender sensibilities is an appropriate choice for you to settle your affections on, sir?"

"She's perfect for me — lovely, charming, demure. Why, I can't think of another lady I'd want to settle my affections on. But even given her delicate nature, she's a lady in very high demand. Gentlemen flock around her, but because of her tender sensibilities, she seems reluctant to enter into a relationship with any of them, in fact, more often than not, she's given them the cut direct."

Bram blotted his lips with a linen napkin. "That right there is why I've been biding my time, waiting for just the right moment to become introduced to her. I don't want to scare her off and lose any chance I might have of securing her interest."

"I think you're forgetting a very important fact, sir. You're Mr. Bram Haverstein, a gentleman in possession of a very fine fortune, your own castle, a summer house on Long Island, more carriages than I care to count, a steamboat, and you're apparently possessed of a face that all the ladies find swoon-worthy. On top of that, I've heard more than one young lady whispering about that fine dark hair you have on your head." Stanley grinned. "Apparently, it's a huge mark in your favor."

Bram rolled his eyes. "I don't believe I've ever caused a lady to swoon before, and honestly, my hair is a very nondescript shade of brown. I hardly think it's unusual enough to have the ladies whispering about it."

"You're missing the point. You're a catch, Mr. Haverstein, and that means this lady of yours, be she in high demand or not, will be more than receptive to accepting your attention."

"I've never gotten the impression this particular lady is impressed by things such as fortunes and handsome faces, let alone nondescript brown hair."

"Every lady is appreciative of a handsome face, sir, and throw in a fortune *and* a castle to go with that face, and you can't lose." Stanley's brow furrowed. "Although, you might not want to tell her straight off that Ravenwood is haunted. That might not be a mark in your favor, unless she enjoys ghosts and creatures of the night, but if she's truly a delicate sort . . . hmm . . . best keep that under wraps until she's fully committed to you."

"Ravenwood is not haunted, Stanley."

Stanley immediately turned stubborn. "Explain all the peculiar events that happen then — like suits of armor moving about, moans in the night, and . . . what about when poor Mrs. Buttermore heard those chains clanking around when she got up early to start the Thanksgiving feast last year?"

"We've never heard any stories about any of the previous owners coming to a bad end. And there haven't been that many previous owners since Ravenwood isn't even that old, so there's no reason for it to be haunted."

"Perhaps the ghosts came over on the boats that brought all the antiquities the last owner acquired and left behind when he sold the castle to you, which is very . . . telling."

"I paid a fortune for those antiquities because I thought they lent the castle a very credible atmosphere."

"Oh . . . I thought the previous owner simply left them when he fled out of fear for his life."

"You've been reading far too many gothic novels," Bram said with a shake of his head, but before he could say more, Ernie suddenly dashed into the room, completely out of breath, and looking a little wild about the eyes.

"The castle grounds have been breached, sir," Ernie finally managed to wheeze as he bent over and sucked in deep breaths of air. "Should we roll out the cannons?"

"I think that might be a bit of an overreaction, especially since I've never really been comfortable blasting unexpected guests hither, thither, and yon about the castle lawn."

"I didn't say we should blast *them,* sir, just fire off a ball or two over their heads in order to scare them a bit," Ernie argued. "And begging your pardon, sir, but I don't believe we should be calling them guests. They're trespassers, plain and simple, and they're not your everyday trespassers either, sir. They went to the very great bother of getting through the back hedge. Those hedges are filled with thorns, not to mention snakes, and it would take someone of a very determined nature to brave obstacles like that."

Bram blinked. "They went through the hedge?"

"Indeed, and they've now made their way past the reflecting pond," another voice said from the doorway.

Looking that way, Bram found Mrs. Macmillan, his less-than-capable housekeeper, slouching in the doorway, looking rather put out at the moment, although, since that was a look she projected quite often, he wasn't taken aback by it in the least.

Why he kept her and her husband, Mr. Macmillan, the butler at Ravenwood, was a discussion he knew the rest of his staff often had. But when he'd purchased Ravenwood, the Macmillans had inquired whether or not they could retain the positions they'd held for the previous owners. And, since Bram was not comfortable turning people out into a world where positions were difficult to come by, he'd agreed to allow them to stay on — though he had regretted that decision a time or two, especially since neither Mr. Macmillan nor Mrs. Macmillan seemed to be especially competent at their jobs.

"Thank you, Mrs. Macmillan," he finally said with a nod, earning a single nod of acknowledgment from her in return. But then she surprised him when she stepped forward instead of getting on her way.

"Mr. Macmillan is already on his way up to the north tower to ready the cannon, per Ernie's suggestion," Mrs. Macmillan continued. "But I thought I should inquire first before I have someone pull up the drawbridges — something Ernie suggested as well — especially since that's such a difficult task, what with all the pulleys and cranks that need to be put into motion."

Sending Ernie a frown, which Ernie staunchly ignored, Bram gave his breakfast one last look before he rose from his chair. "Thank you, but no, Mrs. Macmillan. We'll leave the drawbridges down since I intend to speak directly to the intruders." He turned and caught Stanley's eye. "Would you be so kind as to seek out Mr. Macmillan and inform him that the decision has been made to stand down and not make use of the cannons today?"

"Of course," Stanley said before he strode from the room, taking a muttering Ernie with him.

"Should I ring for fresh tea?" Mrs. Macmillan asked.

"I'm not sure I'll be asking the trespassers in for refreshments, Mrs. Macmillan. While I certainly don't want to fire cannonballs at them, offering them tea might be taking the social niceties a bit too far." With that, Bram walked past his housekeeper and down a long hallway lined with ancient suits of armor.

Pushing open the heavy door that led to the back gardens, Bram squinted against the late-morning sun and scanned the surrounding area, his gaze settling on two figures who had, indeed, made it past the reflecting pond and were even now approaching the moat.

Since both intruders seemed to be on the small side, and neither was carrying any weapons that he could see, he felt no trepidation in the least about approaching them. His approach came to a grinding halt, though, when howling suddenly rent the air. Turning toward the sound, he saw a side gate swing open. Though a gate opening didn't usually constitute a dire emergency, because this particular gate kept his pack of mangy-looking and less-than-well-behaved dogs contained, the situation at hand had taken a definite turn for the concerning. Before he could call out to discover exactly who had opened the gate, four dogs came charging across the lawn. His yells telling them to stop did nothing to slow them down, and the next thing Bram knew, the dogs were scrambling across the draw-bridge, their goal obviously that of getting to the gentleman now standing stock-still about halfway across that bridge.

From what Bram could tell, the man seemed to be saying something to the dogs, but whatever he was saying, instead of calming the beasts, sent them into what could only be called a frenzy. The poor man was now well and truly trapped since the dogs had taken to circling him — something Bram had been teaching them to do, but with the hope that they'd use the training to herd sheep, not people. Breaking into a run as Igor, the largest of his dogs, suddenly crouched, Bram yelled, "Igor, no."

Unfortunately, Igor was a little hard of hearing at times — unless there was mention of chicken, his favorite food — and before Bram could reach him, he leapt at the intruder, who stumbled backward and then over the small ledge that marked the side of the drawing bridge, disappearing into the moat a second later with a very loud splash.

Increasing his pace as water flew up from the moat, Bram skidded to a stop at the edge of the drawbridge, searching the water in the hopes that the man would resurface at any moment. When he didn't, and when all of the dogs suddenly abandoned their howling to jump into the moat as well, Bram had no choice but to follow them, dodging paddling paws before he dove underneath the surface.

Just when his lungs began to burn and he thought he wasn't going to be successful on his first dive, the man shot into him. Unable to believe his good fortune, he grabbed hold of what felt like hair, and surprisingly long hair at that, and kicked as hard as he could, pulling the man up with him. Breaking the surface, he gulped in a breath, released his hold on the hair, and taking a firm grip on the man's arm, tried to tow him to shore.

Unfortunately, the man didn't seem to be receptive to that idea and immediately began fighting him, which had Bram tightening his grip.

"Stop . . . trying . . . to drown me," he heard the man rasp in an unexpectedly high voice between bobs of his head lifting and sinking through the water.

"I'm trying to save you."

"Is that what you call this?"

Intending to reassure the obviously distressed and certainly panicked man, Bram opened his mouth, but soon found himself incapable of speech, a direct result of suddenly finding himself underneath the water. Taken completely by surprise by the idea the man had dunked him, he dodged the man's kicking legs, as well as a few dog paws, and sputtered his way back to the surface, discovering as he did so that the man he'd thought was drowning was swimming his way quite competently to shore.

Striking out after him with his dogs paddling on either side of him, Bram soon reached the side of the moat. Clawing his way up the dirt bank, he flopped onto the grass and turned his head, his attention settling on the man he'd been trying to save. That man was already on his feet, but the longer Bram watched the man, the more it became clear he was no man at all. He, or rather she, had lost her greatcoat in the moat, and her wet clothing was currently plastered against a form that was . . . curvaceous. When she shoved a hunk of long hair away from her face, exposing whiskers, of all things, Bram suddenly found it very difficult to breath because . . .

Standing only feet away from him was none other than Miss Lucetta Plum, one of the most intriguing ladies to ever grace the stage, and a lady who had captured his very great esteem.

She was looking a little worse for wear, especially since she had mud on her face mixed in with the whiskers, and she also had clumps of algae in her hair, but even in such a sorry state, she was beautiful.

She was also the lady he'd been slightly in love with ever since he'd first seen her take to the stage a few years back. Her delicate and refined nature had pulled at his very soul, and the very idea that such a fragile creature was forced to eke out a living on her own had been unfathomable. That was what had prompted Bram to set into motion ways to improve Miss Plum's circumstance in life, those ways including . . .

A wet tongue licking his face had him immediately returning to the situation at hand as he rolled from his stomach to his back, an action he regretted a mere second later when Igor began licking his face in earnest.

"Thank you, Igor, but that'll be quite enough of that." He was not surprised when his dog gave him a few more licks before he finally abandoned his task, ambling a mere foot away before he began shaking out his fur, the shaking sending water flying Bram's way.

Pushing to his feet in an effort to avoid some of the water, Bram gave his wet and distinctly smelly dog a pat before he straightened, his breath becoming lodged in his throat when Miss Plum began walking toward him.

Regret settled in as the thought struck him that there was really no way to avoid finally making her acquaintance even while smelling much like his dog. Summoning up a smile, he was about to offer her a greeting when a trace of smoke coming from one of the castle towers captured his attention. Knowing full well there was only one reasonable explanation for the smoke, he stepped toward Miss Plum just as a yell split the air.

"Watch out below."

As the roar of a cannon sounded, Bram

did the only thing that sprang to mind. He yanked Miss Plum close to him, locked his arms around her slender body, and . . . jumped back into the moat.

5

Gasping for breath when her head broke the surface of the water, Lucetta twisted and turned before she finally managed to extract herself from the man who seemed determined to drown her. Striking out for shore once again, she reached the bank and crawled her way up it, lying on her stomach in the grass as wet and extremely exuberant dogs licked her wherever they could find a spot of skin. Laughing when the licks began to tickle, she rolled over, struggled to a sitting position, and gave one of the smaller dogs, one missing a large chunk of its ear, a pat, earning a lick on the nose in return as the dog scrambled its way onto her lap.

"Forgive me for tossing you into the moat so unceremoniously. I'm afraid the cannon took me by surprise, and getting you out of harm's way had me reacting somewhat irrationally."

Shifting her attention away from the dog

in her lap, Lucetta settled it on the man now rising from the moat. As he straightened and shoved a hand through dark hair that was obscuring his face, Lucetta completely forgot what she'd been about to say when she got her first good look at him.

Standing before her was the very picture of a dashing pirate come to life, a pirate complete with a charming, yet somewhat roguish smile, and . . . he was wearing a patch over his left eye.

Oddly enough, Lucetta found herself feeling a bit more charitable toward the man, perhaps because she'd always been drawn to flawed people, probably because she was fairly flawed as well. Realizing that the patch she was staring at was evidently covering some horrible disfigurement — a disfigurement the poor man undoubtedly didn't care to have people fixating on — Lucetta dropped her gaze, settling it on a chest covered in a dripping wet shirt made of what appeared to be fine lawn material, and . . .

"Goodness," she whispered past a throat that had taken to constricting the moment her gaze settled on an incredibly well-defined form. Lifting her attention the tiniest bit, she found herself, curiously enough, intrigued with the small bit of skin exposed above the man's collar. It was lightly tanned, a circumstance that could mean only one thing — the gentleman standing before her obviously spent a great deal of time outside, which would make him . . . the gardener.

That notion had her feeling even more charitable to the man who'd tossed her into the moat, especially since there was nothing Lucetta appreciated more than a man who was not afraid to put in a hard day's work.

"I say, you're not about to faint, are you, miss?"

Shaking herself from her musings, and ignoring the fact that heat had taken to traveling up her neck because she'd been caught gawking at the man, Lucetta frowned as she realized the man had addressed her as *miss,* even though she was dressed as a coachman, with whiskers on her face, no less.

With a feeling of foreboding settling over her, she lifted her head and settled her attention on his face again, completely forgetting what she'd been about to say as she found herself pinned beneath a brilliant blue eye, the concern resting in that eye leading her to the notion that even though the man had the look of a pirate about him, he seemed to be a rather compassionate sort.

She absently noted that his lips were moving, clear proof that he was speaking to her, but she found herself unable to concentrate on what he was saying because he had the most delightful dimple, right at the corner of his mouth, a dimple that drew attention to the strength of his jaw and the sharpness of his cheekbones, as well as . . .

". . . and if you'll just take my hand, I'll help you to your feet, and then I'll get you straight into the castle, where I'm sure you'd appreciate a nice cup of tea, and maybe . . . a towel."

For some reason, the thought of taking his hand had the heat traveling from her neck to settle on her face. Snuggling the dog closer to her, she shook her head and scooted ever so slowly backward. "Thank you, sir, but I'm not certain I'll survive another instance of your assistance. You've attempted to drown me, and twice at that, and . . ." She lifted her head and frowned up at him. "Is it a normal occurrence for your visitors to be greeted with flying cannonballs?"

His hand dropped to his side. "I wouldn't say it's a *normal* occurrence." He smiled a charming smile, displaying some rather nice teeth in the process. "In all honesty, I think we should look at the whole cannon episode as an unfortunate accident."

"Forgive me, but I don't believe you can fire cannons accidentally. One must first stuff them with a cannonball and then light a fuse. In all honesty, there's really relatively little that can happen with a cannon that's anything but deliberate."

His smile dimmed. "You might be right."

"I also find it interesting that the dogs were set on me, which . . . I don't believe was an accident either."

The man directed his attention to the dog sitting in her lap. "You very well might have a valid point there. I've only recently acquired the dogs, and freely admit they're a collection of scamps at the moment. That's why they're normally confined to a large, fenced-in area on the side of the castle, unless they're with me up in the sheep pasture, or sleeping in the great hall at night."

The idea that the man kept his collection of motley scamps inside at night had her smiling ever so slightly, the smile causing the mustache she was wearing to tickle her nose. Reaching up, she realized it was falling off — most likely due to her two plunges into the moat — so drew in a breath and yanked it off, leaving stinging skin behind. Pulling off the matching beard a moment later, she lifted her gaze and found the man watching her curiously, as if he didn't know what to make of her.

"I'm Miss Plum, by the way" was all she could think to say to break the silence that had now settled around them.

"I know."

Wariness seeped into her every pore, but before she could question him about how he'd already come to recognize her, the little dog on her lap let out a yip and settled more comfortably against her.

"That's Montresor."

Lucetta looked up. "Named after the narrator in Edgar Allen Poe's 'The Cask of Amontillado'?"

The man's one eye blinked back at her. "You're an admirer of Edgar Allen Poe's work?"

"I'm not sure I would call myself an admirer, but I have read all of his work."

"And the name Montresor happened to stick with you?"

"You'd be surprised at how much sticks with me," she muttered before she summoned up a smile when he began to look a little confused again. She nodded to the large, incredibly shaggy dog stretched out right beside her that seemed to be a mix of a sheepdog and some type of poodle. His tongue lolled out of his mouth as he sent her innocent looks out of his big doggy eyes. "What's this handsome gentleman's name?"

"He's Igor."

Lucetta reached out and gave Igor a good scratch, earning a whine of sheer bliss in the process. "I was certain when I first saw him that he was intending on ripping me limb from limb, but he's not frightening at all, just a little rambunctious."

"You didn't happen to see who opened that gate and let the dogs out, did you?" the man asked.

"I'm afraid not, as I was, again, thinking I was about to lose a few limbs." She looked to the right and found the other two dogs racing away toward the forest, but before she could ask what their names were, Montresor slid to the ground and yipped out a greeting. Looking around to see who, or what, was about to join them, she saw Abigail strolling her way, not appearing to be in any hurry, which was odd, since Abigail had elected herself Lucetta's chaperone. Chaperones didn't usually allow unknown gentlemen to get anywhere near their . . .

"Thank goodness you're not dead, my dear," Abigail began, stopping a few feet away from Lucetta. "I was certain you were going to drown when you went into the moat the first time, given that you were wearing such a heavy coat. But wasn't it just so fortunate that my grandson was there to jump in and rescue you?"

The reason behind the lack of urgency in Abigail getting to Lucetta immediately became clear. Shooting a glance to the man she'd assumed was the gardener — although the quality of his shirt should have been an indication he was nothing of the sort — Lucetta turned back to Abigail. "*This* is your grandson?"

Abigail sent her a less than subtle wink. "Too right he is."

To Lucetta's absolute relief, the grandson in question stepped forward before Abigail had an opportunity to begin waxing on about what a dish her grandson had turned out to be, a subject that would have embarrassed Lucetta no small amount, and probably the grandson as well.

"Grandmother, this is certainly an unexpected surprise," the man who was apparently Bram Haverstein said.

Abigail beamed a smile Bram's way and held out her hands, her beaming increasing when Bram immediately strode to her side, picked up both of her hands, and kissed them.

"I'm sure you *are* surprised to see me, dear, just as I'm sure you meant to say *delightful* surprise, not *unexpected,* but enough about that. Even though you and Lucetta are dripping wet, we mustn't ignore the expected pleasantries, so do allow me to formally introduce the two of you. Bram, this is my darling friend, Miss Lucetta Plum, and Lucetta, dear, this is my grandson, the one I've been telling you so much about, Mr. Bram Haverstein."

Trepidation was immediate when Bram flashed a big smile her way. Rising to her feet, Lucetta inclined her head. "It's a pleasure to meet you, Mr. Haverstein."

"The pleasure is mine, Miss Plum," Bram responded as he moved right up beside her and took her hand firmly in his, the heat from his skin sending a jolt of what she could only assume was alarm straight up her arm. "Do know that I'm a great, *great* admirer of your work."

Her sense of alarm promptly increased. Gentlemen who had no qualms admitting they were great, *great* admirers of her work were known to be rather . . . zealous. The very last circumstance Lucetta needed, or wanted for that matter, was to add another great admirer to her unwanted collection of them.

Disappointment stole through her as Mr. Haverstein lifted her hand to his lips and placed a lingering kiss on her knuckles, that disappointment increasing when he lowered her hand and began speaking.

"I must admit that I do think your role in *The Lady of the Tower* is your best to date. Why, I've come to the conclusion that Mr. Grimstone, the playwright, obviously had you in mind to play the part of Serena Seamore from the moment he began penning the story."

Abigail, apparently realizing that her grandson was not making a favorable impression — which certainly wouldn't aid her matchmaking attempt — squared her shoulders, looking quite determined. "How lovely to discover you're already familiar with my dear Lucetta and her work," Abigail said. "But as both of you are dripping wet and certain to catch a cold if we linger, I'm going to suggest we repair to the castle and leave further talk of, uh, theater behind us."

She took a firm grip of Bram's arm. "Perhaps you could explain a bit about the history of your castle as we walk."

With all of the confusion of having to burrow under pesky hedges to gain entrance to the grounds, then being set upon by a pack of misbehaving dogs, not to mention almost drowning a couple times in a moat, Lucetta had completely neglected to take a proper

74

look at Ravenwood. Falling into step beside Abigail, she turned her attention to the structure rising in front of her. The sheer size of it was impressive, even though Lucetta found the castle as a whole to be slightly . . . disturbing.

Three stories of gray stone were styled in a distinctly gothic manner. Flying buttresses added a melodramatic air, while numerous gargoyles squatted from the ledges of the two tall towers that anchored the castle — the expressions on their sculpted faces being nothing less than fierce.

The many windows, all of various sizes, were set with stained glass, and when a flock of ravens suddenly flew from one of the towers, Lucetta couldn't suppress a shiver.

"Bram purchased the castle over a year ago and has been working diligently to update the interior, even going so far as to hire workers to put modern plumbing up in the top tower rooms," Abigail said, pulling Lucetta's attention away from the ravens.

"I imagine it must have been difficult to get plumbing all the way up to the top of the towers, Mr. Haverstein," Lucetta said.

Bram smiled. "It was quite a feat, Miss Plum. I had to consult with three architects, and the project took over a month to complete. My parents bought an estate not far from Ravenwood a few months back, but before that my mother stayed here quite often. She claimed one of the tower rooms as her own, loving the view from the windows, but she didn't appreciate the inconvenience of not having running water at her disposal."

"I didn't know Iris had purchased a home in Tarrytown," Abigail said, coming to a sudden stop, which had Bram and Lucetta doing the same.

Bram immediately took to looking uncomfortable. "Well, uh, yes, she and Father decided they wanted to live at least part of the year in New York."

"But not in the city?" Abigail demanded.

"Uh . . . apparently not."

Abigail's lips thinned before she nodded, just once. "Do they still own that place down in Cuba?"

"If you mean the sugar plantation, yes, they do. Although Hugh" — Bram looked at Lucetta — "my older brother, has been given the responsibility of running the plantation, while Father has moved into an advisory role." He smiled. "Handing over responsibility to Hugh has given my parents quite a bit of discretionary time — time they've been using to enjoy life to the fullest."

"Your mother never once mentioned to me that your father was taking a less active role in the plantation," Abigail said with a distinct edge to her tone.

Bram reached out and took hold of Abigail's hand. "I'm sure she meant to, Grandmother, just as I'm sure she intended to let you know she purchased a home in Tarrytown."

"You and I both know that's not true," Abigail said before she lifted her chin and frowned as she considered him for a long moment. "What happened to your eye?"

"My eye?" Bram repeated slowly.

"Of course, dear — your eye. You weren't wearing that patch the last time I saw you, which means you've evidently suffered some type of horrible accident."

Reaching up, Bram touched the patch in question, his hand stilling a second later. "Honestly, I forgot all about this." To Lucetta's complete and utter horror, he stuck a finger underneath the patch and flipped it up.

She immediately took a marked interest in Montresor, pretending that his sniffing in a clump of weeds was downright fascinating.

"Why in the world would you be sporting an eye patch when there's absolutely nothing wrong with your eye?" Abigail asked slowly.

Shooting a look back to Bram, Lucetta found the man flipping the patch back over an eye that was apparently fine.

"That's a little difficult to explain," he said, but before he could elaborate, Stanley — the man who'd so rudely fired his rifle over her head, scaring her horse in the process when they'd first arrived at Ravenwood — dashed into view.

"You'd better come quickly, sir. We've got another situation. . . . You're not going to believe what just showed up on the dock." With that, Stanley spun around and raced from sight, Igor and Montresor scrambling after him, howling so loudly more ravens flew out of a nearby tree.

"Excuse me" was all Bram said before he dashed off as well.

"How very curious," Abigail said.

"Everything about our arrival here at Ravenwood has been curious," Lucetta said as she took Abigail's arm. "But . . . care to brave a stroll down to the docks and have a look at what's shown up there?"

"But of course," Abigail said with a grin.

Returning the grin, Lucetta moved in step with Abigail to the side of the castle, finding a cobblestone path in the process. Shadows from the castle wall blanketed the path and produced a chill that had Lucetta shivering as she and Abigail hurried along. Reaching the front lawn, Lucetta felt an immediate sense of relief when they finally stepped from the shadows and back into the sunlight.

She wasn't a lady who possessed a dramatic nature, even given her profession, but there was just something about Ravenwood that kept the fine hairs on the back of her neck standing at attention.

Before she could contemplate why she found the castle so disconcerting, a large crowd of people walking across the front drawbridge drew her attention. Lifting a hand to shield her eyes, an unusual sight met her gaze.

The people — most armed with pitchforks — were prodding three apparent captives across the bridge. Unfortunately, those captives were all too familiar to Lucetta, especially since one of them was wearing one of her favorite gowns.

She turned toward Abigail, who was watching the scene unfold in front of them with eyes that had grown rather wide, and said, "The good news is that Archibald, Mr. Skukman, and Mr. Kenton were apparently successful in evading Silas, but . . . I don't imagine they counted on being captured by your grandson's staff."

Lucetta winced as a man she thought was named Ernie — who had also greeted Abigail and herself less than enthusiastically when they'd arrived at Ravenwood — prodded Mr. Skukman with his pitchfork. Unsurprisingly, Mr. Skukman ripped the pitchfork straight out of Ernie's hands and tossed it over the side of the drawbridge.

"Oh . . . dear," Abigail whispered. "And here I was so hoping everyone would get a favorable impression of my grandson and his castle, but . . . pitchforks, I ask you?"

Squaring her shoulders, Abigail tugged Lucetta forward in order to join Bram, who was standing in front of the drawbridge. "Honestly, dear, this is completely beyond the pale. Those are friends of mine." Abigail motioned toward the men. "The tall gentleman is none other than Mr. Archibald Addleshaw; the gentleman wearing the yellow gown is my loyal butler, Mr. Kenton; and the man not wearing a gown but looking quite annoyed with the situation is none other than Lucetta's personal guard, Mr. Skukman."

Abigail raised a hand and sent a wave toward the gentlemen, which Archibald and Mr. Kenton returned, although Mr. Skukman simply nodded his head.

Abigail immediately took to clucking. "Mr. Skukman is obviously not seeing the humor in this situation. Before he tosses someone over the drawbridge, quite like he did to that pitchfork, I'm going to suggest you step in, Bram, so that no one gets hurt. Mr. Skukman's a perfectly pleasant man when he's not riled, but I don't think we should test his patience, especially given his size."

Bram considered Mr. Skukman for the briefest of seconds before he stepped forward and raised a hand, drawing everyone's attention.

"You can set aside the pitchforks!" he yelled. "Those men don't mean us any harm."

"Then why are they dressed as women?" someone bellowed back.

"Yes, Bram, why *are* they dressed like women, and . . . what in the world is my *mother* doing at Ravenwood?"

Turning ever so slowly, Abigail blinked and raised a hand to her chest. "Iris . . . what are *you* doing here?" She asked before Bram could respond.

Directing her attention to where Abigail was looking, Lucetta discovered a woman dressed in the first state of fashion standing a few feet away from them. She looked remarkably like Abigail, and . . . she looked completely furious.

"I'm here to visit my son, of course. And I'm beyond curious to discover what *you* are doing at Ravenwood. I thought I was perfectly clear at Father's funeral, when you began questioning me about my children and their marital aspirations, that I wanted you to maintain your distance and allow my children to make their own choices, with no meddling from you."

"Did you mention that you didn't want me to meddle?" Abigail asked somewhat weakly.

Realizing that Abigail — given that she'd had relatively no sleep the night before — was in no state to deal with an irate daughter, Lucetta did the only thing she could think of. She drew in a deep breath, closed her eyes, then summoned up every acting ability she had at her disposal, right before she released a moan and dropped to the ground.

6

Silence reigned over the front lawn, until Abigail released what almost sounded like a snort right before she turned on her elderly heel and hurried off across the lawn. That reaction was so unexpected that Bram just stood there and watched her for a moment — stood there until he recalled that poor, delicate Miss Plum had fainted dead away. Knowing that the ground beneath Miss Plum could hardly be comfortable and wanting to remedy that unfortunate situation as quickly as possible, Bram bent over, scooped Miss Plum up into his arms, and then staggered just a bit due to the unexpected weight of her.

Regaining his balance, he tightened his grip and headed for the castle, frowning when he passed his mother and saw that she was rolling her eyes at him. Realizing that now was not the time to stop and question his mother — since Miss Plum wasn't growing any lighter — he pressed onward.

Stumbling up the few steps that led to the castle door, Bram was pleasantly surprised to find that Mr. Macmillan, his sometimes questionable butler, was actually at his post, holding the door open for him. Nodding his thanks, Bram carried Miss Plum through the doorway and down the long, *long* hallway, finally reaching the great room. Stepping into the room, he found his housekeeper, Mrs. Macmillan, supervising what seemed to be a dusting of the armor, her face sporting another sour expression as she glanced up and sent a single nod his way.

"I see you changed your mind about allowing at least one of the trespassers into the house, sir. Shall I ring for that tea I suggested before?" she asked, as if it was of little consequence that the trespasser she'd just mentioned was lolling about unconscious in his arms.

Coming to a stop because he needed to shift Miss Plum around, and take a second to catch his breath, he sent Mrs. Macmillan a frown. "Tea might actually be needed in this situation, Mrs. Macmillan. But to clear the air, oddly enough, the trespassers turned out to be unexpected guests that we've unintentionally abused quite dreadfully. As one of these guests is currently suffering from a bit of a swoon — that would be Miss Plum, whom I'm carrying — I need to get her settled straightaway. What tower room would you suggest I take her to?"

Mrs. Macmillan stared at Bram for a moment before she turned her gaze on Miss Plum. "That's Miss Plum, as in the actress Miss Lucetta Plum?"

"Indeed."

"What in the world is she doing at Raven-wood?"

"I haven't gotten all the particulars just yet, Mrs. Macmillan." He felt a droplet of sweat run down the side of his face. "I assume my grandmother, Mrs. Hart, who accompanied Miss Plum to Ravenwood, will soon divulge those particulars to me. But since Miss Plum has suffered not one but two dips in the moat, was set upon by the dogs, had a cannon fired at her, and then came face-to-face with my mother, which might have been the most frightening experience she's had today, I really do need to get her settled."

"If she's here for a visit, you should put her in a guest room, not the tower," Mrs. Macmillan said, even as Bram's arms began to quiver.

"I want her in one of the best rooms, which you and I know are the tower rooms, so . . . which one would you recommend?"

Mrs. Macmillan crossed her arms over her chest, even as she let out a sniff. "Actresses are known to be a demanding lot, especially one with Miss Plum's reputation. I highly doubt the staff is going to appreciate having to run up and down all of those steps to the top of the tower when we have plenty of guest rooms that are more convenient."

"I'm beginning to lose my patience with you, Mrs. Macmillan."

"Fine, the south tower was cleaned just last week, and I'll send a maid up to freshen the linens."

"That would be appreciated, as would the tea you offered to send for."

"Will you want to give that grandmother you mentioned the other tower room?"

"I think the stairs might be a bit much for my grandmother, so we'll give her one of the guest rooms in the main castle."

"Very good, sir."

By the disgruntled tone of voice Mrs. Macmillan was now using, he doubted she found anything good about the situation. However, since Miss Plum was growing heavier by the second, he knew now was not the time to argue with his housekeeper. Turning around, he headed for the door again.

"Good luck negotiating all of those steps," Mrs. Macmillan called after him, apparently determined to have the last word.

Refusing to rise to the urge to retort, which he knew full well was pointless with a woman of Mrs. Macmillan's disposition, he allowed himself a moment to ponder why he *did* keep such a disagreeable housekeeper on staff, even *if* positions were difficult to come by.

When a small voice in his head, one he had a feeling came directly from God, reminded him that unhappy people tended to lash out at others because of wounds their hearts had sustained, he released a breath, sent up a quick prayer asking for patience with his staff, and shifted Miss Plum around yet again in his arms.

Reaching a back hallway, he walked as quickly as he could over the marble floor, wondering for the first time ever why he'd thought buying a large castle with very long hallways and cavernous great rooms that took forever to cross had been a stellar idea. By the time he finally reached the stairs, he'd begun to perspire . . . profusely.

Eyeing stairs that now seemed downright daunting, he drew in a breath, hitched Miss Plum up a little higher in the hopes it would distribute her weight more evenly, then began to climb, counting the steps as he did so.

". . . forty-seven, forty-eight, forty-nine . . . You're really quite sturdy, aren't you, Miss Plum? Fifty . . ."

By the time he eventually reached the tower room, he was completely out of breath, perspiration was dribbling down his face, and his arms were no longer simply quivering, they were now downright shaking. Stepping through the door of the tower room, he faltered for a moment, wondering what he should do next.

"You can just set me down right here, Mr. Haverstein."

Miss Plum's voice took him by such surprise that he almost dropped her right on the hard stone floor of the tower room. Looking down, he frowned when he saw something in her lovely eyes that he'd never, not once, expected to see, something that resembled, if he wasn't much mistaken . . . amusement.

He'd always been under the impression that Miss Plum, being a fragile sort, possessed a somber and serious demeanor, spending her time away from the theater in a subdued fashion, embroidering samplers, or perhaps pillows, as she lounged on a settee, or learning her lines from the comfort of her bedchamber, but . . . what if he'd been wrong?

What if Miss Plum was not as delicate as he'd believed, and what if the woman he'd been enamored with for what seemed like a very long time, turned out to be completely different than what he'd imagined her to be?

"How long have you been out of your swoon?" he asked.

"Would you be very upset to learn that I never swoon?"

His mouth immediately took to gaping open. "Do you mean to tell me that you allowed me to scoop you up off the ground — which wasn't an easy task by the way — carry you into the castle, and then all the way up a tremendous number of steps when there was absolutely nothing wrong with you?"

"I did."

"I could have suffered an injury."

"You seem to be remarkably fit, Mr. Haverstein, and I certainly couldn't own up to the fact I was feigning my condition, especially since I was doing so to aid dear Abigail."

Bram set her on her feet and rubbed his arms. "My arms feel like jelly."

"I'm sure they do. You carried me a

remarkably long distance, and I will admit that I was concerned you were going to drop me a time or two." She pursed her lips. "Quite honestly, I was going to tell you to put me down right about step number forty-nine, but then you made that remark about how sturdy I am, and . . . I changed my mind."

"I said that out loud?"

"Indeed."

"I do beg your pardon."

Miss Plum waved his apology straightaway with a delicate flick of her far-sturdier-than-he'd-believed wrist. "Think nothing of it. I've never been what anyone could call a waif. Truth be told, it takes an entire theatrical village to stuff me into those corsets so that they can then stuff me into those costumes my fervent admirers apparently enjoy seeing me in, but . . . that's not a subject we should be delving into — especially since I seem to be missing my self-proclaimed chaperone at the moment. I'm sure she'd be appalled to hear me discussing unmentionables with you."

"I'm right here, dear, and yes, I do most heartily disapprove of unmentionables being brought up in polite conversations, as you very well know," Abigail said as she took that moment to breeze into the room. She stopped and beamed at Bram. "Unmention-ables aside, though, aren't you just a dear for taking such excellent care of my darling Lucetta when she was in distress and I was, er, unavailable?"

Bram felt his lips begin to curl. "I have a feeling, Grandmother, that you were fully aware of the fact your *darling* Lucetta had absolutely nothing wrong with her and was simply putting to good use her acting abili-ties in order to spare you a confrontation with my mother."

Abigail stepped to his side, lifted her chin, and reached up to pat his cheek. "You're a dear boy, with a chivalrous heart, even if you have yet to explain why you're wearing this patch when you have no need of one."

Since he certainly wasn't comfortable tell-ing his grandmother the truth, he settled for summoning up a smile. "It's difficult to explain."

"Is it now?"

"Indeed, and since I do seem to be drip-ping all over the Aubusson rug, which is surprising since it seems like forever ago that I took those dips in the moat, I'm go-ing to excuse myself and leave you to see after Miss Plum."

Beating a hasty retreat, even as he thought Miss Plum muttered something about a coward, he headed down the tower stairs and turned into the main section of the castle. Striding to his room, he opened the door and found Stanley waiting for him, laying out clean clothes from the looks of it.

He stepped farther into the room and shut the door firmly, causing Stanley to jump almost a foot into the air before he spun around.

"You have to stop sneaking up on me like that, sir."

"Forgive me, Stanley, I didn't mean to take you by surprise."

Stanley raked a hand through his hair. "I'm sure you didn't, sir. It's just with the ghosts running amok at all hours of the night, ladies descending on us in droves while participating in all types of unladylike shenanigans, and now a grandmother I never knew you had showing up out of the blue, and in the company of Miss Lucetta Plum no less . . . well . . . I'm a little on edge."

"There are no ghosts inhabiting Raven-wood."

"We'll have to agree to disagree on that, sir. But speaking of your other grandmother, why is it that none of us have ever met or heard of her before?"

"My mother does not enjoy an amicable

relationship with my grandmother, so in order to maintain a peaceful existence with my mother, I've had to keep my grandmother at arm's length. My grandmother, however, has been going to fairly great lengths of her own over the past few years to get to know me better."

Stanley tilted his head. "How so, sir?"

"She *happens* upon me at the oddest of times and places when I am in the city, and has even been known to steam past the dock here at Ravenwood, although she's never stopped before."

"And you haven't taken the time to invite her in?"

"I'm not proud of that, Stanley. I just haven't really known what to do, given that acrimonious relationship my grandmother shares with my mother. But now that both ladies are here, under Ravenwood's roof, at the same time, we're either going to see them set aside their differences once and for all, or . . . someone's probably going to get arrested."

"A cheerful thought, sir."

"Indeed, and on that cheerful note, I should go clean up."

Pulling his wet shirt over his head, Bram headed for the bathing chamber, pausing as he passed a mirror and getting a glimpse of his reflection — the glimpse reminding him of something he had no idea how to address. Lifting up the patch that covered his eye, he directed his attention to Stanley again.

"Why didn't anyone mention to me that I was wearing this before I charged out of the castle?"

Stanley scratched his head. "Begging your pardon, sir, but since your vision has to be obscured while wearing that patch, I assumed you knew you were wearing it. Quite honestly, I thought you kept it on in order to appear more intimidating. You know — a pirate look, if you will."

"I had to admit to Miss Plum that there's nothing wrong with my eye."

"And . . . that was difficult for you, sir?"

"Do you know how odd she must find me now, learning that I run about with a patch over a perfectly good eye?"

"She wouldn't find you odd if you just told her the truth."

"I can't tell her the truth — or anyone else for that matter. Why, it would kill my mother if she found out."

"Now you're being a little overly theatrical, sir. But speaking of theatrics, you could tell Miss Plum that you were trying to get into the role you'll be expected to play later

94

on this week during the theatrical event your
mother is hosting here at Ravenwood."

"Mother's hosting another one of those
theatrical events at Ravenwood?"

Stanley released a loud sigh. "Do you ever
check the calendar I keep for you?"

"I thought we agreed that you'd discontinue acting the part of my secretary?"

"I never agreed to that, but do know that
when someone more capable of being a
secretary or even a valet, for that matter,
comes looking for a position, I'll gladly
abandon those duties. For now, though,
you're a gentleman with severe limitations
on your time, which means you need all the
assistance you can get."

Bram smiled. "And while I appreciate
that, Stanley, I don't like the idea of you
spending so many hours every week working in order to make life easier for me, while
making it more difficult for you."

Stanley lifted his nose in the air. "Since it
is my time, sir, it's up to my discretion how
to use it, and until I feel I've sufficiently
repaid your kindness for rescuing me from
a life that would have eventually seen me
locked away behind bars, you'll just have to
humor me."

Knowing he'd lost the battle before it had
really even begun, Bram blew out a breath.

"Fine. Have it your way. But getting back to the theatrical event, do you think Miss Plum would believe me if I told her I was wearing that patch in order to get comfortable with a role?"

"I imagine she would, although, now that I think about it, using that as an explanation might turn problematic if the play that's to be performed doesn't have a pirate in it." Stanley frowned. "But pirates aside, sir, why are you so overly concerned about what Miss Plum thinks of you?"

"I never said I was *overly* concerned."

Stanley's eyes widened. "She's the lady you hold in high esteem — isn't she!"

Seeing absolutely no benefit in denying it, Bram shrugged. "I might hold her in a bit of esteem."

"Good heavens, sir, I would have never guessed Miss Plum was the lady we were only recently speaking about, and . . . how peculiar that we were just speaking about her and . . . she shows up in your moat."

"It is an odd coincidence to be sure."

Stanley suddenly looked a bit too knowing. "Your affection for the lady certainly explains much, especially your interest in the theater and . . . using that interest to delve into different aspects of your work."

"I'm sure I have no idea what you could

be suggesting."

"And I'm sure you know exactly what I'm suggesting, sir. Nevertheless, since you seem unwilling to explain what prompted you to take on work you had little time to take on, we'll save this discussion for another time."

"Must we?"

Stanley sent him a sad shake of his head. "You're burying yourself in secrets, Mr. Haverstein, and secrets have a way of rising to the surface when we least expect them to do so. You might want to consider divulging a few of those secrets, before they slip out on their own and cause you all sorts of difficulties."

With that rather ominous statement, Stanley sent Bram a single nod, brushed a piece of lint from the jacket he'd laid across the chair, then turned and quit the room.

7

"I know I said it just a few minutes ago, but it truly does deserve repeating. Your quick thinking and subsequent swoon when Iris arrived so unexpectedly was completely brilliant. You, my darling girl, saved me from a most unpleasant encounter with my daughter."

Scooting down into the bubbles, Lucetta peered over the rim of the claw-foot tub, not really surprised to discover that Abigail was actually dragging a chair into the bathing chamber. It was a normal occurrence these days for Abigail to use the bathing chamber as the perfect place to hold a chat, the perfection of the plan being that the person in the bath was held completely at Abigail's mercy.

"So, tell me, what did you think of my Bram?" Abigail asked as she settled herself in the chair, looking as if she fully intended to stay for a while.

"Don't you think we should discuss your daughter first?"

Abigail immediately turned stubborn. "Not particularly. There's nothing much to say about Iris other than that she loathes me and we don't share an amicable relationship. Now Bram, on the other hand, is a delightful subject to speak about."

Lucetta settled into the bubbles. "Why do you imagine he was wearing that patch when there's evidently nothing wrong with his eye?"

"It was so gallant of him to whisk you into the castle and bring you up to this tower room, wasn't it?" Abigail countered, as if Lucetta hadn't posed a question.

"Do you believe he enjoys assuming a pirate persona when he's at his leisure? Although . . . now that I consider the matter, what does he do when he's not at his leisure?" Lucetta countered right back.

Abigail crossed her arms over her chest and immediately took to looking a little grumpy. "I'm not exactly certain what Bram does, dear. My son-in-law, Phillip — Bram's father — made a rather large fortune when he invested in a sugar plantation years ago down in Cuba. Because of that fortune, Bram, along with his brother and sister, aren't required to pursue professions, or make advantageous marriages, although . . . I'm sure Bram does something to occupy his time."

"And the fact that your family is well-set financially annoys you because . . . ?"

"Phillip's surprising procurement of a fortune — when I was quite certain he would never amount to much — made any assistance from me, or my late husband, Charles, unnecessary or, more importantly, unwanted."

"Ah, now I'm beginning to understand. You don't care for your daughter's husband."

"I'd really prefer not to discuss Iris *or* her husband, if it's all the same to you."

"You must know that you're not going to be able to avoid Iris for long. I didn't get the impression she was the type of woman to be content with not having her say. And I do believe she has quite a few things she wants to say to you."

Abigail took to looking even grumpier. "I'm sure she does, which is why it's so disconcerting to discover there is so much I haven't been informed about — such as the fact that she recently bought an estate not far from here, or that she apparently no longer spends the entire fall in Cuba. If I'd been apprised of those situations, well, I certainly wouldn't have suggested we seek refuge at Ravenwood. But . . . we're here now, and I intend to hide out with you in this lovely bathing chamber until Iris gets tired of waiting to speak to me."

"You do know that we could be stuck up here for quite some time, then, don't you?"

"Which is why it's a fortuitous circumstance that the tower is so well-appointed, as is the rest of the castle from the small glimpse I got as I was making my way — very stealthily, of course — up here." Abigail suddenly took to inspecting the sleeve of her gown. "I couldn't help but notice that Ravenwood would make a splendid spot to hold a wedding. Why, this tower room would be the perfect place for a lady to get ready, and then . . ." Abigail looked up, a faraway expression in her eyes. "The bride could descend the staircase with a train flowing gently behind her . . . Why, I can picture it in detail."

"You should put those types of details straight from your mind, Abigail," Lucetta said. "I have no intention of getting married anytime soon, nor would my choice of groom be your grandson."

"Why not? Bram's a delightful gentleman."

"Who happens to be a great, *great* admirer

of my work."

Abigail leaned back in her chair. "I knew you were going to take issue with that."

"And for good reason. If you haven't noticed, most admirers of my work — gentlemen admirers, that is — have the unpleasant habit of holding me in high esteem, that circumstance brought about through the unfortunate infatuations they develop for me." She blew bubbles off her hand. "Once they become acquainted with the real me, I'm afraid they quickly lose all interest and never darken the steps of the theater again."

"I'm sure Bram will appreciate everything about you even when he does get to know you better."

Lucetta wrinkled her nose. "Thank you, I think, but Bram didn't seem to appreciate carrying me up all of those steps, especially since he made mention of how *sturdy* he found me to be."

"He did not."

"I assure you, he did, although in his defense, he believed I was unconscious when he uttered the whole sturdy non-sense."

"Well, that's a relief, and . . ."

A knock on the bathing chamber door interrupted whatever else Abigail had been about to say. Rising from the chair, Abigail walked across the room. "Who is it?" she called through the door.

"It's Mrs. Macmillan, ma'am, the house-keeper."

Opening the door, Abigail poked her head into the main tower room. "Ah, Mrs. Macmillan, how wonderful to make your acquaintance. I'm Mrs. Hart, Mr. Haverstein's grandmother."

"Yes, I know" was Mrs. Macmillan's only response before she cleared her throat. "I'm here to tell you that Ernie has located your carriage in the forest and driven it back to Ravenwood. Your horse is being cared for in the stables, and I've taken the liberty of having your trunks, Mrs. Hart, taken to the blue room. If you'll look behind me, you'll see that I also had some of the staff cart Miss Plum's trunks all the way up many, many stairs, delivering them to the tower room."

"How very efficient you seem to be, Mrs. Macmillan," Abigail said with a touch of amusement lacing her tone.

"Quite."

Abigail pulled her head back into the bathing chamber and began to close the door.

"I wasn't done yet, Mrs. Hart."

Abigail straightened her spine and lifted her chin, something that would have had a normal housekeeper thoroughly cowed. It quickly became clear that Mrs. Macmillan was no normal housekeeper, though.

"Mr. Addleshaw asked me to tell you, Mrs. Hart, that your butler, a Mr. Kenton, I believe, is having difficulties with Mrs. Haverstein. Mr. Addleshaw believes you might need to come to the main drawing room in order to help sort out that concerning situation."

"Why in the world would Mr. Kenton have gone anywhere near my daughter when he knows full well that Iris still holds a great deal of animosity toward him?"

Mrs. Macmillan let out what sounded exactly like a sniff. "I'm sure I have no idea. Now, if you'll excuse me, I need to inform our cook that we're going to have more people than expected for lunch today."

As the sound of Mrs. Macmillan's footsteps retreated from the tower room, Abigail turned from the door and blew out a breath. "What an interesting choice of a housekeeper my grandson has made, but —" she blew out another breath — "I'm afraid I'm going to have to leave you to your own devices, dear. Tensions between Mr. Kenton and Iris go back decades. I really can't leave him to deal with her unpleasantness on his own, even if I'm sure Archibald is keeping an eye on the situation."

"I'll be down as soon as I get dressed," Lucetta said, earning a smile from Abigail.

"There's no need for you to rush, dear. I'd hate for you to join everyone looking anything but your best. And speaking of looking your best . . ." Abigail hurried through the door and was back in a remarkably short period of time, holding a lovely walking dress of ivory in one hand and what looked like a corset, petticoat, chemise, and stockings in another. Placing them on the chair she'd recently abandoned, she beamed a smile Lucetta's way.

Lucetta did not return the smile as her gaze lingered on the walking dress. "Why have I never seen that particular dress before?"

"Because it's one of the ones I ordered from Worth, and was only delivered from Paris a few days ago."

"You ordered me a dress from Worth?"

"In all honesty, I ordered you more than one, as well as a few items from Jacques Doucet, and some adorable tailored suits that I know you'll enjoy from John Redfern."

"How did you fit them in my trunks? They

were quite full with items I personally packed for this trip."

Abigail batted far too innocent lashes Lucetta's way. "Would you be very put out with me to discover I took it upon myself to take out all of those ratty-looking clothes you seem to enjoy wearing when you're at your leisure, and replaced them with the new items I procured for you?"

"You know I never get put out with you, but . . . didn't you do the exact same thing to poor Millie when she went off to Newport?"

Abigail gave a flutter of her lashes. "Did I?" With that, Abigail spun on her heel and practically pranced out of the room, humming, if Lucetta wasn't mistaken, a wedding march.

"She's far more diabolical than people give her credit for," Lucetta said to the room at large before she dunked underneath the water to wash the rose-scented soap out of her hair and off her skin. Stepping from the tub a short time later, she dried off with a soft piece of linen before wrapping the linen around her. Moving to the chair where Abigail had left the new clothing, Lucetta pulled the chemise over her head, pulled drawers up her legs, and then reached for the corset. Soft satin met her touch, and after adjusting the laces in the back, she pulled the corset around and over the top of the chemise, thankful that there were clasps along the front of the garment, which prevented her having to ring for help. After the less than subtle lecture Mrs. Macmillan had delivered regarding the trunks, Lucetta shuddered to think what the woman would say if someone had to climb up to the tower in order to help Lucetta get dressed.

Struggling into the walking dress, she began buttoning up the back the best she could, but when she got to just below her shoulders, she couldn't reach the remaining buttons. Eyeing the bell, she stepped toward it but stopped when she heard what sounded like something moving — from inside the wall of the bathing chamber. With a heart that had taken to beating a rapid tattoo, she tiptoed up to the wall and pressed her ear against it, frowning when only silence met that ear. Stepping back, she eyed the wall for a moment, moved close to it again, and gave it a sharp rap.

When nothing rapped back at her, she felt her lips curve as she made her way to the door, the thought flashing to mind that the gothic nature of the castle was obviously affecting her. Turning the knob, she stepped into the tower sitting room, coming to an immediate stop when she saw, much to her dismay, that she was no longer alone.

Standing smack-dab in the middle of what had to be a very expensive Aubusson rug was . . . a goat. It was watching Lucetta with eyes that seemed a little wild. Realizing that the poor thing was obviously as surprised to see her as she was to see it, she took a step forward and held out her hand, intending to give the goat a reassuring pat.

She realized almost immediately that she'd made a rather large mistake, because the goat let out what sounded like a shriek, right before it lowered its head and charged her way.

8

Feeling more the thing after having washed the moat water off him and changed into the clean clothing Stanley had left out for him, Bram headed out of his room, brushing an errant strand of hair from a now patch-free eye.

He still had no idea how he was going to explain that matter, because even though Stanley had come up with a plausible explanation, Bram wasn't comfortable, and had never been comfortable, fabricating the truth. Granted, he could always volunteer to play a pirate at his mother's theatrical event, but . . . there really was no guarantee the play was of a nautical bent, and . . . he'd draw his mother's suspicions for certain given that he never volunteered to perform in any of the local performances. She would definitely realize something was amiss, and then . . . she'd throw herself into the process of trying to puzzle out exactly what that something was.

While he loved his mother dearly, she was very opinionated regarding what she felt was, and was not, appropriate for her children. Bram had the sneaking suspicion she would not be pleased to discover he was enamored with Miss Plum. Especially since mothers were rarely keen on their sons forming alliances, no matter how respectable, with actresses.

"Ah, Mr. Haverstein, I was just coming to look for you."

Lifting his head, he found Mrs. Macmillan heading his way, holding a feather duster in one hand and a piece of armor, oddly enough, in the other.

"I'm just now returning from delivering a message to your grandmother — a message I was forced to deliver all the way up to the tower room, I might add." She continued with a telling narrowing of her eyes his way. "The message concerned a troubling situation that is currently transpiring between your mother and Mr. Kenton. As you are the head of Ravenwood, I thought you should be apprised of the situation posthaste, or as quickly as I was able to seek you out after having traveled down all of those many, many stairs leading from the tower."

"I appreciate your dedication to your position as housekeeper," Bram said, doing his best to keep his lips from curving, even though that's exactly what they wanted to do as he faced his extremely cantankerous housekeeper.

"Your mother is in the red drawing room."

"I'll go straight there."

Mrs. Macmillan lifted her chin. "See that you do."

Continuing down the hallway even as he reconsidered his position on keeping unsuitable members of his staff in his employ yet again, Bram made it to the first floor and walked down another hallway, finally coming to the red drawing room a few moments later. Moving through the door, he scanned his surroundings, barely noticing the dark and heavy furnishings he'd paid a small fortune for, or the ornate tapestries of bloody battle scenes that hung from each and every wall. As his gaze settled on his mother, who was sitting in an ugly chair upholstered in brown tweed, and then drifted to the man sitting in a chair opposite her, he wasn't able to resist a grin.

The gentleman, curiously enough, was wearing a cheery gown of yellow, paired with a matching hat, but the hat had taken to listing to the right while the white wig the gentleman was wearing was listing to the left, giving the man a lopsided look. Upon closer observation, Bram realized that the man truly was Mr. Kenton, his grandmother's butler, and a man Bram had spoken to a few times when he'd unexpectedly encountered his grandmother out and about around New York.

He'd once come across Mr. Kenton and his grandmother while he'd been riding a horse in Central Park, although it had been more of a case of almost being run down by them. They'd been in an open phaeton, which had taken him aback, given that phaetons were fast vehicles normally reserved for the younger set. But there Mr. Kenton had been, holding the reins in hands that had clearly been shaking while Abigail beamed back at Bram from her seat beside her butler.

Another time he'd come across her in the gentlemen's suit section at Arnold Constable & Company, where she'd immediately sought his assistance in helping Mr. Kenton choose the perfect suit, even though, in Bram's opinion, Mr. Kenton hadn't been aware he was suit shopping until that very moment.

The last time he'd encountered Mr. Kenton had been on the Hudson River, right

112

beside Bram's private dock. He'd been about to board his steamboat when a horn had blasted, and the next thing he'd known, Abigail was waving madly to him from a steamboat she was on, calling to him that she and Mr. Kenton were on their way to visit friends. Before he'd been able to invite her to come in and enjoy a cup of tea with him at Ravenwood, she'd turned and yelled something to the captain of the boat and they'd quickly chugged away down the Hudson.

Her behavior had seemed somewhat peculiar to him, but after further reflection, Bram had come to the conclusion that Abigail had most likely been trying to sneak a peek at Ravenwood and had gotten caught in the process, which had evidently left her flustered and fleeing. That's when Bram had begun to realize that his grandmother might be trying to build some type of relationship with him, and had also realized that she wasn't nearly the ogre his mother had always made her out to be.

"They've been staring at each other without speaking for the past twenty minutes."

Tearing his attention away from his mother and Mr. Kenton, who were, indeed, staring, or rather, glaring at each other, Bram turned and settled it on a distinguished older gentleman. This gentleman was looking completely at his ease, even while wearing a gown of ivory trimmed in lavender that Bram was fairly certain he'd seen Miss Plum wear a time or two. When the gentleman rose to his feet, Bram moved to join him, shaking the man's extended hand.

"I'm Mr. Archibald Addleshaw, Mr. Haverstein, but since your grandmother and I are fast friends, do feel free to call me Archibald."

"It's a pleasure to meet you, sir, and you must call me Bram." Bram withdrew his hand. "May I assume you're related to Oliver Addleshaw?"

Archibald nodded before he settled himself once again into the wing-backed chair positioned in front of floor-to-ceiling stained-glass windows. Gesturing to a matching chair right beside him, he waited until Bram took a seat before he leaned forward. "Oliver's my grandson, and I'm delighted to learn you're acquainted with him."

"I'm afraid I don't know him well, sir. Oliver and I never mingled in the same social circles, although I have run across him in some of the gentlemen clubs throughout the city. I did hear rumors he'd gotten himself engaged lately, so please pass along my best wishes to him when you see him next."

"He's actually married now, to Miss Harriet Peabody, a great friend of Lucetta's and a dear friend of your grandmother's." Archibald smiled. "Abigail will probably tell you at some point that she was responsible for bringing Harriet and Oliver together, as well as having a bit of a hand in seeing one of Oliver's best friends, Mr. Everett Mulberry, and Miss Millie Longfellow well settled."

Bram frowned. "When you say responsible . . . ?"

Archibald's smile turned into a grin. "She fancies herself something of a matchmaker these days." After speaking those slightly concerning words, Archibald leaned back in the chair and crossed a leg in a very unfeminine manner, the crossing having the skirt of his gown lifting up a few inches, showing a remarkably white leg in the process. That the leg sported a black sock that was currently pooled around the man's white ankle had Bram grinning.

"I don't mean to be forward, sir, but I'm more than willing to lend you a change of clothing if you have nothing of your own to change into," Bram said. "I've never actually worn a gown before, but I have to imagine they're not as comfortable as trousers. And since it's clear you're not wearing, er . . . petticoats, I have to imagine you're experiencing a few drafts here and there."

Archibald returned Bram's grin. "Gowns do seem to be a little breezy, and while I thank you for the offer of a change of clothing, I did bring a trunk of my own." He nodded to Iris and Mr. Kenton and lowered his voice. "I just didn't feel comfortable leaving Mr. Kenton alone with your mother, since I'm well aware of the strained relationship those two share."

Before Bram had an opportunity to ask a single question about the strained relationship his mother apparently shared with Abigail's butler, his grandmother suddenly sailed into the room. She immediately looked her daughter's way, shuddered ever so slightly, and then made a beeline for Bram and Archibald.

Stopping beside Bram as he rose to his feet, she sent him a lovely smile and reached up to pat his cheek. "I'm so glad you've abandoned that patch, dear. You have such a handsome face — though the patch did lend you a rather rogue-about-town appearance." She patted his cheek again in a very grandmotherly fashion. "Do be sure to avoid the patch subject if at all possible the next time you're with Lucetta, though. I'm fairly sure you don't actually have a reasonable explanation as to why you were wearing it, and it won't earn you her esteem if she decides you're too peculiar."

"How do you know I want to earn Miss Plum's esteem?" he asked slowly.

"You'd be a fool not to, dear, *and* I'm your grandmother — we know everything, especially as pertains to our grandchildren, as well as their love —"

Whatever else she'd been about to say got lost when Iris suddenly let out a loud huff, shot to her feet, and advanced toward them with a look on her face that had Bram longing to make a hasty retreat.

"It's about time you decided to put in an appearance, Mother."

Abigail seemed to swell on the spot. "If you must know, Iris, I've been seeing to Miss Plum. If you've forgotten, she did recently suffer from a swooning attack. I, being responsible for the young lady and her welfare, needed to stay with her until I felt she was somewhat recovered from her ordeal."

Iris released a snort. "Miss Plum, as even I know, is an accomplished actress, her skills unrivaled on the stage. Because of that, it was obvious to me that Miss Plum's swoon was nothing more than a ploy to divert attention away from you, as I'm sure you knew from the moment she sank so perfectly to the ground. Furthermore, I'm sure you've been making yourself scarce in an effort to readjust whatever madcap scheme you're currently involved with, a scheme that has you bringing an actress of all people to Ravenwood." Iris crossed her arms over her chest. "I think some explanations are in order, Mother."

Abigail crossed her arms over her chest as well. "And I will be perfectly happy to oblige after you explain to me what you were trying to do to poor Mr. Kenton."

"We were communicating," Iris said with a sniff.

"By glaring at each other?" Abigail pressed.

"I think Miss Iris is still put out with me over the whole pulling her from the window episode," Mr. Kenton said, walking slowly their way on legs that looked anything but steady.

Striding forward, Bram took hold of the elderly gentleman's arm and steered him to the nearest settee, helping him take a seat. "Would you like me to ring for someone to show you to a room, Mr. Kenton? I have yet to be apprised of all that has happened, but I'm assuming all of you have experienced some long hours. Because of that, I'm sure my mother would agree that any discussion of past events can surely wait until you've rested." He leaned closer to the gentleman. "You'll not win an argument with her if you're not at your best."

To Bram's surprise, Mr. Kenton sent him a smile. "I do appreciate your concern, Mr. Haverstein. Do know that even though I haven't had much to do with your mother over the past thirty years or so, I well remember how difficult it is to win an argument with her. Truth be told, that is exactly why I resorted to muteness for the past half hour."

Iris let out another snort, but when Bram looked up at her, the very corners of her lips were curving — until she turned her attention to him and wrinkled her nose as her gaze lingered on his eye, the eye that had recently been covered with an unexplainable patch. To his relief, she shook her head and returned her attention to Mr. Kenton, quite as if she wasn't up to discussing her son and his peculiar ways at this particular moment.

"There would be no need for us to argue

about anything, Mr. Kenton, if you'd only apologize for thwarting me in my desperate attempt to run away from home."

Abigail immediately began *tsk*ing. "Honestly, Iris, that thwarting happened decades ago and since you still managed to become Mrs. Haverstein, you were obviously successful with the running-away-from-home business in the end. Because of that, I'm not certain I understand your continued animosity toward Mr. Kenton, who was simply trying to prevent you from breaking that all too stubborn neck of yours."

Abigail moved to the chair Bram had recently abandoned and took a seat, gesturing Archibald into the seat right beside her. Waiting until he'd rearranged the skirt of his gown, she looked back at Iris, who'd plopped down on a light pink fainting couch that didn't actually suit the décor of the room. "If you've forgotten, dear, Mr. Kenton stopped you in your attempt to climb out your *third*-floor bedroom window. The tree you'd intended to climb down was little more than a scraggly sapling, so in all fairness, you should be thanking the man for saving your life."

"I'd climbed out that window numerous times without a single mishap. And if Mr. Kenton had not stopped me when it was imperative I make my escape, I wouldn't have been forced to run away in the midst of my engagement party."

Bram's ears perked up. "I never knew you had an engagement party."

"That's because it was not a party of my choosing, nor was the intended outcome seeing me engaged to your father." Iris shot a glare to Abigail before turning her attention back to Bram. "Your grandmother came to the unfortunate conclusion that your father was not good enough for me. She staunchly refused to listen to my professions of love for Phillip and insisted that I would outgrow my feelings for 'that German man,' as she referred to him. She then proceeded to go about the troubling business of arranging a marriage for me — one that would see me wed to a Mr. Wilbur Something-or-Other. It was completely archaic, the notion of her handling my future, which is why I took matters into my own hands and ran away."

"It was Mr. Wilbur Gilbert, a gentleman with stellar connections, and a distant relation of the Schermerhorn family," Abigail said. "Poor Mr. Gilbert was completely distraught after you left him floundering in the middle of the ballroom floor with a ring in his hand, but no blushing fiancée in sight."

Iris's eyes turned dangerous. "There would have been no cause for him to become distraught if he'd simply approached me about the whole engagement matter instead of taking your advice and trying to spring it on me in the midst of a ball. I was completely appalled by the events of that evening, and have yet to recover from the idea that you, my mother, tried to corral me into a marriage I didn't want."

Iris drummed her fingers against the curved edge of the fainting couch. "Do you honestly believe that I would have been better served to turn my back on the man I was desperately in love with — and still am, mind you — and marry your Mr. Gilbert, whom, again, I barely knew and had nothing in common with, so that I could . . . what . . . attend all the right parties in town?"

To Bram's surprise, Abigail nodded. "At the time, yes, that's exactly what I thought was best for you, as did your father, God rest his soul. If you'll recall, your Mr. Haverstein wanted to sweep you off your feet and all the way to Cuba, a land I thought was somewhat savage, and a land where he'd gotten involved with a sugar refinery, of all things."

"Since that sugar refinery, along with the sugar plantation we eventually purchased, ended up making us millions, and continues to do just that, Mother, I'm not sure you're aiding your case by bringing it up."

Abigail narrowed her eyes. "Can you truly say that if Ruby, your one and only daughter, came to you and told you that she wanted to marry a man you knew absolutely nothing about, and that the gentleman wanted to spirit her away to the wilds of some mysterious land, that you and Phillip wouldn't try to put an end to her nonsense?"

"We're not talking about my daughter at the moment, Mother. We're talking about you and your meddling ways."

"A subject that, in my opinion, is less than riveting and certainly doesn't need to be discussed further." Abigail narrowed her eyes another fraction. "Why don't you want to discuss Ruby?"

For a second, Iris looked a little shifty, but then she lifted her chin. "I never claimed I didn't want to discuss Ruby. But, I do believe, given the odd circumstance of you being here at Ravenwood, as well as bringing Miss Lucetta Plum along with you, that we have more important matters to discuss than my daughter."

Abigail's gaze sharpened on Iris's face. "Ruby's causing you difficulties, isn't she?"

Before Iris had an opportunity to respond, a loud noise, one that almost sounded like some type of animal, suddenly drifted into the drawing room from the hallway — mixed with the sound of what could only be pounding feet.

Immediately heading for the door, Bram stopped in his tracks when he reached the hall and a sight he'd certainly not been expecting to see met his gaze.

Miss Plum was running toward him, her gown practically falling off her, as if it hadn't been fastened all the way up in the back. She didn't seem at all concerned with the idea that she was giving him, and anyone else, an eyeful of her chemise, corset, and . . . charms — probably because she was running as if her very life depended on it, holding up the skirt of her dress as she flew ever closer to him, the lifting of that skirt giving him an unobstructed view of legs that were well turned out and feet that were . . . bare.

"Don't just stand there, Mr. Haverstein. Do something about your goat," she yelled as she pounded past him.

The word *goat* had him looking down the

hallway, and sure enough, a goat was charging his way, and not just any goat, but Geoffrey — one of the meanest goats Bram had ever had the misfortune of owning.

What the beast was doing inside the castle, he really couldn't say, but since Geoffrey held an intense dislike for females, or more specifically, females wearing dresses, Bram surged into motion, hoping to intercept the goat before it managed to catch up with Miss Plum.

Unfortunately, Geoffrey seemed determined to get past Bram, so with a butt of its head, it sent Bram sprawling and continued charging after its prey, bleating in a menacing sort of way.

Running as fast as she could, even though her lungs were beginning to feel as if they were on fire, Lucetta yelled a word of thanks to the man dressed in formal black attire who was holding the front door open for her. A few seconds later, though, she longed to call her thanks back because the man, for some unknown reason, had kept the door wide open, making it possible for the rampaging goat to continue charging after her.

Lifting her skirt a little higher, she headed for the drawbridge, sending up a quick prayer of gratitude when she made it to the other side without taking another dip in the moat. Dashing across the well-manicured lawn, she set her sights for the trees but slowed her pace when Mr. Skukman burst out of those trees and ran her way. Looking over her shoulder when he blazed past her, she slowed to a stop because while she'd been running, Bram had somehow managed to catch up with the goat and was even now lying on top of the creature. That state of affairs was probably responsible for the mournful bleats the goat was now emitting, as if he couldn't believe his quest of running Lucetta down had come to such a rapid end.

Lifting her head, Lucetta saw Abigail, Archibald, Iris, and Mr. Kenton hurrying out of the castle.

"Everyone wearing dresses, stay back," Bram called, which Lucetta found to be a slightly curious thing to say. Before she could contemplate it further, though, Mr. Skukman reached Bram's side, and as calmly as could be, pulled a length of rope out of his jacket pocket, the sight causing Lucetta to grin.

Mr. Skukman was the only man she knew who always had the right tools available to him, no matter the circumstance.

Looping the rope around the goat's neck, Mr. Skukman nodded to Bram, who rolled off the goat and rose to his feet, earning a bleat of reproach from the goat as he did so. To Lucetta's annoyance, the goat then moved right up next to her guard and actually nuzzled the man with its head.

"Aren't you a good boy?" Mr. Skukman crooned as he began leading the goat directly Lucetta's way.

"He's a horrible boy," she called. "Had murder on his mind from what I could see, and don't even think about bringing him over here to me."

"Honestly, Miss Plum, get ahold of yourself," Mr. Skukman said as he veered to the right and walked the goat around her, although it looked as if he was having to exert some extra pressure to keep the goat moving. "I'm taking him to the barn that's right past those trees behind you."

"How do you know that?"

"Found it when I was scouting the perimeter, checking for safety issues."

With that, Mr. Skukman tugged the goat along, completely ignoring the fact that the creature kept turning its head to eye Lucetta in a very disturbing manner.

"Your Mr. Skukman is a man of few words, isn't he?" Bram said as he walked up to join her.

"It's one of the reasons I hired him."

Bram frowned. "You prefer men who don't speak much?"

"Would you be insulted if I admitted I do?"

To Lucetta's surprise, instead of looking insulted, Bram sent her a look of understanding as he stepped closer to her. "You're obviously overcome by the shock you've recently experienced because of my goat. And while I would love to be able to say that Geoffrey was just out of sorts today, I'm afraid he's been out of sorts ever since someone abandoned him at Ravenwood a few months back, in the middle of the night."

"Your goat's name is Geoffrey?"

"My sister, Ruby, named it after a gentleman she'd once set her sights on, but a gentleman who turned out to be a bit of a disappointment." Bram shook his head. "The man had the audacity to go off and marry some well-connected society miss, breaking Ruby's heart in the process."

Lucetta smiled. "I do believe I'm going to like this sister of yours, Mr. Haverstein, especially since it appears she has no qualms about naming a cranky beast after a gentleman she no longer holds in high esteem."

"Please, since you've been set upon by my dogs, and practically mauled by my goat, feel free to call me Bram."

"Very well, since I have experienced all of that madness at the paws and hooves of your animals, I will call you Bram and you may call me Lucetta." Her smile began to fade. "But pleasantries aside, why do you think your goat tried to attack me, and what was it doing in the tower room in the first place?"

Bram blew out a breath. "Geoffrey attacked you because he has a problem with dresses — something we learned when he chased poor Mrs. Macmillan, who'd been trying to help get Geoffrey to the barn the morning we discovered him." Bram shook his head. "Mrs. Macmillan has not been back to the barn since. As for what Geoffrey was doing in the tower room, I must admit that I can't even fathom how he got up there without someone noticing."

"It's certainly a mystery," Lucetta said as she stepped forward, wincing when something sharp dug into her foot. Looking down, she felt heat traveling up her face when she saw that, in her mad dash to get away from the goat, she'd completely neglected to realize that not only had she forgotten her shoes and stockings, she'd also forgotten that she hadn't buttoned her gown up all the way.

"Goodness," she muttered as she yanked the neckline of her dress up as high as she could.

"If it makes you feel better, I don't believe anyone took note of your somewhat questionable state of *dishabille.*"

Her head shot up as she met Bram's eyes.

"You obviously noticed."

He sent her a charming smile. "Noticed what?" He extended her his arm. "There's a lovely grove right through those trees, which is nowhere near the barn, I might add. It'll afford you a bit of privacy to set yourself to rights since I don't believe you'll be keen to face all the people still lingering outside the castle doors."

Glancing to where Bram was now looking, Lucetta found a small cluster of people looking her way, although Mr. Kenton and Archibald were walking back toward the castle, the skirts of their dresses fluttering in the breeze. Abigail, however, seemed to be in the midst of a heated conversation with her daughter, both women gesturing wildly with their hands as the remaining members of Bram's staff edged ever so slowly away from them.

"Should we intervene?" she asked with a nod Abigail's way.

"I willingly admit I'm not that familiar with my grandmother when she's in a temper, but my mother is not a woman who would appreciate an intervention. I suggest you get yourself straightened about, and then I'll take you for a lovely walk around the grounds. By the time we get back, they'll have hopefully settled a few of their differences from the past thirty years."

"It's fortunate your grounds seem to be extensive."

"Quite," Bram agreed as she took the arm he was still holding out to her. He turned his attention back to Abigail and Iris. "I'm taking Miss Plum for a tour of the grounds," he called. "We'll be back in an hour or two."

Abigail and Iris stopped arguing and turned their attention Bram and Lucetta's way. It was immediately clear that Abigail took no issue with Bram giving Lucetta a tour of the grounds. She lifted her arm and sent them a cheery wave before she spun on her heel and headed back toward the castle, spinning around again a moment later. Putting her hands on her hips, she marched her way back to Iris — who'd not moved at all — took her daughter's arm, and with what looked to be a bit of wrestling, hauled Iris inside with her.

"Perhaps we'll mosey around the grounds for more than an hour or two," Bram said as he steered Lucetta toward the trees. "We can always pass some time visiting my herd of sheep."

"I think I've seen all the animals I care to see today, thank you very much, and even though the thought of avoiding whatever unpleasantness is transpiring between Abigail and Iris is tempting, I really won't be comfortable leaving Abigail for long, even with Archibald and Mr. Kenton to keep an eye on her."

"That's very thoughtful of you," Bram said, sending Lucetta a charming smile that had her knees going a little wobbly.

Shoving aside the idea that he was far too attractive when he smiled, and ignoring the curious condition of her knees, Lucetta fell into step beside him and began chatting about the weather, of all things. As they walked into a stand of trees, the temperature dropped, easing some of the heat that still remained on Lucetta's neck, heat that immediately returned when Bram drew her to a stop and smiled at her again.

"If you'll turn around, I'll help you with those buttons," he said.

His suggestion had the heat traveling up her neck and settling on her face, a reaction that took her by complete surprise. Being an actress, she'd become used to having many people button her up over the years, male and female, but their assistance had never bothered her before. Out of necessity, she'd rarely given much thought to modesty over the past few years, but now, surrounded only by trees and a gentleman who had one of the nicest smiles she'd ever seen, thoughts of modesty were pushing their way to the forefront of her mind.

"Tell me about your sheep," she said as she stood rooted to the spot, unable to turn around, and unwilling to take him up on his offer to help with her buttons just yet.

She was thankful when Bram didn't press her to turn. "It's a diverse herd, made up of a wide variety of once abused and neglected sheep, all of them having a mistrust of humans." He shook his head. "They're becoming fairly well adjusted now, and I have high hopes that the longer they're here, the more they'll realize they're finally safe and will settle into happy lives, chomping high grass on the castle grounds."

"Where did you get them?"

Bram shrugged. "Here and there. It's become known that I'm always willing to take in strays, so . . . people drop off all sorts of animals at Ravenwood, or people send me letters, letting me know of animals that might need my help. My staff and I spend a lot of time tracking down neglected animals, and once we find them, we bring them here to live out the rest of their lives."

Lucetta's heart gave a lurch. "You're a collector of misfits."

Bram smiled. "I like misfits, probably because I've always been a bit of a misfit as

134

well." He moved an inch closer to her. "Shall I button you up?"

"I should probably do it myself."

His smile turned remarkably sweet. "I won't look, in fact, I can close my eyes if it'll make you feel better."

Drawing in a deep breath even as she realized she was being a complete ninny because there was no way she could reach the buttons on the back of her gown, she presented Bram with her back. A second later she nearly jumped out of her skin when his finger slid against the nape of her neck, pushing hair still wet from her bath out of the way before he began securing one button after another.

"There, all done, and I didn't peek — not once." He put his hands on her shoulders and turned her around to face him.

Still feeling a little jittery from his touch, she lifted her head, trying to think of something witty to say. She found herself at a complete loss for words, though, when she looked into his eyes — both of them now twinkling back at her — and lost herself in his gaze.

While he'd previously had the look of a pirate about him that she'd found rather appealing, she now found him to be devastatingly handsome — not simply because he'd been born far too attractive, but because she believed she saw genuine nice-ness residing in his very soul.

When he suddenly lifted a finger to push a damp strand of hair off her cheek, his touch caused any reasonable thoughts she still retained to flee from her mind, and everything surrounding her disappeared except Bram.

"You're very beautiful."

Just like that, the world returned in a flash.

"Thank you," she said before she stepped back from him and felt a sliver of temper — not at him, but at herself — begin flowing through her veins.

She'd known he was infatuated with her, as most of her admirers were. And yet, instead of nipping that immediately in the bud, she'd allowed herself to believe he was different, different because his touch sent her pulse racing and his smile turned her knees a little weak, which, in actuality, did make him a touch different, although . . .

"Forgive me, Lucetta, but have I done something to upset you?"

Lucetta caught Bram's eye. "To be per-fectly honest, I'm more upset with myself."

Bram's brow furrowed. "I'm afraid I don't understand."

"I should have addressed the misconceptions I'm certain you're holding about me straightaway, and yet . . . I've let matters fester too long."

"You do recall that we only met a few hours ago, don't you?"

"Indeed, but I'm quite certain you've been harboring misconceptions about me from the moment you saw me step foot on stage, which I'm going to assume was a year or two ago."

The furrow deepened. "I'm still not sure what you're trying to say."

"I'm not a lady who enjoys being told I'm beautiful, nor am I a lady who enjoys being pampered, catered to, or treated as if I'm fragile. I'm also nothing like any of the characters I've ever played on stage."

"You're exactly like the character in *The Lady in the Tower*," he argued. "Charming, demure, and delightful."

Resisting a sigh, she moved to a fallen tree lying off the path and took a seat. "I would never be content to remain a prisoner in a tower, waiting for my very own prince charming to rescue me, which is exactly what Serena Seamore, my character, does. I've been on my own, Bram, for a very long time, and I'm quite capable, thank you very much, of taking care of myself." She held up her hand when it looked as if he wanted to argue. "What you need to remember is that I'm an actress. Playing a part is what I do, and I'm successful because I can play parts very, very well. I've also been given an unusual face, expressive if you will, and that expressiveness allows me to convince people I'm someone I'm not."

"Your face is lovely, not unusual."

Lucetta waved away his compliment. "I'm not getting through to you, am I."

"Of course you are."

Lucetta drew in a deep breath and slowly released it. "I'm afraid I'm not the lady you think you hold in high esteem."

"I don't think I hold you in high esteem, I *know* I do."

"Oh . . . dear," she muttered before she squared her shoulders. "I'm peculiar."

"I highly doubt that."

"Oh, believe me, I am, and . . ." She patted the spot beside her on the log. "Perhaps you should take a seat."

Lowering himself ever so slowly beside her, Bram frowned. "Why do I get the distinct feeling you're about to tell me something I'm not going to care to hear?"

"Because I am, and while I truly don't want to hurt your feelings, you need to understand that the last thing I need at the moment is another admirer."

"You don't care for people who admire your work?"

"I don't think it's only my work you admire, Bram."

His only response was to consider her for a drawn-out moment, until he released a bit of a sigh and began scrutinizing the trees that surrounded them.

Not being a lady who ever cared to hurt a person's feelings, she reached out and touched Bram's arm.

"I would enjoy being friends with you, though."

He stopped scrutinizing the trees and pinned her beneath a brilliant blue gaze. "You want to be my friend?"

"I don't have many friends, especially male friends, but the few I do have . . . well, I enjoy their company tremendously." She took a second to pat his arm again. "Although, to be clear, if you and I become friends, you'll need to stop admiring me."

"Most ladies enjoy admiration."

"Most ladies don't attract admirers who want to acquire them, even going so far as to coerce a weak-minded stepfather into a game of cards in order to cheat him and have said stepfather offer his stepdaughter up as a means to honor a debt."

Bram arched a brow. "May I assume we're

talking about something other than my admiration for you now?"

She nodded, just once.

Leaning forward, he frowned. "May I also assume you're the stepdaughter in question in this particular instance, and that one of your admirers expects you to . . . honor your stepfather's debt?"

"Unfortunately, you may make that assumption because Silas Ruff — one of my most repulsive admirers — expects just that, which should, I would hope, be a sufficient explanation as to why I don't care for admirers."

"Are we speaking about the Silas Ruff who left the city a few months back because of unbecoming behavior on his part at some society event?"

"One and the same, and you should know that his unbecoming behavior happened at a ball your own grandmother hosted."

Bram leaned even closer. "Silas Ruff behaved poorly in the company of my *grandmother*?"

"Indeed he did, but Archibald's grandson, Oliver, handled the matter, although it's quite clear now that Silas wasn't handled for good. That is why Abigail and I have descended on you unannounced, abusing your hospitality in the process since we certainly didn't give you an opportunity to refuse us." She released a sigh. "Silas seems more determined than ever to secure a relationship with me, so do know that I truly appreciate your allowing me to seek refuge here at Ravenwood, at least until I can figure out a way to deal with Silas once and for all."

Bram looked away from her, his attention settling on a squirrel that was watching them from a nearby tree. Nodding as if to himself, he turned back to Lucetta. "You're welcome to stay at Ravenwood for as long as you need, and I'll do whatever I can to assist you."

"Thank you, Bram. I certainly appreciate your offer, although I'm not sure anyone can assist me with Silas. He's a very influential man, has unsavory contacts throughout the country, and doesn't know how to take no for an answer. I've been at my wits' end for years trying to figure out a way to get away from him once and for all, but I've yet to come up with a viable plan."

For a moment, Bram said absolutely nothing as he continued watching her with a considering look in his eyes. Then he took hold of her hand, giving it a good squeeze. "I believe one of the best solutions available to you, and one that will rid you of Silas

Ruff once and for all, is this." He sent her a charming smile as his hand tightened on hers. "You're going to have to get married, and as circumstances would have it, I would be perfectly willing, and incredibly honored, of course, to offer you the safety of my name."

10

"Mr. Skukman, you're a man."

Mr. Skukman backed out of the floor-to-ceiling fireplace he'd been investigating in the tower room and sent Lucetta a frown. "I didn't realize that was in question."

Lucetta winced. "Well, no, it's not. I was simply pointing out that you're a man, and as such, I'm hoping you can explain to me why another man would offer to marry me — after I explained to that man how peculiar I am, and that I don't take kindly to admirers."

"I see we're back to what happened yesterday with Mr. Haverstein."

"He offered to *marry* me."

"So you've said, numerous times."

"Abigail is upset with me because I graciously rejected Bram's completely ridiculous suggestion."

Mr. Skukman quirked a brow her way.

Lifting her chin, Lucetta quirked a brow

right back at him. "I *was* gracious."

"If you say so. But in my opinion, he offered you a reasonable solution to the very real problem you're facing with Silas Ruff."

"You cannot truly believe I should have accepted his proposal, can you?"

Mr. Skukman's brows drew together. "Of course not, but I would have expected you to show a bit more appreciation for his willingness to sacrifice himself for *your* benefit." He ducked back into the fireplace, tapping against the stone with a hammer he'd pulled out of one of his numerous jacket pockets. "I was certain we'd find evidence of a hidden passageway in here, but it sounds remarkably solid."

Leaning over, Lucetta stuck her head in the fireplace. "What do you mean . . . sacrifice?" she asked, her voice echoing eerily around her.

"I've been in your employ for quite some time, Miss Plum. I, probably more than anyone, know your true nature, and . . . you can be difficult — downright cantankerous, some might say."

"Your days of being in my employ could very well be numbered," Lucetta muttered.

Mr. Skukman turned and caught her eye. "You would never get rid of me."

Withdrawing her head from the fireplace,

Lucetta wrinkled her nose. "You're probably right, but I still don't understand why Bram offered to marry me. As I mentioned a time or two already, I explained to him that I don't care for admirers, and yet . . . less than ten minutes after I did all that explaining, he offered me his name."

Mr. Skukman withdrew from the fireplace again as well. "I think what you need to understand, Miss Plum, is that Mr. Haverstein is one of those rare gentlemen, a throwback, if you will, to the days of knights in shining armor. One only has to look at that staff of his, or take a trip to one of his many barns filled to the brim with the oddest assortment of animals I've ever seen, to know he possesses a strong sense of chivalry and honor. You, my dear, can't blame him for offering to marry you, especially not after you presented him with a classic damsel-in-distress scenario."

With that, Mr. Skukman sent her a rather stern look before he nodded to a bookcase that took up an entire wall on the opposite side of the room. "Now that we've settled that, make yourself useful. Since it doesn't appear there's a passageway hidden in the fireplace, we'll try the bookcase next."

Lucetta frowned. "Don't you think that would be a little too obvious, hiding a secret passageway behind a bookcase?"

"It's so obvious that it might very well be the most logical choice. And, given the architecture of Ravenwood, it's evident the original owner possessed a sense of the dramatic. I imagine he would have enjoyed hiding a secret passageway behind the proverbial bookcase, as well as riding across the misty moors with a pack of snarling wolves nipping at his heels."

Lucetta tilted her head. "Have you been reading Lord Byron again?"

Mr. Skukman gave a brief nod. "Funny enough, I have. I recently finished Lord Byron's 'Manfred,' although I also recently discovered 'Nightmare Abbey' by Thomas Love Peacock." His eyes went a little distant. "What a fascinating story, filled with characters who were inspired by real-life acquaintances of Thomas Love Peacock, such as that master of romantic poetry himself, Lord Byron."

Lucetta resisted a grin. "That sounds fascinating indeed, but if we could return to the marriage proposal subject for just another moment . . . ?"

Mr. Skukman nodded to the bookcase again. "I think we've covered all there is to cover regarding that, Miss Plum. Off you go."

Feeling a little put out that Mr. Skukman did not care to continue the discussion surrounding Bram and his proposal, but knowing if she argued the point she'd be proving Mr. Skukman right about her being a touch difficult upon occasion, Lucetta blew out a breath and marched across the room. Eyeing the books, she saw a copy of *Wuthering Heights* by Emily Brontë and pulled it out, opening it a second later and quickly becoming immersed in a story she'd somehow neglected to read before.

"I've never really understood how you're able to read so quickly."

Snapping the book shut, Lucetta lifted her head, found Mr. Skukman watching her, and said, "What a disturbing story Emily Brontë penned. I think it is one you — what, with your appetite for anything gothic these days — will enjoy. Although . . . that Heathcliff character is fodder for some deep contemplation."

"You didn't address my previous statement," Mr. Skukman pointed out. "You've obviously almost finished that entire book, yet less than an hour has passed since you picked it up, and . . . clearly you were reading and comprehending what you'd read."

Lucetta stuck the book back on the shelf. "I've been reading for almost an hour?"

"Still not explaining how you read so quickly."

Knowing Mr. Skukman could be incredibly stubborn when he put his mind to it, Lucetta shrugged. "It's not a secret, even though I don't share it often . . . or . . . ever. You see, even though I casually tell people I'm peculiar, the truth of the matter is, I really am. I remember every word, or every number, I see, which means that when I read a book, it's almost like my mind is taking a photograph, and that photograph is stored away in my memory forever."

Mr. Skukman sent her a rare smile. "That's not a peculiar gift, Miss Plum, it's an extraordinary one."

Intent on arguing that point, because she'd learned firsthand how unfortunate it was to have her particular gift, Lucetta opened her mouth but was interrupted before she could say a single word when someone rapped on the door.

"Miss Plum, it's Mrs. Haverstein. I'd like a word with you, if you please."

Lucetta's nerves immediately took to jittering. She'd not had an opportunity to speak with Iris, Bram's mother, as of yet. When she'd returned to the castle with Bram the day before, he'd escorted her straight up to the tower room before bid-ding her a very pleasant — albeit slightly chilly — good afternoon. After she'd watched him beat a hasty retreat, she'd walked into the tower room and found a lovely luncheon tray waiting for her, as well as Mrs. Macmillan, the housekeeper. Finding it a little odd that the housekeeper would have been standing guard over her lunch, Lucetta soon discovered that the woman had lingered in order to tell Lucetta that Abigail, Archibald, Mr. Kenton, and even Mr. Skukman, had repaired to their respective rooms to eat a peaceful meal, and then to take a rest.

Quickly coming to the conclusion that a rest was a very good option indeed, especially since she'd been very short on sleep, Lucetta had thanked Mrs. Macmillan for providing her with a lunch, ignored the woman's sniff, and had seen her rapidly out the door. After eating the delightful lunch provided for her, she'd lain down on the bed, appreciating the softness of the blankets covering it, and had fallen straight to sleep.

She'd not woken up until the morning. When she'd gone down to the dining room, she'd been told by a very disappointed Abigail that Bram was not about, Iris had gone back to her own home the day before and had not returned, and Mr. Kenton and Archibald were both beginning to show symptoms of colds so they were going to have a restful day in bed.

Abigail had been so disappointed regarding Lucetta's rejection of Bram's offer of marriage, that she'd spent the entire breakfast sighing loudly into her eggs, the sighs finally having Lucetta excusing herself to get ready for the day.

She'd been at the whole getting-ready business for a few hours, but wasn't keen just yet to seek Abigail out, knowing that woman had now been left to her own devices for quite some time, and during that time, Lucetta was fairly certain Abigail had taken to plotting again.

Reluctantly, Lucetta's thoughts returned to Iris waiting at the door. "What do you think Mrs. Haverstein wants to speak with me about?" she finally whispered, eyeing the door but making no effort to move toward it.

To her surprise, Mr. Skukman strode to her side, took her by the arm, and the next thing she knew, she was standing behind thick brocade curtains.

"You may consider this, Miss Plum, my apology for calling you difficult, but do try to keep quiet while I deal with Mrs. Haverstein," he cautioned before he pulled his head out from the curtain, gave it another yank as if to make certain Lucetta was well covered, then moved away, the soles of his shoes clicking against the stone floor. The door gave a squeak, and . . .

"Mr. Skullduggery. I certainly wasn't expecting to find you up here."

"It's Skukman, Mrs. Haverstein."

"Is it really?"

"Indeed."

"Hmm, forgive me, then. Although . . . *skullduggery* fits you admirably, given your daunting appearance. But that's neither here nor there. I'd like to have a word with Miss Plum."

"Begging your pardon, ma'am, but I'm fairly sure you'd like more than a word with her."

"You may be correct."

Silence settled around the tower after that, becoming more and more uncomfortable as the seconds ticked away, punctuated by the large clock that graced the wall right beside where Lucetta was hiding.

"Don't you believe it's a little untoward, you being up here in rooms Miss Plum is currently occupying?" Iris suddenly demanded.

"Not at all. I'm searching for clues as to

151

how that goat got up here."

"You're a man."

"That has been pointed out quite a bit today."

"Pardon me?"

Mr. Skukman cleared his throat. "I am Miss Plum's personal guard, Mrs. Haverstein. As such, it is my duty to keep her safe. I'd be incredibly derelict in that duty if I didn't investigate threats to her safety, and Geoffrey the goat was a distinct threat and could have caused Miss Plum serious injury."

"I suppose that is a valid point."

"Indeed."

More seconds ticked away.

"Would you happen to know where Miss Plum is?" Iris asked.

"I do."

"Well?"

"I'm not at liberty to disclose that information, Mrs. Haverstein."

"Whyever not?"

"Because again, my main objective, as her personal guard, is to keep her safe."

"I'm not going to harm her."

"Best not to chance it."

A loud sigh reached Lucetta's ears. "Very well. Since you won't divulge her location, answer me this. Why would Miss Plum turn down a respectable offer of marriage from a gentleman such as my Bram?"

"Why is it that ladies seem to believe I enjoy discussing these types of personal matters?" Mr. Skukman countered.

Iris continued as if Mr. Skukman had not spoken. "Bram is a wealthy, eligible, and influential gentleman who owns his own castle — not to mention his stellar good looks."

"You're his mother. Of course you're going to believe he has stellar good looks."

"You don't believe my Bram is handsome?"

"Yet another topic I'm not comfortable discussing, but . . . I suppose if I really consider the matter, yes . . . Mr. Haverstein's features are adequately arranged, but Miss Plum is not a lady who is impressed by a handsome face."

"She's an actress."

Mr. Skukman let out a bit of a growl, which had Lucetta immediately stepping from behind the curtain. "Thank you, Mr. Skukman, but I think it might be for the best if I take it from here."

"Were you hiding behind the curtains?" Iris demanded.

"Obviously," Lucetta said as she headed across the room, stepping in between Iris, who was looking indignant, and Mr. Skukman, who'd adopted his most intimidating pose — a pose that didn't appear to intimidate Iris in the least.

"Now then," Lucetta began, sending Mr. Skukman a frown when he cracked his knuckles, "from what I overheard, you're here, Mrs. Haverstein, to learn why I rejected Bram's offer."

Iris lifted her chin. "That's one of the reasons I've sought you out."

"Lovely, and before we address those other reasons, allow me to say that the reason I refused Bram's proposal was because your son was offering to marry a woman who doesn't exist. He simply has yet to realize that."

Iris narrowed her eyes. "Bram could provide you with everything."

"I'm fairly good at providing for myself, Mrs. Haverstein."

Iris's eyes narrowed to mere slits. "What are you really playing at? Are you, by chance, hoping that because you turned him down, he'll make you a better offer?"

Lucetta's brows drew together. "What else could he possibly offer me that would be more appealing than his name?"

For a second, Iris looked a little taken aback, but she rallied quickly. "You may be the type of woman who prefers the freedom spinsterhood provides, so I would imagine you're holding out for a nice place in the city, replete with all the fashionable amenities."

Even though Lucetta was well aware of the reputation most actresses were assumed to enjoy, and even though such insinuations normally never bothered her, a sliver of hurt wormed its way into her heart. Before she could summon up a suitable response, though, Abigail suddenly breezed into the room.

"Lucetta is like a granddaughter to me, Iris, and as such, you will treat her accordingly, as well as apologize for your serious lack of manners," Abigail said as she plunked her hands on her hips and scowled at her daughter.

At first, it seemed that Iris wanted to argue the point, but then she blew out a breath and nodded Lucetta's way. "My mother is quite right. That was unkind of me, and unfair. Forgive me."

Lucetta lifted her chin. "I'm sure discovering that your son extended his name to an actress has you feeling out of sorts, Mrs. Haverstein, but . . . if you'll recall, I did refuse him, so I don't exactly understand why you're so put out with me."

"She's not put out with *you,* dear," Abigail said before Iris could respond. "She's put out with *me* but taking her frustrations about that out on *you.*" She held up her hand when Iris opened her mouth. "You see, I made the mistake of telling her I felt that you and Bram would suit each other admirably, which is why she is now dead set against the two of you making a match of it."

"Because you have no skill at all when it comes to the delicate art of matchmaking, Mother," Iris began. "That, if you'll recall, was proven many years ago when you tried to pull off what would have been the tragedy of the century by trying to match me with Mr. Gilbert." Iris turned to Lucetta. "You were not present when this bit of history was brought up yesterday, but do know that my mother chose a completely unsuitable gentleman for me to marry, one who had all the right social connections but didn't stir my heart in the least. She even went so far as to convince this Mr. Gilbert to spring a surprise proposal on me in the middle of a society ball. That embarrassing episode is exactly what had me fleeing New York, marrying my Mr. Haverstein, and vowing to forsake New York society forever."

Missing pieces of the puzzle that surrounded Abigail began falling into place.

Lucetta had always known there was something in Abigail's past, some unfortunate event that Abigail regretted, that had been behind her taking in three young ladies from the Lower East Side. While the claim had been made that Abigail had been so generous simply because of her friendship with Reverend Thomas Gilmore, a dear man who'd saved Lucetta from the streets when she'd been little more than a child, it was now becoming clear that the true reason behind Abigail's generosity might have had more to do with her seeking redemption for a past wrong than for fulfilling any favors requested.

Reverend Gilmore, being a very intuitive sort, had likely known what Abigail's heart had needed all along. By asking Abigail to help Lucetta and her friends get on their way to a better life, he'd given Abigail a purpose and a way to compensate for the mistakes she'd made in the past with her own daughter.

What was certainly going to be fodder for future contemplation was this: Because Abigail had become involved in Lucetta's life, and that involvement had led to their being at Ravenwood — which had put Abigail in direct contact with her daughter — it almost seemed as if God was orchestrating some type of plan. What that plan was exactly . . . well, it was far too soon to know, but Lucetta was fairly sure it had something to do with healing the wounds of the past.

Further thoughts on the matter were pushed firmly aside when a young lady took that moment to sweep into the room, dressed in the latest fashions. Her suit was tailored to perfection and drew attention to her small waist, the tasteful bustle attached to her backside further emphasizing that smallness. The wide-brimmed hat she wore perfectly matched the green in her suit, but unlike most fashionable hats of the day, this hat did not sport so much as a single feather, having, instead, a large piece of ribbon drawn up into a bow. Her dark hair, styled to perfection, complemented a creamy complexion, and the young lady's blue eyes were filled with excitement as they glanced around the room.

"I do hope I haven't missed anything of importance," the young lady said as she breezed up to Iris, gave her a kiss on the cheek, and then let out a laugh before she hurried to greet Abigail.

"Grandmamma, it's wonderful to see you. Mother told me yesterday that you were here, but . . . she wouldn't let me visit, saying you were exhausted from your travels or some such nonsense."

"Ruby!" Abigail exclaimed, leaning forward to accept the kiss the young lady planted on her cheek. "You are looking charming as ever." Abigail stepped back and took hold of Ruby's hand. "Come, I want you to meet a friend of mine." Pulling the young lady farther into the room, she brought her to a stop right in front of Lucetta. "My dear Ruby, this is —"

"Miss Lucetta Plum," Ruby finished for Abigail before she moved closer to Lucetta and beamed a smile filled with delight her way. "I'm Miss Ruby Haverstein, Abigail's granddaughter." She sent Lucetta an unexpected wink. "Rumor has it that you and I may well be sisters someday soon."

Iris released a sigh. "Honestly, Ruby, we've been over this a hundred times in the past day. Bram and Miss Plum will not be getting married. Your brother was simply being chivalrous, something he tends to do on a far too frequent basis."

"You say that as if chivalry is not a welcome trait for a gentleman to have," Ruby said slowly. "Why, having been involved with a gentleman who turned out to have not a single chivalrous bone in his body, I can well attest to the allure that an old-fashioned gentleman with old-fashioned values has to a woman in these trying times."

"Hear, hear."

Lucetta blinked and glanced around Ruby, her lips curving when her gaze settled on Mr. Skukman. He'd apparently been responsible for the *"Hear, hear,"* yet he was now looking as if he didn't quite understand how those words had slipped from his mouth.

Ruby glanced around as well, and to Lucetta's surprise, the young lady stepped directly up to Mr. Skukman and dipped into a curtsy. "I do beg your pardon, sir. I'm afraid I neglected to notice there was someone else in the room, even though . . ." She stepped back and considered him for a moment, the consideration likely the reason Mr. Skukman's face began to turn an interesting shade of red. "You're quite intimidating, aren't you."

"Ruby, what a thing to say," Iris muttered, stepping up beside her daughter. "This is Mr. Skukman, Miss Plum's personal guard. Mr. Skukman, this is my daughter, Miss Ruby Haverstein."

"It's a pleasure to meet you, Miss Haverstein. Now, if you'll excuse me . . . I think I've had quite enough of ladies for the day."

Mr. Skukman strode for the door, handing Lucetta the hammer he'd been using to test the fireplace wall as he passed her. "You can have them help you," he said before he disappeared from sight.

"He seems like a delightful man," Ruby said to no one in particular. "Is he married?"

Abigail sent a knowing look Iris's way. "And this would explain why you didn't want to discuss Ruby yesterday." She shook her head. "*Not* having difficulties, I ask you?"

"Ruby has been in an unusual frame of mind ever since Mr. Geoffrey Jensen discontinued his association with her. It certainly didn't help matters much when he took up with Miss Darla Crofter while we were just beginning our holiday in Paris this past spring," Iris said.

"He didn't *take up* with Miss Crofter, Mother," Ruby said, pulling the gloves from her hands. "He married her, abandoning me in the process." She moved over to a chair situated by the fireplace and took a seat. "I suppose we can be thankful I haven't been introduced into society quite yet, which allowed that unfortunate abandoning to go unremarked."

"You want to become introduced to society?" Abigail asked slowly as she lowered herself into the closest available chair to her, almost as if her legs were about to give out from shock.

"Ruby will not be traveling within society," Iris said, plopping down into a chair right beside Abigail. "I turned my back on society long ago, and I will not go begging on bended knee to my old friends, asking them to sponsor Ruby simply because she wants to teach Mr. Geoffrey Jensen a lesson."

Lucetta absently took a seat, watching as Ruby seemed to swell on the spot.

"I'm twenty-three years old, Mother. A spinster, for all intents and purposes, since I wasted so much time on Geoffrey. I have no prospects at the moment, even given Father's large fortune and the extremely large dowry he's offered to any gentleman who might care to take me away. Why, it's little wonder I've developed the peculiar habit of considering any gentleman under the age of fifty with a discerning eye, especially since I don't travel in circles that allow me to be in the regular company of suitable gentlemen."

"Oh, here we go," Iris muttered.

Ruby completely ignored her mother's remark as she directed her attention Lucetta's way. "Since my mother has refused to arrange my introduction into society, I've decided to take matters into my own hands, and . . ." She suddenly beamed a bright smile Lucetta's way. "You're exactly the lady who can help me."

Keeping her gaze staunchly fixed on Ruby, especially since Iris had begun to sputter, Lucetta cleared her throat. "Am I to understand, Miss Haverstein, that you want me to question Mr. Skukman for you and see how old he is?"

"Please, call me Ruby, and no, that's not what I had in mind at all. However . . . how old is Mr. Skukman?"

"I think he may be around thirty, but . . . I'm not swearing to that."

"Ah, that's not old at all, especially considering I'm twenty-three, but . . . I'm getting completely distracted from the subject at hand." She leaned forward. "You see, without the proper backing of a society matron, if I have any hope of being invited into society, I need to show that I'd be a welcome addition to any and all society events." She nodded determinedly. "Which means I need to become the belle of the ball."

"Oh . . . dear," Iris said as she buried her head in her hands.

"How do you plan to do that?" Lucetta asked slowly.

"I need an escort who everyone will want

to meet, and that escort needs to be a gentleman of consequence." She beamed another smile Lucetta's way. "That's where you come in. I've never been introduced to the gentleman I have in mind, but since everyone knows he specifically wrote *The Lady in the Tower* for you, I'm quite certain you're well acquainted with him."

"You want me to introduce you to Mr. Grimstone?" Lucetta asked.

"Indeed."

"And . . . then what?" Lucetta asked slowly.

"We must convince him that his greatest desire is to marry me, of course."

11

"Igor, round them up," Bram called, watching as Igor released a sharp bark and then began tearing around the small cluster of sheep Bram had brought with him to the far pasture. He'd never taken the sheep to this particular pasture before, and it had been quite the feat, getting his less than trained band of mutts to herd them such a distance. But he'd needed to get as far away from the castle as possible — or rather, get as far away from Miss Lucetta Plum as possible — because quite honestly, he'd needed to seek out a place of peace and quiet in order to finally sort out his thoughts.

Lifting his face to the late October sun, he realized that the only thing he'd managed to sort out during the numerous hours he'd been avoiding the castle was the fact that he'd made a complete idiot of himself with Lucetta.

He certainly hadn't intended to offer her

a marriage proposal in such an impulsive manner. It had just happened. But then, when she'd very kindly turned down his offer, in a tone of voice one usually reserved for the very ill, he'd begun to get the most unpleasant feeling that he might have spent three very long years pining after a woman who didn't actually exist.

The woman he'd thought he was in love with was a most delicate sort, fragile, needy, a bit melancholy upon occasion, and too beautiful for words, of course.

While Lucetta's beauty was even more impressive close up, that was seemingly the only thing he'd gotten right about the lady. She was not delicate in the least, and didn't appear to possess a melancholy demeanor. The case couldn't even be made that she was fragile, considering she'd managed to outrun a goat bent on bodily harm, without dissolving into a bout of hysterics.

In all honesty, the best word to describe Miss Lucetta Plum was . . . *practical.*

It was a disappointing word — *practical* — not romantic at all, and certainly not a word he'd ever thought he'd be using in regard to Lucetta.

The bleating of the sheep shook him out of his thoughts. Turning his attention back to the flock, he blew out a breath. Igor was

166

still dashing around the sheep, in rapid circles, his tail wagging furiously. While his herding attempt was certainly enthusiastic, the only progress he was making was to make the sheep dizzy, except for the one that had actually stretched out across the brown grass of the field and seemed to be on the verge of falling asleep.

"I see training is going well."

Looking over his shoulder, Bram felt his stomach drop when he caught sight of Lucetta walking his way, no hat on her head, or parasol to protect her skin from the rays of the sun.

He found he was not really surprised by that, nor was he surprised by the fact her hair was styled in two simple braids, those braids making her appear remarkably young and certainly not the sophisticate everyone assumed her to be.

Turning to face her, the unexpected thought flickered through Bram's mind that, even if she wasn't what he'd thought her to be, he was finding himself more and more intrigued by her, as if she were a mystery he desperately needed to solve.

That idea had him shuddering ever so slightly.

He'd never considered, not once, that he'd ever find Miss Lucetta Plum to be a mysterious soul. In fact, when he'd considered her — and he'd considered her quite often — it had always been with the certainty that, if he were successful in winning her over, she'd be a lady for him to take care of for the rest of her life, not a lady that he'd be able to converse with, laugh with, or heaven forbid, appreciate her opinions.

Igor suddenly let out a sharp bark of welcome right before he abandoned the sheep and dashed Lucetta's way. Montresor yawned before he got up from where he'd been lying on the ground watching the sheep, while Bram's other two dogs, Brutus and Victor, scampered way.

Lucetta bent down, gave Igor a good scratch, then straightened, only to bend down again when Montresor caught sight of her and scampered over to greet her. Scooping the little dog up, she snuggled it close as she straightened, sending Bram a smile. "They may not have gotten the herding business down yet, Bram, but my goodness, they sure are adorable." She nodded to where Brutus and Victor were sitting quite a distance away now. "Do they not care for ladies either, just like Geoffrey?"

"They don't really care for anyone and only tolerate me because I feed them."

Walking toward him, Lucetta smiled. "You

really are a rather nice man, aren't you. And speaking of nice, I can see why you've chosen this spot to hide out today. It's beautiful out here — what with the colors of fall surrounding you and the last days of what has to be an Indian summer warming the air. And . . ." She grinned. "It's very quiet."

He couldn't help but return the grin. "My grandmother's finally rested up?"

"Indeed, and your mother and sister have arrived at the castle as well."

"Oh . . ."

She looked around the pasture and then walked up to a spot where the grass had been well and truly trampled and took a seat. Taking a second to settle Montresor on top of her skirt, she patted the spot beside her. "Come join me."

"I don't know if that's a good idea."

"I thought we'd agreed we were going to be friends."

"I don't recall us actually getting around to agreeing to that."

"You're trying my patience. Take a seat."

Knowing he'd come across as churlish if he refused, Bram lowered himself down beside her. "I never realized you have a propensity for bossiness."

"It's part of my charm."

"I'm not certain I'd agree with that."

Lucetta surprised him when she grinned again. "You're just out of sorts because I'm not what you imagined me to be, and now you're probably embarrassed over the whole offering to marry me business — and relieved as well, I might add."

"I would *still* marry you, even if I'd come to the conclusion you were a complete and utter lunatic."

"You think I'm a lunatic?"

"Well, no, I was just giving you the first example that sprang to mind."

Her nose wrinkled. "Which means you actually do believe I might belong in an asylum."

Blowing out a breath, Bram smiled. "Of course I don't. The point I was trying to make is that, as a gentleman, I'm bound by a gentleman's code to honor my offer of marriage to you. And even though I'm quite certain you'll argue with me, I still believe marriage is the best option you have to put the Silas Ruff problem to rest. As we've mentioned, he's a dangerous man and isn't simply going to go away."

"Mr. Skukman mentioned to me this morning that he knows some . . . men."

Bram blinked. "I'm sure he does — as do I, if you want to know the truth of the matter — but I'm also sure you'd be more comfortable attending a wedding over a funeral."

Lucetta leaned over and kissed the top of Montresor's head, earning a lick of affection in return. "I have no issue with attending weddings. I just have no desire to be the lady walking down the aisle to meet a groom at the end of that aisle."

"I always thought every woman's greatest dream was to get married."

"And I'm sure that was my dream when I was twelve." She shrugged. "Life has a way of turning out differently than we expect, though, doesn't it?"

The urge to soothe her was immediate, an urge he staunchly pushed aside, knowing she would turn all prickly again if he tried.

"Mr. Skukman told me I should have been more appreciative of your sacrifice," Lucetta said, her tone decidedly disgruntled. "And that sacrifice, according to him, was you offering to marry me."

Bram felt his lips curl. "Did he now?"

She caught his eye. "He did, and I hate to admit this, but . . . he might be right about me not showing you the appropriate appreciation." She blew out a breath. "Apparently, I'm difficult."

He couldn't hold back a laugh. "Such

conclusions can be surprising, but . . . truth be told, *difficult* may be part of your charm. It's far more delightful than bossy."

Rolling her eyes, Lucetta leaned back on her elbows, earning a rumble of dissent from Montresor in the process as he resituated himself in the folds of her skirt. "Difficult though I may very well be," she began, "I find myself curious about you. Tell me something interesting about Bram Haverstein."

"There's not much to tell."

"I'm sure that's not true. You live in a castle. There must be a riveting story behind that."

"I'm afraid it's a rather dull story, not riveting. I loved the look of the place and knew it would provide me with enough room to keep a few animals and provide me with the calm atmosphere I need to . . . Well . . . who doesn't enjoy a calm atmosphere?"

"From what I've experienced since arriving at Ravenwood, the atmosphere here is anything but calm. And I don't think that's the real story behind why you bought the place." She considered him for a long moment. "Quite honestly, I've come to the conclusion there's far more to you than meets the eye."

Bram blinked. "Ah . . . well, I'm sure that could be said about most people."

"Why did you really purchase Ravenwood?" she pressed.

Bram leaned back. "Fine, since persistence also seems to be part of your charm, I'll tell you. But it's hardly a riveting tale. You see, the previous owner, Mr. James Woodward, was desperate to sell because his wife had come to the conclusion Ravenwood was haunted. After one too many encounters with what she claimed were otherworldly beings and otherworldly experiences, she had Mrs. Macmillan pack her a bag and she left for the city, vowing to never step foot in Ravenwood again — which, I can honestly tell you, she never did."

"Mrs. Macmillan worked for the previous owners?"

"She and her husband did."

"And you thought keeping them on was a good idea because . . . ?"

Bram shrugged. "They asked if they could remain, and since I didn't have a housekeeper or a butler, I didn't see any harm in allowing them to retain their positions."

"Well, they certainly do fit the roles for caretakers of a haunted castle, but you have yet to truly explain why you bought the place."

Plucking a long piece of grass out of the ground, Bram rolled it between his fingers. "Who doesn't want to live in a haunted castle?"

Lucetta arched a perfect brow his way.

"Oh, very well," he said. "I'll tell you, but only because I'm not certain I'm quite ready to add *nagging* to the long list of supposed charms I've had to accept about you recently."

"I don't nag," Lucetta muttered.

"That may well be debatable, but . . . back to my story. You see, the previous owner, Mr. Woodward, had recently suffered some extensive losses in the market, and because of that, he did not have the luxury of taking a financial loss on Ravenwood once rumors spread that it was haunted. However, since his wife refused to step foot inside the castle once she came to the belief it was well and truly haunted, he found himself in a bit of a bind, so . . . I stepped in and bought it from him."

"Good heavens, Mr. Skukman was right. You do enjoy rescuing people," he heard Lucetta say under her breath before she lifted her head and sent him a smile that showed a great deal of teeth. "It was very nice of you to buy Ravenwood from that man."

Bram shoved aside the peculiar thought that she didn't actually seem to like the idea that he enjoyed rescuing people, and summoned up a smile of his own. "I had the means to buy Ravenwood, and I love the castle, so helping out Mr. Woodward wasn't an act of any great consequence."

"I'm certain it was to him."

He turned his attention to the sheep, all of which were back to grazing as Igor slunk around them. Looking back at Lucetta, Bram caught her eye. "Just as I've come to discover you don't care to have people remark on your skills on stage, I don't particularly care to talk about the assistance I extend to people." He smiled. "Reverend Gilmore, a dear friend I met about a year ago, once told me that he believes God puts people on certain paths. And when you cross paths with a person who is in need, and you have the solution to that need, well, God expects you to put that solution to use. I don't know about you, but I'm not one to argue with God."

Lucetta's mouth had dropped open. "You're acquainted with Reverend Gilmore?"

"Shouldn't I be?" Bram asked slowly.

"He's friends with your grandmother, and . . . he's the man who helped me get

175

safely settled when I first landed in New York years ago."

"That is a curious coincidence, but I don't believe he's deliberately sought me out for some nefarious scheme — something that horrified expression on your face clearly suggests you are considering. It's well known throughout the tenements that I'm willing to hire a person if they have a desire to work, and that's how Reverend Gilmore heard about me. Since he's a gentleman who has dedicated his life to serving the poor, and I'm willing to employ people from the slums who are desperate for work, it's little wonder that he'd make a point of meeting me."

"He sends you prospective employees?"

"He does."

"It still seems a bit too coincidental to me," she muttered.

Smiling, Bram rose to his feet and held out his hand to Lucetta. "You may very well have a point, and there be something Shakespearean in motion, however, the day is quickly getting away from us. The dogs and sheep will need to eat soon, so shall we continue our discussion of unlikely coincidences as we travel back to the castle?"

Lucetta sat up, set Montresor aside, and took Bram's hand, allowing him to pull her to her feet. "I'll walk with you to feed the animals, but I'm not going back inside the castle just yet. When I fled Ravenwood less than an hour ago your mother and grandmother were entrenched in the tower room I occupy and were arguing about Ruby, and Ruby was arguing right back to both of them. In the midst of all that Mrs. Macmillan came in. She'd climbed all the way to the tower in order to introduce me to Tilda — an employee of yours who is going to be acting as my lady's maid, even though I told Mrs. Macmillan I don't have need of a personal maid."

"Tilda's a young woman Reverend Gilmore sent me."

"And she seems quite lovely. However, I really have no need of a lady's maid, but I never imagined Mrs. Macmillan would be so adamant about me taking Tilda on. And don't even get me started with what happened when your housekeeper discovered what Mr. Skukman had been doing with the hammer she saw me holding."

"She reacted unpleasantly?" Bram asked slowly.

"That's a bit of an understatement. Quite honestly, she completely lost her head."

"That doesn't sound like Mrs. Macmillan."

Lucetta shrugged. "All I can fathom is that she takes her position as your house-keeper far too seriously and was obviously worried Mr. Skukman and I were going to harm the castle walls when she discovered we'd been searching for secret passageways."

Of anything he'd been expecting her to say, that hadn't been it. "Why were you looking for secret passageways?"

"That goat didn't fly up to the tower. And since Mr. Skukman questioned half the staff this morning and no one saw the goat being led up the stairs, well, a secret passageway is the only reasonable solution we could come up with."

"Don't you think your time might be better spent with Mr. Skukman trying to come up with a plan to deal with Silas Ruff?"

"We discussed options as we searched for the passageway, but since we've been less than successful coming up with a viable plan, solving the mystery of the goat seemed a pleasant way to pass the time." She smiled. "There's nothing like a good mystery to help settle a person's thoughts. I normally settle my thoughts by taking to the stage, but since a stage isn't exactly available to me, I'm hoping that as I sort through the mystery of the tower, a plan will subconsciously develop in regard to what to do about Silas."

"Do you intend on hammering through a tower wall in order to seek out this supposed passageway?"

"Of course not. Mr. Skukman was using the hammer to tap on the stones of the fireplace, but he's now convinced a passageway probably exists behind the bookcase." She released a sigh. "I was unable to investigate that idea fully, though, given all the arguing."

"Ah, yes, the arguing. Should I want to know why my mother, grandmother, and Ruby were arguing?"

"I'm not certain I understood everything about that situation, but from what I could gather . . . your mother was appalled that Ruby is trying to orchestrate an introduction to Mr. Grimstone, your grandmother was appalled that Ruby didn't even consider her when she decided she wanted to enter New York society, and Ruby was annoyed that neither her mother or grandmother thought pursuing Mr. Grimstone was a good idea. And she got even more annoyed after I told her I couldn't introduce her to Mr. Grimstone. But her annoyance disappeared in a flash after I explained — over a great deal of shouting, I might add — that I have never met Mr. Grimstone, which was why I couldn't introduce them."

Bram abruptly sat back down on the grass, motioning her to join him. "Why in the world would my sister want to be introduced to Mr. Grimstone?"

"Well, at first I thought she wanted him to marry her."

Bram's mouth dropped open. "What?"

"Exactly the reaction I had, but it turns out that your sister has a very curious way of devising plans."

"You do realize that explains absolutely nothing, don't you?"

Lucetta smiled a charming smile, one filled with mischief that had him completely losing his train of thought.

"Ruby has come to the somewhat unusual conclusion that, in order to get back at Geoffrey — the man, not the goat — she needs to enter New York society. In order to do that, since she apparently neglected to realize that Abigail can get her accepted with a crook of her little finger, Ruby decided that she needs Mr. Grimstone to become enamored with her, and then escort her to all the best society events, which will have all society doors opening to her in no time at all."

"That's one of the most absurd plots I've ever heard in my life."

"That's what I thought too, at first, but after further contemplation, I've decided it's not absurd at all. Everyone in New York society is completely enthralled with Mr. Grimstone and his delicious gothic novels, along with his first play, that" — she smiled — "yours truly is in.

"Quite honestly, it was a brilliant move on Mr. Grimstone's part to remain incognito, that state lending him a most mysterious air. If Ruby could, indeed, become introduced to the man and then have him escort her around town, well, all the doors of all the best houses — excluding Mrs. Astor's, of course, because everyone knows she doesn't care to entertain the artistic set — would be open to your sister."

Bram opened his mouth to argue the point, but before he could voice a single argument, something moved a few feet away from them, attracting his attention. As that something came into focus, a sense of alarm soon followed.

Geoffrey — the goat, not Ruby's false-hearted gentleman friend — was standing only one good leap away from them, his attention centered on Lucetta. How the goat had managed to escape the barn and then find them was a complete and utter mystery, but not one Bram had time to consider at the moment.

"Don't move," he whispered — which had Lucetta immediately turning around.

"Is that . . . Geoffrey?" she demanded right before Geoffrey pawed a hoof against the ground and then . . . charged.

12

Feeling quite like she was in the midst of some outlandish dream, one where she kept getting chased over and over again by a goat, Lucetta leapt over a tree stump while being mindful not to land on Montresor as the little dog scampered by her feet. Running as fast as she could across a pasture painted in the lovely colors of fall, she crested a small rise and saw Mr. Skukman and Stanley striding her way.

"Geoffrey is determined to kill me again," she yelled, which had Mr. Skukman — who seemed to be brandishing a sword — breaking into a run. As he disappeared over the rise she'd just crested, she slowed to a walk and drew in a sharp gasp of much-needed air as she pressed a hand against a stitch that was developing in her side. To her dismay, only seconds later Geoffrey charged over the rise, bleating as if his very life were in danger as Mr. Skukman tried to catch him.

"Mr. Skukman, Geoffrey is afraid of swords," Bram yelled as he ran into view.

His words had Mr. Skukman coming to an immediate stop and lowering the sword, but Geoffrey continued forward, galloping past Lucetta, clearly having abandoned all interest in her.

"That's not something one sees every day," Stanley remarked as he moved up to join her.

Nodding, Lucetta watched as Geoffrey continued his flight across the pasture, disappearing into a grove of trees before she caught Stanley's eye. "I'm quickly coming to the conclusion one sees many odd things here at Ravenwood."

Stanley sent her a weak smile right as Bram joined them.

"Are you all right?" Bram asked.

"A little short on breath, but besides that, perfectly fine," she said before she looked Mr. Skukman's way. He was walking backward, still holding a sword in his hand, his attention settled on something Lucetta couldn't see. A mere moment later, that mystery was solved as sheep began cresting the rise, followed by Igor, Brutus, and Victor, who, surprisingly enough, seemed to be doing a credible job of herding them.

"Would you look at that," Bram said, raising a hand to shield his eyes as the sheep, and then the dogs, now joined by a tail-wagging Montresor, wandered by them.

"May I suggest we follow them back to the castle, sir?" Stanley asked, eyeing the dogs somewhat warily. "There's really no telling where the dogs may herd the sheep, and you must remember how distressed Mr. and Mrs. Plinkhurt were the time the sheep made it off Ravenwood's property and ended up in Mrs. Plinkhurt's rose garden." Stanley shuddered. "I don't believe I've ever seen a lady dissolve into such hysterics over a few eaten bushes, and that was after we assured her we'd replace them."

"That might be for the best," Bram said, turning to offer Lucetta his arm.

Taking the offered arm, she fell into step beside Bram, Mr. Skukman falling into step on her other side.

Glancing at the sword Mr. Skukman was carrying, Lucetta tilted her head. "I know I'll probably regret asking this, but why are you carrying that sword, and why are you and Stanley walking about the grounds with a sword in the first place?"

"We've been looking for you," Mr. Skukman said. "Young ladies, along with quite a few of their mothers, have descended on

Ravenwood. Since you're not in disguise at the moment, I felt it prudent to track you down. We'll need to slip you into the castle and back to your tower as stealthily as possible so that no one gets an opportunity to recognize you."

Bram frowned. "It seems quite out of character for Ernie to allow ladies entrance into the castle, especially given that he's been apprised of the importance of keeping Lucetta's presence here a secret."

"In Ernie's defense, sir," Stanley began, "the ladies had an invitation to call at Ravenwood, from your mother. Although in Mrs. Haverstein's defense, what with all the chaos of the last day or two, she forgot she'd extended these ladies an invitation to tea."

"Why did she invite them to Ravenwood instead of her own house?" Bram asked.

"They're here to discuss plans for the theatrical event, sir. I overheard that the first rehearsal for that event is to be held at the castle tomorrow, which explains why the ladies are here today." Stanley nodded in a very knowing way. "From what I understand, they need to get the lay of the land."

"We can't still host a theatrical event, not since we need to keep Lucetta hidden," Bram argued.

"Your grandmother brought up that very

same argument, sir," Stanley began. "But when your mother tried — and very graciously, I might add — to cancel the event, the ladies, each and every one of them, turned . . . suspicious."

"Why would anyone's suspicions be roused simply from an event being canceled?" Bram asked.

"I think it might have had something to do with your grandmother implying you were soon to make an announcement," Mr. Skukman said, speaking up.

"What?" Lucetta and Bram asked together.

Mr. Skukman's lips twitched ever so slightly. "Mrs. Hart seems determined to see you well settled, Miss Plum, and I think she may have planted that particular seed for her daughter's benefit — so that Mrs. Haverstein will have time to adjust to the idea of you and Mr. Haverstein making a match of it."

"We have no intention of making a match of it," Lucetta said firmly.

"There's no need to declare that quite so adamantly," Bram mumbled.

Lucetta sent him a smile. "Forgive me, Bram. You and I have agreed to become friends, and that was hardly friendly of me, was it? Still, I've seen Abigail maneuver

187

events to her satisfaction before, and we cannot let our guard down — not when it's now become clear she's still determined to see us well settled, and well settled together."

"I believe the two of you would make a lovely couple," Stanley said, sending a smile to Lucetta before he sent a not-so-subtle wink to Bram.

Bram cleared his throat. "Yes, thank you for that, Stanley, but my grandmother's matchmaking schemes aside, we still can't host an event. We can't chance Lucetta being recognized."

"Don't worry about me," Lucetta said with an airy wave of her hand. "I'm very good at disguise, and quite honestly, I've never been invited to attend a local theatrical event before, and I find the very idea of that intriguing."

Bram's eyes narrowed on Lucetta's face. "You can't *go* to it."

"Of course I can. As I just mentioned, I'm a master at disguise. No one will have the faintest idea that a notorious New York actress is in their midst."

Bram's eyes narrowed another fraction. "You wouldn't happen to be considering trying out for a part, would you?"

"Is that how it works?" she asked. "How

188

marvelous. I'm now quite curious to discover whether or not I'll be able to win a part if no one knows that I'm Lucetta Plum."

Bram slowed his steps. "Absolutely not."

Unwilling to continue the argument, especially since she was rapidly coming to the conclusion that Bram Haverstein possessed a bit of a stubborn streak, Lucetta turned to Mr. Skukman and abruptly changed the subject. "I find myself curious about that sword, Mr. Skukman. Why, you look as if you're about ready to join a swashbuckling brigade of pirates. All you're missing is a patch like the one Bram was wearing when we first met him. Might it be that you've found a band of motley pirates here at Ravenwood, and that they're practicing their pirating skills in the hope that they'll win a part in this upcoming theatrical event?"

Mr. Skukman sent her a look that suggested he thought she'd lost her mind. "No, I've not found a band of pirates here, nor would I even consider joining them if I had. Although" — he shot a look to Bram — "practicing up for a theatrical role would explain why you were wearing that patch when, clearly, you didn't need one."

"Ah . . . hmm . . ." was Bram's only reply

to that, making him, in Lucetta's opinion, seem almost guilty about something.

Before she could question him, though, Mr. Skukman returned his attention to her. "As for what I'm really doing with the sword, strange as this is most likely going to sound — it fell off a ledge in the fireplace chute, almost impaling poor Mrs. Macmillan in the process."

Lucetta came to an immediate stop, as did Bram and Stanley, although the sheep and dogs continued moving forward. "I beg your pardon?"

"That sword fell out of *what* fireplace?" Bram asked, now looking closely at the sword in Mr. Skukman's hand, right before he shot a look that could only be described as darkly significant to Stanley — although what was behind the significance, Lucetta had no idea.

"The fireplace in the tower room Miss Plum is currently using," Mr. Skukman said with a sad shake of his head. "It's a troubling situation to be sure, sir, especially since, if you inspect the sword closely, there appears to be droplets of dried blood on it."

"Good heavens," Lucetta breathed.

"Indeed" was apparently the only response Mr. Skukman thought necessary.

"But . . . what was Mrs. Macmillan *doing*

in the fireplace?" Bram asked slowly.

Mr. Skukman nodded in clear approval. "Excellent question, sir, and one I asked her myself, after I'd made certain she hadn't suffered a wound when the sword crashed down on top of her."

"And her reply was . . . ?" Bram prompted when Mr. Skukman seemed to get lost in thought.

Shaking himself ever so slightly, Mr. Skukman shrugged. "That's a bit difficult to explain, sir. Quite honestly, I found the entire situation to be rather curious. From what I could gather, Mrs. Macmillan was originally upset because she'd learned Miss Plum and I had been searching for a secret passageway. For some reason, she came to the conclusion that I'd caused damage to the fireplace, which is how she explained what she was doing in there. However, after the sword fell, and I ducked back into the fireplace to assess if any real damage had actually been done, I noticed a loose stone a foot or so above my head, and that is when Mrs. Macmillan turned downright difficult. She ordered me out of the fireplace. But since I've never been one to take ridiculous orders, I went ahead and pulled out the stone, finding something concerning hidden behind it."

Mr. Skukman handed Stanley the sword, reached into his pocket, and pulled out what appeared to be a diamond-and-emerald-encrusted necklace. Holding it up, he arched a brow Bram's way. "Any thoughts as to why this would have been hidden in the tower fireplace?"

Bram reached out to touch the necklace Mr. Skukman was displaying. "You say you found it behind a loose stone?"

"I did, which does seem to suggest it was put there for a reason."

Lucetta took the necklace from Mr. Skukman and looked it over. "How interesting. It's a piece by Tiffany, because that's Tiffany's mark on the back, and . . . I don't think it's very old." She handed the necklace to Bram. "If I were to hazard a guess, I'd say what we're looking at is a piece of stolen goods."

"An interesting conclusion," Bram said slowly.

"Indeed, and we mustn't forget the sword," Lucetta reminded him. "It might have been used to pull off the jewelry caper."

"I doubt that," Bram mumbled under his breath before he lifted his head and sent her a strained smile. "But even though this is a morning of revelations, we're quickly nearing the castle, which means further speculation about what dropped out of the fireplace will need to wait for a later time, since we apparently have a houseful of ladies taking tea at the moment." He nodded to Mr. Skukman. "You'll see Lucetta inside, and keep her from being seen by our guests?"

"Of course."

"Thank you," Bram said before he turned to Lucetta. "If you'll excuse me, I do believe it might be for the best if I were to go have a word with my staff." He turned and walked away without another word, slipping the necklace into his jacket pocket. Stanley walked off as well, carrying the sword.

"Are you going to contact the authorities?" Lucetta called after Bram, her question having him turn back to her.

"I don't think there's any need for that quite yet."

"A bloody sword dropped out of your fireplace, along with a mysterious necklace from Tiffany & Company . . ." she reminded him.

"I'm hardly likely to forget that, Lucetta." With that, Bram turned around again and walked rapidly away even as he began discussing something with Stanley, their voices so low that Lucetta couldn't hear a single word of what they were saying.

As the two men disappeared from sight, Mr. Skukman released a sigh. "I don't mean to come across as the bearer of gloom and doom, but I'm coming to the conclusion that, not only does Ravenwood seem to be a haven for neglected and abandoned animals, it might also be a haven for criminals."

As Lucetta took Mr. Skukman's arm, she found she couldn't disagree, especially since she'd just been coming to that very same conclusion.

13

By the time he got the sheep safely situated in the barn, made certain the dogs had clean water and food to eat, spent time with Geoffrey — his far too neurotic goat that *had* shown back up in the barn but was shaking from head to hoof — an hour had passed since he'd parted ways with Lucetta. During that hour, he'd had plenty of time to think, the result of that thinking leaving him feeling distinctly disappointed.

Someone in his employ had obviously reverted back to their old ways, and in so doing, had brought scrutiny to Ravenwood — and scrutiny by the authorities, if Lucetta had her way.

The last thing he or his staff wanted was scrutiny.

Stashing the sword in an obscure corner of the barn, even as he patted his jacket pocket to make certain the necklace was still there, Bram made his way outside and trekked up the steep path that led to the back of his castle. By the time he reached the manicured lawn of Ravenwood, his mood could only be described as dismal.

The very idea that someone had abused his trust and had hidden what was clearly a stolen necklace in his home was almost too much to take in.

He'd given the members of his staff an opportunity for a second chance, pulled them out of the meanest tenements in the city and had only asked that they put their criminal ways behind them in return.

He was fairly certain that stealing a necklace and then stashing it in a fireplace was not exactly abiding by the rules he'd set up.

Trudging across the lawn, he suddenly heard what sounded like giggling. A desire to avoid the source of the giggles at all costs had him darting behind an ostentatious statue of a winged beast that Stanley liked to tell visitors came alive at night and flew about the towers. Peering around the beast's wing, he found a group of young ladies — all dressed in ivory day dresses and twirling matching parasols — meandering over the cobblestones of the formal courtyard. They kept looking this way and that, and knowing full well that what they were looking for was him, he pulled back and decided his only option, since he was in no frame of mind to participate in idle chitchat, or fend off the attentions of young ladies with marriage on their minds, was to wait them out.

Sinking to the ground, he leaned back against the statue . . . and stifled a yelp a moment later when a young lady suddenly appeared right in front of him — a young lady, it turned out, he wasn't opposed to seeing, until she opened her mouth.

"I see you're embracing a cowardly attitude today," Ruby said before she plopped down next to him. "It was fortunate for you that I told those young ladies that you like to spend time in the gazebo past the reflecting pond. That information was undoubtedly why they didn't see you over here, focused as they seemed to be on finding that gazebo."

"You told them I spend time in the gazebo?"

"They were beginning to annoy Grandmamma, and you must have realized by now that she's not a woman one wants to annoy." Ruby shuddered before she smiled. "Besides, it's not as if you're actually in the gazebo at the moment since you're clearly hiding here."

"If you've forgotten how to count, sister dear, allow me to point out that there are six young ladies now strolling around Ravenwood's lawn. If I were to hazard a guess, I'd say they're all unmarried. You'd take to hiding too if you were a man and were facing that many threats to your bachelorhood."

"Yes, it must be quite the trial to be so sought after."

Remorse was immediate. Reaching out, Bram rubbed Ruby's arm. "You're a beautiful, intelligent, somewhat amusing young lady — when you're not exasperating me, that is. You'll find your special someone someday."

"I wasn't aware we'd changed the subject to me."

"Weren't you?"

Ruby blew out a breath. "Forgive me. I don't mean to come across as a bitter shrew all the time. I clearly haven't come to terms with Geoffrey Jensen rejecting me in such a cavalier fashion, and for a snooty lady of society, no less. Since I didn't begin an association with him until I was twenty, and with all the time I wasted on him, I'm now, much to my dismay, twenty-three — and well on my way to being considered firmly on the shelf."

"You were never a young lady to embrace the idea of marrying directly out of school,

Ruby. If I need remind you, you spent two years touring Europe after school, and only began spending time with Geoffrey because so many of your younger friends were getting married."

She sent him a rather sweet smile. "I did enjoy touring Europe."

"Of course you did. And returning to the being-on-the-shelf business, from what I've been told, you've already come up with a plan to change that dastardly situation, a plan that will see you squired about town on the arm of Mr. Grimstone."

Ruby smiled. "Ah, it seems you've encountered Miss Plum this afternoon. I was so hoping you wouldn't hide away from her forever after that ill-advised marriage proposal you extended her."

"I hate to disappoint you, Ruby, but I didn't seek Lucetta out. I was perfectly content to hide away from her as long as possible, but she ran across *me* in the far pasture, where I'd taken the dogs to run through their paces with the sheep."

"You *do* know how to spend a fun afternoon. But be that as it may, I'm still glad you got to speak with her." Ruby's smile widened. "May I assume the two of you have come to some type of an understanding?"

"I think it's safe to assume Lucetta and I aren't going to wed."

Ruby reached out and patted his arm. "I wouldn't give up all hope just yet, Bram. I, probably more than anyone — since I've attended so many of her performances with you — know how long you've held Lucetta in high esteem. Quite frankly, now that I've met the *real* Lucetta, I do believe she's entirely more fascinating than everyone, myself included, assumed her to be."

Frowning, Bram tilted his head. "Why do you say that?"

"Because I think she's far more accomplished then she lets on, seems to be incredibly intelligent, and . . . I didn't get the impression that she's overly concerned with her appearance, which, coming from a lady as beautiful as Lucetta, is well and truly telling." She smiled. "And, she's definitely not fragile, nor does she seem to be the weepy type. I always expected her to be weepy for one reason or another."

Bram nodded. "I thought she would be weepy as well, but that certainly doesn't seem to be the case. Truth be told, now that I consider the matter, she seems very similar to you, except for the whole shrew business. I don't get the impression Lucetta is much of a shrew."

"You find me as accomplished as Miss Lucetta Plum?" Ruby asked slowly.

"Of course you are. You've taken over a large chunk of the investments for the family. And according to my bank account, you're very good at buying and trading in the financial market."

"Stocks are easy, Bram. You'd do well with investments too if you'd simply put your mind to it."

"I'm not really one for numbers — or any other normal business endeavor, for that matter."

"And that right there is the crux of your problems," Ruby said as she wrinkled her nose. "Do you know that Mother is now under the impression that you've been spending your time here at Ravenwood pursuing endeavors of an illegal nature?"

"What?"

Ruby blew out a breath. "She'll be very annoyed with me if she discovers I've told you this, but . . . quite honestly, I'm getting a little tired of listening to her many and varied suspicions. At this very moment, she's decided that you're playing Robin Hood — you know, stealing from the rich to give to the poor."

"I beg your pardon?"

Rolling her eyes, Ruby shook her head. "I

201

suppose her believing you're a Robin Hood type is better than what she thought just yesterday — that you hire questionable employees to further your own criminal pursuits. But since Mr. Skukman pulled that necklace out of the fireplace today, Mother's now convinced you spend your time breaking into society members' homes, stealing a few items here and there, and then spreading the wealth around."

"That's ridiculous, unless . . . There haven't been a rash of robberies in this area of late, have there?" he asked slowly.

Ruby shook her head. "I haven't heard of any, nor has Mother mentioned anything about robberies."

A sense of relief swept over Bram, but before he could question Ruby further about the matter, she took to completely changing the subject.

"What do you think of that Mr. Skukman?"

"Ah, well, he seems to be a dependable sort, from what little I can tell, although he doesn't speak much. But . . . getting back to Mother — why do you suppose she's been under the belief I'm up to no good?"

"It's either think you're up to no good, or think you're aimless without a purpose in life."

"I have purpose in my life."

Ruby arched a single dark brow his way.

"I am not playing Robin Hood" was the only response he could think of to say.

"That was convincing."

He shifted on the hard ground. "I'm not."

"Then what have you been doing all these years since you left the university, Bram? You certainly never continued on with pursuing your law degree, and . . . no one seems to know what you do to pass the time during any given day."

"I rarely have enough hours in a day to complete everything I need to accomplish."

Ruby's other brow rose to join the first one. "If you're not up to illegal activities, explain the necklace."

"I can't, because I have no idea where that necklace came from, or who might have stashed it in the fireplace."

"What about the sword?"

"What about it?"

Ruby rolled her eyes again. "Now you're just being difficult."

"I might be a little difficult, but I can assure you, I'm not doing anything illegal, nor have I been pursuing a life of crime since I left university."

"Fine, don't answer the question about the sword. We'll talk of your personal life instead." She smiled grimly. "What are you going to do to win Lucetta's favor?"

"What are you going to do to draw Mr. Grimstone's interest or even discover who he is?" he countered.

For a moment, Ruby looked as if she wanted to continue arguing with him, but then her shoulders sagged ever so slightly. "I was hoping Lucetta could introduce me to him, but oddly enough, she's never met the man, even though he wrote *The Lady in the Tower* specifically for her. Now I'm not sure how to proceed. Although . . . would you find it curious if I develop feelings of an affectionate nature for a gentleman who doesn't possess a fortune, or speak very much, for that matter?"

"Speaking can be overrated, and . . . you have been known to speak enough for three people, but . . . we're not talking about Mr. Skukman now, are we?"

Ruby's face turned just the slightest shade of pink before she shook her head. "Don't be silly. I barely know that man. But getting back to another man that no one seems to be familiar with — Mr. Grimstone — do you think it might be possible that when he penned *The Lady in the Tower* he had an unrealistic impression of Lucetta as well?"

"I'm not certain I'm following you."

"Well, the character Lucetta is playing, Serena Seamore, is fragile, sensitive, and dissolves into tears three times during the play. Since Mr. Grimstone has let it be known that he wanted Lucetta, and only Lucetta, to play the part of his Serena, doesn't it stand to reason that he wrote the play with her in mind all along, and that he wrote the part exactly how he believes Lucetta really is — delicate and in need of a protector?"

"It almost sounds as if you no longer care for the character Lucetta has been hired to play."

"Well, I still find Mr. Grimstone's writing to be brilliant, but as I've been thinking about him so often of late, and thinking of his work, I've finally realized what would make him more brilliant in my humble opinion."

Bram frowned. "I quite enjoy the work he's done on *The Lady in the Tower.*"

"I didn't say I didn't enjoy it, but if you consider his whole body of work, the themes of his stories are remarkably the same. The hero is always the rescuer, the heroine is always the victim in need of rescuing, and there's always a great deal of swooning and tender feelings going on. I mean, if you consider the matter, it's no wonder Lucetta thought to swoon when faced with Mother for the first time, since she's spent so much of her time swooning on stage."

Ruby drew in a seemingly needed breath of air and continued. "Quite honestly, I believe Mr. Grimstone needs to write a novel, or another play, with the heroine as a strong, independent lady, one who is perfectly capable of saving herself. She will then, of course, meet a gentleman she can love, and together, they save the day before riding off to their happily ever after."

Bram felt his mouth drop open as everything he'd thought he believed or knew shifted.

He'd been so convinced that Lucetta was a victim in the play called Life that he'd completely neglected to take the time to see past his misconceptions.

She was not searching for a knight in shining armor, she was searching for a partner, someone she could share her experiences with — not someone who'd want to take over her life and make everything easy for her.

Miss Lucetta Plum was certainly not a lady who would enjoy easy, at least not all of the time. She was too complicated, too accomplished, and too intelligent to live a life of mundane pleasantness.

She was also a lady who deserved an equal partner, not a gentleman who wanted to set her up on a shelf, away from the messiness of living, something he'd been determined to do.

"That's exactly where I've been going wrong, and why I haven't been able to . . ." He stopped when he realized he was speaking out loud, and with Ruby sitting by his side.

Knowing he needed to get right to work, while the inspiration was still flowing through his thoughts, he rose to his feet. Pulling Ruby up beside him, he sent her a smile.

"I know you're going to find this curious, but I have to bid you good day."

"Right this very minute?" Ruby asked slowly.

"Right this very minute."

"What about all of the ladies who are hoping to see you this afternoon?"

"They're going to be disappointed."

"What should I tell Mother about dinner? She's expecting all of us to sit down together, because I think she wants to question you about your chosen path in life."

"The questioning will have to wait, but do extend everyone my sincerest apologies. And if Mother badgers you about why I'm unavailable, tell her a matter of urgent business has arisen that I have no choice but to address." Giving Ruby a kiss on the cheek and leaving her with a very confused expression on her face, Bram headed for the castle, anxious to get back to work.

14

To say that matters had gotten a little peculiar at Ravenwood was a bit of an understatement.

Lying in the enormous canopied bed that was the centerpiece of the tower bedchamber, Lucetta pulled the counterpane up to her nose as she debated whether or not she truly wanted to chance life and limb by trying to get off a bed that was several feet from the floor.

Granted, there was a set of steps a person could use to get on and off the bed. But since the gas lamp Lucetta had intentionally left burning in the abutting bathing chamber seemed to have been extinguished, negotiating those steps in a pitch-black room was not an option she wanted to embrace.

However, when another mournful moan rang out, followed by what seemed to be the clinking of armor, Lucetta pushed aside her trepidation and flung back the counter-pane. Scooting along until she felt the edge of the bed, she swung her legs over that edge and jumped.

Landing harder than she'd intended, she limped across the room, keeping her hands out in front of her as she tried to find the door. Running into that door a moment later, she fumbled for the doorknob and gave it a twist. Relief was immediate when she opened the door and saw that moonlight was flooding the sitting room, making it possible to see. Her relief was short-lived, though, when a suit of armor suddenly sauntered into view, swinging a battle-axe.

Raising a hand to eyes evidently seeing things that weren't there, Lucetta gave them a good rub but found when she returned her attention to the situation at hand, there was still a suit of armor in front of her. Edging slowly backward, she stopped when the suit of armor turned her way, sent her a nod, and then, as calm as you please, continued across the sitting room, only to disappear through the door that led to the tower staircase.

A loud crash had Lucetta jumping almost out of her skin, until the thought came to her that the crash might have just been the suit of armor running smack into a wall, which meant it was only . . . human.

Determined to get to the bottom of the matter, Lucetta pushed her fear aside and darted forward, her darting coming to a quick end when the door she was aiming for slammed shut before she reached it. The clear click of the lock turning in place had temper stealing over her.

Jiggling the knob to make certain it wouldn't turn, she spun around and headed to her bedchamber, turning on a gas lamp and then blowing out a breath of annoyance when she discovered the key to the room was missing from the hook right beside her bed.

Pushing aside the case of the willies over the idea that someone must have been remarkably close to her while she slumbered, Lucetta squared her shoulders and marched into the bathing chamber. Setting her attention on a small box of hairpins, she plucked one of them out and strode back to the locked door.

Making short shrift of the lock, thanks to the lock-picking tutorage she'd received from her good friend Millie Longfellow, she tugged the door open, cocking an ear in the hopes of hearing sounds of retreating armor. To her frustration, not a single clink could be heard.

Unwilling to allow the suit of armor to go on its merry way, Lucetta fetched a wrapper, slipped her feet into comfortable shoes, and left the tower, pleased to discover that the gas sconces lighting the steep staircase had been left burning.

Reaching the ground level, she heard the hoot of an owl and, surprised to find that the castle door had been left open, followed the hoot outside. A second later, she was feeling all sorts of foolish when *that* door slammed closed, leaving her standing outside in her wrapper. Squaring her shoulders, she marched her way over to the door, grabbed hold of the handle, and felt temper begin to boil through her veins when she discovered she'd been locked out of the castle.

"I'm not finding this amusing," she called through the heavy wood, unsurprised when she received not a single peep in response.

Tugging the wrapper up around her neck and ignoring the chill breeze that had taken to swirling around her, Lucetta turned and headed down the few steps leading to the lawn, using the moonlight to guide her way as she walked to the front of the castle, hoping there was a bellpull she could use to summon some assistance.

Rounding the corner of the castle, she

stopped in her tracks as the distinctive *clip-clop* of a horse sounded in the distance. Lifting her wrapper so she wouldn't trip, she dashed after the sound, resisting the urge to call to the rider just in case it wasn't someone she knew. She found herself stopping yet again, though, when the moon hit the rider exactly as he turned to look back at the castle and she found herself staring at none other than . . . Bram.

What he was doing out and about at this time of night, she couldn't even hazard a guess. She'd not lain eyes on the gentleman since they'd parted ways that afternoon, when Bram had assured her he was off to question his staff about the mysterious necklace and sword.

From what she'd been able to gather through Stanley — who'd been sent up to the tower room to inform Lucetta that the ladies who'd come for tea had departed for the day — Bram had gotten distracted from questioning his staff because some mysterious matter of business had arisen. That matter of business had also been the explanation given to excuse his absence from the dinner table, as well as his absence from the conversations that had taken place after dinner in the drawing room.

Although Iris hadn't spoken a single word

about his absence throughout the lovely dinner Mrs. Buttermore, the cook, had provided, it had been clear she'd been less than pleased. But when they'd repaired to the drawing room, Iris had become quite vocal regarding her disappointment with her son. She'd taken a seat right beside Abigail and had launched into a conversation with her mother regarding how she was obviously not very good with the whole mothering business, given the curious nature of her middle child, Bram, and the contrary nature of her only daughter, Ruby — at which point Iris had turned away from Abigail and sent a pointed look Ruby's way.

Ruby, bless her heart, had strolled over to the piano and declared that what the evening needed to liven it up — and drown out opinionated mothers — was music. Sitting at the piano, she'd cracked her knuckles right before she'd begun pounding out tune after tune, seemingly oblivious to the fact she wasn't in the least proficient at the keys. While Lucetta had moved her chair closer to Abigail and Iris to distract herself from the horror coming out of the piano, Mr. Skukman, surprisingly enough, had pulled his chair closer to the piano and had taken to watching Ruby play, an expression of great appreciation on his face even when

Ruby missed her fair share of notes.

While Lucetta had found Mr. Skukman's behavior unusual, indeed, she hadn't dwelled on it long. Instead, she'd taken to watching Iris and Abigail, both ladies seemingly content to spend their evening sitting beside each other — on the same settee — sharing ideas pertaining to family matters, their voices rising louder and louder as Ruby continued banging on the keys with more and more enthusiasm.

What had become evident to Lucetta the longer she'd watched Abigail was that, even if their trip to Ravenwood did not produce a solution to the Silas Ruff situation, it had allowed Abigail an opportunity to repair some of the hurts she'd caused in the past, and repair — or at least start to repair — the relationship with her daughter. Because of that, as she stood shivering in her wrapper in the middle of the night, Lucetta couldn't regret the trip, even if she did regret lowering her defenses ever so slightly, which had allowed Bram to worm his way — and his obviously criminal ways, at that — into a little piece of her heart.

She was rarely taken in by any gentleman, but Bram had almost convinced her, in a relatively short period of time, that he was kind, generous, and compassionate, all the while hiding what could only be explained as a Machiavellian nature.

Suddenly realizing that Bram and his horse were now nowhere in sight, Lucetta shook away those unhelpful thoughts, squared her shoulders, and headed down the drive. By the time she reached the gate-house — the one resembling a mausoleum — she was short on breath and long on temper.

"Miss Plum, my goodness, what are you doing out and about at this time of night, and without your Mr. Skukman, from the looks of it?"

Stumbling to a stop, Lucetta found Ernie ambling her way from the front of the mausoleum, rubbing his eyes and looking exactly as if he'd just been woken from a sound sleep.

"I could ask you the same thing, Ernie," she said. "Surely you're not required to attend to the front drive at all hours of the day and night."

"Of course not. I volunteered to sleep out here for a night or two, given that I'm to blame for that swor . . ." He clamped his mouth shut and didn't say another word.

"Blame for . . . Were you going to say . . . *sword*?" Lucetta finally asked.

Ernie blinked big eyes back at her in a far

too obvious attempt to look innocent. "I was going to say," he continued, "that there are shenanigans going on here at Ravenwood, and Mr. Haverstein, well, he's powerfully worried about them." Ernie puffed up his chest. "He trusts me, though, Miss Plum, which is why I've been given the task of making certain there aren't any suspicious comings and goings at odd hours of the night, and . . ." He reached up and scratched his head. "Begging your pardon, but you being out at this hour is . . . suspicious."

"I got lured, and then locked out of the castle, after being scared half to death by a walking suit of armor."

Ernie stuck his hand into his jacket pocket, pulling out a small pad of paper, which he immediately opened before he pulled out a pen and sent her a nod. "That sounds like a case of shenanigans to be sure, Miss Plum. Now . . . tell me, what did the suit of armor look like?"

"It looked like a suit of armor, of course."

"Was there anything of a distinguishing nature about it?"

"It was walking across the room."

Ernie scribbled something into the notebook. "Suspicious indeed, and not something one expects to see when they're a guest at Ravenwood."

"It was certainly an unexpected sight, and while I'd love to provide you with additional details, I really need to speak with Mr. Haverstein. Did you happen to notice him passing by a few moments ago?"

"Of course."

"And you're not concerned about *Mr. Haverstein's* suspicious comings and goings?"

"Heavens no. There's nothing suspicious about Mr. Haverstein riding Storm — that's his horse — out and about at this hour. They do it almost every night."

Lucetta blinked. "What else do they do almost every night?"

"I'm not at liberty to say, especially since I've never accompanied him on his nightly rides."

"Do you happen to know where he might be heading this evening?" she pressed.

"He's probably heading off toward town, but I'm not completely certain about that."

Unwilling to admit defeat just yet, Lucetta glanced down the empty road. "How far is town from here?"

"Not far, but . . . you can't go walking off by yourself, Miss Plum. Mr. Haverstein wouldn't like that at all, and . . ." He shuddered. "I hate to think what your Mr. Skukman would do if he learned I'd let you waltz away on your own."

Looking around, Lucetta smiled. "Is that your horse and pony cart over there?"

"Sweet Pea isn't a horse, Miss Plum. She's a mule."

Lucetta considered Sweet Pea for a moment. "May I borrow her?"

"Ah, well . . . I really think it might be for the best if you were to return to the castle and wait for Mr. Haverstein there."

"But then I'd miss this prime opportunity of finding out what he's really up to."

Ernie frowned. "That almost sounds as if you think he's up to something questionable."

"Isn't he?"

"Of course not. But since it's clear you're not going to listen to me, you may use Sweet Pea, but only if you promise to tell Mr. Skukman — if he asks you, that is — that I let you use the mule under duress."

Much to Lucetta's delight, she soon found herself sitting in the pony cart as Sweet Pea practically pranced down the road, evidently enjoying the crisp night air.

Lucetta, on the other hand, was beginning to wish she'd had the foresight to grab a jacket, because to her, with the wind swirling past her as Sweet Pea continued her prancing at a remarkably fast clip, it was becoming downright chilly.

Rounding a bend in the road a good fifteen minutes later, Lucetta was considering giving up her quest due to the fact she'd taken to shivering, when Bram and Storm came into view.

Oddly enough, Bram had dismounted and was standing to the side of the road, gesturing wildly to Storm and shouting phrases like "You cowardly cur" and "Unhand me at once." Finding that to be a slightly peculiar conversation to be holding with a horse, especially when Storm kept tossing his head as if he was in perfect agreement with Bram, Lucetta steered Sweet Pea toward them, unable to help but notice that when Bram finally did catch sight of her, he stopped speaking at once even as he took to looking slightly . . . guilty.

"Lucetta!" he exclaimed, as his guilty look was replaced with a charming smile when she brought Sweet Pea to a stop. "What in the world are you doing out here, and . . . are you in your wrapper?"

Not waiting for her to reply, he shrugged out of his top coat and moved close enough to her to draw the coat around her shoulders.

Lovely warmth seeped into her every pore as the scent of sandalwood, lime, and something distinctly male tickled her nose.

When she realized he was waiting for some type of reply, she pulled herself from thoughts of warmth and manly smells. "I got locked out of the castle, and when I saw you leaving, I thought I'd try to catch up with you."

Bram frowned. "What do you mean you got locked out of the castle? And what were you doing wandering around the castle at this hour of the night anyway?"

"I wasn't planning on wandering around the castle," she said with a bit of an edge to her tone. "In all honesty, I'm sure I'd still be fast asleep if a suit of armor hadn't decided to take a nighttime stroll through the tower."

"What?"

"A suit of armor . . ."

"Yes, I heard you, but . . . why would a suit of armor be walking through the tower? Or better yet, how would it have gotten up there in the first place?"

"Probably the same way Geoffrey did, although *why* they were in the tower room, well, that's fairly obvious."

"Not to me."

"Someone wants me gone from Ravenwood."

"Surely not."

"Why else would someone don a suit of armor and try to scare me half to death?"

Bram blew out a breath. "I suppose someone was inside the armor, since it couldn't have been walking about on its own. But why they did such a thing is a bit of a mystery."

"As could be said for numerous recent situations at Ravenwood — including why you've chosen to ride your horse around in the middle of the night."

The horse in question moved up to join them, practically knocking Bram over as it nuzzled him. Regaining his balance, Bram smiled and gave his horse a good pat. "This is Storm, and there's nothing mysterious at all about me riding him at night, even if the good folk of Tarrytown have taken to making up tales about me and my nightly rides."

He patted Storm again. "Storm, if you must know, hasn't tolerated sunlight well for the past couple of years. His eyes have turned sensitive to the light, but I didn't want him to grow old before his time, which is why we ride when it's dark."

A rather warm and mushy feeling began traveling through Lucetta, a feeling that had her knees going a tad weak, until she remembered she was talking to a man who'd yet to explain why he'd been wearing an eye patch when she'd first met him, or why questionable jewelry and a bloody sword had been stashed in his fireplace. Add in the fact that there was now a suit of armor meandering around, scaring unsuspecting guests in the middle of the night, and she had no business allowing her knees to go all wobbly.

". . . and since you have managed to track me down, would you care to join us as we continue on with our nightly adventure?"

"Adventure . . . ? What kind of adventure?" she asked slowly.

Bram leaned down and placed his mouth directly next to her ear, his closeness sending a chill, and one she didn't think was from the cold air, down her spine. "We'll just have to make that up as we go."

A thread of disappointment stole over her as he straightened, moved to Storm's side, and then swung up into the saddle.

"What type of adventure sounds fun to you?" he asked.

"I'm not certain what you're asking."

He gave a sad shake of his head. "Oh dear, you've forgotten how to have fun, haven't you."

Annoyance was swift. "Of course I haven't."

"Prove it."

Not one to back down from a challenge, Lucetta smiled. "Very well, off the top of my head, I believe it would be great fun to visit Sleepy Hollow Cemetery, and . . . walk amongst the gravestones."

Smiling, Bram sent her an approving sort of nod. "Very good, Miss Plum, you're obviously a lady after my own heart, although I will admit I didn't take you for the type who'd enjoy places that embrace a rather gothic nature."

"Or *morbid,* one might say," she added.

Nodding in agreement with that, he turned Storm around and urged him into motion. Lucetta clicked her tongue, and Sweet Pea fell into step right next to Storm. It quickly became clear that besides not tolerating the sun, Storm didn't tolerate a fast clip for very long, and before Lucetta knew it, she was slowing Sweet Pea down to such an extent that the mule actually turned its head and sent her a reproachful eye.

"Now then," Bram began, looking down at her from his seat on Storm, "in the spirit of keeping with our theme of adventure, we're going to create a story as we ride."

"A story?"

"Yes, you know, use our imaginations and come up with some riveting tale to keep us entertained."

"Is that what you were doing when I first came upon you?"

For a second, he simply looked at her, and then, oddly enough, he smiled his charming smile at her again. "It was indeed, and . . . since I have already begun a story, we'll use what I've come up with thus far and continue on with it."

"I'm not very good with creating imaginary stories," she admitted slowly.

"Nonsense, you create imaginary scenes every time you take to the stage."

"That's different. I have a script I've memorized, but I certainly wouldn't be able to create those words written in that script." She shook her head. "Why, if I tried to create my very own story the end result would be too awful to even contemplate."

Bram considered her for a moment. "You really are very much like my sister, as I actually pointed out to Ruby earlier today. She — I'm sure you'll be surprised to learn, given her exuberant nature — has not an ounce of artistic talent in her entire body, and whatever you do, ignore any offer from her to play the piano for you. It's an event your ears will never forget."

"She played for us after dinner this evening, which you would have known if you'd joined us."

Bram looked anything but contrite. "It truly is unfortunate that I had important matters to attend to that demanded my full attention, making dinner, as well as entertainment in the drawing room afterward, an impossible event."

Lucetta frowned. "Why is it that your staff — as well as your family — seems to be rather vague when talk turns to you and important matters, which I'm going to assume are business matters?"

"I'm sure they're a little vague because they assume their guests will be bored if the conversation turns to matters of business."

"Does that mean you're involved in a business that most people find less than exciting such as . . . finance, perhaps?"

Bram actually shuddered. "I don't care for finance in the least. Ruby is the one in the family who has a proficiency for numbers. Growing up, she'd spend hours in Father's office, poring over his ledgers. She'd considered going to a university to study finance but found that the universities she wanted to attend would not admit a lady to their finance departments." He released a sigh. "Truth be told, I believe the only reason she became involved with Geoffrey Jensen was because he works on Wall Street. While she claimed to be fascinated with the gentleman, I believe she was more fascinated with the talk they shared regarding the market than anything else about him."

"Your sister enjoys the stock market?" Lucetta asked.

"Indeed, and she has recently taken over a few of our family investments, I'm pleased to report, which have shown substantial growth under her watch."

Lucetta smiled. "I imagine Mr. Jensen would be most put out if he were to learn she's successfully playing the market."

Frowning, Bram tilted his head. "He already knows. He came to dinner one night months ago right after Ruby had learned a railroad stock she'd chosen to invest in was beginning to show promise of a nice return."

"Then it's little wonder he discontinued his association with her. Gentlemen — especially those who fancy themselves experts in the area of finance — don't care for ladies who involve themselves in the market, believing that finance is unfitting for a true lady to participate in."

"You say that as if you're personally acquainted with just that situation," Bram said slowly.

"Yes, I did, didn't I? But enough about me. I'd much rather talk about you and your family. Tell me more about your father, and . . . now that I think about it, you mentioned something about a brother. Where are they, and what do they do?"

"Father's currently in Cuba, as is my brother, Hugh. Hugh's the eldest and is in the process of taking over the family sugar business."

"Didn't *you* want to have a hand in running your family business?"

Storm suddenly wandered over to the side of the road, and for a moment Lucetta thought she'd offended Bram and he was putting some distance between them, until she realized that Storm had gotten distracted by a patch of weeds.

"I was never interested in the sugar business," Bram continued as Lucetta brought Sweet Pea right up next to him. "Granted, I enjoyed running through the sugarcane fields when I was a boy, but I had no interest in the factories, preferring to spend my time on the white beaches of Cuba, watching the clouds drift by."

"It sounds as if you might be a bit of a dreamer."

Smiling, Bram shook his head. "There's no *might* about it, Lucetta. I am a dreamer, much to the disappointment of my parents, which is why I enjoy spending my time out here on this deserted stretch of road in the middle of the night, creating my own stories and such. And speaking of stories . . . let us return to the one you're going to help me to create."

"I told you, I'm not good at thinking up stories."

"You will be a great help with creating our story since you often assume the identity of a damsel in distress when you take to the stage," he countered.

"I *always* assume the identity of a damsel in distress," she corrected.

"Which is an excellent point and is also why we'll make our story a little different." He lapsed into silence for a moment. "Instead of having your typical knight in shining armor, especially since you might be a little predisposed to take issue with a man sporting armor at the moment, why don't we make our hero a pirate?"

"Is he a real pirate? Because real pirates probably smell, and that's not a characteristic a true hero should possess."

"Another excellent point, so . . . he'll only be masquerading as a pirate. His real profession is a . . . spy for the Crown."

"Which Crown?"

Bram waved the question away. "We don't need to concern ourselves with details just yet."

"Details are what make a story interesting."

"Fine, he's from Romania."

"That seems a bit farfetched. What would a pirate be doing in Romania?"

Bram ignored her question even as he seemed to begin grinding his teeth. "Working as a spy, he soon finds himself captured by . . ."

"Members of Ravenwood's staff," Lucetta finished for him — yet another suggestion Bram ignored.

". . . captured by dastardly criminals, and they take him to a dungeon, where they proceed to threaten him."

"Threaten him? They need to hang him from the ceiling, from his feet."

Bram's brows drew together. "Who are you?"

Clearing her throat, Lucetta gave an airy wave of her hand. "Continue, if you please."

Sending her a look of disbelief right before Storm began drifting back to the road again, Bram waited for her to get Sweet Pea back into motion before he continued. "As I was saying, before you injected a rather disturbing plot point into the story, our hero gets captured, and . . . here's where I'd really like your opinion — although given your other opinions, I'm not actually certain

230

about that any longer. . . ."

He looked somewhat intently her way, as if the fate of the world rested on this particular question and, subsequently, her answer. "How would the heroine of the story react to this dastardly situation?"

Giving the question the attention Bram obviously felt it deserved, she wrinkled her nose after a few seconds had passed. "The heroine I *normally* play, or the heroine I'd *like* to play?"

"The heroine you'd like to play."

She smiled. "She'd slip into the jail, cut the hero down from where he was still hanging from the rafters, pull a pistol on the criminals who'd been holding the hero captive, and then spirit him away to a remote location, where she'd then hire a caretaker to tend to his wounds."

"Why doesn't *she* tend to his wounds?"

Lucetta let out a snort. "Please, practically every romantic story written these days has the heroine tending to the hero's wounds, or fever, or whatever else could possibly be laying him low, and . . . she's usually weeping. If she brings in a caretaker to see to the injuries, there's no need for the whole weeping scene, which I'm sure most readers would find refreshing in this day and age."

"You really are very frightening, aren't you."

Laughing — a response that felt delightful — Lucetta launched into other ideas, charmed in spite of herself when Bram, after mentioning a few more times that he was coming to the conclusion she was slightly deranged, threw himself back into the creation of their story. Before she knew it, Bram was leading them down a gravel lane, stopping in front of a stone archway that had a wrought-iron sign swinging from it — a sign that sported the words *Sleepy Hollow Cemetery.*

Slipping off Storm, Bram looped the reins around a nearby tree, then moved to Lucetta and helped her out of the pony cart.

"Storm isn't keen on cemeteries," he said, taking Lucetta's arm. "They make him jittery, so it's best if we leave him here, as well as Sweet Pea. They can keep each other company."

Heading for the archway, they walked through it and into the cemetery, Lucetta immediately steering Bram over to a line of grave markers that were gleaming in the moonlight.

Time slipped away as they studied one marker after another, each of them pointing out interesting tidbits that they found engraved on different stones.

"You might find this one interesting, Luc . . ." Bram suddenly reached out and pulled her close when the sound of wheels crunching over gravel disturbed the peace surrounding them. Before they had a chance to dart behind a grave marker, a carriage — one that looked all too familiar — rumbled into sight.

As Abigail's carriage skidded to a stop, Mr. Skukman jumped to the ground and advanced their way, stopping right in front of her. He sent her a shake of his head before he looked to Bram and let out a grunt.

"Would you be so kind as to explain to me why — when it is well known that Silas Ruff has gone to extraordinary means to get close to Miss Plum and is probably even now scouring the eastern coast for her — you thought it would be a good idea to spirit her away from the safety of the castle and bring her to a cemetery, of all places?"

When Bram didn't seem to have a ready answer to that, and Lucetta couldn't seem to think of a reasonable way to explain the suit of armor, which had well and truly been the reason she'd left the castle, Mr. Skukman let out another grunt before he took her by the arm and hustled her away.

15

"I'm afraid I still have no idea why you've decided that I need to be in disguise to attend the theatrical rehearsal tonight," Mr. Skukman mumbled as Tilda, a delightful young woman Mrs. Macmillan had insisted Lucetta use as a lady's maid, applied a pair of hot tongs to Mr. Skukman's hair, creating a style that was . . . interesting.

Lucetta looked up from the wig she'd been in the process of fluffing. "Since you've been so vocal regarding keeping me safe, as can be seen by your overreaction to events last night, we certainly don't want to risk anyone recognizing you now. Why, that might lead to unwanted questions about what Mr. Skukman, Miss Plum's incredibly recognizable personal guard, is doing at Ravenwood."

Mr. Skukman's only response was a grunt, probably because Tilda seemed to have gotten the tongs stuck and was obviously pulling Mr. Skukman's hair as she tried to get the tongs released. Stumbling back a moment later, Tilda held up the tongs and blew out a breath.

"This tong business is far trickier than I ever imagined," Tilda said as she set aside the tongs and patted Mr. Skukman's head. "But you still have most of your hair, so no harm done."

Mr. Skukman rubbed his head and frowned Tilda's way. "Are you suggesting that you've never used hot tongs before?"

"I'm not *suggesting* anything. I've only recently been elevated to lady's maid, so this fixing hair and doing up gowns business is quite new to me." Tilda grinned. "Why, up until a day ago, I was a scullery maid, only responsible for cleaning out the fireplaces, and before that . . . Well, let me simply say that I was involved in the . . . stealth business, although . . ." Her grin faded. "Mr. Haverstein has been the only person in my life to ever give me an honest opportunity, so I've put my days of stealth — and all that went with that — behind me for good."

"How delightful for you, Tilda," Mr. Skukman said before he arched a brow Lucetta's way, a brow that rose above the squiggly curls that now covered his forehead, a forehead that normally never saw hair touch it, as Mr. Skukman preferred to keep his hair combed away from his face. "However, I'm finding it less than delightful that you, Miss Plum, have apparently set a woman armed with hot tongs — and yet having no skill to wield those tongs — on me."

Lucetta smiled and picked up a stick of kohl, using it to darken her brows. "You annoyed me, so Tilda and hot tongs was my way of making you completely aware of that annoyance."

"You pay me to keep you safe," he reminded her.

"I was hardly in any danger with Bram, and since I know full well that Ernie told you I'd gone out to find him, you had no reason to believe I was in any danger."

"We know relatively nothing about Mr. Haverstein, and given the disturbing shenanigans that have been happening in this very castle, you cannot blame me for doubting the motives of a man who has questionable jewelry and bloodied swords dropping out of fireplaces."

"And don't forget cannons blasting off unexpectedly," Tilda added. "I'm sure the neighbors were startled out of their sleep last night when the cannon fired off just as you and Miss Plum returned to the castle."

Mr. Skukman nodded. "That was unfortunate, although I've been hoping the cannon was simply fired as a way to allow the staff to know that they could discontinue searching for Miss Plum, and not for any other reason."

Tilda shook her head sadly. "Clearly you've not lived amongst the criminal — or rather, *former* criminal — element, Mr. Skukman. If you had, you'd realize that the cannon blasting off last night was to notify someone that you and Miss Plum had been spotted coming home."

Lucetta's brow drew together. "As in a warning to someone who might have been searching the tower room?"

Tilda shrugged. "That's my guess. I could always be mistaken, but since someone went to great lengths to get you out of the tower and then out of the castle, I'm fairly certain I'm right."

"What would anyone want from the tower room?" Lucetta asked slowly. "I assure you, I brought nothing of value with me."

"You're living with reformed criminals, Miss Plum," Tilda explained. "While most of us have set aside our questionable ways for good, I'm afraid the lure of additional treasures hidden throughout the castle may be too great of a temptation for some." She shrugged. "If I was still in the, well, stealth business, I'd search the tower room first. Specifically" — she nodded to the fireplace — "that."

"Because there might be more treasures stored up there," Lucetta finished for her, rising to her feet. Making her way over to the fireplace, she stuck her head in, withdrawing it a second later. "Everything seems to be in order."

Tilda shook her head. "They wouldn't have left traces, Miss Plum. They'd be too careful for that."

"I wouldn't think donning a suit of armor was careful, if you really think about it," Lucetta said. "Why, if I hadn't been so taken aback by the sight, I could have very well confronted it. Being rather cumbersome, the person inside would have been hard-pressed to beat me to the door, and we could have easily discovered who is behind this mystery."

"Which is what the perpetrator has probably concluded as well," Mr. Skukman said. "Especially since you said it sounded like he ran into the wall."

"But where did he go?" Lucetta asked, more to herself than anyone in the room. "He disappeared, which means there has to be a hidden passageway somewhere up here."

"You don't have time to search for a passageway now, Miss Plum," Tilda said. "It's nearly seven, and the guests will be arriving soon." She ruffled Mr. Skukman's hair and then eyed him critically. "Well, it's not a style anyone could consider fashionable, but I do think the curls are enough of a distraction that you won't be recognized, especially after you put on the spectacles Miss Plum dug out of her trunk for you."

Picking up the spectacles, Mr. Skukman put them on and got to his feet. "I'll meet you downstairs," he said to Lucetta. "I want to do a preliminary walk-through, make sure nothing's out of place."

"*Everything's* out of place in the ballroom," Ruby suddenly said as she breezed into the room with what looked to be a dress thrown over her arm. She came to an almost immediate stop and looked Mr. Skukman over from head to foot. "And you're supposedly disguised as . . . ?"

Mr. Skukman blinked. "I'm supposed to be a man about town, one who owns his own steamboat and stopped by to visit his very good friend Mr. Haverstein."

Ruby's lips twitched ever so slightly. "Hmm . . . of course you are." With that,

239

she headed Lucetta's way, handing over the gown. "I found this in the attic. It's a little musty, but as you and I discussed over our lunch this afternoon, people might find it curious, given the look you want to achieve, if you're wearing Worth cut in the latest styles."

"Indeed," Lucetta agreed.

"What look *are* you trying to achieve this evening?" Mr. Skukman asked slowly.

Lucetta smiled. "You'll see. But now, if everyone will excuse me, I need to finish getting ready, and in order to truly get into character — as you well know, Mr. Skukman — I need the room to myself."

"Oddly enough, I keep forgetting you're an actress," Ruby said, more to herself than to Lucetta. Shrugging, she smiled and turned back to Mr. Skukman, offering him her arm, which, Lucetta was surprised to see, he took rather quickly, actually smiling as Ruby spirited him out of the room.

"That's an interesting turn of events," Tilda said with a nod to the door.

"And a much nicer turn than the event Ruby originally had in mind, the one where she was going to seek out Mr. Grimstone and have him squire her about."

Tilda opened her mouth, seemed to think better of what she'd been about to say, and took the dress Ruby had brought for Lucetta. "I'll just go give this a light pressing." With that, she headed out of the tower room, closing the door behind her.

Thinking Tilda's behavior was a little curious, but knowing she was growing short on time, Lucetta drew in a deep breath, exhaled it slowly, and began assuming the identity of the woman she'd decided to become that evening.

Not quite an hour later, Lucetta had completely transformed herself into the character she'd chosen to play. Her posture was less than perfect, her gait impeded by a slight limp, a limp she'd not forget to keep since she'd put a few stones in her right shoe, and her red wig was styled in a fashion that had gone out of fashion years before. Looking over the top of the deliberately smudged spectacles she'd put on to disguise her eyes, she considered the table of sweets that Bram's staff had set up for the guests, debating what delicacy the character she was playing would prefer. Choosing a cookie dipped in chocolate, she was about to take a nibble when a delicious scent tickled her nose, a scent that was a mix of sandalwood, lime, and . . . Bram.

"If Ruby hadn't described the dress she'd

found for you to wear, I'd never have been able to pick you out of the crowd," Bram whispered in her ear, the warmth of his breath sending curious little tingles down her spine.

Nerves had her popping the entire cookie she'd just picked up into her mouth, regretting that decision almost immediately when she realized her mouth had gone remarkably dry. Her heart had also taken to pitter-pattering at a most uncomfortable rate, and her hands inside the confines of a most hideous pair of lace gloves had taken to turning a little clammy.

It was very baffling, the unusual antics of her body, but antics that she knew full well were a direct result of Bram's whispering in her ear while standing remarkably close to her.

That right there was the crux of the problem.

His nearness was having an unusual effect on her, especially considering she was not a lady prone to clammy hands simply because a gentleman had whispered in her ear, his breath tickling that ear as each and every word escaped his mouth. Choking on that piece of nonsense, along with the cookie she'd shoved into her mouth, Lucetta staunchly banished the whole breath-tickling-her-ear idea because it was not helping the state of the pitter-pattering, or the state of not being able to catch her breath.

A sound pounding between her shoulder blades had the air whizzing back into her lungs, even as she realized that Bram seemed to be trying to apologize to her.

"It was completely unacceptable for me to steal up on you like that, Lucetta, and I do apologize for causing you to choke, but . . ." His words trailed to nothing when she lifted her head, giving him an unobstructed view of her face.

"And . . . you are not who I thought you were, so I fear I must apologize again," he continued a little weakly, taking a large step back from her.

"Don't you worry about that for a single second, sir," she said in a nasally drawl, having no idea why she wasn't telling him her real identity, but seeming to have no control over what was pouring out of her mouth at that moment.

When his eyes widened as his gaze settled on the mole she'd added right above her lip — a mole that had a long hair sprouting from it — it took every acting ability she had at her disposal to keep a straight face. "I'm just pleased as punch that you made such an honest mistake, although I have to wonder what lady you mistook me for since I've been told I'm one of a kind." She took a second to look him up and down, even going so far as to tip her spectacles just a bit, but not enough to where Bram would get a good look at her eyes. Tapping a gloved finger against her chin, she smiled a very wide smile, knowing full well she was presenting Bram with a mouth that appeared to be missing quite a few teeth.

To give the man his due, he barely winced as he returned her smile with one of his own.

"I'm Bram Haverstein, at your service, and you would be . . . ?"

"Enchanted, Mr. Haverstein, simply enchanted, and you may call me . . . Fauna."

"As in Mrs. Fauna?" he asked somewhat hopefully.

"I'm not married, Mr. Haverstein, but . . ." She tipped her spectacles again and sent him a wink, one he pretended not to notice. "I wouldn't mind if that circumstance were to change in the near future."

Bram smiled a little weakly. "I'm sure you must have many suitors."

"Nary a one, but my mother is still holding out hope. And speaking of my mother — would you be a dear and help me find her? The last I saw of her, she was in the ballroom, watching the ladies of Tarrytown set up the stage." She sent Bram another wink and fanned her face with a gloved hand. "She's a dear, dotty thing, but I bet she'd enjoy meeting you, and she'd adore seeing me on your arm." She lowered her voice. "My mother has been worried for years that I'm destined to remain a spinster, so it will do her old heart good to see that I've procured the attention of such a *dashing* gentleman." She smiled again as Bram's face turned a little pale, but then, to her very great surprise, he took her arm and even gave it a most reassuring pat.

"It would be my sincere pleasure to meet your mother, Miss Fauna."

For a second, Lucetta couldn't breathe, or move, or even think, at least not clearly.

It was rare to find genuine kindness in the world, and yet she'd seen Bram offer just that very thing time and time again.

The urge to bolt was immediate, an urge that was completely ridiculous, but one that stemmed from the fact she was beginning to find Bram just a little too appealing.

From what she'd discovered about the gentleman thus far, he was a man who thrived on taking care of people, and that was the last thing she wanted — especially given that she'd vowed to herself after her father had died that she'd never allow anyone to take care of her again.

Her father, while he'd been alive, had taken excellent care of Lucetta and her mother, making certain they had all the creature comforts in life, while giving Lucetta all the love and attention she craved.

She'd loved him more than anyone else in the world, but then . . .

He'd left her.

Not only had he left her, but he'd made her promise to take care of everything, including her mother, and . . . because Lucetta had loved her father so very, very much, she'd made him that promise — and her life had been forever altered because of it.

"Miss Fauna? Are you feeling unwell?"

Shoving aside the dark thoughts that had no business popping out of the deep recesses of her mind when she was smack in the midst of a social event, Lucetta cleared her throat. "I'm fine," she said as she dropped her nasal tone. "Even if you've put a damper on what should have been a most amusing bit of frivolity by going and turning all noble on me."

Bram stopped patting her arm. "Lucetta?"

"One and the same."

Bram leaned closer to her, peering intently into her face before he grinned. "That was a brilliant performance, some of your best work to date, and as we both know" — his grin widened — "I've seen a good deal of your work."

Her pulse immediately took to rushing through her veins, that circumstance due to the idea he was comfortable with addressing his past infatuation with her and wasn't opposed to poking a bit of fun at himself in the process.

It was quickly becoming clear that — after their amusing antics of the night before and now seeing the ease in which Bram dealt with a subject that had to still be a little painful to him — he was a gentleman in possession of a wonderful sense of humor.

There was something very appealing about that side of him, something that tugged at her heart and had those curious little tingles running down her spine again. Realizing she'd lapsed into silence for quite some time, and that that silence was earning a close look from Bram in the process, she shoved the spectacles back into place and lifted her chin. "I'm delighted you're enjoying my performance this evening, and . . . to go along with that performance, since Ruby's putting it about that I'm a distant cousin of yours, allow me to properly introduce myself. I'm Fauna Fremont, I've never married, I have an overabundance of cats that live with me, and . . ." She grinned. "This is the most interesting tidbit of all about me — I am currently enthralled with the study of plants that consume insects."

Bram frowned. "Do you know anything about plants that consume insects?"

"Only what I read in the book Ruby thrust into my hands a short time ago."

"Why would Ruby make up such a peculiar tidbit about you?"

"Apparently Mr. Skukman enjoys the study of plants, as well as poems by Lord Byron, and he suggested the book about plants for Ruby to read. She then evidently came to the conclusion that I'd be seen as more eccentric if I had the ability to wax on and on about carnivorous plants."

"But you haven't had time to study that book yet," Bram pointed out. "So you won't be able to wax on and on about them."

Unwilling to admit that she'd already read the book, and in a relatively short period of time, Lucetta summoned up a smile, that smile turning into a laugh when Bram shuddered ever so slightly at the sight of her missing teeth.

"Shall we go look over the other delicacies

your mother had your staff prepare?" she asked when Bram didn't seem capable of looking away from her face.

"I'm afraid I might be put off food for a while," he admitted slowly before he extended her his arm. "But I wouldn't be opposed to squiring you around to peruse the delicacies, as long as I don't have to watch you eat them."

A sliver of delight rolled over her when Bram linked his arm with hers and walked with her through the receiving room. She knew she looked a complete and utter fright, and yet, he still wanted to spend time in her company. That idea left her feeling far too warm and tingly, especially since there was still so much mystery surrounding Bram, mystery that included diamond necklaces, bloody swords, and armor that went bump in the night, not to . . .

"Why would Mr. Skukman suggest a book to my sister?" Bram suddenly asked, pulling Lucetta straight from her musings.

"Oh, uh . . . hmm" was all she could think to respond.

"He doesn't have romantic intentions toward her, does he . . . or . . . she for him?" he asked, bringing them to a stop directly in front of a rather disturbing tapestry. It appeared to portray some epic battle scene, the blood spilled from that battle a brilliant shade of red.

Pulling her attention away from the violent scene spread out above her, she caught Bram's eye. "You would have to ask Ruby or Mr. Skukman that question, since neither one of them have chosen me as their confidante in the matter."

"That's a wonderful idea," Bram said as he tightened his grip on Lucetta's arm and hustled her across the room.

"You're just going to find your sister or Mr. Skukman now, and . . . badger them about their interest in each other?"

"I'm not going to badger Mr. Skukman about it, since I obviously don't know him well, and . . . he's a little frightening at times. But my sister, on the other hand — as her older brother, I have every right to question her about her, uh, interests."

"I haven't gotten the impression Ruby's the type of lady to enjoy interference," Lucetta said as Bram released a grunt of satisfaction and steered her to the right, stopping abruptly when they were still a few feet away from where Ruby was sitting on a vivid red round divan.

"Someone's given her a script."

Lucetta wrinkled her nose. "It's a theatrical event. Of course someone gave Ruby a script."

"I would have thought they'd have learned from past events that Ruby should never be given a script. She can't act . . . at all, and . . . she can be . . . difficult."

"It's a local event, Bram. How bad could she be, and . . . I'm sure Ruby's not difficult."

Bram's only answer to that was a shudder before he urged her back into motion again, coming to a stop directly in front of Ruby.

For a moment, she didn't acknowledge them as she continued reading the script, squinting a second later at something on the page. Picking up a pen, she scribbled out a line, adding in one of her own over the top of the printed words.

"One would have thought after what happened the last time you tried to change a script that you would have learned your lesson," Bram said after Ruby finished writing.

Looking up, Ruby sent them a sad shake of her head. "It's an even shoddier story than the last one we were forced to perform, and I have to say, I'm beginning to question the taste of the Tarrytown ladies who formed our theatrical group."

Bram frowned. "It's simply a social group, Ruby. If you want a serious production, you'll have to go to the city."

"And maybe I'll do just that," Ruby said with a wink sent Lucetta's way. "I'm sure Fauna would be more than happy to put in a good word with her theater company, which would then see me landing a choice role to play."

Before Lucetta could do more than release a single sputter, Bram shook his head. "You may be brilliant with investments, sister dear, but an actress you'll never be, so . . . leave the script alone."

Waving his admonishment away as she rose to her feet, Ruby looked past Bram right before her smile widened. "Oh, look, it's" — she lowered her voice — "Mr. Skukman. Although he and I decided he's to be a Mr. Smith this evening. If you'll excuse me, I want to show him this script, because there's a part I believe he'll be perfect for."

With that, Ruby hurried away, looking over her shoulder a second later. "Nice wart by the way." Laughing, she turned her head and continued forward, taking hold of the arm Mr. Skukman offered her. With heads bent closely together, they walked into the crowd gathering in front of the ballroom and disappeared.

"Well, I suppose that answers the question I was going to pose to my sister," Bram said. "And since that's that, shall we repair to the ballroom and find a seat to watch the drama I'm certain is about to unfold? I know my grandmother and Archibald are already there."

"I thought Archibald was still under the weather."

Bram smiled. "He claims to be fit as a fiddle, although I've been told that Mr. Kenton's rheumatism is now acting up, which is why Grandmother has ordered him to stay in bed, read books, and not give her any trouble about following her orders."

Lucetta smiled. "They're very sweet together, your grandmother and her butler."

"I'm surprised they haven't killed one another over the years, and honestly, you're going to have to stop smiling, because those teeth . . ."

Pressing her lips together, she took the arm he extended and walked with him toward the ballroom, stopping when a well-dressed young lady reading a script suddenly wandered right in front of them, lifting her head as she mouthed one of the lines, her eyes widening when she caught sight of Bram. Lowering the script, she immediately turned a bright smile Bram's way.

"Mr. Haverstein, everyone was so hoping you'd come to rehearsals this evening. Dare

I believe that you've decided to actually try out for a part?"

"I'll think I'll leave all the parts for my guests, Miss Cooper, but I do thank you for thinking about me." He pulled Lucetta forward. "Have you met Miss Fauna yet?"

"Fremont," Lucetta corrected.

"Exactly, Miss Flora Fremont," Bram corrected.

"It's Fauna," Lucetta whispered, even though she knew Miss Cooper wasn't paying a bit of attention, given that the lady was gawking at the wart on Lucetta's face.

"It's a pleasure to meet you, Miss Cooper," Lucetta finally said when Miss Cooper actually leaned forward, with a finger raised, as if she was about to touch the wart on Lucetta's face.

Pausing with her finger only inches away from Lucetta's wart, Miss Cooper scrunched her brows together. "It's a pleasure to meet you as well, Miss, uh . . ."

"Fremont," Bram supplied. "She's Miss Fauna Fremont, a dear friend of the family."

"I'm your distant cousin," Lucetta said, smiling back at Miss Cooper, who blinked and immediately took to looking a little queasy.

"Perhaps the two of you should go find a

seat, before they're all taken," Miss Cooper said as she edged ever so slowly away from Lucetta.

"Thank you, dear," Lucetta said.

Ushering her quickly into the ballroom, Bram laughed. "You're a very odd woman, Miss Fauna Fremont," he said before he walked her across what was normally the ballroom floor, but was now lined with a few rows of chairs. Bringing her to a stop in front of two chairs that had been placed out of the way by a stained-glass window, he saw her seated, then sat down beside her.

To pass the time, Bram took to telling her about different Tarrytown residents who'd shown up for rehearsals, all of those residents bent over their scripts and looking quite serious about the business at hand. When Lucetta remarked on the seriousness, Bram smiled.

"Local events are not to be discounted as frivolous endeavors, Lucetta. The ladies who are in charge of our theatrical shows take these events very seriously, and there have been many a hurt feeling when people have been turned down from a role they particularly wanted."

Lucetta blinked. "They really do turn you down?"

Bram blinked right back at her. "You're

255

not truly considering trying out for a part, are you?"

"Of course I am. I've never been one to sit in the audience."

"What if you don't get chosen?"

She rose to her feet and smiled back at him, causing him to wince again. "That sounds like a challenge, so . . . be prepared to be amazed by the incredible acting abilities of Fauna Fremont, your . . . cousin."

Bram glanced around and then frowned. "Everyone else trying out seems to have a script."

"Please, I've already read the script, and I've chosen the bit part of Mrs. Nesbit. She has two lines, although it's an interesting part since she's been written as an annoying neighbor who drops in to borrow tea every day."

Lifting her chin, Lucetta was about to recite her lines to prove her point but was interrupted when someone clapped their hands, drawing everyone's attention.

"If we could have everyone who'd like to read for a part come up to the stage, we'll get our readings and then subsequent rehearsal under way," a voice called from where a stage had been erected at the far end of the ballroom.

"Well, this is it," Lucetta said. "Time to

see what Fauna can do." With that, Lucetta
drew in a deep breath, adjusted her posture
so that she was slouching exactly how she
imagined Mrs. Nesbit, the character she
wanted to play, would slouch, and then
limped away, smiling ever so slightly when
she heard Bram release what sounded
exactly like an appreciative laugh behind
her.

16

"I never thought I'd say this, but I do believe I've suddenly acquired the most unusual desire to tread the boards."

Rising to his feet when he realized Abigail had joined him, Bram saw her settled into the very chair he'd just vacated before he grinned. "If you'd really like to give it a go, Grandmother, I do have a small bit of influence with the ladies who are organizing this event, although . . ." His grin widened. "I might have to offer one of them the full benefit of my name to get you a *lead* part." He winked. "Those parts are incredibly sought after."

Abigail returned the grin as she gestured to the chair Lucetta had been sitting in. "You're a bit of a scamp, dear, but I do enjoy you. Care to keep your old grandmother company?"

Taking a seat, Bram nodded. "I'd be delighted to keep you company, Grandmother, but . . . where's Archibald?"

Abigail's eyes began to twinkle before she gestured to the stage. "That poor dear got coerced by some sweet young ladies into trying out for the role of butler. Apparently they have not had enough gentlemen show up this evening, which begs the question of how you got out of taking to the stage."

"I've let the ladies host their event in my castle."

"Your mother offered up the castle."

Bram smiled. "Well, true, but . . . weren't we talking about Archibald?"

Abigail wagged a finger his way. "I see how you are now, but . . . yes, Archibald." She looked to the stage, and Bram wasn't certain, but he thought he heard her release just a bit of a sigh — and one of those romantic sighs, at that. "Bless his heart, the poor man's barely recovered from his cold, and yet, there he is, up on a stage, taking on a most daunting part."

"If I'm not much mistaken, you mentioned he was taking on the role of the butler and . . . I wouldn't think that would be a daunting role to play."

Abigail nodded to the stage. "If you'll direct your attention to what is already unfolding on the stage, you'll notice that Miss Dunlap, a young lady with a rather bossy attitude, has apparently decided that, even given Archibald's many years spent on this earth, he's apparently less than proficient at the whole opening and closing of a door."

Looking up, Bram found that his grandmother was speaking nothing less than the truth. Miss Dunlap, a young lady who often declared herself in charge of the theatrical productions, was opening and closing the stage door, gesturing wildly with her hands, while Archibald nodded his head every now and again, and once even reached out and patted Miss Dunlap on the back. Turning back to his grandmother, Bram smiled.

"Your Mr. Addleshaw seems to be a likeable sort."

Abigail's cheeks took on an interesting hue of pink. "Oh, go on with you now. He's not *my* Mr. Addleshaw."

"He suits you."

Abigail waved his observation aside with a flick of her hand, although when she immediately took to waving that hand in front of her face, Bram thought he might have actually made a valid point.

"Speaking of suiting one another," Abigail suddenly said with a far too casual glance his way as she stopped fanning her face. "How are you and Lucetta getting along?"

"I'm sure you'll be pleased to discover she and I are well on our way to becoming . . . friends."

"Friends?" Abigail demanded in a rather affronted tone of voice.

"A person can never have enough friends."

"That's not what I want you and Lucetta to be at all."

"Clearly, but . . ." Bram stopped speaking when the lights suddenly dimmed and Miss Dunlap marched her way to the center of the stage and held up a hand. As silence descended over the ballroom, she smiled and dipped into a graceful curtsy.

"We're almost ready to begin, which is why I'm now going to request that any and all conversations come to an end as we go about the difficult business of choosing just the right person for each and every part." With that, Miss Dunlap brought a finger to her lips and seemed to look directly in Abigail's direction.

"She's very bossy," Abigail whispered before she waved at Miss Dunlap, who was now scowling their way.

Miss Dunlap drew herself up, seemed to shake herself, and then gestured to the parlor scene set up behind her. "To set the stage, our play — *An Evening in a Fifth Avenue Parlor* — opens up in present day, with a hint of winter in the air." She turned her head to the right, waved her hand at someone behind the scenes, then snapped her fingers and began to look rather cross. "The rattling of the windows, if you please, to allow everyone to know that bad weather is rolling in."

Bram swallowed a laugh when somewhere backstage someone banged together what sounded like two pans.

"At-home performances were all the rage when I was young," Abigail whispered in a voice that still carried. "We enjoyed them tremendously, although I suppose that was due to the fact there wasn't as much available to entertain a person back then."

"If everyone would please remember that there is to be no speaking," Miss Dunlap shouted as she looked Abigail's way again.

Abigail snapped her mouth shut, and even though her face was cast in the shadows, Bram was fairly sure she'd taken to looking a little grumpy. Reaching out, he took hold of her hand, giving it a quick kiss but not letting go as the audition began in earnest.

The next ten minutes were somewhat uncomfortable as Miss Dunlap truly did turn into a very bossy lady. She had an opinion about everything, wasn't shy about sharing that opinion, and more than one young lady left the stage in high dudgeon, as well as a few of the men. Archibald, much to Bram's amusement, seemed to be enjoying himself immensely, even with Miss Dunlap barking instructions at him every time someone was supposed to come through the door. A glance at Abigail found her leaning forward ever so slightly whenever Archibald went to open the door, a move Bram found very telling indeed.

Returning his attention to the stage after he'd watched Abigail lean forward yet again, he found that while he'd been distracted, Lucetta had taken the stage.

That she was not looking her best, there could be no debate. Her wig was a dull shade of red, and possessed a bit of frizz, the frizz seemingly becoming more pronounced as the evening wore on.

Fluffing up the frizz with a gloved hand, Lucetta moved to the spot Miss Dunlap was pointing to, lifted her chin, and opened her mouth. " 'I do beg your pardon, Miss Sonnenberg, but I've run short on tea. May I borrow some?' "

A mere second after Lucetta had spoken her lines, Miss Dunlap was standing directly in front of her.

"Miss Frizzmont," Miss Dunlap snapped. "Where, pray tell, is your script?"

Lucetta's chin lifted a notch. "It's Miss Fremont, and I left my script on a table somewhere."

Miss Dunlap's chin lifted a notch as well. "This, my dear Miss Fuddlemere, is an audition, and as such, proper actresses keep their scripts about their person at all times."

Bram held his breath as Lucetta stepped toward Miss Dunlap, but to his surprise, she simply smiled at the woman. The distance that separated him from the stage made it next to impossible to see her face clearly, but given that Miss Dunlap took a good three steps back from Lucetta, he got the distinct impression Lucetta was putting her toothless disguise to good effect.

"Forgive me, Miss *Doolittle*. I certainly didn't mean to slow the process by not having my script ready. If you could give me my lines, as I've heard they do with actresses who've forgotten their lines on a New York stage, I'll try it again."

"It's Miss Dunlap, and —"

"You said the line just as it's written in the script, Miss Pl . . . er . . . Fremont," someone called from somewhere behind Bram, someone who sounded remarkably like Tilda.

Turning, Bram found most of his staff gathered in the back of the ballroom, nodding in unison, which meant they'd evidently decided to claim Lucetta as one of their own.

That was not an honor they granted lightly, but before he could contemplate the action further, Abigail sat forward.

"Is that Ruby?" she asked.

Sitting forward as well, Bram winced when he realized that his sister had joined everyone on stage, and she now seemed to be in the midst of arguing with Miss Dunlap, gesturing to Lucetta every other second as she argued. Miss Dunlap, apparently taking issue with Ruby's interference and obvious defense of Lucetta, immediately took to shaking her finger Ruby's way.

Before Bram could get to his feet to intervene, he saw Mr. Skukman striding across the stage, his sheer size having the immediate effect of Miss Dunlap's finger shaking stopping midshake as the entire ballroom fell silent. Coming to a stop directly by Ruby's side, Mr. Skukman folded his arms over his impressive chest and did what he did best — look intimidating, somehow being able to still accomplish the look while sporting a head filled with curls. Although . . . from what Bram could tell from the distance that separated them, some of the curls were beginning to come undone, giving Mr. Skukman a rather deranged appearance, or one that suggested he'd been caught in a nasty windstorm, which wouldn't explain his appearance this evening since there was relatively little wind.

It was soon clear that Miss Dunlap was made of surprisingly stern stuff because she did not back down for long. Stepping closer to Ruby, which Bram thought was a huge mistake on Miss Dunlap's part, she opened her mouth, but before she could speak, Lucetta stepped forward.

"May I suggest that we just start again — from the part where I enter the room? I'll be sure to get my two lines right this time."

"You got your lines right the first time, as you very well know," Ruby said.

Lucetta tipped her spectacles down. "Do you want to be here all night?" she asked before she nodded to Mr. Skukman, who immediately held out his arm. And even though it seemed as if Ruby was less than thrilled to end the argument with Miss Dunlap, she did take the offered arm and allowed Mr. Skukman to escort her from the stage.

"From the start of that scene?" Lucetta asked, and without waiting for an answer, she breezed her way across the stage and disappeared through the door Archibald had managed to get open for her without any guidance from Miss Dunlap.

"Is it my imagination, or . . . is Mr. Skukman paying Ruby a bit too much attention?"

Looking up and to the right, Bram found his mother standing beside him, her eyes narrowed on the stage. Rising to his feet, he offered his mother his chair, and after she'd taken a seat, he knelt down next to her as Miss Dunlap called for the rehearsal to resume.

"I haven't heard anything of a specific nature, but I've gotten the impression that Mr. Skukman holds Ruby in high esteem, an esteem Ruby seems to return."

"I thought Ruby had set her sights on Mr. Grimstone."

"Well, yes, I do think she had set her sights on him at one point, but since she's never met that man before, Mr. Skukman might actually be a better option for her."

"And here I was finding myself hoping we'd get to have a writer in the family, even if it was only through marriage," Iris muttered before she blew out a breath, shook her head, and then turned to Abigail. "Tell me everything you know about Mr. Skukman."

Abigail smiled in obvious delight over her

daughter seeking her council, and immediately launched into a whispered dissertation regarding what she knew about Mr. Skukman, which, surprisingly enough, turned out to be quite a bit.

With their heads now bent together, Bram couldn't help but think that Iris and Abigail looked exactly as they should — mother and daughter engaged in a brisk debate regarding a potential suitor for one of their own.

Not caring to interrupt the healing that the whispering and the exchanging of opinions was creating, Bram straightened. Sending his mother and grandmother a nod they neglected to notice, Bram walked across the ballroom, nodding to the people sitting about here and there who weren't trying out for a part but had simply come to watch. Reaching the far end of the room, he moved into the shadows created by the stage. Leaning back against the wall, he smiled as Archibald opened the door again, revealing Lucetta. This time she was clutching a script in her gloved hand, and with a lift of her chin, she walked determinedly across the stage, stopping exactly where she'd stopped before, even as she, interestingly enough, brought the script up to her face, as if she wanted to leave no doubt about the fact that she'd brought the script with her.

"I do beg your pardon, Miss Sonnenberg, but I've run short on tea. May I borrow some?" Lowering the script, she glanced his way, and he couldn't be certain, given the disgusting amount of smudges on the lenses of her spectacles, but he thought she sent him a wink right as Miss Dunlap began marching across the stage again.

"You need to put some emotion into that line, Miss Fuddlecakes," Miss Dunlap proclaimed. "I want to feel the anguish you're experiencing over not having any tea at your disposal."

"It's Fremont, Miss Dimplekins, and I'll see what I can do." Spinning around, Lucetta marched off the stage again, reappearing ten seconds later through a door Archibald was once again holding open for her, although to Bram's eye, it almost seemed as if Archibald was beginning to have a difficult time maintaining the dignified demeanor of a butler. After Lucetta flounced through the door, he had to turn his back to the audience as his shoulders took to shaking suspiciously.

Taking her spot on stage, Lucetta spoke her lines, and . . . was sent back by Miss Dunlap to do it all over again.

Bram could only watch in stunned incredulity as Lucetta was sent back time after time as Miss Dunlap lamented the sorry state of Lucetta's acting abilities. To Lucetta's credit, she didn't bother arguing with the ridiculousness of the situation, she just kept smiling and marching on and off the stage with increasing frequency. By the fifth time, though, Bram noticed that the marching was beginning to turn more into stomps, and Lucetta's smile didn't exactly come across as being all that pleasant, especially since whatever she'd used to blacken her teeth seemed to be slipping, and . . . it made for a most interesting sight.

Just when he thought Lucetta might have had quite enough of the irritating Miss Dunlap, that woman declared she thought Lucetta might be improving, if only a little bit, so because of that, and because she'd proven herself willing to take direction, she had won the role of Mrs. Nesbit.

Grinning in pure delight after hearing that news, Lucetta practically skipped right off the stage.

As he watched the back of her skirt vanish from sight, Bram suddenly realized that the woman who'd just been absolutely thrilled to win a two-line part in a local play was, without a doubt, the real Lucetta Plum, and . . . she was absolutely nothing like he'd imagined her to be.

She wasn't possessed of a delicate or whimsical nature, wasn't fragile in the least, and . . .

He found her absolutely fascinating.

She had a wicked sense of humor, a keen intellect, no vanity at all when it came to her appearance, and . . . she was the heroine gothic novels deserved, the heroine of the future, and . . .

She was the heroine he needed to include in his next novel — a novel that would, hopefully, bring fresh life to the Mr. Grimstone books he'd been penning for years.

The story he'd been struggling to write for months now suddenly didn't seem all that daunting as ideas flowed through his thoughts, ideas that he'd begun to formulate the day before when he'd been with Ruby, but ideas that hadn't fully festered as much as he'd needed them to fester.

A sense of relief traveled over him as he realized he might not be completely washed up as an author after all, an idea he'd been considering quite seriously after his editor had been less than pleased with the manuscript he'd sent him a few months back — a manuscript that had been returned to him a few days before Lucetta had arrived at Ravenwood with enough suggestions written all over it that there were barely any empty spots on the pages.

Phrases like *doesn't move the story forward, heroine quite bland,* and *you've written this same story before but with different characters* had been scrawled in the margins by Bram's editor, and . . . that man had been exactly right.

Ever since Bram had seen Lucetta take to the stage three years before, he'd been writing all of his heroines with her as his inspiration, but that inspiration had never been a flesh-and-blood woman — she'd been a fantasy he'd created. That fantasy woman, however, couldn't hold up book, after book, after book, because, well, quite honestly, perfection got a little boring after a while, which was . . .

"Bram . . . over here."

Blinking out of his thoughts, he looked to the right and found Lucetta stepping through a door that led to the backstage area.

"What are you doing?" he asked as he joined her.

"I slipped away to warn you about something rather disturbing."

"You've seen another suit of armor walking about?"

Her brows drew together. "No, this is

more disturbing than even that." She leaned closer to him. "I've discovered that the reason all these young ladies keep showing up here at Ravenwood is because someone has started the rumor that you're actively searching for a wife, and — this is the worst part — you'd like to complete your search before the holidays."

"What?"

Lucetta took hold of his arm. "Someone is obviously trying to drive you away from Ravenwood, and unfortunately, all the signs point to someone on your staff."

"Not that I care to argue with you, but why would anyone choose such a ridiculous way to do that?"

Shrugging, Lucetta tilted her head. "If I were to hazard a guess, I'd say that the person behind this is getting desperate, probably because the whole ghost about the castle business hasn't chased you away yet."

"The rumors about the ghosts have been swirling for a while. If you'll recall, they're what chased the previous owners away."

"Which is . . . interesting, now that I think about —"

"Is someone talking?" Miss Dunlap suddenly called out.

"We should take this conversation elsewhere," he whispered.

Nodding, she took the hand he offered her, and they hurried across the ballroom, slipped out one of the back doors, and headed down a dimly lit hallway. Opening another door, one that led to the silver polishing room, he pulled her inside and flicked on the gas lamp.

"You have an entire room dedicated to polishing silver?" Lucetta asked, looking around as he closed the door.

"We mostly use this room to polish and fix up the armor."

"Which I'm sure is a most daunting task, but . . ." Lucetta smiled. "Getting back to our conversation, the one about the rumor spreading around that you're actively searching for a wife, you're really going to have to be careful around the Tarrytown ladies. From what I overheard, competition is fierce to win your attention, so I wouldn't suggest you go off and shut yourself away in a storage room with any of *them.* That could very well see your bachelor days coming to a rapid end."

"Aren't you concerned someone will discover us together?"

Lucetta rolled her eyes. "I've seen a mirror recently, Bram. I don't believe we have anything to worry about there, but . . . getting back to how I think you should ap-

proach the ladies of Tarrytown, you probably . . ."

As Lucetta continued going on and on
about what he should do, in that rather
bossy manner he'd never imagined she possessed, he found himself having a bit of a
difficult time concentrating on what she was
saying. Her lips were moving rapidly, and
while he was certain she was probably giving him sound advice, he found himself
more concerned with the idea that it seemed
to him as if she'd done something to her
lips — something that made them seem
quite spinster-looking, as if their very
plumpness had been squeezed right out of
them. The lips he was looking at now truly
did seem to belong to a woman who'd sport
a wart on her face, but . . . how had she
managed to make them appear so unattractive, so . . .

Taking a step closer to her, he leaned
forward, trying to puzzle out the mystery
behind her lips. They looked thin, which
was very peculiar, although . . . perhaps it
was the wart she'd so cleverly put right
above the upper lip that was . . .

"Why are you staring at me like that? Has
the wart moved?"

Dragging his attention away from the wart
in question, he looked up and caught her

eye through the smudged lenses that he had
no idea how she could see out of. Instead of
answering her, though, his hand rose,
almost of its own accord it seemed, and the
next thing he knew, he'd plucked the phony
wart straight off her face.

"What has gotten into you?" she demanded. "I need that wart, and . . . did you
just throw that over your shoulder?"

"It was disgusting," he said, dusting his
hands together, pleased with himself over
taking control of the wart even though
Lucetta looked about ready to strangle him.

"It was meant to be disgusting."

"Well, now it's gone."

Lucetta let out a grunt before she tried to
scoot around him, seemingly intent on looking for the wart he'd just tossed aside.
Before she could pass him, though, he
reached out, took hold of her shoulders and
felt her tense.

"What are you doing?"

Instead of answering her, he drew her
closer, smiling just a touch when he heard
her take a swift intake of breath.

"Bram . . . really . . . what are you doing?"

"Trying to figure something out," he said
as he moved one of his hands from her
shoulder and used a single finger to take a

poke at her lip.

"It's still full," he said, more to himself than to her. He poked it again before he pulled at her lower lip, exposing her teeth in the process. "You no longer appear to be missing your teeth."

"Stop that." She smacked his hand away. "I knew I shouldn't have snuck that second cookie backstage. It must have knocked the gum off."

"You used gum?"

Lucetta nodded. "I did, Black Jack gum, created by Mr. Thomas Adams, who opened the first gum factory with his sons in 1870, although I suppose now is not actually the time to recite history when faced with such a concerning situation." She blew out a breath. "I'm normally very careful when I use gum to make it appear as if I'm missing teeth, but I must have swallowed it when I ate that cookie."

"Do you think that'll hurt you?" Bram asked slowly.

"Hard to know at this point." She closed her eyes and shook her head a mere moment later. "No, I haven't read anything regarding a medical condition one can expect after swallowing gum."

Bram frowned as Lucetta opened her eyes. "You know it's really not a normal occurrence for people to be able to summon up random tidbits like that at will, don't you?"

A ghost of a smile played around Lucetta's mouth. "I've never claimed to be normal, Bram."

That smile struck him straight through his heart.

It was a genuine smile, with a bit of a self-deprecating edge to it, and . . . Without allowing himself a second to reconsider, he leaned toward her as his hand moved from her shoulder to her waist, and pulling her ever so slowly against him, he lowered his lips to hers.

17

Even though a part of Lucetta knew she really shouldn't be kissing Bram Haverstein in the middle of an isolated storage room, another part of her, the part that seemed to be melting against him, wasn't allowing her an opportunity to put up much of a fight.

To complicate the whole melting into him dilemma was the pesky fact that her mind, a part of her that was usually in fine working order, had apparently taken this particular moment to turn rather . . . fuzzy.

She'd never had a fuzzy mind before, had never known such a thing was even possible, and . . . given that all sense of logic seemed to have absorbed straight into the fuzziness, well, it was . . .

The distant sound of what she thought might be a door creaking tickled at what little rational thought she had left, but the tickling vanished almost as soon as it had begun, because, well, Bram was kissing her in a rather delicious fashion. And since she'd never been kissed before, even though she was twenty-six years old, and even though everyone assumed her to be a bit of a flirt, an assumption that was completely wrong, well . . .

"Miss Fremont! What in the world are you doing to poor Mr. Haverstein?"

For a second, Lucetta found herself wondering who this Miss Fremont was. But then a clear sense of panic struck straight through the fuzziness as Lucetta's mind snapped back into fine working order and she realized that she was supposed to be Miss Fremont and . . . she and Bram had apparently been found out. Untwining her hands from around Bram's neck, Lucetta stepped away from him and turned, finding Miss Dunlap, in the company of Miss Cooper, glaring back at her.

"Ladies, this is an unexpected surprise," Bram said in a remarkably casual tone of voice, as if he'd not just been discovered in a completely inappropriate situation. Stepping forward, he pulled Lucetta ever so discreetly behind him. "May I assume there's a perfectly good reason as to why you've abandoned the rehearsal?"

"Miss Cooper and I saw you leaving with Miss Fremont," Miss Dunlap began. "And quite frankly, we found that to be most suspicious." She leaned to the right and nodded to Lucetta, who'd taken to watching the conversation unfold from the safety of Bram's shadow. "Clearly you used some unusual excuse to lure poor Mr. Haverstein away from the ballroom, which you should feel very ashamed about now." Miss Dunlap switched her attention back to Bram even as she, curiously enough, sent him a beaming smile. "Do know, though, Mr. Haverstein, that we won't speak a word of this to anyone."

"There's absolutely no reason to keep the matter hush-hush now, Miss Dunlap," a voice said from the doorway. "Especially since you and Miss Cooper neglected to shut the storage room door behind you."

Swinging her attention to the doorway, Lucetta discovered Ruby marching into the room, followed by Mr. Skukman, who at least had the presence of mind to close the door after him, which drew mutters from all the people who'd gathered outside that very door.

"Oh . . . dear" was all Lucetta was able to utter as Mr. Skukman sent her a quirk of a brow before he took up a position in front of the door in an obvious attempt to keep anyone else from entering the room. Curiously enough, he was looking even more intimidating than usual, what with his hair having lost most of its curl, which gave him a somewhat menacing appearance, and the spectacles he was wearing pushed down past the bridge of his nose as he set his attention on, not Miss Cooper or Miss Dunlap, but Bram.

It was not reassuring to Lucetta in the least when Mr. Skukman took to cracking his knuckles . . . twice.

Ruby stepped forward with fists on her hips. "What I find myself compelled to ask, even though I'm sure I'm going to regret the question, is this. . . . What possessed you, Miss Dunlap and Miss Cooper, to sneak off after my brother in the first place?"

Miss Dunlap lifted her chin. "That's a little harsh, Miss Haverstein, accusing us of sneaking. We were only looking after your brother's reputation, because we had a feeling Miss Fremont, being the confirmed spinster type, might very well take it upon herself to get caught with Mr. Haverstein in a compromising situation."

Her chin lifted another notch. "Clearly, she's done just that, but . . ." She suddenly beamed another smile Bram's way. "The details of what has transpired in this very room are sketchy at best, which means if there are rumors already swirling around about someone being compromised, I would be more than happy to step forward and claim to be that compromised person even though my reputation will surely suffer for it."

Silence settled over the room until Miss Cooper started tapping her toe against the stone floor even as her face began to mottle. "Why do you get to step forward and claim to be compromised?" she demanded of Miss Dunlap. "I would be just as willing to step forward as well, and . . ." She looked to Bram and fluttered her lashes. "I believe I would add a welcomed bit of charm to the fairly dark and gloomy nature of Raven-wood."

"I've always been considered far more charming than you," Miss Dunlap bit out.

Deciding that the situation was only going to deteriorate the longer the two ladies were allowed to quibble over who was the most charming, Lucetta stepped forward, intent on intervening.

"Ladies," she began with a smile, catching Miss Dunlap's eye, "while I'm sure every-one is grateful for your more than generous —"

"What happened to your teeth?" Miss Dunlap interrupted.

"My . . . teeth?"

"You seem to have acquired more of them."

Lucetta immediately pressed her lips together. "How very unusual," she managed to get out through the side of her mouth.

"Where's your wart?" Miss Cooper demanded as she, along with Miss Dunlap, inched Lucetta's way, the ladies' animosity toward each other apparently forgotten.

"Uh . . ." Lucetta could think of nothing else to say, but she was spared further response when Bram stepped in front of her again.

While a part of Lucetta found his actions to be high-handed — especially since she firmly believed she could take care of herself — the other part of her, the part that had recently had her lips firmly attached to Bram's, well . . . that part of her found his protectiveness rather sweet, even nice, which was quite concerning when she considered the —

"While I'm very, er, touched," Bram began, "that the two of you are evidently very worried about my welfare, and my future, from the sound of it, I believe at this point it truly would be for the best for all of us to return to the ballroom and continue on with rehearsal."

"But what about . . . her?" Miss Dunlap asked as she craned her neck and set her sights on Lucetta again.

Lucetta craned her neck right back since Bram refused to budge even when she'd tried to nudge him out of the way. "Since only the two of you saw anything, and you've both promised Bram you're not going to say a word, I say we simply allow everyone their speculations as we go on our merry way and really dig in to the meat of that play."

Miss Dunlap took a single step Lucetta's way, completely ignoring everything that had just been said. "Who are you?"

"Mr. Haverstein's distant cousin, Fauna Fremont," Lucetta said promptly.

Miss Dunlap tilted her head. "I think not, especially since you've suddenly been able to regrow teeth and lose a wart."

"I don't believe a person can actually regrow teeth" was the only response that came to Lucetta.

"Which means you're in disguise, and . . ." Miss Dunlap's gaze shot from Lucetta to settle on none other than Mr. Skukman, who'd assumed his usual stance — arms folded across his chest, shoulders thrown back, and a scowl on his face. She inched his way. "I've seen you before. At the New

285

York Theater a few weeks ago. You were guarding that actress, that . . ." Her eyes widened as she looked back at Lucetta again. "On my word, you're Lucetta Plum."

Miss Cooper's mouth dropped open. "Why, you're right. She is Lucetta Plum. I can see it now, but . . ." Her eyes narrowed. "Why would you try out for our meager little play when you perform in the city on a renowned stage?"

"That, my dear, as I'm sure you're quite aware, is none of your business."

Looking up, Lucetta found Abigail edging into the room, followed by Iris and Archibald, who immediately put his recent instruction regarding opening and closing doors to good use by shutting the door behind him.

"We've been hearing outlandish tales," Iris began as she looked around before settling her sights on Miss Dunlap and Miss Cooper. "You two . . . out."

Miss Dunlap's mouth went slack. "Why . . . I never . . ." She squared her shoulders. "Miss Cooper and I walked in on your son kissing none other than" — she pointed a bony finger Lucetta's way — "Miss Lucetta Plum, the . . . actress."

Iris blinked, just once, right before she raised a finger of her own, pointed to the door, and said in the iciest voice Lucetta had ever heard, "Now."

In a flurry of skirts, Miss Dunlap and Miss Cooper quit the room, their mutters ending abruptly when Archibald, who'd returned to his door duties and had opened the door for their exit, closed it as soon as the last flurry of skirt disappeared over the threshold.

"What could you have been thinking?" Iris demanded a mere moment later, advancing on Bram with her hands on her hips. "You have, in case you've forgotten, a castle filled with local Tarrytown folk, your grandmother in residence, no less, as is a young lady whose identity we were supposed to be protecting." She stopped right in front of him and actually poked him with her finger. "Why would you have chosen this particular time, and this" — she gestured to the storage room at large — "particular place to try to woo Miss Plum? A lady, if you'll recall, who we've told all those gathered is your cousin, which makes all this" — she gestured around the room again — "seem rather tawdry."

"She's supposed to be a *distant* cousin," Bram reminded her.

"And one with a wart and no teeth," Ruby added, her lips curving ever so slightly.

"I don't believe you're helping my situation," Bram muttered.

"Goodness, you're right." Ruby smiled before she moved to Mr. Skukman, took his arm, and attempted to prod him toward the door. "Since the storage room is quite crowded at the moment, and since outlandish rumors are probably even now spreading like wildfire out there, Mr. Skukman and I will go assess the situation and see if there's anything that can be done to stem the amount of damage done to both of your reputations."

Mr. Skukman hadn't moved a single inch even with Ruby trying so determinedly to get him to the door. He sent a single nod Lucetta's way. "Would you like me to stay with you?"

"I think assessing the situation might be a better use of your time," Lucetta said. "Especially since I'm fairly sure Miss Dunlap and Miss Cooper are even now spreading the word regarding my true identity."

Cracking his knuckles again, Mr. Skukman released a grunt. "Would you like me to dissuade them from spreading the word?"

"Goodness, Mr. Skukman, get ahold of yourself," Ruby said before Lucetta could respond. Grabbing him with both hands, she tried yet again to get him to move,

288

releasing a pent-up breath of air a moment later when he refused to budge.

Sending Ruby a look that seemed to have a touch of amusement mixed in with clear exasperation, Mr. Skukman turned and caught Lucetta's eye. "Just call if you decide you have need of me." With that, he headed for the door with Ruby still firmly attached to his arm.

"I believe, since this is a family matter and I'm not a family member — at least not yet — I'll go help Mr. Skukman and Ruby assess the situation." With those cryptic words — words that left Abigail standing with her mouth slightly open — Archibald opened the door with a flourish, strode over the threshold, and pulled it closed behind him.

"What do you think Archibald meant by . . . *yet*?" Bram asked slowly.

"This is not the time to be pondering anything other than what you're going to do now," Iris said with a distinct edge to her tone as she shook her head at her son. "You've been caught in a compromising situation with Miss Plum, and . . . there's no getting around what has to be done now — you'll have to get married."

Lucetta's eyes widened. "Oh, I don't think there's any need for us to be hasty about anything, Mrs. Haverstein. Bram and I barely know each other. Add in the fact that I'm an actress, for heaven's sake, and . . . well, it's not as if I enjoy a pristine reputation, so no harm done, and that's that."

Iris plopped her hands on her hips. "What about Silas Ruff?"

"I don't want to marry him either."

She wasn't certain but she thought Bram's lips twitched just a touch. But, seeing those lips suddenly reminded Lucetta that she'd recently been very close to those lips, and . . .

"Your identity has now become public knowledge, Miss Plum," Iris continued, pulling Lucetta abruptly away from thoughts of lips, heat, and . . . closeness. "It will not be long until Silas learns your direction, and from what I've been told, he's determined to acquire you."

Lucetta shot a look to Bram, hoping for some assistance, but she found that Bram, curiously enough, was looking vacantly about the room, his thoughts clearly not on the present and oh-so-concerning situation. Resisting the urge to smack him back to the conversation at hand, she drew in a breath and returned her attention to Iris.

"I'm not certain why you're pursuing this idea of marriage between me and your son so adamantly, Mrs. Haverstein. Clearly, I'm not the type of lady a mother would actively seek out to become her daughter-in-law, and again, Bram and I barely know each other."

Iris lifted her chin. "My mother heartily approves of you."

Abigail drew in a sharp breath and raised a hand to her chest as her eyes turned suspiciously bright. "What a lovely thing to say."

Iris smiled. "I've seen that you truly do have only the best interest for your grand-children at heart, Mother. And since you care so deeply about Miss Plum, and my son apparently cares about her — because he's never been caught kissing a lady in a storage room before — who am I to stand in their way?"

Alarm traveled through Lucetta's veins, increasing by the second as Iris and Abigail turned her way and began beaming bright smiles in her direction. Realizing that she was not getting through to them, she turned to demand assistance from Bram, discover-ing that he'd moved stealthily away from everyone and was now . . . furiously scrib-bling something down on a crumpled piece of paper that seemed to be covered in silver polish.

"What are you doing?" she demanded.

Bram stopped scribbling, lifted his head,

blinked a few times, then straightened as he stuffed the piece of paper into a pocket and smiled at her. "Just had a thought" was his only reply.

"And you didn't want to lose it," Abigail said with a fond smile sent Bram's way. "I do the same exact thing when something important strikes me."

"Which is lovely to be sure," Lucetta said slowly. "But this is hardly the time for random thoughts, Bram, unless they pertain to the abominable situation at hand. That situation, if you've neglected to realize, is that the general consensus seems to be that we, as in you and I" — she gestured between herself and Bram — "have no choice but to get married."

"You don't have a choice," Iris said before Bram could respond. "You were discovered *kissing.*"

"Well, yes, I suppose we were, but . . ."

"There's no *suppose* about it, Lucetta," Bram said with the faintest hint of a smile. "You and I were caught in the act so to speak, which is exactly why we'll be getting married."

"I don't particularly care to be *told* I'm going to marry you."

Bram's brows drew together even as his eyes turned distant again. "Right. Because

292

independent ladies don't like to be told things, they prefer to be asked, and . . ."

To Lucetta's absolute confusion, and a good bit of annoyance, Bram suddenly pulled out the crumpled piece of paper he'd stuffed into his pocket, set it on a table that held a variety of silver-polish bottles on it, scribbled something else on the page, then straightened.

"Right," he said again. "Well, I need to go attend to something, so I'll leave you ladies to finish up with all the details of planning a wedding."

Unable to summon up a single question regarding what was obviously complete and utter lunacy, Lucetta watched in speechless disbelief as Bram headed her way. He stopped directly in front of her, kissed her on the cheek, leaned back, considered her face for a second, then leaned toward her again, and pressed a kiss right on her mouth. He seemed completely oblivious that Lucetta had taken to sputtering, while Abigail and Iris had taken to *tsk*ing, although Abigail's *tsk*ing seemed to have a rather pleased tone about it. Stepping away from her, he nodded, just once.

"That would work better — definitely on the lips," he said to no one in particular before he seemed to shake himself. "Now then, if everyone will excuse me . . ."

With that, Bram strode from the room, vanishing from sight before she had the presence of mind to call him back.

"This is turning out to be a very peculiar evening indeed," Abigail finally said, breaking the silence that had fallen over the room.

"It's not *peculiar,* Abigail — it's downright insane," Lucetta argued. "And . . ." She turned her head and caught Iris's eye. "What in the world was that all about? Who just walks off in the middle of a life-altering conversation?"

Iris sent her a faint smile. "Perhaps Bram has gone off to compose a more suitable marriage proposal."

Abigail immediately nodded in clear agreement with that. "I bet that's exactly what he's done."

"I got the impression he thinks matters are settled between us," Lucetta said slowly.

"And they will be," Abigail returned. "Just as soon as we get all the wedding details in place."

As Lucetta stood there with her mouth hanging open, Abigail and Iris linked arms, and then, chatting furiously in whispered tones, they hurried out of the room with phrases like "She'll make such a lovely

bride" and "We should hire Monsieur La-
mont for the cake" trailing after them.

18

"While I don't claim to be an expert regarding matters of a romantic nature, I'm afraid you, Mr. Haverstein, have made a complete disaster of the situation with Miss Plum."

Lifting his head from his Remington Model 1 typewriter, Bram found Tilda marching into the dungeon, wearing, oddly enough, a black skirt and blouse over which was a perfectly pressed white apron, an outfit normally only required for late afternoon and evening service. "Isn't it a little early to be wearing black?" was the first thing to enter his plot-encumbered brain.

"It's almost four . . . in the afternoon," Tilda returned, coming to a stop directly in front of the medieval desk he'd purchased because he'd known it would be a great source of inspiration for his gothic novels, what with all the deep gouges and stains littering the surface of it.

"Is it really?"

"Indeed," Tilda returned, crossing her arms over her chest. "On . . . Saturday."

Bram blinked. "It's only Friday."

Tilda sent him a pitying look. "And that right there is why you're in a great deal of trouble with Miss Plum. She's beyond irritated that you've been nowhere to be found over the past *two* days. Believe me, she's been trying her very best to wheedle that information out of every member of your staff — all of whom, you'll be pleased to learn, have yet to give in to her wheedling."

She shook her head. "Just so you know, Mr. Macmillan has promised everyone on staff a substantial bonus if they remain strong against the charm Miss Plum is now being suspected of plying rather heavily in order to pry information out of people."

"How much trouble do you believe I'm in?"

"Nothing you can't recover from — at least that's what your grandmother said this morning before she and your mother went off to look at fashion plates at your mother's house."

"Ah, so do you believe Lucetta has accustomed herself to the idea of marrying me?"

Tilda arched a brow. "Not at all. I believe

your mother and grandmother are refusing to face the truth — that truth being that Miss Plum never agreed to marry you. And after she got over the shock of being found in the storage room with you, she began to feel very put out indeed that anyone would assume, and I think you may be included with that whole anyone business, that she'd" — Tilda tapped a finger against her chin — *" 'blithely sit back and allow everyone else to plan out my life when I'm fully capable, as well as willing, to plan out that life on my own.' "*

Bram winced. "Am I to assume those were her exact words?"

"Or close enough," Tilda said. "I'm afraid you've really made a muddle of this, Mr. Haverstein, and I'm also afraid that you won't be marrying Miss Plum anytime soon, if ever." She leaned closer to him. "She talks quite often to herself when she's alone. Because of that, I've been privy to some interesting conversations, all of which center around the idea she's not a woman who wants to lose her independent identity through marriage." As an afterthought, Tilda added, "And . . . she's come to the firm belief that you're demented."

"What?"

Tilda shrugged. "Can you blame her? You

298

proclaim the two of you are going to get married — without asking her if that's what she'd like, mind you — while allowing your mother and grandmother to believe they should start planning the wedding festivities. That, Mr. Haverstein, is not how it's done. The bride gets a say in this day and age, and then, add in that pesky business of you disappearing and it's little wonder Miss Plum is questioning your sanity."

"Why didn't someone simply tell me I was losing track of so much time?" Bram asked as he settled back in his chair.

"Because you *are* slightly deranged when you're in the midst of writing, and everyone on your staff knows better than to approach you unless you ring for us," someone who sounded very much like Stanley said from the far side of the dungeon, Bram's room of choice to churn out his work.

With a sense of dread settling over him, Bram rose to his feet and craned his neck, wincing when he discovered Stanley lying on the dungeon floor. "You're not still shackled to that piece of railroad track I set up, are you?"

"While I would love to be able to say *no*, that hairpin I told you I was certain I would be able to free myself with . . . didn't exactly work out as planned."

"But I must have shackled you to that railroad tie hours ago," Bram said weakly.

"Oh, you did, but it's been fine down here on the floor. It's not overly cold, just a bit chilly."

"Why didn't you tell me you couldn't get free?"

"And interrupt what will probably be your best work to date?" Stanley let out a grunt. "Not likely. And that's exactly how you'll need to explain your less than chivalrous behavior of the past two days to Miss Plum. She's an industrious soul, she'll understand that, and it'll go far in soothing her indignation over your leaving her to deal with the repercussions of what Miss Dunlap did after you, she, and Miss Cooper parted ways."

Bram winced. "There were repercussions?"

"Indeed," Tilda said. "Miss Dunlap, you see, put on quite a dramatic display after she went back to the ballroom, far more dramatic than anything that dreary production she was trying to direct could have achieved. You won't like hearing this, but the woman actually took to the stage and told everyone the rehearsal, as well as the final production, had been canceled. Then she told everyone in the ballroom about you and Miss Plum — and that Miss Plum had

300

been the very unattractive Miss Fremont —
and that Miss Plum had obviously gone to
great lengths to pull the wool over everyone's eyes, embarrassing the good folk of
Tarrytown in the process by mocking their
theatrical efforts."

"Oh . . . no," Bram said.

"Indeed," Tilda agreed. "And unfortunately, it gets worse."

"Maybe you shouldn't tell me everything
all in one sitting, Tilda," Bram said a little
weakly.

"Don't be a coward, Mr. Haverstein. It's
always best to hear all the bad instead of
parceling it out bit by painful bit."

Retaking his seat, he buried his face in his
hands. "Very well, carry on."

"Well, you see, Miss Dunlap was clearly
distraught, as well as disappointed, that
you'd been discovered kissing Miss Plum.
Because of that, she said some very dispar-
aging things about Miss Plum, and before
long Mr. Skukman joined her on stage."

"Oh . . . no."

"Exactly. Well, Miss Dunlap didn't take
kindly to him arguing with her, and she . . .
attacked him."

Bram lifted his head. "She . . . attacked
him?"

Tilda nodded. "She did, but to give Mr.

301

Skukman credit, he didn't bat an eye as she went about the unpleasant business of pummeling him. It wasn't harming him at all, of course, but when she started throwing things — and not just at him but at members of your staff as well — Mr. Skukman saved quite a few people from suffering injuries by picking up Miss Dunlap, tossing her over his shoulder, and carting her offstage."

"Should I ask what happened next?"

"He was run out of Tarrytown by a horde of angry townswomen, and . . . to add further chaos to the evening, someone let Geoffrey out of the barn again and he chased Miss Dunlap and Miss Cooper all the way down the drive, until they were rescued by Ernie. Although . . . he was apparently in the process of creating some new gravestones for the back graveyard in case you needed some disturbing inspiration some night, and . . . there is now a rumor swirling about town that we're up to some concerning shenanigans here at Ravenwood."

"The graveyard's just a muse to me," Bram pointed out. "It's not as if we're actually burying people in it. Why, one only has to read the *Countess of Devonshire Heights* to find half the names Ernie's etched on the stones."

"Forgive me, Mr. Haverstein, but since no one except you, your editor, and your staff knows you're Mr. Grimstone, you can't actually blame people for finding you a bit . . . curious — nor can you expect anyone to assume the graveyard we have here at Ravenwood doesn't have any graves in it." Tilda released a breath. "Although, if you want my opinion, I think it's past time for you to disclose your secret to your friends and close family. It would save a lot of speculation, and your poor mother wouldn't be wondering if you're up to criminal activities."

Bram released a breath of his own. "You might be right."

"Of course I am, but now is not the time to ponder the matter further. You need to make amends with Miss Plum before you lose her for good."

"Before you do that, though, sir," Stanley called from where he was still lying on the floor, "could you possibly be bothered to unshackle me?"

"I do beg your pardon, Stanley. Once again I seem to have forgotten all about you languishing down there." Bram opened the top drawer of his desk and rummaged through it. "I seem to have misplaced the key, though."

When Stanley began sputtering, he hurried to continue. "But not to worry. I know I have a spare one in the kitchen, and I'll go fetch it straightaway."

Rising to his feet, he headed out of the dungeon and pulled the door closed behind him. Walking up the narrow flight of stairs that led to the ground floor, he reached the top and opened the door that led into the kitchen ever so slowly. Sticking his head around it to make certain the coast was clear, he froze on the spot when his gaze settled on none other than Lucetta.

That she was just as surprised to see him, there was no question, since she'd frozen as well. But unlike him, she wasn't frozen for long. Advancing his way with absolutely delightful curls tumbling around her beautiful face, she stopped right before the door and plunked her hands on her hips.

"Your hair looks very lovely today" was the only thing that sprang to mind to say to her.

"I've been bored, which led to my experimenting with the hot tongs, but . . . where have you been?"

"Working."

Lucetta lifted her chin. "I didn't ask what

you've been doing, I asked where you've been doing it."

"Oh, uh, well . . ."

"What's behind that door?"

"Who says there's anything behind it?"

"Step aside."

"I find this bossy side of you to be incredibly charming."

"I'd hate to have to hurt you, but I will if you don't get out of my way."

"I find ladies who seem to have no qualms about threatening a gentleman to be just as charming as bossy ones."

"I'm beginning to lose patience with you."

Bram edged his way through the door, opening it just enough to squeeze through, but then Lucetta brushed right past him, and since he certainly wasn't a gentleman who was comfortable physically restraining a woman, he simply stood there, resignation stealing a breath from him as he watched her hurry down the steps . . . until he realized what she'd find down there. Rushing after her, he caught up to her right as she caught sight of the black door leading to the dungeon.

"Why is that door painted black?"

"Uh . . ."

"What's in there?"

"Nothing you'd find interesting."

She reached out and jiggled the knob. "It's locked."

"I guess that means we should go back to the kitchen. I, for one, just realized I'm starving, and I'm also dying to learn what happened to Mr. Skukman, only recently learning that he got run out of town."

"Honestly, Bram, he's Mr. Skukman. Do you actually believe he wouldn't have found a way back to Ravenwood — pitchfork-carrying townsfolk or not? He, unlike some people we know" — she sent him a pointed look — "is very diligent when it comes to his responsibilities. Which is why he's currently searching for that secret passageway up in the tower — so that I won't be taken unaware again by some misbehaving member of your staff."

She drew in a breath and continued. "But enough about that. I'm far more interested in what happened to you. Why are you still wearing the same clothing you had on two nights ago, and" — she narrowed her eyes — "how could you have forgotten the disaster you and I landed ourselves in? Because of your disappearance over the past couple days, your mother and grandmother are under this misimpression that you and I are truly going to get married. They've been plotting and planning almost nonstop, actually repairing to Iris's house today so that they could plot in peace, seemingly annoyed by the fact I keep telling them there's not going to be a wedding."

She smiled somewhat unpleasantly at him. "You may just find yourself in the midst of a wedding they've taken great pains to plan, and having to explain to those dear women why they were allowed to continue planning such a wedding when you have no fiancée to meet you at the end of the aisle."

Bram took a single step toward her but froze on the spot when she let out what almost sounded like a hiss. "I know I haven't been very attentive," he began. "But I have a reasonable explanation for that — or fairly reasonable. However, explanations aside, surely you haven't forgotten that your good name has been compromised, which means, given that we were discovered in a tricky situation, we have no choice but to get married."

"Surely you haven't forgotten that I'm an actress. There is very little that can be done to harm a reputation I haven't seen for about a decade."

Not caring at all for the direction the conversation seemed to be heading, and truly wanting to kick himself for allowing his writing to consume him over the past two days instead of settling things properly with Lucetta, Bram summoned up a smile. "I have a feeling your reputation is very important to you — why else would you have gone to such extremes to discourage all of your admirers over the years?"

Instead of answering him, Lucetta jiggled the knob to the dungeon again. When it didn't budge, she took to knocking on the door.

"Who is it?" Tilda's voice called through the door.

"It's Lucetta, Tilda. Open the door."

For a second, dead silence rang out, but then, "There's no one here right now, especially no one by the name of Tilda."

"Honestly," Lucetta muttered before she plucked a hairpin from her curls and bent down to the lock. Less than thirty seconds later, the lock clicked, she turned the knob, and before he could stop her, she stepped into the dungeon.

"Where did you learn how to do that?" he asked after he forced himself to trail after her into the dungeon.

"My friend Millie taught me, but . . ." Lucetta drew in a sharp breath. "What's going on in here?"

Stepping up beside her, Bram winced. Stanley, unfortunately, was still lying on the ground, shackled to a railroad tie, no less, while Tilda, for some unknown reason, was spread out on the rack that had once been used for stretching people, and . . . she'd even gone so far as to stick her hands through the holes at the head of the rack, which made her look as if she was in the process of being tortured.

It was not how he would have liked to have gone about the business of introducing Lucetta to his real life, because, well, looking at it through her eyes, it was a menacing scene indeed, and . . .

He snapped back to the situation at hand when he realized Lucetta was now moving through the very large dungeon, her eyes enormous as her gaze drifted from one unusual device to the next — all procured with a specific plot point in mind, but . . . devices that a supposedly normal person certainly wouldn't have collected.

"This is going to break your grand-mother's heart," she finally said, lifting up a heavy chain that had spikes attached to the end of it. "I have no idea how I'm going to divulge to her that you, her treasured grandson, are nothing more than some . . . crazed lunatic."

"That's a bit harsh, and all of this" — he gestured around the room — "is not exactly what it seems."

"It's not a dungeon filled with every type of torture device devised in the last five hundred years?"

"I think the oldest I've managed to find is three hundred years old, and . . ."

"You're not helping your case, Mr. Haverstein," Tilda called out to him.

"Uh yes, probably not."

"I'm confused about the railroad tie Stanley's attached to," Lucetta tossed at him, causing him to blink at the rapid change of topics.

"Uh . . ." he began.

"It's not that confusing, Miss Plum," Stanley said, speaking up when Bram continued floundering. "I'm trying to see how long it takes to get freed from being shackled to a railroad track with only a hairpin to get undone."

"Why would anyone need to know that?"

"Well, it might come in handy if, well . . . hmm . . . That is a difficult question to answer," Stanley said as he sent Lucetta a rather strained smile.

"May I assume you have a reason for practicing such a thing?" Lucetta pressed.

"Uh . . ." was all Stanley seemed capable of replying, which had Lucetta marching right up to him.

"What is your area of expertise, Stanley?"

"Well, that depends, Miss Plum. I'm very good at assuming a variety of different roles, one of those being Mr. Haverstein's acting valet at the moment. Although . . . now that I think about it, since he's not changed his clothing for two days, that might not have been the best example to give you regarding what I'm good at."

"What did you do before you began working for Bram?"

"A . . . uh . . . bit of this and that."

"*Criminal* this and that?" she pressed.

"I grew up in the Lower East Side, Miss Plum. I'm fairly certain that over the years I lived there a few of my positions would have, possibly, been considered less than reputable. But when I came to work for Mr. Haverstein, I had to promise to put aside my less than honest ways, and that's what I did."

He nodded. "Reverend Gilmore, a very wise man, once told me that God forgives us for the sins of our past if we ask for forgiveness. He also told me that God expects each and every one of us, after we've acknowledged our wrongdoings, to try and walk the straight and narrow. That right there is what Mr. Haverstein expects from those he hires, and I can say with all certainty that I'm a better man now than I've ever been."

"You know Reverend Gilmore too?" Lucetta demanded.

"Of course. He's a familiar figure in the tenements. He's just tickled to death to have found a gentleman like Mr. Haverstein, a gentleman who is kind, compassionate, willing to always lend a hand, a true champion for the weak and downtrodden, and . . ."

"I think she gets the point," Bram said quickly when it started becoming a bit too obvious that Stanley had descended into a touch of embellishing when it came to Bram's character. Squaring his shoulders, he moved to his desk, the one where his typewriter sat, opened his mouth, and was just about ready to reveal all when . . . Ernie strolled into the dungeon, carrying a shovel over his shoulder and whistling a bit of a happy tune under his breath.

"Finished burying that sword, Mr. Haverstein, just like you asked me to, and there'll be no finding it now, not with it being buried in the graveyard . . . Oh . . . hello, Miss Plum. I wasn't expecting to find you down here in the, um, dungeon." Ernie shot a glance to Bram, who only had a grimace to send him in return. Shifting the shovel to his other shoulder, Ernie blinked far too innocent eyes Lucetta's way. "How goes the wedding plans?"

"I'd rather discuss why you were burying the sword, and where this graveyard is, and exactly what, or who, is buried in it," Lucetta returned.

"I've always thought a wedding right around Christmas would be lovely," Ernie continued as if Lucetta hadn't spoken.

"I'm sure Abigail and Iris would agree with you, Ernie, which is why I'm also sure they're going to be incredibly disappointed to learn that there will be no wedding, at least not one that will ever see me married to your boss — Mr. Madman Haverstein."

Bram frowned. "The whole *Madman* business is a bit severe, don't you think? Because there truly is a rational explanation regarding all" — he gestured around the room — "this."

Lucetta's eyes turned stormy. "If you think I'll believe anything you have to say from this point forward, Mr. Haverstein, you're more delusional than I'm giving you credit for. Although, do know that I'm not blaming you for everything. I will take some responsibility for being caught in a compromising situation."

"I'm the one who stole you away from the rehearsal."

"True, you did, but . . ." Lucetta drew herself up. "In hindsight, it was a mistake on my part to accompany you there so readily. You're obviously not a gentleman I can trust, and that means . . . I expect you to keep your distance from me until I can make arrangements to depart Ravenwood for a safer environment."

With that, she spun on her heel and was out of the dungeon before he could even consider stopping her.

"Don't just stand there, go after her," Tilda said.

"She's not going to listen to me."

"You'll have to tell her the truth. Tell her you're Mr. Grimstone."

"I was about to do just that, but . . . well, matters seemed to get quickly out of hand."

"That's because Miss Plum thinks you've lied to her, sir," Ernie said.

"I have lied to her — I've lied to everyone, for that matter, by keeping Mr. Grimstone a secret."

Ernie shifted the shovel to his other shoulder. "Perhaps it's time for you to make amends for that. I believe your family will be more accepting of having an author in the family than you've given them credit for, sir."

"Except for maybe Ruby," Tilda said,

speaking up. "Especially since she was considering tracking Mr. Grimstone down and convincing him he should court her."

"Good thing she's been showing a bit of interest in Mr. Skukman," Stanley pointed out from his position on the ground. "That way you won't be dealing with a sister nursing a broken heart over a love that can never be hers."

Bram's lips quirked ever so slightly "Yes, thank you for *that*, Stanley." Heading for the door, he looked over his shoulder and caught Ernie's eye. "Will you see Stanley released? I wasn't able to retrieve the spare key from the kitchen."

"Don't you give it another thought, sir," Ernie said with a nod. "And don't fret over what you need to tell Miss Plum. Just remember what Reverend Gilmore was preaching the last time we were back in the city — the truth shall set you free."

Bram smiled. "A good reminder. Thank you, Ernie." With a nod meant for everyone, Bram strode out the door with additional words of encouragement drifting after him from his eclectic, yet good-hearted, staff. Taking the steps two at a time, he walked into the kitchen right as a distinctive boom sounded from outside the castle.

Heading immediately down the hallway, Bram came to an abrupt stop when Mrs. Macmillan rushed into view.

"Mr. Haverstein, thank goodness," she breathed. "We didn't know what to do. Mr. Macmillan and I were up on the north tower because . . . Well . . . no time to explain that, but . . . we saw a bunch of riders approaching. They went right by the gate, which means Ernie's either dead or he abandoned his post. So while Mr. Macmillan got the cannon ready to draw attention, I rushed down the steps, but . . . I was too late. Someone knocked on the door, and before I could stop her, Miss Plum answered it, and . . . they snatched her straight out of the castle."

19

To say the rooms she'd been held captive in for three days were the height of gaudiness was a definite understatement.

Pink was the color of choice for the sitting room, deep purple had been lavishly used in the bathing chamber, and the bed-chamber . . . Well, it was a garish nightmare with all the black, red, and gold papering the walls, hanging from the windows, and making up the counterpane that covered the canopied bed.

The only bearable element in what was, in reality, her jail, was the large bookcase that ran along an entire wall in the sitting room, filled with leather-bound books, most of them with their spines intact.

At first, assuming that Silas had picked out each and every one of them for her as he'd pictured her cozied up on the pink divan reading them had kept her from open-ing up a single book. But then, when Silas didn't put in an appearance and the hours had ticked slowly by and anxiety had begun to build, Lucetta had turned to the books as a source of distraction.

Unfortunately, given that she was an incredibly fast reader, and given that she'd now been held against her will for three very long days — her only company being the rather masculine-looking women Silas had hired to watch out for her — she'd run out of books to read.

Having no desire to pick up a book she'd already read, especially since all the words she'd read were firmly engraved on her mind, Lucetta blew out a breath, rose off the divan, and moved to the window, one that had been painted pink, and one that had been nailed shut. Since all the windows on the building she was being held in had been boarded over, having seen them from her vantage point of being slung over the shoulder of one of the menacing brutes who'd snatched her from Ravenwood, she knew it would be useless to break the window — something she'd contemplated numerous times anyway over the time she'd been held captive.

She'd also been contemplating her relationship with God quite often, that contemplation brought about because she'd taken to praying for help . . . frequently. But as the days slipped away and Silas continued on with what could only be described as a cat-and-mouse game by not putting in an appearance, Lucetta had come to the conclusion that God might have abandoned her. Not that she could blame Him, of course, especially since, uncomfortable as it had been to admit it to herself, she'd faltered in her faith walk, had been faltering for a very long time, and simply kept up the pretense that she was a woman of faith because she hadn't wanted to delve into the reasons behind her annoyance with God.

Clearly, God had known of her annoyance with Him. What she was becoming more and more ashamed of, though, as the hours ticked away, was that she, like so many people who'd faltered in their relationship with God, had had no qualms about asking Him for assistance when disaster had fallen. And that —

The sound of a creaking door pulled Lucetta from her thoughts. Turning from the window, she watched the door open, expecting to find one of the women Silas had paid to deliver meals entering the room. Unfortunately, as the door opened wider, it revealed none other than Silas Ruff, looking as confident as ever as he strode into the room, his gaze traveling from the top of her head to the tips of her shoes that were peeping out from beneath one of the red crushed-velvet gowns he'd left for her to wear.

"Aren't you just a vision," Silas said, the intensity of his gaze causing Lucetta's skin to feel as if it were about to crawl right off her body and hide behind one of the tacky pink drapes.

Lucetta inclined her head, forcing down the bile rising in her throat as she summoned up her most arrogant demeanor. "Silas, how nice of you to come calling."

Silas smiled. "I knew if I left you to your own devices for a bit, you'd be anxious for my company."

"I'm anxious to be *released,*" she countered. "I've grown tired of my prison and have matters of great importance to attend to, so I demand you let me go." Lucetta forced herself to meet his gaze, doing her very best to ignore the fact her knees had taken to knocking underneath the hideous gown she'd had no choice but to wear.

She'd actually considered refusing to don any of the clothing Silas had provided, but since one of the women who'd been looking after her had made off with the clothing she'd been wearing while she was taking a bath, she hadn't had much choice in the matter.

Languishing about unclothed was certainly not a state she'd wanted Silas to discover her in.

"I'm afraid you're in no position to demand anything, my darling, and I have no intention of releasing you — now or in the foreseeable future." Silas gestured to the divan. "What say you we get comfortable?"

"I'm fine where I am."

"Sit down."

The ice in his voice chilled her to her very soul, and since her knees were now about to give out on her instead of simply knocking about, she moved to the divan and sat. Dipping her head, she took a moment to adjust the skirt of her gown, a moment she needed to collect her composure.

It would not do to allow Silas to see her fear. He was a man who thrived on intimidation, depravity, self-indulgence, and cruelty. Giving him any ammunition would not serve her well in the end, which was why she knew she needed to present him with the Lucetta he thought her to be — cool, reserved, and . . . haughty. Lifting her head when she was relatively certain she'd gotten her emotions under control, she sent him an arch of a single brow.

Taking a seat in a poufy chair upholstered in pink floral that was right next to the divan, Silas considered her for what felt like forever. The tip of his tongue darted out of his fleshy lips, moistening them, the sight of that tongue prompting bile to once again rise up in Lucetta's throat.

"I've decided to make you my mistress."

A small thread of temper mixed in with the fear traveling through her veins. "Have you now?"

"I bought this building just for you, and had the top floor decorated in a manner I was quite certain, given your dramatic attitude, you'd appreciate."

Lucetta drew in a breath — refusing to allow Silas the satisfaction of even glancing at some of the more gaudy pieces in the room he was pointing out — and waited until he'd run out of words before she lifted her chin another notch.

"I'd like to know, if you please, how you came to the conclusion I'd be receptive to the idea of becoming your mistress."

Silas settled back in the chair, folding his hands across a stomach that strained against the buttons of the jacket he was wearing. "Come now, dear. There's no need to continue playing coy. You've led me on a merry chase these past few years, never af-

fording me an audience after your performances, and neglecting to answer the notes
I sent asking you to join me for a late-night
dinner here or there." He wiggled a finger
in her direction. "You and I know full well
that you did so in order to increase your
value."

"I wouldn't be so certain about that."

He continued speaking as if she hadn't
voiced a reply. "I'm willing to allow you to
live here, amongst this lavish setting, and
will provide you with your very own personal maid, a carriage with matching bays,
a driver for that carriage, and . . . give you
the pleasure of my company until I tire of
you."

She dug her fingernails into the tender
skin of her palm so that she wouldn't be
tempted to rake them across the man's face.
"I have my own carriage, thank you very
much, as well as a lovely place to stay, and
while I'm flattered you want to spend time
in my company, I do have a profession I
need to get back to. That means I am —
regretfully, of course — going to have to
refuse your simply charming offer to become your mistress."

Her head snapped back from his slap
before she'd even realized he'd gotten up
from his chair. Blinking to hold back tears

that longed to fall, she lifted her chin and ignored the pain in her cheek as Silas retook his seat and immediately took to staring at her.

His eyes were filled with something hot, something she was certain verged on the edge of true insanity, and that insanity chilled her straight through her bones.

"It wasn't an offer, my dear," he finally said quite pleasantly. "But enough about that." He nodded to a piano across the room. "Since I've paid a small fortune to track you down, after spending far too much time on that wild goose chase your guard sent me on, I find myself in need of soothing. A nice tune by Bach would be lovely right about now. You'll find the sheet music in the bench."

For a second, she thought about refusing, but the stinging in her cheek and the knowledge that he wouldn't be opposed to slapping her other cheek if she didn't comply with his demand had her rising from the divan. Shaking out the folds of her skirt, she made her way to the piano and found the sheet music exactly where he'd said. Not bothering to tell him that, even though she knew how to read music, she didn't exactly have a light hand on the keys, she sat, squared her shoulders, and began to play.

Before she'd made it through an entire page of notes, Silas was standing by her side, his face mottled and his eyes blazing. "Play it properly," he demanded when she lifted her fingers from the keys.

"That *was* me playing it properly."

Bracing herself for another slap when his eyes narrowed, Lucetta was spared another bout of pain when a knock sounded on the door right before it opened and one of the women Silas had hired stepped into the room.

"The dinner you ordered is ready, sir."

"Wonderful!" Silas exclaimed. "We'll eat at the small table, if you please."

While another woman pushed a tray filled with silver-domed dishes into the room, Silas turned back to her and offered her his hand. Not quite brave enough to decline the offer, Lucetta placed her hand in his, refusing a shudder when their skin made contact. He tightened his fingers around hers before tugging her to her feet, and then, with a hand settled against her back, he ushered her over to the small table, and then into a straight-backed chair. Taking his seat opposite her, he smiled as he nodded at all the dishes being set before them, too many to actually fit on the table, which had the two women leaving some of them on the cart. Bobbing curtsies to Silas, they left the room on silent feet.

"We'll be dining on terrapin tonight, my dear. A delicacy I'm certain you will enjoy, as well as the Madeira that will bring out the flavors of our meal."

Snapping a linen napkin open, Lucetta placed it over her lap. "I would have thought you'd choose a merlot, what with the rather unusual taste of terrapin."

"Are you bringing into question my ability to choose a proper wine?"

Lucetta forced a shrug. "Not at all. I was just making polite dinner conversation, although I should tell you that I don't actually enjoy terrapin, so there'll be no need to serve me any. I'll content myself with the vegetables those lovely women you've hired brought."

"Your father enjoys terrapin," Silas returned. "And enjoys Madeira as well. Although . . ." Silas shook his head sadly. "It is a shame that Nigel overindulges in alcohol so frequently."

"Nigel is not my father, Silas, as I'm sure you discovered when you had someone run him to ground."

Silas leaned his elbows on the table as he pressed his fingertips together. "Of course he's not. My mistake. Your father died when you were quite young, didn't he — of an unexpected case of blood poisoning, from what I've been told?"

Frowning, Lucetta tilted her head. "Did Nigel tell you all of that?"

"Nigel doesn't speak of your father, dear. I learned about your father, as well as a good deal about your entire family, from a tracker I hired to look into your past. I thought he was well worth his exorbitant fee, what with the discovery of Nigel. But then . . . after I won you fair and square in that card game, you did the unthinkable and fled."

"You and I both know that you didn't win anything *fair and square.*"

When Silas sent her a wink, she almost choked on the small bite of bread she'd put in her mouth. "Come now, dear, surely you've figured out that all of this" — he gestured around the room, and at the meal — "as well as the money it took to track you down, was my way of proving to you once and for all that you and I are meant to be together."

Lucetta narrowed her eyes. "Rumor has it around town that you've been short of funds ever since you and Oliver Addleshaw parted ways."

Silas narrowed his eyes back at her until

he, curiously enough, laughed. "Is that why you've given me such a difficult time, my girl? You think I'll be unable to keep you in style?"

Blinking, Lucetta found she had no response to that piece of ridiculousness, but she was spared the need to respond when Silas continued.

"You'll be relieved to learn that my wife, harridan that she is, has a great deal of money — although she can be tightfisted with it at times, which means I have to *encourage* her to send money my way when I'm short on funds." His smile widened. "But she's learned over the years it's easier to simply hand me money rather than have me *encourage* her to hand it over. That means I'll have no problem keeping you knee-deep in lovely gowns and whatever other frivolous items you may want."

His words had Lucetta setting down the rest of the bread, unable to eat another bite. For a man to speak so casually about *encouraging* his wife, which could only mean abusing her, made Lucetta physically ill.

"And while I'm sure that you'll miss the theater, dear, do know that after you've accustomed yourself to me and my . . . needs, I may return you to the theater — if only to allow all of those gentlemen who salivate over you, and have done so for years, to see you performing for me, and only for me as I sit in a private box and watch your every move, and . . ."

Whatever else Silas intended to say was lost when there was another knock on the door.

"Go away," Silas yelled. "Miss Plum and I are in the midst of dining and do not care to be disturbed, nor will we want to be —"

Whatever he'd been about to say was cut off when there was a very loud explosion and the door blew straight off its hinges.

As she dove underneath the table, Lucetta heard someone calling her name — someone who, even though she thought him to be a bit of a lunatic, was a far safer lunatic than the man who'd abducted her and had been holding her captive. Scrambling away from Silas, who was trying to grab hold of her leg, she crawled her way to the middle of the sitting room through smoke that made her choke. Pushing to her feet, her gaze settled on a most welcomed sight.

Bram was striding through the smoke, covered in soot, with his hair standing on end, and he looked downright . . . dangerous.

Gone was the affable gentleman who had such a charming smile, replaced with a man who had rage in his eyes and determination in every step as he strode ever closer to her.

Lunatic or not, no one had ever looked more appealing to her than Bram did at that very moment, and when he stopped a foot in front of her and opened his arms, Lucetta didn't hesitate to jump directly into them.

20

As soon as Bram's arms closed around Lucetta, he felt a strong sense of relief sweep over him.

Over the past three days, he'd imagined her experiencing one horror after another at the hands of her abductors, but finding her alive eased a little of the terror that had been his constant companion ever since she'd been taken.

It didn't ease the fury that still coursed through him, though — fury at Silas Ruff for having the audacity to steal Lucetta from Ravenwood, but also fury at himself for not being able to protect her from Silas in the first place.

If only he'd been truthful with Lucetta, if only he had told her why he had a dungeon and torture devices and employees who were shackled to the ground, she wouldn't have felt compelled to storm away from him, and . . . she wouldn't have been in that hallway at the exact moment abductors, of all things, had come to call, and . . . she'd never have been in such peril.

"I think you might be cracking my ribs," Lucetta mumbled into his chest, her words having him release his death grip on her before he took a step — but only a step — away from her.

"You have no idea how happy I am to see you" was all he could think to say.

Lucetta smiled. "You have no idea how happy I am to see you as well, and" — she nodded to Stanley, Ernie, and Mr. Skukman, who were currently sitting on top of Silas Ruff, while Tilda stood guard at the door they'd blown open, looking rather menacing as she kept a pistol at the ready — "I'm delighted to see you brought some assistance as well." She nodded toward the blown-apart door. "Assistance proficient in the use of dynamite, if I'm not mistaken."

"That was me," Ernie said, sending Lucetta a grin. "Not that I use dynamite all that often anymore," he hurried to assure her. "But my expertise with the substance does come in remarkably handy at the oddest of times."

"Should I ask why Ernie's an expert with dynamite?" Lucetta asked, turning back to Bram.

"I would suggest not," Bram said.

Wrinkling her nose, Lucetta nodded. "You're probably right, but tell me, how did you find me?"

"Using a wide variety of interesting contacts spread throughout the city." Bram blew out a breath. "Everyone's been so worried about you."

"I've been fine," Lucetta began, nodding when he quirked a brow her way. "Honestly, I have been. I mean, yes, the men Silas hired to abduct me scared me half to death — especially the man I heard was some sort of tracker — but as soon as they delivered me here, they left and I never saw them again. Truth be told, until today, it's just been me along with a pack of intimidating women Silas hired to make certain I didn't escape from this cozy little nest he's been holding me in."

"Silas left you alone until today?"

"Curious as that may seem, yes. He only showed up about an hour ago." She smiled. "I do believe he had a most romantic dinner planned for the two of us, but matters got off to a rough start when he demanded I play him a piece by Bach, and discovered I . . . . Well, let's just say that, if you'd compared my playing with Ruby's, your sister would sound downright competent at the keys."

Brushing a strand of honey-golden hair from her face, he returned the smile . . . but felt it fade almost immediately when he got a closer look at her cheek. "Is that a hand-print on your face?"

Lucetta waved it off. "It's nothing.

He leaned closer. "Did Silas hit you?"

"It was more of a slap, but considering I was expecting far worse, well . . ."

Bram's hand clenched into a fist. "He touched you?"

"Well, yes, slapping a person does entail touching, but again, it could have been much worse."

"Excuse me." Stepping around her, he nodded to Mr. Skukman, who was sitting on Silas's back, arms folded across his chest as if it were an everyday occurrence to lounge around on the back of a man he undoubtedly wanted to strangle. Bram couldn't help but admire Mr. Skukman's restraint even though Bram had no intention of following in the man's footsteps.

"Would you be so kind as to stand with Lucetta for a moment?" he asked Mr. Skukman.

"Of course." After making certain Stanley and Ernie still had Silas firmly under control, Mr. Skukman stood, walked around

Bram, and then, to Bram's surprise, pulled Lucetta into an enthusiastic hug, so enthusiastic that Lucetta's feet left the ground even as she laughed.

Realizing that the poor man had obviously been just as distraught as Bram had been over Lucetta's abduction, Bram couldn't help but smile at their reunion. His smile faded almost immediately, though, when Silas began trying to squirm his way free.

"I demand you release me at once. I'm Silas Ruff, an influential man about the country. Believe me when I tell you I'll use that influence to see each and every one of you pay for your interference and careless disregard for my person."

Bram walked closer to him and looked down. "I'm afraid your influential days are numbered, Silas. You see, kidnapping is a serious offense, which is why you'll be spending quite a few years in jail."

Silas had the nerve to smile. "I didn't kidnap anyone."

"No, you paid a Mr. Cabot to organize and implement the abduction. And before that you paid him to track down Lucetta's family, which allowed you to learn her stepfather is a notorious gambler with a bit of a drinking problem."

The smile slid off of Silas's face. "How do

you know that?"

"Mr. Cabot told me, of course."

"How do you know Mr. Cabot?"

"His family lived right down the street from me growing up," Stanley said, re-arranging his backside just a smidgen as he continued to sit on top of Silas. "When Miss Plum got snatched, we figured it was you behind the snatching, so we hightailed it to the city and started asking around the old neighborhood if anyone had heard any-thing." Stanley nodded. "Sure enough, my mother had heard that Mr. Cabot was back in town, visiting his dear mama. And since his reputation as a tracker and man who'll do anything for a substantial fee precedes him, and there aren't that many men offer-ing up those substantial fees in the city at the moment, well, we had a feeling Mr. Cabot was just the man we needed to speak with. It took us a couple days to find him in the hole he'd crawled into, but when we did —"

"A man like Mr. Cabot would never divulge the secrets of any of his clients," Silas said.

Stanley began inspecting his nails. "Well, I don't know about that, Mr. Ruff, because after Mr. Skukman, an intimidating gentle-man in his own right" — Stanley sent an

336

appreciative nod Mr. Skukman's way —
"got done with him, well, Mr. Cabot divulged just about everything I imagine he knew about you." Stanley returned his attention to his nails. "You'll have plenty of time to take him to task about that, though, as I'm sure you'll be seeing each other quite often in jail."

"Mr. Cabot's been taken to jail?" Silas asked.

Stanley looked up and smiled. "Indeed, and since that's where you're headed, you'll be reunited with him shortly."

Bram felt a rush of satisfaction run through him when Silas's face began to pale. Nodding to Stanley, Bram stepped forward. "Get him to his feet."

A moment later, Silas was standing before Bram, rage evident in his eyes as Stanley and Ernie kept firm holds on him. Summoning up what Bram hoped would come across as a pleasant smile, even though what he really wanted to do was rip the man limb from limb, Bram nodded to where Lucetta was standing next to Mr. Skukman.

"Before we see you off to jail, though, Silas," Bram said, "I do think I'm going to have to insist you extend Miss Plum an apology for . . . well . . . everything you've put her through over the past few days, and for all the bother you've caused her over the past few years as well."

Silas considered Bram for the briefest of seconds before he spat on the floor. "That's the only apology she'll ever —"

Before Silas could finish the sentence, Bram's fist firmly connected with the man's jaw. All of the fear, fury, and frustration of the past three days was behind the punch, the strength of it sending Silas straight to the floor, where he remained . . . not stirring a single muscle.

"Impressive," Mr. Skukman said as he moved forward and, with Ernie and Stanley's help, hefted Silas's unconscious form straight off the floor and carted him from the room. In the doorway Mr. Skukman stopped for just a second to catch Bram's eye. "I'll help Ernie and Stanley get him into a carriage and off to jail. Then I'll meet you at your carriage." As he continued through the doorway, he was less than careful with Silas's head, allowing it to connect with a piece of what might have been part of the doorframe before Ernie's dynamite tore it apart.

"Shall I follow you down, Mr. Haverstein?" Tilda asked. "Just in case we run into unexpected trouble?"

"That would be greatly appreciated,

Tilda," Bram said.

He walked back to join Lucetta, offering her his arm. "I'm sure you've had all the trouble you want to experience for years to come."

"Indeed," Lucetta said, taking his arm.

"We'll go to Abigail's house," he told her as they picked their way through the debris the blasting of the door had created and headed down the stairs. "She, along with Archibald, my mother, Ruby, and Mr. Kenton, insisted on traveling to the city in order to be kept updated on any progress we were making."

Reaching the sidewalk, he led her to his waiting carriage, surprised when she stopped in her tracks and looked around. "But we're right by my theater, just off Broadway," she said slowly.

"We are."

Temper flashed in her eyes. "Silas had been planning this for a very long time, hadn't he?"

"I'm afraid he might very well have been."

Muttering something about the madness of overzealous admirers, Lucetta climbed up into the carriage.

"I'm sure she wasn't including you in with those overzealous admirers, sir," Tilda said quietly when Bram paused outside the carriage.

"She might after she learns what *I've* done for her," he said.

"You can't compare what you've done to an abduction," Tilda argued.

Sending Tilda a faint smile as she climbed up to join the driver on the carriage seat, Bram turned and waited as Mr. Skukman joined him, both gentlemen watching the carriage that held Silas, Ernie, and Stanley depart for the jail before Mr. Skukman took a position on the back of Bram's carriage, while Bram ducked inside to take a seat opposite Lucetta.

"Are you certain you're unharmed?" he asked as the carriage surged into motion.

"My nerves are a little rattled, as can be expected, but other than that, I'm fine." She caught his eye. "I'm incredibly grateful that you and everyone else worked so hard to find me, and were able to rid me of Silas once and for all." A smile tugged at her lips. "I'm sure after a few weeks have passed, or . . . maybe a few years, when it's not so very fresh to me, I'll be able to laugh about it and tell people I was able to participate in my very own gothic-style story, quite like one our favorite author, Mr. Grimstone, might pen."

The mention of Mr. Grimstone had him leaning forward. "We have much to discuss."

Lucetta immediately took to looking wary. "Why do I have the feeling we're no longer talking about me and . . . my abduction?"

"Because we need to talk about us, and talk about where we go from here before we get back to Abigail's house and everyone distracts us."

Lucetta's wariness immediately increased. "I'm not certain there's any need for that, Bram. The danger to me has passed, which means I'm free to return to the theater, and . . . you and I are free to go on our merry ways — and our separate merry ways, at that."

Bram settled back against the carriage seat. "I never took you for a coward, Lucetta."

Temper flashed in her eyes. "I'm not a coward."

"Then why aren't you willing to at least see where whatever this is between us leads?"

"There's nothing between us."

"Your lips said differently a few days ago, and . . . you enjoy my company — you can't deny that."

"Perhaps I do enjoy your company, but we'll leave my lips out of further discussion, if you please. The truth of the matter is that I don't trust you, I don't like secrets, which you're obviously keeping, and . . . I have no desire to become attached to a gentleman who spends time in a dungeon, of all places, and has a mausoleum marking the entrance to his drive."

"Ah, well, yes, but you see, those are some of the things I'd like to discuss with you." He sent her what he hoped was a most charming smile, but one that only had her arching a brow his way again. Clearing his throat, he sat forward. "To continue, I have to admit that I've thought out my explanation regarding all of the things I need to explain in a certain order. So . . . if you'll humor me, I wrote down a list, and . . ." Digging a hand into his jacket pocket, he pulled out the list and read it through, nodding before he lifted his head.

"First, I need to say that —" he blew out a breath — "I've bungled practically everything with you so far, starting when I almost drowned you in the moat, er . . . twice."

"You won't get an argument from me on that."

"I neglected to warn you about my goat."

Her lips twitched right at the corners. "That might be being a little hard on yourself, Bram. You couldn't have known someone would turn Geoffrey loose on me up in the tower room."

"True, but I should have mentioned that I owned a goat with a curious dislike for ladies in skirts."

"I don't believe Geoffrey is really at the root of the issues I have with you and Ravenwood, Bram."

He caught her eye and nodded. "I'm at the root of your issues, Lucetta — me and all of my secrets — which is why . . ."

He consulted his notes again before he lifted his head. "I'm going to tell you everything, and then . . ." He glanced one last time at his notes before he looked her way. "After you hear me out, I'd greatly appreciate it if you'd consider allowing me to . . . court you."

"Court me?" She began inching toward the carriage door, which was rather disturbing considering the carriage was traveling at a fast clip down the road.

Stiffening his resolve, and ignoring the disbelief in her eyes, he nodded. "It would be my greatest honor to court you, especially since I should have asked to court you before I kissed you, and certainly before I offered to marry you . . . twice."

"You offered to marry me once, and then told me we'd have to get married after we were found in a compromising situation."

"That was not well done of me."

"Again, I won't argue with you there, but I'm really afraid, given all the secrets you've kept from, well, everyone, and the dodgy nature of your castle, I don't see that we have much of a future ahead of us."

"I'm Mr. Grimstone." The words burst out of his mouth before he could stop them.

She stiffened. "I beg your pardon?"

"I'm Mr. Grimstone."

A single blink was her first response, before she leaned ever so slowly forward. "As in . . . the author?"

He summoned up a smile. "One and the same."

Her eyes flashed in a most ominous fashion. "You penned a play specifically for me and never once allowed me to know your identity?"

"It would have defeated the goal of me wanting to remain anonymous if I'd disclosed my identity to you."

"Your sister wanted to meet you and have you squire her about society."

"And isn't she going to be surprised when she finds out that won't be a possibility? Although, I'm not sure she'll be that fussed about it, given her apparent interest in Mr. Skukman."

Lucetta leaned back. "Ruby's still showing an interest in Mr. Skukman?"

Relieved to have the topic move to someone besides himself, Bram smiled. "She does seem to enjoy his company, and when we've stopped by Abigail's to give them reports of our progress, Ruby always makes a point of speaking with him before we depart."

"They'd probably suit each other well, and you'll not find a more reliable man, but . . . *Mr. Grimstone,* you do realize that penning a play for a woman you'd never met in person can be considered an act of a less than sane individual, don't you?"

Seeing little point in avoiding the question, since he had vowed to disclose everything, he shrugged. "I only did so because I wanted to make certain you'd have a steady income."

"What?"

"I knew that if I penned a play, everyone would want to see it because of Mr. Grimstone's popularity. And, if I specifically requested you as the star, well, you'd have access to a steady income for quite some time because *The Lady in the Tower* was almost certain to be an immediate success."

"Just how infatuated with me were you?"

He sat forward and caught her eye. "I've

done a lot of thinking regarding that while I've been searching for you, and . . . I don't believe we can say I was infatuated with *you,* since you're not anything like I imagined you to be. You're not demure, or delicate, or possessed of a gentle spirit."

"Is that supposed to make me feel better?"

"Of course it is, because you see, the truth of the matter is this — the woman I thought I was a touch in love with is a shell of the woman you turned out to be."

Her lips curved into the faintest of smiles, something she quickly tried to hide by dipping her head, but he'd seen the smile and it gave him just a tiny ray of hope.

Lifting her head a second later, she frowned. "What I don't understand is why you've kept your writing a secret from your family. There's nothing shameful about being an author, especially not given the fame you've earned."

"My family has always found me to be a rather curious being, not caring for business matters, and spending my time lost in imaginary worlds. They were incredibly disappointed when I didn't finish pursuing a law degree, but halfway through law school I had this dream, one that turned out to be my first novel, *Murder at Highcliffe*

Hall." He smiled. "I disappeared for nine months to write that book, renting an isolated cottage by the ocean, and then it took me another year to find a publisher."

Lucetta wrinkled her nose. "I know writers who've written dozens of books and have yet to get a single one of them published after years and years of trying. You were fortunate indeed to get a first novel picked up so quickly."

Bram leaned back. "Perhaps I was, but it was a stressful time for me, and again, I knew I'd disappointed my parents by abandoning the law, a profession they both thought would be a suitable and respectable option for me."

Lucetta tapped a finger against her chin. "I suppose I can see why you withheld the information then, but why not disclose all after your books began to get such great acclaim and became in such high demand?"

"By the time I started making money off my work, a few years had gone by and I'd started traveling to the tenements to search out story ideas. It was while I was in the tenements that I realized I could be of assistance to a great many people, and help those people turn their lives around, so . . . I didn't want the notoriety of Mr. Grimstone to affect what has turned out to be the most important work of my life."

"But surely you realized that your family would find your desire to save people a noble calling. You've done them a disservice by keeping them in the dark." She shook her head. "Your mother believes you're involved in some type of criminal enterprise."

"I know, and you're right. But it became harder and harder to disclose the truth the longer I kept it hidden from everyone."

To his surprise, she nodded glumly. "I can understand that, but tell me — that dungeon — is it where you go to find inspiration for your work?"

"It is. I had Stanley tied to the railroad track to try to puzzle out a plot point." He smiled. "I was going to go with your idea about hanging him from the ceiling by his feet, but for some reason, Stanley flatly refused to participate in that idea, even for a riveting scene in my next novel."

"You were thinking about using my idea?"

Bram nodded. "Until Stanley balked, and until it became clear that no one else wanted to help me work out the particulars of seeing how the hero could get undone from the ceiling." He smiled. "I think their lack of willingness might have had something to do with me suggesting they dangle from the ceiling for unspecified amounts of time."

"The heroine was supposed to cut him down."

"Well, yes, that was your suggestion, but I'm still not completely sold on the idea that readers want to see that strong of a heroine, or if ladies and gentlemen in general truly believe a lady should be the one to save the day in the end."

"Perhaps you need to draw up a list about areas to avoid while attempting to court a lady. If I were you, I'd put 'Adopting a condescending attitude toward independent ladies' right at the top of such a list."

"You might have a point," he muttered before he summoned up a smile. "But getting back to the dungeon and why I have one, it's a wonderful place to plot out a story because, what with all the staff members I've accumulated ever since I bought Ravenwood, it's difficult to find places that afford me any measure of quiet."

For some reason, Lucetta suddenly closed her eyes, kept them closed for the merest of seconds, and then opened them. "That's what's been bothering me about the dungeon scene. You have a typewriter down there mixed in with all the torture devices."

"You remember that?"

She didn't bother to answer his question. "Explain the mausoleum as a gatehouse."

Bram smiled. "That was Ernie's idea, as was the graveyard we've built in the middle of the forest at the back of Ravenwood. I was working on *The Bell Tolls at Midnight,* one of my best-received novels, and I couldn't picture the scene of the crime, let alone write it out descriptively, so . . . Ernie loves to build things, all kinds of things, and . . . we'd been talking about adding a gatehouse, and the next thing you know, he'd built one that looked exactly like a mausoleum." He shook his head. "It's been quite the talk of the neighborhood."

"I'm sure it has been, but how do you explain the bloody sword stashed in your fireplace?"

"It wasn't blood, it was red stain, and Ernie stashed it in the fireplace because I needed a new plot idea, and he thought if I had to search for the sword after he'd hidden it, I'd get some good ideas."

"The eye patch?"

"I was contemplating a pirate-laced plot, but . . . writing a hero with a disfigurement like that — well, it just wasn't working."

"And the necklace?"

Bram released a sigh. "I've never seen that necklace before in my life."

"Ah, so all the mysteries can't be solved on our ride to Abigail's, can they?"

"I'm afraid not, but . . . to return to the subject of . . . us. . . . Since I have now divulged my deepest and darkest secret, how do you feel about my previous suggestion, the one regarding me courting you?"

Lucetta regarded him for a long moment before she released the smallest of sighs. "This would be so much easier if you really were a madman, but since you've been so forthcoming with me, it's only fair that I'm now forthcoming with you."

Of anything he'd been expecting Lucetta to say, that had not been remotely close.

"You have secrets of your own?"

She smiled just a ghost of a smile. "Most people do have secrets, Bram, and I'm afraid my secrets are going to put a rapid end to your desire to court me."

Drawing in a deep breath, she looked out the carriage window for a moment, nodded, just once, and then turned and caught his eye.

"While it's true that I'm one of the most sought-after actresses in the city, there's a lot about me that no one in New York knows. I did not grow up in the tenements, nor did I have to claw my way out of the stews, using my unusual looks to procure a

351

role on the stage. What I don't tell anyone is that I grew up on a plantation in Virginia."

"Your parents worked on a plantation?" he asked slowly.

"My parents owned the plantation."

Bram's eyes widened. "Did it burn down during the Civil War, and that's when your father died of that blood poisoning that Mr. Cabot mentioned, and then you were forced to live in a one-room hovel, where your mother then married that horrid Nigel person, and you ran away to New York to finally escape the poverty you were living in?"

"Goodness, you really do have an imagination, don't you," Lucetta said before she seemed to stifle a grin and continued on with her tale. "While your version of my life would make a most riveting tale, that's not even close to what happened. You see, my father was not your typical plantation owner. We did not own slaves, nor did we produce much in the way of crops. My father bred horses, but he was also a well-respected attorney who worked in Washington when Congress was in session. Because of that, when the Civil War began, both sides agreed that our plantation, Plum Hill, would not be touched, and it wasn't."

Bram frowned. "I'm afraid I don't understand then how you came to work as an actress when you were destined to become a southern belle."

"Ah, yes, the allure of the belles. I did, at one time, believe I would take my place amongst those lovely ladies, presiding over one ball after another. But alas, it was not meant to be for me, especially after my father died of blood poisoning, as you mentioned. But he didn't die until I was thirteen and —"

"And that's when you found out his fortune had disappeared and you were left with nothing?"

"No . . . and rein in that imagination of yours, if you please, so I can finish the true tale without becoming overly distracted."

"I won't say another peep," Bram assured her.

"Wonderful. To continue, Plum Hill, our plantation, survived the Civil War, as did everyone in my small family, and as I grew older, it became obvious that I'd inherited something from my father that I don't discuss often, if at all, because it's what most people find a rather unsettling gift." She smoothed out a wrinkle on the velvet gown she was wearing and then lifted her head to catch his eye. "I have a perfect memory."

Bram blinked. "A . . . what?"

"A perfect memory — which means I can recall pages I've read years ago word for word, and . . . I can not only remember numbers, but I can tally them up in my head without having to use pen and paper or an abacus."

"I've never heard of anyone capable of doing such things," he said slowly.

"I'm a bit of an anomaly, but the reason I said you'd soon have no desire to court me is this. . . . Not only was I born into a well-respected, socially acceptable family — which is why I do know how to manage my way around a formal table setting and dance the quadrille — I'm very good at, and have been very successful with . . . investments. That means I am not one of those poor, unfortunate souls you enjoy saving from dismal circumstances."

Bram simply looked at her for a long moment, feeling as if he'd lost all control of the conversation. "I would think being successful with investments is a mark in your favor," he finally settled on saying, earning a rolling of the eyes from her in the process.

"Well, yes, normally that would be true, but . . . you're a gentleman who receives a great deal of satisfaction from providing better lives for others." She smiled ever so slightly. "I'm financially independent — don't actually need to work in the theater any longer because of that — and . . . I'm not sure I'm a lady you'd actually care to court since I don't need a knight in shining armor to swoop in and rescue me."

Bram narrowed his eyes. "I don't remember making the claim that my deepest desire in life was to swoop in and rescue you."

"You enjoy playing the hero."

"You say that as if there's something wrong with having a chivalrous nature."

"I don't think you'll be happy with me," she finally said in a small voice.

For a second, he had no response to her words, but then, he felt his lips quirk into a grin. "For an apparently overly intelligent sort, you're remarkably obtuse about some things."

"I'm not sure I understand."

"Well, it is true that I enjoy saving people, lifting them up so to speak, but I also enjoy spending my time with flawed people, especially if they are amusing as well. And you, my dear Lucetta, are incredibly flawed, but you make me laugh. That's the person I'd like to court, if you'd give me the opportunity.

"And while I must admit that I'm incredibly disappointed to discover you're financially independent — because who wouldn't be disappointed to learn that the lady they wish to spend their life with is somewhat clever — well . . . I suppose I'll just have to learn to struggle along with my disappointment and perhaps encourage you to pair up with Ruby to increase all of our fortunes. And then . . . we'll have more money to hire on additional people from the tenements, and maybe procure an entire herd of goats to keep Geoffrey company."

Lucetta's brows scrunched together. "I don't believe you're understanding the true nature of the problem. You relish being the knight in shining armor, but I'll never care to be your damsel in distress."

Bram nodded. "Because you're much too intelligent for that."

She leaned forward. "Are you smiling, because my oddness is a true obstacle that . . ."

As Lucetta launched into all the reasons behind why he wouldn't be comfortable courting her — reasons that he didn't agree with in the least, even if he'd been slightly taken aback to learn she really had just as many secrets as he did — the carriage slowed, coming to a stop a mere moment later.

Before he was able to jump back into the

conversation to assure her that he'd be willing to face whatever obstacles were thrown their way — especially since he'd come to the realization that she was the most fascinating woman he'd ever met in his life — the carriage door burst open. A young lady stood on the other side of the door, a young lady he'd seen a few times at the theater but had never been introduced to before. Her identity became clear, though, when Lucetta let out a shriek of pure delight and scrambled out of the cab.

"Millie!" she yelled before she snatched the young lady into a hug.

Even though Bram couldn't resist a smile at the sight of Lucetta being reunited with one of her best friends, he also couldn't resist a small sigh of regret, because with the arrival of Millie, and their arrival at Abigail's brownstone, further talk of courtships was certainly going to be set aside for the foreseeable future.

21

"What in the world are you doing here?" Lucetta demanded when the former Miss Millie Longfellow and present Mrs. Everett Mulberry, gave Lucetta a final squeeze and stepped back, even though she did not release the hold she had on Lucetta's hand.

"Abigail sent me a telegram stating that Silas had absconded with you." Millie shuddered. "I barely took a second to pack before I hopped on a train and headed to New York. Everett, I'm afraid, did not make the trip with me, staying back in Boston with the children. We didn't want to put them in harm's way again, not after all they've been through over the past year."

"Indeed not, although I'm confident Silas won't be a threat for some time to come, especially since he's currently on his way to jail to face kidnapping charges."

Millie smiled as she shoved brown curls out of her eyes. "Thank goodness he's finally getting exactly what he deserves — jail. And I can't put into words how wonderful it is to see you unharmed. I kept envisioning — which I recently learned means *picturing* — you tied up and stowed in a dirty room, with a leering Silas pacing back and forth in front of you as he rubbed his hands together and chuckled rather menacingly, while maybe rattling some chains."

Lucetta blinked. "Have you discontinued reading those sweet romances you've always been so fond of reading in lieu of something a little darker?"

"Funny enough, I have." Millie grinned. "I've decided to bridge out a little, explore different genres, if you will. And because you, my very good friend, are starring in a play penned by none other than the renowned — which I'm sure you know means *celebrated* — Mr. Grimstone, I decided to try a few of his gothic novels."

"What did you think of the Grimstone stories?" Bram asked from behind them.

Turning, Lucetta found that Bram had stepped out of the carriage and was looking dashingly rumpled, with his hair standing on end and his face streaked with soot here and there. Glancing at Millie, Lucetta found her friend considering Bram closely, right before she nodded at Lucetta and arched a brow.

"The mysterious grandson, I assume?"

"One and the same." Lucetta pulled Millie forward, stopping right in front of Bram. "Millie, I'd like to introduce you to Abigail's grandson, Mr. Bram Haverstein. Bram, this is one of my very dearest friends, Millie Mulberry, formerly Millie Longfellow."

"It's a pleasure to meet you, Mrs. Mulberry," Bram said, bringing Millie's hand to his lips and placing the expected kiss on it. "Lucetta and my grandmother speak most highly of you."

Millie smiled, the action causing a dimple to pop out on her cheek. "It's a pleasure to meet you as well, Mr. Haverstein. I won't embarrass you by relaying all the things your grandmother told me and Lucetta about *you* over the past few months. Although I will admit I thought she was exaggerating your attributes — and that means *features* — but . . . never mind about that." Her smile widened. "I'm very relieved to discover that you appear to be relatively normal, and that you're not sporting a humped back or any other peculiar deformity, something Lucetta and I were afraid your grandmother was trying to hide."

Bram quirked a brow Lucetta's way.

"You'd thought I'd be deformed?"

Smiling, Lucetta shrugged. "Abigail made you out to be so mysterious, who could blame us for concluding the worst?"

"She kept calling you a dish," Millie added with a grin. "Which only goes to show how determined she is to see you, as well as any other eligible person within her direct vicinity, well settled, but —"

"Honestly, Millie," none other than Abigail interrupted as she hurried down the sidewalk toward them. "When you said you heard a carriage and were going to investigate, I thought you'd come right back and tell us what you'd discovered, not stand around discussing my matchmaking propensities."

"You're exactly right, Abigail, but I fear I got horribly distracted by a topic that Lucetta and I have always found slightly alarming — your matchmaking schemes," Millie said, earning a shake of her head from Abigail right before the older lady pulled Lucetta into an embrace and gave her a good squeeze.

"You shall promise me here and now, young lady, that you will never do that to me again." Abigail relaxed her hold and stepped back, but only to tuck Lucetta's arm in hers. "You're not hurt?"

"I'm fine, a little tired, a little rattled, but . . . Bram and his staff did a wonderful job of rescuing me."

Abigail nodded. "Tilda just ran inside to tell us you were back safe and sound, apparently realizing someone" — she sent a pointed look to Millie, although she softened it with a smile — "had gotten distracted."

"You can't truly blame me for getting caught up in the moment, Abigail," Millie argued. "I mean, honestly, with Lucetta being gone for so long it was all looking very grim just a short time ago, and yet now . . ." She beamed Lucetta's way. "Here she is, standing in front of your brownstone — wearing one of the most hideous gowns I've ever seen, but still standing here nevertheless."

"Speaking of standing here," Mr. Skukman suddenly said, drawing everyone's attention. "Evening is fast approaching, it's getting dark, and if none of you have noticed, even though it's still October, but just barely, it's downright brisk tonight. While I'm delighted we've gotten our Miss Plum back, and that certainly is a cause for a joyful celebration, I'm now going to suggest we take the celebration into the warm confines of Mrs. Hart's home before our feat of rescuing Miss Plum becomes all for naught when she catches her death due to a cold."

Millie blinked before she walked right over to Mr. Skukman, gave him a hug — which had his eyes widening just a touch — and then linked her arm with his. "I do believe that's the most words I've ever heard you string together, Mr. Skukman. May I hope you've been following my example and have taken to studying them?"

"Studying . . . what?" Mr. Skukman asked slowly.

"Words, Mr. Skukman, words." Millie prodded him toward the house. "There's nothing like a good grasp of the English language to make a person feel more confident about life." With that, they headed toward the front door, Millie's offer to lend Mr. Skukman one of her many dictionaries drifting back to Lucetta on the breeze.

"She enjoys words?" Bram asked as he offered Abigail one arm and Lucetta his other.

"Millie's been improving her vocabulary for quite some time," Lucetta said as they moved up the sidewalk. "She grew up in an orphanage and didn't have access to a proper education, so she decided to learn on her own. She's an avid reader these days, and has apparently taken to reading Mr.

Grimstone novels." She sent Bram a wink, which he pretended not to notice as Lucetta turned her attention to Abigail. "May I assume everyone is still gathered here?"

Abigail nodded. "Indeed. Iris and Ruby rode down from Tarrytown with me, along with Archibald of course, and Mr. Kenton. Archibald has been traveling back to his house every evening, but he comes back first thing in the morning, bless him." She got what almost seemed to be a dreamy look in her eyes for all of a second but then seemed to shake herself. "Everyone will want to make certain you're quite alive and well, but after you've allowed everyone to hug and exclaim over you, I want you to head up to your room for a good soak in the tub. I'll send Bertha up to get that dress you're wearing and . . . have her burn it."

"That would be most appreciated."

Walking through the front door, Lucetta found herself greeted with a chorus of cheers, and she spent the next ten minutes being hugged and fawned over by Iris, Ruby, Archibald, Mr. Kenton — although he insisted on maintaining his distance in case his cold was still lingering — and all the members of Abigail's staff. After being given a strong hug by Abigail's coachman, who assured her she was not to worry about his greatcoat that she'd lost in Bram's moat, or his pistol that she just then realized she'd lost as well, she found her arm taken by Millie as Abigail shooed them up the stairs, telling everyone else it was time for some tea, coffee, and treats in the drawing room.

After assuring everyone she'd join them soon, Lucetta walked with Millie up to the second floor, strolling arm in arm down a narrow hallway until they reached the suite of rooms Abigail had so generously given to Lucetta. Stepping over the threshold, Lucetta grinned when she caught sight of numerous glossy boxes with French names stamped on them that were stacked in a corner.

"I see Abigail hasn't quite finished with the new wardrobe she apparently believes I need," Lucetta said.

Millie grinned. "I think she ordered all of that" — she nodded to the boxes — "a few months ago, and it's just now showing up in the States. I've had numerous deliveries from Paris and England at my home in Boston, and I have to say, Abigail does have a keen sense of style."

Stepping into the bathing chamber a moment later, Lucetta discovered Bertha, one of Abigail's maids, already there, readying the bath for Lucetta. Dipping a hand in the water to evidently check the warmth of it, Bertha straightened, looked Lucetta over from head to toe, and immediately began clucking.

"We need to get you right out of that garish rag," Bertha declared, setting to work on the buttons that marched down the back of the gown. "How in the world did you get into this, dear, or . . . is that a question you'd rather not answer?"

Slipping out of the gown once Bertha had it undone, Lucetta caught Bertha's eye. "I know everyone must be so concerned that Silas took unacceptable liberties with me, but I barely saw the man while I was being held captive. In fact, he only showed up a few hours ago at the rooms he'd stashed me in. We spent less than an hour together having a meal, and then . . . Bram showed up and saved the day, along with Mr. Skukman and Bram's staff, of course, and . . . here I am. Tired, but fit as a fiddle."

She smiled at Bertha. "As for how I got into this gown, Silas, being the incredibly untrusting type, apparently didn't want me to be kept around any men, so he hired women to watch over me, and they are the ones who helped me get dressed every day."

"Well, I'm here to help you get dressed now, but I'll leave you in peace while you take a good, long soak in the tub. Just ring for me when you're done." With that, Bertha quit the bathing chamber, promising to throw the dress into the nearest fireplace.

Slipping out of her unmentionables, Lucetta slipped into the tub, sighing in satisfaction as the warm water drifted over her. The sound of a chair being dragged across the floor had her looking up, unsurprised to find that Millie was the person dragging the chair, which she positioned exactly so in front of the tub before taking her seat. Leaning forward, Millie suddenly looked a little too determined.

"I've heard the most interesting rumors regarding you and the oh-so-dishy Mr. Haverstein," Millie said.

"I don't believe *dishy* is a real word" was all Lucetta could think to respond.

Millie waved that away with a flick of her dainty wrist. "I can't be expected to know all the right words, Lucetta, and you're stalling."

Lucetta blew out a breath, stirring the bubbles. "What have you heard?"

"That you and Mr. Haverstein were caught in a most interesting situation in a storage room of all places, that he tried to save you from drowning twice in his, uh, moat from what I've been told, and . . . that he did save you once from a mad goat by the name of Geoffrey. I've also heard that you seem to enjoy his company, so much so that there's been talk of marriage — but you rejected the marriage idea because of mysterious happenings occurring at Ravenwood."

"Bram didn't save me from drowning twice. He almost caused me to drown both of those times."

"Again . . . stalling."

Tracing a finger through the bubbles, Lucetta took a second to gather her thoughts. "He's explained away practically all the mysteries surrounding him, which has allowed me to come to the conclusion he's not insane."

Millie's eyes turned the size of saucers. "You had reason to doubt his sanity?"

"He maintains a dungeon and has a castle where suits of armor go strolling about in the middle of the night — what else was I to conclude?"

"A . . . dungeon?"

"Yes, but I can't explain that in any further detail, since the dungeon is part of a rather large secret that Bram has yet to divulge to anyone except his staff — and now me, of course."

Millie settled back in her chair and crossed

her arms over her chest. "Fair enough, but . . . tell me this, how do you feel about the man, especially since his sanity is no longer in question?"

"That's a little tricky to answer."

Millie sent her a look that had exasperation stamped all over it. "It is not. And since you're the one who insisted Harriet and I dwell on exactly what our feelings were for Oliver and Everett just a few months back, I'm going to extend you the same courtesy. So . . . feelings — yours for Mr. Haverstein — what are they?"

"He, uh . . . did mention that he'd like to court me."

"Court you?"

"Yes, you know, call on me, take me for drives, bring me flowers, and . . . well . . . court me."

"That's incredibly romantic."

"Well, yes, it is, but . . ."

"You don't want to be courted because you see that as a weakness of being female."

"What?"

Millie rolled her eyes. "Lucetta, you and I have been friends for a very long time, and while you never talk about yourself much — as in *ever* — it's always been clear to me and Harriet that you've got this attitude, if you will, about being a female. It's one of the reasons I believe you've held yourself so distant from any gentleman who has ever shown an interest in you. And, it's why you're incredibly wary of men like Bram Haverstein, who clearly — and this is without me even knowing that much about him — is an old-fashioned man, one who enjoys swooping in and saving the damsel in distress."

"There's that romance novel lover I've been missing."

Millie sat forward. "You know I'm right."

"So . . . how are those delightful children you and Everett are doing such a wonderful job raising?"

Narrowing her eyes, Millie regarded Lucetta for all of a second before she nodded. "Very well, I see how we're going to proceed. So . . . Everett's wonderful, as are the children. They're very well adjusted these days, don't cause hardly any trouble at all, except for the normal trouble children tend to get into, and they've come to adore Everett as their guardian, and seem to enjoy having me about as well." She brushed her hands together. "Now that we've gotten that out of the way, back to you."

"There's really nothing else to add."

"Courting . . . you . . . Mr. Haverstein, and . . . what you've decided to do about it.

You may now proceed with giving me answers in whatever order you'd care to proceed."

Lucetta tried to think of another diversion but couldn't come up with a single thing, so she ended up shrugging instead. "I divulged most of my well-guarded secrets to the man, and not only did he refrain from throwing himself out of the carriage after I was done, he didn't react as if I'm some curiosity one should view in a circus show."

"Ah, you told him about your memory."

"You know about that?"

Millie released a snort. "Please, you read a script one time and never look at it again. But tell me this . . . have you told him about Wall Street?"

"You *know* about Wall Street?"

"Bits and pieces, but enough to know that if you'd been a man, you'd be a king in the investment industry."

"I thought I was being so stealthy."

"Lucetta, we lived together for years in a tiny little suite of rooms in a rickety boardinghouse. Stealth isn't always possible under those conditions, especially when a woman such as Hetty Green, the so-called Witch of Wall Street — who, by the way, even I know — comes to pay you a visit. When I saw her taking tea with you and then heard her asking your opinion about a railroad stock, well, let me simply say it wasn't difficult to figure out you've been dabbling in more than just theater over the years."

Lucetta smiled. "Hetty's a curious woman. Do you know she was actually impressed by the idea that I'd chosen to live in such mean surroundings even though I had the where-withal to move to a more fashionable area?"

"She's not the only one some might consider odd," Millie said with a pointed look Lucetta's way. But, before she could continue on with the odd business — something her expression clearly stated she wanted to do — the door to the bathing chamber opened just a crack as Tilda stuck her head in.

"I beg your pardon for interrupting, ladies, but we have a small situation unfolding in the drawing room that I don't believe you're going to want to miss."

"A situation?" Lucetta repeated warily.

Tilda nodded. "Mr. Haverstein chose to disclose everything to his family, and . . . I think they may very well be in some unusual state of shock. I'm afraid he might need a bit of help, Miss Plum. You were the only person I could think of to help him, since I know he told you all about his big secret. I may have unintentionally overheard most of your conversation in the carriage, probably because we'd forgotten to close the small sliding door that makes it possible for the rider to speak with the driver."

Knowing full well that no one had forgotten anything, and peculiarly enough, finding herself liking Tilda all the more because the woman certainly did possess a bit of cheek, Lucetta sat up in the tub and reached for the towel Millie was already holding out for her.

"Shall I tell him you'll be down in fifteen minutes?" Tilda asked.

"Tell him I'll be down in ten."

Less than ten minutes later, with damp strands of hair that had already escaped the knot she'd arranged on her head, Lucetta headed for the drawing room with Millie by her side. She was now dressed in a lovely gown of deep green, one that she'd pulled directly from the first box she'd opened from the stack in her room, and one that had a label proclaiming it to be a Jacques Doucet creation.

Stepping into the drawing room a second later, she came to an immediate stop as the most peculiar urge to laugh settled over her.

Everyone seemed to be frozen in place. Iris was sitting beside Abigail on a settee done up in brown tweed, both ladies sporting rather dazed expressions on their faces, while Ruby was standing right behind them, her eyes blazing and her lips thinned. Archibald, on the other hand, looked slightly amused as he sat in a wing-backed chair, peering over a newspaper that he'd seemingly forgotten he was reading.

Poor Bram was standing smack-dab in the middle of the room, facing everyone and looking for all intents and purposes as if he might just be reconsidering his decision to disclose everything to everyone at this particular moment in time.

Clearing her throat, Lucetta stepped farther into the room. "What a cheerful scene. I, for one, am certainly glad to be back in Washington Square."

Bram sent her a slight twist of his lips, which might have been his attempt at a smile, while everyone else just continued sitting there, or in Ruby's case, standing, remaining completely mute.

"Uh, well, speaking of Washington Square . . ." she began, trying to break the strained silence. "While I was languishing away — having been abducted, no less — I had quite a lot of time to catch up on my reading, and it just so happens there was a book I read that had facts about the city, and some of those facts dealt with Washington Square."

She gazed expectantly around the room, earning not so much as a blink in response, although she thought Archibald's paper fluttered a little.

"What were some of those facts?" Millie chirped, her eyes wide and looking exactly as if she had no idea what she should do next.

"Well, thank you for asking, Millie." She shut her eyes, summoned up the pages she'd read, opened her eyes, and nodded. "The story goes, at least according to a Mr. Greeley who researched the matter, that Washington Square was not always a posh part of New York City. It was, I'm sad to report, a potter's field, purchased clear back in 1797 by the New York government in order to provide a burial site for the indigent, poor, or members of the criminal persuasion."

"Dead people used to be buried underneath where we're standing?" Millie asked, her eyes going from simply wide to as big as dinner plates.

"Unfortunately, they still are," Lucetta admitted.

"That sounds like something right out of a Mr. Grimstone novel," Millie muttered, and that was all it took for the room to burst into noise.

"How could you have withheld the fact you're Mr. Grimstone, especially after I let it be known I wanted that man to squire me about the city?" Ruby demanded.

"Keeping such important secrets from your own family," Iris said, rising to her feet as she shook a finger Bram's way. "You should be ashamed of yourself. Do you know that your father and I have worried about you for years, wondering how you turned out so aimless, and then . . . thinking you were up to matters of a criminal nature?"

"At least you can now thank the good Lord above that he's not doing anything criminal," Abigail said, rising to her feet as well, even as she started to smile ever so slightly.

Archibald sent Lucetta the faintest hint of a wink before he snapped open the newspaper and disappeared behind it.

"You're Mr. Grimstone?" Millie finally asked, her question over all the others that were still being tossed Bram's way the one he decided to answer.

"I am."

Millie beamed back at him. "But how delightful to meet you in person. Why, I cannot begin to express how in awe I am of people who are able to create stories in their heads, and then — here's the best part — put down those stories on paper." She shook her head. "I have plenty of stories rolling around my mind, but the few times I tried to gather my thoughts and write them down, well, chaos — which means *turmoil,* by the way — is all I succeeded in creating."

Bram smiled. "Thank you, Mrs. Mulberry."

Millie returned the smile. "Please, call me Millie." She turned her attention to Iris, Abigail, and Ruby. "I'm afraid I don't understand your outrage with this extraordinarily talented gentleman. Everyone knows authors are an extremely neurotic lot, so I'm not surprised in the least that Bram . . ." She turned and quirked a brow his way. "You don't mind if I call you by your given name?"

"Not at all."

"Lovely," Millie said with a nod before she directed her attention to the three ladies now watching her a bit warily. "As I was saying, being a creative sort must be incredibly difficult, and just think about all the pressure poor Bram must be under, expected to turn out a book better than the last one he turned out time, after time, after time. Why, it must be exhausting being him, but I, a true lover of books, am thankful the world has people in it like Bram, and all of you should be as well."

Iris took one step forward. "Well, of course we're thankful for our Bram, dear, but surely you understand why we're put out with him? I've been under the impression he's been dealing in illegal activities for years, while his father has been concerned that Bram's been aimlessly drifting through life, not having a true purpose."

"I thought you and Father would be disappointed to learn I'd chosen writing as a profession over the law or over helping Hugh manage the family's business interests," Bram said.

"We could never be disappointed in you, Bram," Iris countered. "Concerned, certainly, but if writing — and being wildly successful at it, by the sounds of things — makes you happy, I, for one, could not be more —"

Before Iris could finish her thought, Ernie, followed by Stanley, who was clutching a bleeding nose, rushed into the room, stopping directly in front of Bram.

"What happened?" Bram demanded as he took hold of Stanley's arm and helped him into the closest chair right as Mr. Skukman dashed into the room, a half-eaten sandwich held in his hand.

"What happened?" Mr. Skukman asked as well, nodding to Ernie.

"We got ambushed," Ernie explained as he dropped into another chair. "By women, no less — the same women Silas hired to watch over Miss Plum."

"We'b neber saw it comin'," Stanley said as he pinched the bridge of his nose with one hand, while accepting the handkerchief Mr. Skukman had fished out of his pocket with the other. "Thank you."

Bram frowned. "We didn't even consider those ladies a threat. I mean, they simply walked out of the building when we showed up, and acted as if they were happy to be gone from the place."

"Women can be tricky," Ernie said with a knowing nod. "But . . . they stole Silas away, and . . . me and Stanley rushed back here because there's no time to waste."

"You think he's coming after Lucetta again?" Bram asked, stepping over to Lucetta to take hold of her arm, as if he expected Silas to burst into the room at any moment and try to steal her away again.

Ernie shook his head. "No, he's not coming after Miss Plum. I overheard him say he's going after her . . . mother."

22

As the private Pullman car Bram had secured for their trip to Greenville, Virginia,
began to slow, he looked across the aisle to
where Lucetta was sitting with Millie, noticing that her hands were clenched and she
was sitting so straight in her seat that she
looked incredibly uncomfortable.

"Nervous?" he asked quietly.

Catching his eye, she nodded. "I am — a
condition I'm afraid isn't going to dissipate
until I discover whether or not we've arrived in Virginia ahead of Silas."

"He's on the run from the law now,
Lucetta," Bram reminded her. "That means
he's going to have to travel carefully, and
who knows how he's going to go about the
tricky feat of funding his trip in the first
place."

"Men like Silas Ruff always have funds
hidden away," Mr. Skukman said, lowering
the paper he'd been reading before he

leaned forward and looked out the window. "Looks like we might have arrived."

As the train came to a complete stop, Ernie, Stanley, and Mr. Skukman fetched their bags, and after Bram told Lucetta and Millie to wait a moment, the gentlemen stepped from the Pullman car and assessed their surroundings.

"Seems to be safe," Mr. Skukman said.

"Not a lot of people milling around," Ernie added.

"I'll go find a carriage to rent," Stanley said, heading off for a weather-beaten building with the words *Greenville Depot* painted over the door, and where a few gentlemen were sitting on wooden chairs on the wraparound porch.

Bram lifted a hand to shield his eyes from the sun, before he nodded at Mr. Skukman. "Do you think this is a good idea, bringing Lucetta here?"

"Not at all."

"I don't remember you voicing a protest back in New York when she insisted on accompanying us to Virginia."

"Miss Plum has been watching out for her mother for years, Mr. Haverstein. She certainly wouldn't have calmly stayed behind while we gentlemen went off to save the day. It's not in her nature, and it's something you need to accept about her."

"I suppose you're right, but . . . have you ever met her mother?"

"Never. Nor has that lady ever come to visit Miss Plum in New York. It doesn't speak well of the woman that she's never seen her only daughter perform onstage, especially since I know for a fact that Miss Plum is responsible for providing her family with . . . Well, I really shouldn't say anything more about that."

"You haven't said anything about anything."

Mr. Skukman's lips twitched. "Too right — I haven't."

"What are you two discussing in such a clandestine fashion?"

Summoning up what he hoped was an innocent smile, Bram turned and found Lucetta and Millie standing right behind him. "Didn't I tell you two to stay in the Pullman car until we got matters settled out here, and until we made certain it was safe?"

"I thought you would have realized by now that I'm not a lady who takes orders well." Lucetta looked around. "Where's Stanley?"

"He went to see about renting a carriage."

Lucetta blew out a breath. "He won't be successful. He's a Yankee through and

through, and" — she smiled — "they can
smell Yankee from a mile away down here."
With that, Lucetta closed her eyes for all of
five seconds and drew in a deep breath.
When she opened her eyes again, Bram
found himself looking at a consummate
southern belle, complete with fluttering
lashes and a gloved hand that took to waving ever so precisely back and forth in front
of her face.

"Mr. Wilkinson, is that you over there?"
Lucetta called in a voice that practically
dripped molasses as she sashayed toward
the gentlemen sitting on the depot porch,
all of whom jumped to their feet and tore
the hats off their heads.

"Why, Miss Lucetta Plum. Good heavens,
darlin', I hadn't heard you were fixin' on
comin' home."

"It was a spur-of-the-moment decision,
Mr. Wilkinson, but tell me, how is that
mama of yours? Is she still making the best
sweet tea Virginia has ever tasted?"

Mr. Wilkinson smiled. "Mama is doin' just
fine, Miss Plum, and her tea is as good as
ever. I'm sure she'd appreciate seeing you
while you're here visitin'."

"You tell her I'll try my best to make my
way over to your plantation, but now, I'd
like to introduce all of you to some friends

of mine." She turned and gestured Millie forward first. "This is one of my very best friends in the whole world, Mrs. Everett Mulberry."

Bram watched while southern charm practically oozed out of each and every gentleman as they took a moment to meet Millie, and exclaim over Lucetta time and time again. Irritation flowed freely as he watched Lucetta's hand get kissed again and again — until he realized that a few of the older men were missing limbs, that telling state of affairs having Bram's irritation evaporating into thin air.

It had been seventeen years since the war had ended, but clearly, for men of the South, there were daily reminders of that war all around them.

"Bram, come meet some of my old neighbors."

Moving to join Lucetta, Bram quickly discovered that while the gentlemen were more than willing to extend their southern charm Millie's way, they weren't willing to offer him anything but the most cursory of greetings. Until Lucetta rolled her eyes and plopped her hands on her hips.

"Honestly, gentlemen, Mr. Haverstein is my very good friend, and besides, while he may currently live in New York, he was raised in Cuba."

That was all it took for Bram to be well and truly welcomed to the town of Green-ville. His hand was shaken by everyone, and a few of the men even slapped him on the back. They were not as gracious to Mr. Skukman, Ernie, or Stanley, when he returned to join them, but since Lucetta had taken to narrowing her eyes at them as she made introductions, they did at least send a few nods around.

"I'm afraid I wasn't able to find a carriage to let," Stanley said, moving up beside Bram. "And . . . the man running the depot didn't have any suggestions as to where I might find one."

Mr. Wilkinson, who'd obviously overheard Stanley, frowned as he stepped closer to Lucetta. "I would have thought, even given the animosity you and Mr. Nigel Wolfe share, that he would have been agreeable to sending a carriage for you. Truth be told, it's not proper that he didn't, not proper at all."

A ghost of a smile teased Lucetta's lips. "As I believe I mentioned, this wasn't a planned visit, so Mother isn't expecting me, which is why a carriage hasn't been sent." She glanced around at the gentlemen still surrounding her. "May I dare hope that one of you has a wagon or something else with wheels that we could borrow?"

"Monty Morrison and his wagon are parked around the front side of the train depot," Mr. Wilkinson said. "He just brought his aunt to town to catch the next train. I would imagine he'd be delighted to see all of you over to Plum Hill."

Lucetta gave another flutter of her lashes, the act so unlike her that Bram had to turn his head to hide the smile he hadn't been able to stifle as she continued. "Thank you, Mr. Wilkinson, and do be sure to tell your mama I was asking about her."

After a chorus of pleasantries and invitations to visit one plantation after the next, Lucetta smiled and nodded to everyone before she took Millie's arm, and with Bram falling into step beside her, and Mr. Skukman, Ernie, and Stanley falling into step behind them, they headed down the boardwalk that ran adjacent to the train tracks.

"How far is Plum Hill from here?" Millie asked.

"About forty minutes or so, depending on the speed of the horse one takes."

"And it's an honest-to-goodness southern plantation?"

"It is."

"And your mother will be happy to welcome all of us to this plantation?" Millie pressed.

"Hmmm . . ." was all Lucetta said to that before she quickened her stride, waving a hand at a wagon pulling out onto the road.

As the wagon Lucetta had been waving down came to a stop, and Lucetta arranged for Mr. Morrison, the driver of that wagon, to see all of them to Plum Hill, Bram couldn't help but wonder why Lucetta hadn't answered Millie's question, or why her mother wouldn't be pleased to welcome her daughter home.

Drawing in a deep breath, he could only hope that Lucetta wasn't about to experience yet another dramatic circumstance.

23

Sitting on the front seat of Monty Morrison's wagon, with Monty sneaking peeks at her every other second out of the corner of his eye, Lucetta couldn't keep from smiling as an image of a very young Monty, who was a good five years younger than she was, kept flashing to mind.

He'd always been a bit of a scamp, never clean for longer than an hour, and had been the bane of his mother's existence, or so the woman had claimed, but it was encouraging to hear him talk about the improvements that were being made on his family's plantation.

"We put in tobacco this year, Miss Plum, and have also taken to raisin' some hogs. Mother finds them a little distasteful and smelly, but there's a profit to be made with hogs, and we could certainly use the money."

"Did you ever get the repairs done to

your house?"

Monty nodded. "The major ones, but some of the smaller repairs that still need to be made will have to wait a little longer, hopefully just until we take our hogs to market, or if tobacco keeps rising in price." He glanced out of the corner of his eye again at her. "You still taking to the stage up there in New York City, or have you come home to stay?"

The word *home* had her nerves jingling, even though a part of her had always considered Plum Hill home.

She just hadn't felt welcome in that home since Nigel had wormed his way into her family a decade before.

She had yet to understand why her mother had married the man, had done so almost the moment her two-year period of mourning for Lucetta's father had passed. Susannah, Lucetta's mother, hadn't even given her only daughter the courtesy of seeking her opinion about the marriage before she'd gone ahead and tied herself to Nigel, even with Lucetta being the one who'd been given the task of keeping Plum Hill afloat after her father had died.

Lucetta had known from the moment Nigel showed up at Plum Hill, claiming he was simply stopping in to pay his respects to Susannah, that he was trouble hiding behind a bushel of southern charm and manners. He'd been impeccably dressed, and had kept being impeccably dressed every time he paid Susannah a visit, even though Lucetta discovered he'd lost everything in the war. That *everything* included the plantation he'd grown up on in Georgia, a plantation that just happened to be right next to the plantation Susannah had grown up on — both of the regal houses that anchored the plantations having the misfortune of being burned to the ground when General Sherman had gone marching through that state.

Nigel had used their common past to burrow his way straight into Susannah's heart. Their glory days were often the focus of their conversations, especially the glory days that centered around talk of Susannah being the most sought-after belle in all of Georgia. Every time he brought up her great success, Susannah fluttered her lashes like the debutante she'd been, instead of behaving like a widow and mother of a daughter who'd almost been old enough to make her own debut.

Susannah had never seen past the flattery Nigel diligently tossed her way, had never seen that the war had changed him in ways that made him so different from the young man she'd known growing up.

Lucetta had never seen the man her mother remembered. She'd only seen a man who was disturbingly broken, and a man who had the ability to break the very small and very tenuous bond that Lucetta and Susannah shared.

Once he convinced Susannah to marry him and vows had been exchanged, Nigel had been able to get his hands on all the money Lucetta's father had left behind, money he couldn't gamble away fast enough.

Lucetta shifted on the wagon seat as a memory she'd purposefully filed away in the deepest recesses of her mind sprang forward, a memory of her begging her mother to talk to Nigel about the money he was losing, large chunks of money that would just disappear into thin air, usually after he'd return from what he liked to call *business trips.*

Susannah had brushed Lucetta's concerns away as she'd walked out the door of Plum Hill, only interested in getting to an afternoon tea she'd been invited to, an event that was obviously far more important than listening to the concerns of her daughter — concerns that centered around the fact that their money would shortly run out and they'd be left with no roof over their heads.

"Miss Plum . . . is something the matter?"

Shaking herself straight from thoughts she'd believed she'd left in the past, although clearly that was not the case, Lucetta summoned up a smile and sent it Monty's way. "I have no idea why you keep calling me Miss Plum, Monty. We've known each other for years."

"You've been gone a long time, so I wouldn't claim to know you at all these days," Monty countered. "But very well, Lucetta it is — only not when your mother is around, because she, I have to admit, still frightens me."

"She frightens everyone," Lucetta muttered.

"I sure did enjoy your father's company, though, back when he was alive. Now, there was a gentleman who made a person feel right at ease." Steering the wagon down a well-tended lane, Monty smiled again. "Just over that rise and you'll be home."

Sitting ever so slightly forward, Lucetta kept her attention front and center, feeling a small ache settle in her heart the moment they crested the rise and Plum Hill was laid out before them.

Monty slowed the horses to a stop, as if

he knew she'd want to take a moment to enjoy the sight of her old home.

The money she'd made in the market and on the stage had been responsible for keeping Plum Hill in good standing. The four pillars that guarded the portico were dazzlingly white-washed and the cobblestone drive that led to the front steps was cleared of all weeds and looking as if it had been swept only that morning. The three stories of red brick had always lent the structure a rather regal air, and with the black shutters that framed the paned windows on the front of the house looking as if they'd recently gotten a fresh coat of paint, the house looked downright stately. The glass in the windows gleamed in the late-afternoon sunlight, giving testimony that this was a house that had a full staff to keep it looking spotless, and she imagined she'd find the interior looking just as impressive.

"And to think you gave all this up for an attic room in a boardinghouse," Millie said from her seat in the wagon directly behind Lucetta.

"Where I spent many a happy year with you and Harriet." Lucetta nodded to Monty. "You may drive on, Monty. While I'd love to linger here for the rest of the afternoon, I have matters to discuss with my mother."

"And since I think that may be your mother stepping out on the portico, you're not going to have to wait long to discuss those matters," Monty said, flicking the reins, which had the horses plodding into motion again.

As they drew closer to Plum Hill, the woman standing on the portico came into focus, and there was little doubt that the years had been incredibly kind to Susannah Wolfe. Her hair was still a lovely shade of gold, although a shade darker than Lucetta's was these days. Her figure was trim, showcased to perfection in a gown that had come directly from Paris, one that sported a small bustle in the back and one that had cost a small fortune, a small fortune Lucetta had been responsible for paying.

For the briefest of seconds, Lucetta felt tears sting her eyes. But knowing her mother would not appreciate any type of emotional display, especially in front of people Susannah did not know, Lucetta drew in a deep breath, and by the time Monty pulled the wagon to a stop a bit of a distance from the entrance to Plum Hill — at Lucetta's request so that she could have a few private moments with her mother — she was in complete control again.

Hopping down from the wagon seat after

she told Bram, Millie, and the others she'd be right back for them, she squared her shoulders and headed for the front steps. "Hello, Mother," she said, climbing the four steps it took to reach the portico where her mother was waiting.

"Lucetta Plum, do not tell me those are honest-to-goodness wrinkles in the skirt of that gown?" was the first thing to come out of Susannah's mouth, even though she hadn't spoken to Lucetta in months.

"It's a long train ride from New York to Virginia, Mother, and I'm afraid I didn't think to bring a maid with me, or . . . Oh, yes, I don't actually employ a lady's maid."

Susannah completely ignored Lucetta's response as she sashayed her way closer. "While this is certainly a *lovely* surprise, having you come to call on me and all, did it ever cross your mind to send me a little note, asking if today would be convenient for me to have you show up at Plum Hill?"

Pushing aside the small bit of hurt over the idea her mother was clearly not ecstatic to see her, Lucetta lifted her chin. "There wasn't time to send a note, Mother, and considering Plum Hill is my home, one would think I wouldn't need to send a note to make certain my presence would be welcome here."

All hints of pleasantness disappeared from Susannah's lovely face. "I know full well you hold the deed to Plum Hill, Lucetta. Must you throw that in my face every time we see each other?"

Lucetta blinked. "I don't believe I said a thing about the deed to Plum Hill, Mother, nor do I believe I've ever mentioned anything about me holding the deed to Plum Hill to you. Now, Nigel and I, on the other hand, recently had a very enlightening chat about the status of Plum Hill, a chat I find myself wondering if he even brought up to you."

"Nigel just got back from a business trip, so we haven't had much time to chat about anything," Susannah said before she suddenly smiled, every trace of unpleasantness disappearing from her face, as if she'd suddenly recalled that Lucetta had arrived with a whole wagon filled with people — those people, Lucetta was quite certain, being the only reason Susannah was currently smiling.

"But speaking of your dear stepfather," Susannah continued with a flutter of her lashes. "We're expected to dine this evening at the old Kerr plantation, which was recently purchased by a family distantly related to the Vanderbilts."

Susannah gave a delicate shudder. "I don't particularly care to socialize with Northerners, but the ladies we vacation with at White Sulphur Springs are itching to get some of our belles invited to one of those Patriarch balls that are held up in New York City. Those ladies are of the firm belief that cozying up to this new family will help us achieve that goal."

"I hate to be the bearer of bad news, Mother, but the Vanderbilts have yet to be accepted into New York high society."

Susannah blinked. "But . . . I've heard that the Vanderbilts are one of the richest families in the country."

"While that is certainly true, they've been deliberately kept out of high society — or what those in the know call the New York Four Hundred — by none other than Mrs. Astor." Lucetta shook her head. "Even with all the money the Vanderbilt family possesses, Mrs. Astor believes them to be uncouth, which is rather amusing when you think about it."

"What in the world would you find amusing about that?" Susannah asked slowly.

"Well, Mrs. Astor enjoys the high position she holds within society, but her husband's grandfather wasn't well-heeled in the least, and the Vanderbilts' grandfather, Cornelius

Vanderbilt, the founder of their fortune, wasn't well-heeled either. So why is the Astor family accepted into society, while the Vanderbilt family is not? Quite frankly, I've seen Alva Vanderbilt out and about in the city, and I cannot imagine her eating her peas with a knife."

Susannah frowned. "I've never understood how you always have so much history at your fingertips, or why you'd even be interested in it, but . . . I find myself curious as to how you know all of this information about New York high society."

Lucetta shoved aside the tiny sliver of disappointment her mother's words caused. Susannah had never understood Lucetta's mind, or her father's, for that matter. She'd even mocked Lucetta's intelligence over the years, telling her time and time again that she'd never find a gentleman to marry, because gentlemen did not enjoy being around women who knew too much.

Forcing a smile, Lucetta shrugged. "I hear and see things at the theater, Mother, especially since society does enjoy its amusements. But besides that, I have a very good friend who has been an accepted member of society for years."

"I really prefer not to discuss your 'very good friend,' if it's all the same to you."

Temper replaced any hint of lingering disappointment as Lucetta hugged her arms around her middle — as if that would stave away the unpleasantness she'd just heard — and stared at her mother, who'd taken to looking affronted.

That the woman had actually given birth to Lucetta but apparently didn't know her daughter or what values her daughter held was beyond telling, but it went far in explaining the less than warm and tender relationship mother and daughter shared.

"I would hope you'd have a bit more faith in me, Mother, than to immediately assume my very good friend is a gentleman, or more importantly, my lover."

"You're being impertinent," Susannah shot back before she smiled one of her lovely smiles and nodded to something off in the distance. "You're also being neglectful of your friends."

Finding herself less than surprised by her mother's response to something she obviously didn't care to discuss, Lucetta turned and walked to the edge of the portico, reining in the temper flowing through her as she gestured for Monty to bring the wagon closer.

It would never do to lose her temper with her mother, because Susannah would no doubt disengage from the conversation and dismiss Lucetta before she could warn her mother about Silas.

As the wagon drew near, Lucetta turned back to her mother, finding her smoothing down her hair, even though there was not a single strand out of place in the tidy chignon her mother preferred to wear when she was at home.

"You look lovely, Mother. There's no reason to fuss with your hair."

Susannah stopped smoothing her hair and frowned. "Thank you, dear. What an unexpected thing for you to say."

"I'm sure I've told you you've looked lovely before."

"Not since you were a small child, back in the days when you liked me."

Lucetta blinked. "When have I ever made the claim that I don't like you?"

Susannah let out what sounded remarkably like a snort. "Please, I may not be as intelligent as you are, or your father was, but I was born with a bit of common sense. That means I can tell when someone doesn't like me, and you, daughter dear, don't like me, just as I can tell you're disdainful of the way I prefer to live my life, finding it far too frivolous for a practical soul like you."

"I'm not always practical" was all Lucetta could think to respond to something she'd never even considered before — the idea that her mother suffered hurts from slights she believed Lucetta had flung her way.

A trace of uncomfortable truth nudged its way into Lucetta's thoughts.

She did find her mother frivolous, and . . . perhaps she had been a little disdainful over the years in regard to her mother's lack of competency with any matters of a business nature, especially matters of finance.

Before she could address the subject further though, she heard footsteps approaching. Turning, she found Bram striding her way while everyone else remained in the wagon.

Her pulse immediately sped up the closer he drew, but she didn't find herself annoyed by that reaction. Quite honestly, she was getting used to her pulse galloping about at the strangest of times, mostly when Bram smiled, or . . . held her arm, or . . . breathed.

They'd not had an opportunity to speak much about anything since learning Silas had escaped, but now that she knew his secrets, knew he wasn't a madman, and knew he wasn't appalled by her rather curious gifts, she'd been thinking over the whole courting business, and . . . truth be told, she'd been . . . considering it.

Blinking straight out of those thoughts, Lucetta realized that Bram had made the decision to approach them on his own, almost as if he'd known Susannah might be a little overwhelmed if she'd been faced with meeting everyone at once.

His inherent kindness had the smallest of sighs escaping from Lucetta's lips, sighs that disappeared in a flash when Susannah let out a sigh of her own.

"My goodness but that is one handsome man," Susannah breathed before she breezed past Lucetta, a brilliant smile spreading over her face. Holding out her arms in clear welcome, she went from disgruntled mother to the image of the quintessential southern woman — all smiles and grace — in a split second.

Lucetta couldn't help but be slightly impressed with her mother's acting abilities.

"You must be Lucetta's mother, although I would have said sister if I didn't already know Lucetta is an only child," Bram said, climbing up the stairs to take the hand Susannah immediately held out to him. He brought her fingers to his lips even as he inclined his head to her. "I'm delighted to meet you."

Susannah dipped her head and peeked out

at Bram from beneath her lashes, an action all southern ladies learned from almost the moment they could walk. The peeking came to an abrupt end, however, when Susannah shot a glance to Lucetta and raised a perfectly shaped brow.

Stepping forward before her mother did something worse than raise a brow over what she evidently thought was Lucetta's grave lapse in manners, Lucetta summoned up a smile. "Mother, I'd like to introduce you to a friend of mine, Mr. Bram Haverstein. Bram, this is my mother, Mrs. Nigel Wolfe, Susannah to her close friends and family."

"Which means you must call me Susannah," her mother all but purred. "Any friend of my daughter's is certainly a friend of mine."

"I would be honored to call you Susannah, and you must call me Bram," he said as he released Susannah's hand, earning a sigh of obvious disappointment in return.

Lucetta had almost forgotten how flirty southern women tended to be, no matter their ages. Before her mother could begin flirting in earnest though, footsteps marching up the steps drew Lucetta's attention, and to her relief, she found that Millie had decided to join them.

"What a marvelous house," Millie exclaimed when she reached Lucetta's side, beaming a smile Susannah's way. "I'm Mrs. Everett Mulberry, Mrs. Wolfe, but please, call me Millie, since I've been fast friends with your daughter for what feels like forever and you apparently feel that any friend of Lucetta's is a friend of yours. Why, I'm sure you must feel as if you and I are fast friends already since I lived with Lucetta for years and years before I got married, which means I know she must have told you all about me."

Susannah's forehead puckered ever so slightly as she looked Millie up and down. "Lucetta has never mentioned a word about you, Mrs. Mulberry."

Millie's eyes immediately took to narrowing, and for such a small lady, she suddenly looked quite intimidating. "Millie, please, and clearly I've arrived just in the nick of time. You and Lucetta are obviously suffering from a less than desirable relationship, which means the two of you need someone to intervene on both of your behalves, and, well . . . here I am."

With that, Millie stepped forward and, with Susannah eyeing her warily, reached out, took a firm hold of Susannah's shoulders, and pulled her into an enthusiastic embrace.

"Oh . . . my" was all Susannah seemed capable of saying as Millie gave her a last squeeze and stepped back, immediately entwining her arm with Susannah's.

"Now then, since it's clear a bit of a heart-to-heart talk is long overdue between you and my dear Lucetta, I'm going to suggest we repair to . . ." She tilted her head. "Do you call them parlors down here in the South?"

"We have a receiving room," Susannah said slowly.

"Excellent. We'll repair to the receiving room, where I'm hopeful some of that sweet tea I keep hearing about will be served as I tell you about the many, many things I don't believe you know about your daughter."

With that, Millie prodded Susannah into motion and disappeared with her into Plum Hill.

"Millie's a little frightening, isn't she?" Bram asked slowly.

"This coming from a man who owns his own dungeon," Lucetta replied right before she caught sight of someone walking around the corner of the house.

Before she could get a single word out of her mouth, however — as in a word of warning to the unfortunate soul who'd rounded that corner — Mr. Skukman came dashing out of nowhere, launched himself into the air, and knocked none other than her dastardly stepfather, Mr. Nigel Wolfe, straight to the ground.

24

Lucetta braced herself for the wrath she knew was about to be unleashed as she watched her mother hover over Nigel, temper having colored Susannah's cheeks a vivid shade of pink.

"I would really like to know why anyone would find it acceptable to accost poor Nigel when the man was simply trying to enter his own home," Susannah suddenly said, pausing in her act of mopping up Nigel's bleeding lip with a wet cloth in order to send everyone now gathered in the receiving room a glare.

Mr. Skukman, who was standing by the floor-to-ceiling window on the far side of the room, pulled his gaze away from studying the back lawn and settled it on Susannah. "I thought he was Silas Ruff." Apparently believing that went far in explaining everything, Mr. Skukman immediately returned his attention out the window again, sipping the sweet tea Susannah had provided him after he'd carried Nigel into the receiving room.

In the South, good manners and hospitality were never to be neglected, not even if the man you were extending those manners to had just knocked your husband to the ground.

Lucetta felt her lips quirk as that odd thought rumbled around her mind, her lips quirking up even farther when she recalled Mr. Skukman's look of complete surprise when her mother had thrust the tea into his hand before marching off to assist her husband.

"Would there be a reasonable explanation as to why you'd want to accost this Mr. Ruff character?" Susannah demanded, pulling Lucetta back to the conversation at hand.

Mr. Skukman took a sip of his tea, pulled his attention away from the scene outside the window again, and nodded Susannah's way. "He's been obsessed with your daughter for years, showing up at all of her performances. That obsession culminated with him recently abducting Miss Plum and holding her captive for days against her will."

Susannah's eyes widened before she closed them, drew in a deep breath, and slowly released it. When she opened her eyes again, she appeared perfectly calm, not a trace of concern or surprise lingering on her face — a tactic Lucetta had put to great use over the years as well, although she normally put that tactic to use when she was on a stage.

It was becoming remarkably clear that she hadn't inherited all of her gifts from her father.

Looking around the room, Susannah's attention settled on Bram. "And what flimsy excuses are you going to tell me, *Mr. Haverstein,* about what compelled you to punch my Nigel in the nose? Clearly, he's not Silas Ruff, nor could he have possibly done anything to you that would have warranted your violence toward him since he told me only moments ago that he's never seen you before in his life."

Bram, who'd been standing directly beside Lucetta as she sat on a divan that had once belonged to her grandmother, crossed his arms over his chest and sent Susannah a pleasant smile. "I'm afraid I have no excuses to give you, Mrs. Wolfe," he said, apparently realizing Susannah's demand of using informal names was no longer in play. "In all honesty, I can't even claim I punched Nigel in error, since I heard Lucetta call out his name right after Mr. Skukman jumped on him."

Susannah blinked and narrowed her eyes. "That almost sounds to me as if you hit him on purpose."

Bram shrugged. "Someone needed to, especially after he tried to serve Lucetta up as a means of honoring a gambling debt to Silas Ruff — a circumstance that led to all the unfortunate events Lucetta's been forced to endure ever since Nigel sat down to play cards with Silas."

Susannah straightened, the wet cloth she'd been using to blot Nigel's lip now all but forgotten in her hand. "Nigel doesn't gamble anymore. Everyone knows that, and I don't appreciate you insinuating otherwise."

"I don't believe I was insinuating anything, Mrs. Wolfe, but since you are evidently unwilling to take my word for it, perhaps you should ask your husband about the details surrounding the incident with Silas." Bram nodded to Nigel, who'd taken to slouching down in the chair he was in.

With mutters of "nasty accusations" and "have no idea what they're talking about" making it past lips that barely moved, Nigel sunk even lower into his chair and settled into a sulky silence, refusing to say another word.

Giving him an encouraging pat on the

arm, Susannah squared her shoulders right before she marched across the room. Dropping down between Lucetta and Millie on the divan, Susannah scooted around in an obvious attempt at getting more comfortable, hardly noticing that her scooting had sent Millie straight off the edge.

Completely unperturbed about that unexpected turn of events, Millie snatched up what had to be her third glass of sweet tea that she'd left on a side table, and clutching it closely to her, she glided across the room, taking a seat in an unoccupied chair.

"Why would Mr. Haverstein believe such a silly tale about Nigel?" Susannah asked after Millie was once again settled. "I told you years ago, Lucetta, that Nigel had given up gambling, and . . . well, he would never lose you in a game of chance even if he *did* still occasionally sit down to a friendly hand of cards."

"While I'm sure most people find your naiveté remarkably charming, Mother, I find it nothing of the sort," Lucetta said as a thread of temper began to weave through her. "You, of all people, should realize that I have more important things to do in my life than compose 'silly tales' about Nigel. Everything Bram said is nothing less than the truth. Nigel is still lying to you about everything, and there is no disputing the fact that he did sit down to play cards with Silas Ruff, losing far more than he had available to lose after he apparently drank to excess."

"Nigel doesn't drink anymore either," Susannah said with a sniff.

"You were just standing inches away from him, Mother. Did you not smell the whiskey on his breath? Because believe me, I smelled it from across the room."

Susannah rose to her feet and presented Lucetta with her back. "It's impossible to hold a rational conversation with you when you turn all dramatic."

Lucetta rose to her feet too, as her temper went from simmering to boiling. "He tried to throw the deed to Plum Hill into his card game, and when it was learned that he didn't have the deed in his possession, he offered me up to Silas Ruff. That, quite frankly, is something I'm convinced Silas was hoping would happen from the moment he conned Nigel into sitting down with him in the first place."

Susannah turned around and narrowed her eyes on Lucetta. "Nigel would never gamble away Plum Hill. He knows it means too much to me."

"He can't gamble it away, Mother. He

doesn't own it."

Susannah's eyes narrowed to mere slits. "Oh, here we go again, you bringing up the deed to Plum Hill. As the man of this family, of course Nigel owns this property, Lucetta. I realize you and he had some type of falling out that ended with him allowing you to hold on to the deed, but that doesn't mean you own Plum Hill."

Lucetta's brows drew together. "Is that what he told you — that I forced him to hand over the deed to me? Honestly, Mother, I know you enjoy playing the southern lady to a fault, and playing it so that no one would ever guess you have a brain in your head, but . . . I didn't get all of my intelligence from Father. Surely you've at least considered the possibility, since I hold the deed to Plum Hill, that I do, indeed, own the place."

Susannah plopped her hands on her hips. "How would you have found the means to buy Plum Hill?"

"I'm very good with investments, something that you should be thankful for since that talent has kept a roof over your head."

Susannah lifted her chin. "I don't believe you."

Considering her mother for a long moment, Lucetta frowned. "Nigel really never

414

told you about any of this?"

"Don't think for a second you can have me turning on Nigel with the lies you're spouting. I've always known that you've never cared for him, never wanted me to marry him, which was really unfair of you since Nigel's always had your best interests at heart."

"Did he have those interests at heart when he realized he'd been going through Father's money far too quickly and was soon going to run out and so decided that I'd be the perfect solution to help him acquire a fortune at the gambling dens?"

"Shut up," Nigel growled as he got to his feet and took a threatening step toward her. He came to an abrupt stop, however, when Mr. Skukman moved across the room in a flash, his menacing stance blocking Nigel from Lucetta and returning him to his seat.

"Go on, Lucetta," Bram said quietly, stepping directly to her side and taking her hand in his.

"It doesn't matter. She's not going to listen."

"And that doesn't matter either," Bram countered. "You need to get your past out into the open so you can finally put it to rest. This is your opportunity."

"Her opportunity to spread her lies,"

Nigel called from his seat, snapping his mouth shut when Mr. Skukman released a growl.

Bram brought her hand up to his lips and kissed it. "Tell us why Nigel wanted you to accompany him to gambling dens."

Shoving aside the absurd thought that she really could get used to the feel of his lips on her hand, Lucetta drew in a deep breath and slowly released it. "I'd just turned sixteen when Nigel presented his idea to me. He needed to replenish the coffers before my mother discovered what he'd been about. They hadn't been married long, you see, but he'd lost his head having the fortune my father had left us at his disposal, and while he was losing his head, he'd managed to lose himself a good chunk of that fortune. Disaster was nipping at his heels, and that, I believe, is what had him watching me so closely."

Lucetta smiled. "I readily admit I probably came across as a most unusual child, what with my habit of studying the financial sections of the newspaper and trying to budget the household expenses and such. I was in the pantry one day, making an inventory of supplies, when Nigel joined me. I found it peculiar that he'd chosen to speak to me in the pantry, but it didn't take me long to figure out why he'd wanted to speak with me well away from my mother's ears."

"Did he touch you?" Bram asked, so quietly Lucetta had to lean closer to him to catch his every word.

"Goodness, no, it wasn't that type of meeting at all. He simply asked me to join him in a friendly game of faro."

Susannah let out a snort. "That's what you've been so upset about? Nigel asked you to play faro?"

"He had an ulterior motive for asking me to play, Mother — that motive being proof of what he'd begun to suspect about me. By the time we were finished, Nigel knew without a doubt that I was capable of remembering every card played out on the table, and could predict the cards that were still left in the deck with remarkable accuracy."

"Her father had that same ability," Susannah said before her lips thinned. "I always found it to be incredibly disconcerting — unnatural, if you will."

Bram looked at Susannah for a long moment, his gaze causing her to fidget before he returned his attention to Lucetta. "It's little wonder you ran away."

"Quite, especially since I didn't see that I had any choice in the matter. Nigel was ecstatic about my *gift* as he'd taken to calling it, and had even gone so far as to pull out maps and circle where the best gambling establishments were throughout the country." She shot a glance Nigel's way. "He saw absolutely nothing wrong with me helping him out, even though I was rather vocal about not wanting to do it since I really didn't believe cheating at cards was right."

"She told me that *God* would be disappointed in her," Nigel said, speaking up even as he kept a wary eye on Mr. Skukman.

"And you told me that God would be disappointed in me for not helping my stepfather provide for the family," Lucetta countered.

Nigel waved that away with a flick of his hand. "We could have made a fortune."

"We could have made a fortune if you would have stopped gambling and allowed me to invest my father's money."

"You were sixteen," Nigel reminded her.

"And I'd made a tidy fortune for myself by the time I was twenty-one."

As soon as the words left her mouth, Lucetta wanted to call them back. She'd never talked about the money she'd made through her investments with her family before, not wanting to allow Nigel information he could use against her. But before she could think of a way to distract Nigel from her blunder, her mother took to *tsk*ing under her breath before she suddenly took to pacing around the room.

"I have no idea where I went wrong with you, Lucetta," Susannah said as she stopped pacing and shook a finger Lucetta's way. "You've turned into a nasty little liar over the years. Clearly, I did not do a very good job raising you."

"You never had anything to do with raising me — my nurse and nanny did. Father was the only one in the family who spent any time with me. But, you put an end to that quickly enough when you insisted on sending me off to boarding school, which made my time with Father almost non-existent."

"Then I suppose we can blame your father, your nanny, and your nurse, along with that school for turning you into a liar."

"I'm not lying about anything. In fact, the only person who seems to be doing that is Nigel." Lucetta drew in a breath of air. "Why you've always chosen to believe him over me, always *chosen* him over me, is beyond my comprehension."

"I love him, and always have, ever since

we grew up together on adjacent plantations."

Of all the things Lucetta had expected her
mother to say, that had never entered her
mind. Lifting her chin, she caught Susannah's eye. "Then why, pray tell, did you
marry my father?"

Susannah gave a delicate shrug. "It was
an arranged marriage. My mother knew
your father, and believed Bertram was
destined to become a man of consequence.
He was wealthy, somewhat attractive, intelligent — although far too intelligent for my
taste — and he was ambitious. Add in the
fact that he became smitten with me the
moment he laid eyes on me, and it was a
match my mother and father were more
than pleased with."

"But you were in love with Nigel."

Susannah's eyes softened as she glanced
Nigel's way. "I must admit that I was deeply
in love with Nigel, but my parents didn't
approve. He was not the eldest son, nor did
he possess any great wealth of his own,
and . . . well, even I must admit that Nigel
has never been overly ambitious." She gave
a sad shake of her head. "His only hope of a
bright future was to marry a wealthy lady,
and since my mother flatly refused to give
me a dowry if I chose to marry Nigel, he

was forced to marry Miss Delia Davidson, and I was left with no choice but to marry Bertram."

"But Nigel got to benefit from your dowry in the end when he married you," Lucetta pointed out. "Although . . . what happened to Delia?"

"I didn't do away with her, if that's what you're going to suggest next," Nigel said, finally speaking up. "Consumption took Delia, and I suppose I did mourn the loss, but I've never been one to dwell on the disappointing aspects of life."

Lucetta narrowed her eyes. "Forgive me if I find it difficult to believe you were disappointed by a death that allowed you to marry my mother."

"One matter of disappointment that I *have* dwelled on," Nigel continued, as if Lucetta hadn't spoken, "is the whereabouts of Grandmother Plum's jewelry." He tilted his head and considered Lucetta for a moment. "You wouldn't know what happened to that, would you, especially since it disappeared right around the time you did?"

Lucetta rose to her feet, resisting the urge to throttle her stepfather. "You know very well that Grandmother Plum left me her jewels, Nigel, and because of that, they were mine to take with me when I left Plum Hill.

Besides, you of all people should be thankful that I did take the jewels, because if I hadn't, I would not have had the funds to make my initial investments. But because I was successful with those initial investments, I had the money to save Plum Hill after you used it as leverage in one ill-fated card game after another."

"I was going to pay you back. You didn't need to demand that I sign over the deed to Plum Hill the last time I got myself in a spot of trouble," Nigel said, his voice decidedly sulky.

Susannah walked across the room and stopped directly beside Nigel. "Darling, surely you didn't truly sign over the deed to Plum Hill to Lucetta, did you? I mean, that would . . ." She raised a hand to her chest. "Well, that would mean she *does* own the plantation."

Nigel once again retreated into stony silence.

Lucetta said softly, "I told you years ago, Mother, that Nigel was gambling Father's money away, and yet you wouldn't listen to me, but I wasn't lying. He did gamble Father's fortune away, and the only way you've been able to stay at Plum Hill is because I made that possible — me, your daughter, not Nigel." She drew in a shaky breath. "You've behaved badly, Mother, and it started when you took up with Nigel not long after Father died."

"I didn't marry Nigel until two years after Bertram died, a completely proper mourning period."

"But Nigel showed up only a few months after Father died, and I knew full well he was living in the guesthouse. You risked bringing shame to Father's good name by associating with and then marrying a drunk with a gambling problem."

Susannah's face began to mottle. "If anyone brought shame on the family, it was you, Lucetta. You chose to keep your real name when you took to the stage in New York, having to know that actresses are considered little better than, well, ladies of ill-repute."

"I kept my name because I was the last of the Plums."

Susannah released a laugh that was less than pleasant. "You kept the Plum name because you knew it would embarrass me if any of my friends traveled to New York and just happened to take in a show that you were performing in. And you also decided to use your real name as a way to get back at a father who left you all alone in the world — except for me, his beautiful wife whom he didn't believe had an intelligent thought in her head."

Lucetta stepped toward her mother, but before she could even begin to argue that point an unwelcome thought flashed to mind, one that left her reeling.

Her mother had just spoken nothing less than the truth.

She *had* kept her name to embarrass her mother — there was no question about that — but . . . she had *also* kept it as a way to leave a black mark on the family name because . . . she'd been furious with her father for years, furious that he'd had the audacity to leave her — to leave her with a neurotic mother. His leaving had forced Lucetta to abandon the dreams she'd had for her life — his death allowing Susannah the opportunity to marry Nigel.

Truth flowed through Lucetta as she finally accepted the fact that, while she'd loved her father with all her heart, loved his kindness and generosity, she'd hated that on his deathbed he'd made her promise to take care of her mother. He should have known that promise was far too heavy a burden to place on the slim shoulders of a girl not yet out of the schoolroom. He should have known that the promise would set Lucetta up for failure, because Susannah was willful, spoiled, and not easily managed.

"I was supposed to be a belle," she whispered as the drawing room turned completely silent. "I was supposed to go to assemblies, dance cotillion dances I'd spent hours rehearsing, and then be presented at White Sulphur Springs, where I'd officially accept the honor of having the title of *belle* bestowed on me. Gentlemen would flock to win my favor and sign their names on my dance cards.

"But I didn't get to do any of that. I had to make my way to New York on my own, go to work at sixteen years old because the prices the jewelers offered me for Grandmother's jewelry were far too low, and . . . I lived in a slum, in a boardinghouse that . . ." Tears clogged her throat as another thought entered her head, but before she could speak it out loud, Bram was at her side, drawing her close to him, his warmth seeping through the coldness that seemed to have taken root in her very soul.

"You need to remember that your father was a dying man, Lucetta, a dying man who'd never intended to die so early, and . . . he was scared," Bram murmured into her ear.

"I was barely thirteen when he died,"

Lucetta whispered into Bram's chest.

"But he knew you were extraordinary, knew you were capable, and I have to imagine that he was trying to protect you as much as he was trying to protect your mother. He knew that you could manage Plum Hill, even as I'm sure he knew it was a very great burden to give a young girl."

Lucetta felt a light hand rubbing her back and pulled away from Bram to find Millie had joined them. Her friend's eyes were wet with tears, and . . .

Lucetta brought her hand up to cover her heart. "Good heavens, Millie, I must apologize to you. I sounded like a complete shrew just now, complaining about living in the slum and the boardinghouse, when you must realize that living with you and Harriet has been one of the greatest blessings of my life."

Millie dismissed that with a sniff. "Please, I'm not so delicate that I'd get upset about something like that. Besides, as you were speaking, something struck me, something wonderful."

Lucetta tilted her head. "What?"

"If you'd stayed here, if you hadn't run away, you'd have gotten your wish and you would have become a belle, but . . . you would have never been happy leading that life, my dear friend. You would have never been content to be some gentleman's pretty wife, worrying about what dress you were going to wear next or what social function you needed to plan or attend." Millie tossed a nod Susannah's way. "No offense, Mrs. Wolfe."

Susannah frowned. "I'm perfectly content with my life."

"I don't know how you could be, what with your husband obviously lying about pretty much everything to you . . . but we're not going to dwell on that at the moment." Millie turned back to Lucetta. "You've experienced things that most people will never experience. And while you might not realize it, your involvement with Wall Street has opened a door ever so slightly for women to follow in your footsteps." She shook her head. "That's something you'd never have accomplished living down here in the South with gentlemen flocking to add their names to your dance card."

Lucetta blinked through eyes that had turned a bit misty. "I do enjoy playing the market."

"Of course you do."

Her lips curved at the corners. "And I *really* enjoy investing money for others and seeing their nest eggs grow."

Millie narrowed her eyes. "Do you now?"

Lucetta smiled. "Indeed. Take for instance that money Harriet left us before she departed for England with Oliver."

"What about it?"

"Well, if you'll recall, you told me to keep an eye on your share since you were rather distracted throughout the summer with Everett and the children."

"Quite."

"And, well, I'm not comfortable with money simply lying about, not earning any interest or gain, so . . . I invested all the money in the Erie Railroad Company." Her smile turned into a grin. "You'll be pleased to learn that our investment has grown substantially."

"What investments have you made for your mother and me?" Nigel suddenly demanded.

Lucetta lifted her chin. "How is it possible you can even think I owe you anything after that debacle you put me through with Silas Ruff?"

"I certainly couldn't have known that he was deliberately seeking me out in order to get to you."

"No, you couldn't have, but you shouldn't have been gambling, and you certainly shouldn't have thrown the promise of Plum

Hill, and then me, into the pot." Lucetta blew out a breath. "Of course I've made investments for my mother, but those will always be managed by me, and you will never be given access to them, Nigel. All of your needs will be taken care of, within reason, of course, but I will not allow you an opportunity to get your hands on the money that's set aside for my mother."

"It's disrespectful, you treating me, your own stepfather, like this."

Deciding that remark didn't deserve a response, Lucetta turned to her mother. "While there is plenty more I could probably say regarding your finances, the mention of Silas has reminded me why I'm here. Silas is probably on his way to Virginia as we speak, deciding that since he was unsuccessful gaining my cooperation, he'd hurt me by coming after you."

Susannah raised a hand to her chest. "Has no one bothered to let this man know that you and I hardly share a cordial relationship?"

"Probably not, but even though we don't share a close relationship, you are still my mother, and I did still promise Father I'd look after you. So this is me, honoring that promise. You and Nigel should go away for a few weeks — perhaps take a trip to White

Sulphur Springs. It might be a little chilly this time of year, but the hot springs would still be nice to visit."

With her eyes narrowing ever so slightly, Susannah stepped closer to Lucetta, but before she had an opportunity to say another word, Mr. Skukman was charging across the receiving room with his pistol already drawn. "Get down. It's Silas," he yelled before he vanished from sight and the sound of gunfire split the air.

Bram shoved Lucetta to the ground before she had the presence of mind to move, did the same to Millie, and then whipped a pistol out from underneath his jacket and caught Lucetta's eye. "Stay here, stay away from the windows, and don't even think about coming outside." With that, he rushed after Mr. Skukman.

No one spoke a word as time ticked by until Lucetta finally lifted her head and looked around, finding Nigel and Susannah hiding under a table. "And this is where gambling and drinking leads a person," she said with a nod to Nigel before she began edging her way inch by inch toward the door.

"Where are you going?" Millie whispered, although why she was whispering was a bit of a mystery since the sound of yelling, along with a lot of cursing, was flowing into the house.

"I'm not just going to sit here while everyone else is fighting my battle."

She made it all the way to the door, crawling on her stomach, no less, before she was forced to stop when she encountered a pair of shoes. They were nice shoes, a little dusty, and unfortunately, they belonged to none other than Bram.

"You weren't trying to sneak out to help, were you?" he asked, squatting down next to her.

"I might have been."

"There's no need. Silas has been secured."

Lucetta frowned. "He came down here on his own?"

Holding out a hand, Bram helped her to her feet before he smiled. "Apparently, yes. I imagine those women he hired weren't too keen to travel the country with him. Aiding and abetting men on the run usually results in a stint behind bars, and they must have decided he wasn't worth that."

"I need to speak with Silas," Lucetta said quietly.

Instead of arguing with her, Bram nodded and took her arm. With Millie trailing after them, they left Nigel and Susannah cowering underneath the table and walked outside.

The first thing to capture Lucetta's attention was Silas standing on the lawn with his hands tied behind his back. Even captured and secured, the rage pouring out of his eyes and turned her way had the hair standing up on the back of her neck.

"This isn't the end, you know," Silas said as he tried to twist away from Mr. Skukman, who appeared to have a death grip on his arm.

Lucetta lifted her chin. "I'm afraid it is, Silas, because —"

Whatever else she'd been about to say was forgotten when — powered by what could only be described as insanity — Silas let out a howl of fury, broke free of Mr. Skukman's hold, and lunged for her. Bram pushed her out of the way, and as she stumbled and caught her balance by grabbing hold of one of the white pillars that graced the front of the portico, she heard a pistol go off, and then there was silence.

With her heart feeling as if it would beat straight out of her chest, her gaze went immediately to Bram, who was standing still as a statue on the bottom step leading to the cobblestone path, staring at Silas. That man was lying on his stomach, completely motionless as a trickle of blood began seeping out from underneath him.

Glancing behind her, Lucetta found that someone had joined them outside, someone who was holding a smoking pistol in his hand . . . and someone who turned out to be none other than Nigel.

Handing the pistol over to Stanley, who'd raced up on the portico and aimed his pistol Nigel's way — that action probably responsible for Nigel being so cooperative — he lifted his head and caught Lucetta's eye.

"I do hope that my shooting Silas means we're finally squared up, you and me, Lucetta. And since I have taken care of Silas once and for all, at great risk to myself, I must add, I wouldn't be opposed to accepting some type of reward from you . . . a reward that should probably come straight from a bank."

25

Four days later

"I must say, that was one of the most unusual trips I've ever taken," Millie said, holding on to the railing of Bram's steamboat as they chugged their way up the Hudson, drawing closer and closer to Ravenwood.

Lucetta smiled. "The South is always an interesting place to visit, Millie, although we normally don't allow our guests to experience the rudeness of seeing a man shot on our front lawn."

"Your mother did keep making a point to apologize about that," Millie said with a grin. "But since Silas wasn't, well, dead, it's not as if we'll be haunted forever by witnessing him being shot."

"Unusual as this may seem, I was relieved that Nigel hadn't fatally injured Silas," Lucetta added as she inched just a little closer to Bram, enjoying the feel of his hand settled against her back and the fact that his large form was blocking her from some of the wind. "He's an evil man — there's no question about that — but . . . I wouldn't have wanted him dead, no matter his transgressions."

Millie turned and considered Lucetta and Bram for a moment. "You do know that, as your acting chaperone, I'm supposed to insist that the two of you maintain a few inches of separation from each other at all times, and . . . I believe the recommended space to be maintained is six inches."

Lucetta blinked. "Is that an actual chaperoning rule, or one you just made up?"

Frowning, Millie wrinkled her nose. "Abigail told me to enforce that particular rule at all times, but . . ." She gave a sad shake of her head. "I'm afraid I've been negligent in enforcing it, what with all the dangerous situations, arguments between you and your mother that pulled at everyone's heartstrings, except perhaps Nigel's — since I'm not certain he has a heart — and . . . Well, let us not forget the emotional toll returning to Virginia took on you in the first place."

Bram's brows drew together as he caught Millie's eye. "And what does that have to do with you being negligent in your duties?"

"Lucetta needed comforting, of course, and I certainly wasn't going to stand in the way of her getting that comfort from you."

As Bram and Millie continued bantering, Lucetta couldn't help but think that Millie was exactly right. She *had* been emotionally exhausted throughout the time they'd spent in Virginia, coming to terms with her anger at her father, and coming to terms with the animosity she'd been holding for far too long against her mother. Bram had been a rock beside her through everything, and . . . oddly enough, she had not been opposed to the idea of leaning on that rock, nor had she been embarrassed that she'd needed his strength to soothe her when she felt a little overwhelmed, and . . .

". . . so don't despair about your chaperoning abilities," Bram was saying, tugging Lucetta straight back to the conversation at hand. "Since I'm fairly certain the six-inch rule isn't a real rule, you've not failed as a chaperone just yet."

"I'm hoping I'm never called upon to chaperone again," Millie said with an exaggerated sigh. "It's far more difficult than I ever imagined, and definitely not for the faint of heart. Although . . . for the most part, you and Lucetta didn't cause me too many difficulties."

Lucetta leaned forward, catching a gust of wind in her face as she did so. "What are you going to do when Elizabeth and Rose come of age?"

"Since I highly doubt Everett will ever allow any gentleman to court our darling girls, my services as chaperone will not be required."

Lucetta placed her hand over Millie's on the railing. "Speaking of Everett, please tell him when you return to Boston how sorry I am for keeping you away from him and the children. I'm sure they weren't expecting you to be away for so long."

Millie brushed that aside. "Don't be silly, Lucetta. Everett expected me to stay for as long as it took to see you found and firmly on your way to recovering from your ordeal. That we had to journey to Virginia to do that, well, I got the added pleasure of meeting your mother and . . . Nigel. I was also privy to a thrilling tale, one where madness ruled the day, until that madness was struck down by a bullet, and good persevered over evil."

Bram laughed and shook his head. "I'm going to send you an advanced copy of my next book, Millie, with just what you said inscribed inside, because you really do have a way with words."

Millie beamed a bright smile Bram's way. "That's high praise indeed coming from such an esteemed author. I'd absolutely adore getting an early copy of your next book, especially if you could perhaps add a character in it who . . . enjoys dictionaries and learning new words, but can solve mysteries as well." She smiled and sent him a nod. "You could name that character Mildred, but you and I would know it's really me."

Tilting his head, Bram seemed to consider that for a few seconds. "Do you think a lot of people are going to expect me to create characters written with them in mind now that I'm doffing my anonymous cloak?"

"Most assuredly," Millie said with a nod. "And *assuredly* means undoubtedly and . . . wouldn't that be a clever bit to add into one of your stories — a character who throws out random meanings of words every now and again."

Bram's lips twitched just a touch. "Maybe I *should* have remained anonymous."

Lucetta shook her head. "You know full well that it was past time for you to come out in the open. And by admitting the truth, there are no more secrets, for either of us." She smiled. "That means we're able to discontinue playing the parts we've been playing for far too long and begin living our lives as they were meant to be lived — you as an author, and me as . . . well, I haven't figured that out exactly yet, but I have a few ideas in mind."

Bram smiled. "I have to hope that I figure in somewhere with those few ideas, but . . ." He nodded to the shoreline. "We're almost to Ravenwood, so now is hardly the time to discuss such matters."

Knowing he was right but finding herself unable to keep from smiling at the idea of having Bram Haverstein as part of her future plans — although what part he would play in her life it was certainly too soon to tell — Lucetta set her sights on the shore, anxious to see Ravenwood from the vantage point of the Hudson.

"Do you think it's a little worrisome that Abigail didn't wait for us in the city, but traveled to Ravenwood with everyone before we were able to return to New York?" Millie suddenly asked.

"I can't imagine something else of a troubling nature could have occurred," Lucetta said with a smile. "I mean, we've had enough chaos to last us for at least a few years to come."

"We ladies of the tenement slum area have certainly seen our share of troubling adventures lately," Millie said, returning Lucetta's smile.

"Which just goes to show that our struggles in life made us incredibly resilient, something I'm sure we'll find —" The rest of what Lucetta had been about to say got lost as a cannon blasted away, sending a flock of ravens flying up out of the trees and straight over the steamboat.

"Goodness, and here I was just about to completely relax my guard," Millie said, ducking her head, with a hand to her chest.

"Curious as this may sound, cannon fire is just a normal way of life at Ravenwood," Lucetta said. "And wait until you meet Geoffrey the goat. Although . . . we might need to borrow some pants from Bram's staff. I've been thinking that Geoffrey might not attack me if I'm wearing trousers, and . . ." She released a sigh. "I do miss the days of living in our boardinghouse when I could practice my lines while experiencing the freedom of trousers without anyone thinking a thing about it."

"The only time I saw you wearing trousers was when you were impersonating a coachman," Bram said slowly.

"Have you seen her when her hair looks like a rat's nest because she's braided it at least a thousand times while she's distracted with her lines or . . . investments?" Millie asked.

To Lucetta's surprise, instead of seeming taken aback by the idea she wasn't always very concerned about her appearance, Bram was watching her now with what looked like clear delight in his eyes.

"I'll see what I can do to find you and Millie some trousers, if you really think that will help you mend fences with Geoffrey." Bram nodded toward shore. "Ernie's come to greet us, which means they all made it back to New York safe and sound."

"I was hoping Miss Haverstein would come down to meet the steamboat."

Turning, Lucetta discovered that Mr. Skukman had now joined them on deck. He had fallen asleep in an uncomfortable-looking chair in an inside hallway, the events of the past month apparently having caught up with him.

Bram eyed the man for a long moment before he frowned. "Forgive me, Mr. Skukman, because I'm fairly sure I should have asked this before now, but . . . what *is* your interest in my sister?"

Mr. Skukman barely blinked. "That almost sounds as if you're asking me what my intentions are."

"Perhaps I am."

"Hmm . . . that'll depend on Miss Haver-stein, I suppose" was all Mr. Skukman said before he sent Lucetta the barest hint of a wink and walked over to where some crew members were getting ready to throw Ernie a rope.

Millie moved closer to Bram. "Do you think your mother would object to Mr. Skukman showing a profound interest in your sister?"

"My mother has surprised me of late regarding many things, so no . . . I don't think she'd mind, especially since my father is planning on settling a large dowry on Ruby, which means they wouldn't have to live a frugal life."

Lucetta rolled her eyes. "I've been managing Mr. Skukman's money for years. Allow me to say that he has no need to live frugally and would certainly be offended if you were to bring up Ruby's dowry. In fact, I imagine Ruby would be offended as well if you brought it up in conversation with Mr. Skukman."

"That's actually rather sound advice, which means I won't mention Ruby's dowry again." He smiled. "I certainly don't want to annoy her further, especially with all the animosity she was tossing my way before we left for Virginia."

Lucetta returned the smile. "I'm sure she's gotten over the fact you're Mr. Grimstone, especially since I don't believe she was really settled on the plan of seeking him out and having him escort her around town in the first place."

"Let us hope you're right about that." Taking hold of Lucetta's hand and offering Millie an arm, Bram walked with them to where Ernie was securing the boat to the dock. Handing Millie over to Mr. Skukman, Bram helped Lucetta off the steamboat and then, with the dock swaying back and forth beneath their feet, they walked to shore.

"Good to have you back, sir," Ernie said with a nod to Bram. "Did you have a pleasant journey?"

"Pleasant enough, but it's wonderful to be home. Although . . . I wasn't expecting to be greeted with the blast of a cannon. May I assume that was Mr. Macmillan's way of welcoming us back?"

Ernie shook his head. "I'm afraid not, Mr. Haverstein. That's Mr. Addleshaw up on the tower with, uh, well, I don't want to ruin the surprise. As for Mr. and Mrs. Macmillan, well, there's been a bit of a situation happening here at Ravenwood with them, a situation that Tilda uncovered after she returned from the city and we were off to

Virginia. Tilda wasn't certain which way to turn with all of us gone, so she ended up sending a telegram to Mrs. Hart.

"Your grandmother, being a take-charge type of lady, stuffed everyone who was staying at her home in Washington Square into a few carriages, and they arrived here a few hours after receiving Tilda's telegram."

"And it's been quite dramatic ever since."

Looking up, Lucetta found none other than Harriet Peabody — or rather, Mrs. Oliver Addleshaw now — standing a few feet away from her.

The mere sight of Harriet took Lucetta completely aback, especially since her very good friend — having only recently discovered she was the long-lost daughter of a duke, of all things — was supposed to be in London, becoming better acquainted with a family she'd never known she had.

Letting out a small shriek, Lucetta bolted forward, soon finding herself wrapped in Harriet's embrace. A second later, Millie nudged her way into the embrace as well, and Lucetta couldn't help but think that her world had turned quite lovely. Stepping back, she grinned at her friends.

"This is an absolutely marvelous surprise, Harriet, but I wasn't expecting to see you until closer to Christmas."

"Oliver and I weren't planning on coming back until then, but I missed the States — missed you two, of course — and . . . it's a good thing we did come back early." Harriet's eyes narrowed. "I could not believe my ears when we showed up at Abigail's brownstone and learned that Silas Ruff was back on the scene." She caught Lucetta's eye. "He's truly been dealt with once and for all?"

"I do believe he has, but . . . did I hear you mention something about a dramatic situation?"

"Unfortunately, you did. However . . ." Harriet nodded to where Bram was standing a few feet away, pretending an interest in the river obviously to allow Lucetta an opportunity to reunite with her friend without interference. "Do not tell me *that* is Bram Haverstein?"

"Indeed it is," Lucetta said, wincing ever so slightly when even she detected the large dollop of . . . something . . . in her tone — something that sounded almost like satisfaction, and something that had both Harriet and Millie looking at her rather knowingly.

Pretending not to notice their knowing looks, she gestured Bram forward. Taking hold of his hand, she took a second to perform introductions.

After the expected pleasantries had been exchanged, she nodded Harriet's way. "So . . . the disastrous situation?"

As everyone began moving toward a narrow path that led up to Ravenwood, Harriet blew out a breath. "Well, I'm not certain of all the particulars, mind you, but we'll need to travel straightaway to the dungeon so that Bram can assess the situation."

Bram stopped moving. "Why do we need to go to the dungeon?"

"Because that's where everyone decided Mr. and Mrs. Macmillan should be held until you got back to Ravenwood, of course."

26

Walking through the great hall of Raven-wood, Bram didn't quite know what to think about all the suits of armor scattered about here and there, the furniture turned on end, or the paintings that had been taken off the wall and were now littering the floor.

"What in the world do you think they were searching for?" Lucetta asked slowly, as Harriet hurried away from them to find her husband, Oliver, and notify him and Archi-bald that everyone had returned to the cas-tle.

"I have no idea, but . . . I have the most curious feeling we're about to discover why everyone believes Ravenwood's haunted," Bram returned.

"I wonder if they were behind Geoffrey getting into the tower room." Lucetta said right as Millie stopped dead in her tracks and let out a gasp.

"Good heavens. Would you look at what

someone has done to the library?" With that, Millie plowed into the library, stepping over books that were lying higgledy-piggledy about, and immediately started tidying up, muttering something about depraved people as she did so.

"I don't think we should encourage her to join us down in the dungeon just yet," Lucetta whispered. "Millie's a charming sort, unless she's . . ." Lucetta nodded back to Millie, who was now red in the face and muttering faster than ever under her breath, looking quite menacing for such a wisp of a lady.

"I think you may be right." Bram took Lucetta's arm, and with Mr. Skukman trailing behind them, they moved through the castle and into the kitchen, finding Iris and Abigail sitting at the kitchen table, of all places, drinking cups of tea and chatting away as if they had not experienced a thirty-year estrangement.

"Ah, there you are," Abigail said, rising to her feet. "We thought the cannon blasting off might have been because you'd returned. Although . . ." She grinned. "Archibald and Oliver have been having far too much fun with the whole cannon-blasting-off business. They apparently have been holding contests to see how far the balls will go."

448

Her grin widened. "I'm fairly certain Oliver will want to speak with you, Bram, regarding selling him one of your cannons, but if you'd like to stay in Harriet's good graces, I'm going to suggest you tell him they're not for sale."

Giving his grandmother a kiss on the cheek, and then one on his mother's cheek, Bram frowned. "Where's Ruby?"

"She's waiting for you down by the dungeon," Iris said.

Bram tilted his head. "Is she still refusing to acknowledge that I'm her brother?"

"Goodness no," Iris said. "Ruby's never been one to hold a grudge, and she wasn't that determined to become acquainted with Mr. Grimstone in the first place. It was just a poorly thought-out plan of hers to get back at Geoffrey Jensen, but . . . she's since moved on, or at least that's what she told me."

"What do you mean she's moved on?" Mr. Skukman asked, stepping forward and looking rather frightening as his face darkened.

Iris, Bram noticed, didn't seem intimidated by the man at all as she arched a brow Mr. Skukman's way. "My mother and I took Ruby to a few society events while we were still in the city, and . . . well, I'm not exactly certain what happened, but Ruby has since decided she does not care for society gentlemen much at all, but prefers the more strong and . . . silent type."

Mr. Skukman blinked, blinked again, smiled, and then headed immediately through the door that led down to the dungeon.

"I didn't know he knew how to smile," Abigail said to no one in particular.

Leaving Iris and Abigail discussing the benefits of Ruby apparently being interested in a strong, yet practically mute type, Bram led the way down the narrow steps with Lucetta right behind him. Reaching the hallway that led to the dungeon, he found Ruby engaged in an actual conversation with Mr. Skukman, that gentleman once again smiling at something Ruby was saying.

"Bram," Ruby exclaimed as she looked up, hurrying over to give him a hug, her animosity with him evidently a thing of the past. "Can you believe the mess the Macmillans made throughout the castle?"

"Do you know why they made it?" he countered.

Ruby shook her head. "They won't answer any questions, and believe me, Tilda, Stanley, and Ernie have been badgering them endlessly."

"Would you like me to have a word with them, Mr. Haverstein?" Mr. Skukman asked even as he gave a single crack of his knuckles.

"Thank you, but no, not unless they refuse to talk to me."

"Very good, sir. Would you like Miss Haverstein and me to wait out here while you question the criminals?" Mr. Skukman sent him a rather innocent look, one at complete odds with his intimidating appearance.

Biting back a grin, Bram inclined his head. "That might be for the best, Mr. Skukman. We wouldn't want to overwhelm our criminals, would we?"

"Off you go, then," Ruby said, waving Bram and Lucetta away right before she moved closer to Mr. Skukman and they immediately returned to whatever conversation they'd been having before Bram had interrupted them, a conversation that seemed to concern . . . favorite poems by Lord Byron from the sound of things.

"They may just be a match made in heaven after all," Lucetta said under her breath as she took him firmly by the arm and practically pulled him into the dungeon and away from his sister.

What he found in that dungeon had him coming to an immediate stop.

Mrs. Macmillan was sitting on the torture rack, a chain attached to her ankle, while Mr. Macmillan was sitting on the floor, leaning up against a wall with his arm shackled to a bolt a little above his head. Stanley was pacing back and forth in front of them, looking disgusted, while Tilda sat at Bram's desk, her feet propped up on it as she twiddled her thumbs. Sending her a smile when she caught sight of him, Bram waved Tilda back in the chair when she jumped to her feet before he proceeded across the dungeon and stopped directly in front of Mrs. Macmillan.

"Would you care to tell me why you and Mr. Macmillan felt compelled to tear apart my castle while I was away?" he asked, seeing no point in beating around the bush. "As my housekeeper, I would have thought making such a disaster of the place you were entrusted to maintain would go against your very nature."

Mrs. Macmillan took him by complete surprise when she actually opened her mouth. "I'm not a housekeeper."

Pulling a hardback chair right up next to her, Bram took a seat. "Which explains a lot, but . . . why have you been masquerading as one, and for quite some time, from what I understand?"

Mrs. Macmillan exchanged a look with Mr. Macmillan and then blew out a breath. "If I tell you the truth, will you let me and Mr. Macmillan go?"

"I'm not certain. It depends on what you've done."

"We haven't really done anything yet, except make a bit of a mess in the castle."

Tilda let out a snort. "A bit of a mess? It's a good thing I came back from New York City when I did or Ravenwood might not still be standing."

Mrs. Macmillan ignored her. Keeping her attention centered on Bram, she released a sigh. "Oh, very well, if you must know . . ." She drew in a deep breath, released it, drew in another, and continued rapidly. "Mr. Macmillan and I were hired by the lover of Ravenwood's previous mistress, Mrs. Woodward, to recover a large collection of diamonds he'd given to her — and a collection Mrs. Woodward would not give back after she severed ties with him."

Bram blinked. "What?"

Waving her free hand in the air, Mrs. Macmillan shook her head. "I know, it's a rather torrid tale, but that's why we came to Ravenwood to work for the Woodwards. However, Mrs. Woodward had hidden the diamonds, you see, obviously wanting to keep them from being discovered by her husband. When we learned that, we had to alter our plan, which is how it came about that Ravenwood suddenly took to being . . . haunted."

"We needed everyone to think ghosts were strolling about so that no one questioned the noise we were making at night," Mr. Macmillan added before he heaved a heavy sigh. "We just didn't realize that Mrs. Woodward would start suffering from a nervous condition due to all the ghostly encounters she thought she was experiencing. That had her moving the diamonds on a regular basis. But the poor dear, well, she eventually forgot where she'd hidden them because she kept them split up, not hidden all together."

"So you're still working on behalf of this . . . lover?" Lucetta asked, stepping forward.

Mrs. Macmillan shook her head. "No, when the Woodwards left Ravenwood, Mrs. Woodward's lover decided it was time to move on. Since he's one of those industrialists, he has more money than he knows what to do with, so recovering the diamonds had only been a matter of principle for him."

She nodded, just once. "We're working for Mrs. Woodward now. She approached us right before they moved out, asked if we'd like to earn a bit of extra money every month with the promise of a bonus if we found her jewels. Well, it was too good of an offer to pass up, so . . . here we are. But she's decided she's getting tired of waiting so gave us until the end of this week to find the diamonds or she's bringing someone else in."

"I think I'll be having a few words with Mrs. Woodward about that," Bram said. "But tell me, did you end up finding the diamonds?"

Mrs. Macmillan smiled. "Well, Mr. Skukman actually found the first of them, when he pulled that necklace out of the fireplace, and then we found the rest of them right before Tilda called everyone back from New York." Her smile faded. "Mrs. Woodward had stashed the majority of her collection in the hems of numerous tapestries hanging on the walls, the absolute last place we thought to look." She gave a snort of clear disgust. "One only had to notice the way they weren't hanging like the rest of the tapestries to realize something was amiss."

"That might have been where having experience as a real housekeeper would have come in handy," Tilda pointed out. "Real housekeepers, you see, have the tapestries beaten and cleaned every so often."

"Perhaps it's time for you to change positions yet again, Tilda, taking over a role I do believe will be available immediately — that being the housekeeper role," Bram said with a nod Tilda's way, earning a delighted grin and a nod back from Tilda in response.

Mrs. Macmillan completely ignored all that as she caught Bram's eye. "What are you going to do with us?"

"Well, I suppose I'll have you return Mrs. Woodward's diamonds to her first."

"You don't think the diamonds should go back to the lover?" Tilda asked.

Bram shook his head. "No, he apparently gave them to Mrs. Woodward, and even though she was not behaving in a respectable manner, a gentleman should never try to retrieve a gift he's given a lady."

Clearing his throat, Mr. Macmillan shifted a little on the ground, the shifting causing his chains to rattle. "We never considered keeping the diamonds for ourselves. I think that needs to be made clear."

"Oddly enough, Mr. Macmillan, I actually believe you," Bram said. "Clearly I have been a little too trusting when it comes to you and your wife. However, since no real harm *has* been done, although you have scared a lot of people during your service here at Ravenwood, I'll let you go on your way after the diamonds have been returned. I'll even make certain Mrs. Woodward honors her promise to you and pays you your bonus. But, I would appreciate it if you'd extend everyone at Ravenwood an apology, especially Miss Plum, who got chased by Geoffrey and scared by a suit of armor, two circumstances that I'm going to assume you were responsible for."

"We are sorry, Miss Plum, especially about Geoffrey," Mrs. Macmillan said with a nod Lucetta's way. "I, for one, remember full well what it feels like to be chased by that beast, which is actually why we chose him to bring up to your room. We thought that type of fright, the type I experienced when Geoffrey chased me, would be enough to send you packing, so we could finish searching the tower room."

"How did you get him up there?" Lucetta asked.

Mrs. Macmillan smiled. "Through the secret passageway that can be accessed from the hidden door in the bookcase, or through stones that move in the stairwell. There's a hidden lever in the bookcase behind the third book on the top shelf, and there's another lever behind one of the gas sconces on the wall of the stairs."

"I knew there were secret passageways."

"That's how I was able to duck out of sight when I was wearing the armor," Mr. Macmillan said. "Mrs. Macmillan is the one who closed the door for me and locked you in the room, while I crashed my way into the secret passageway, then stood as still as a statue until I heard you run down the stairs."

"Where Mrs. Macmillan then lured me out of the castle and locked me out of that as well?" Lucetta finished for him with an arch of a brow Mrs. Macmillan's way.

Mrs. Macmillan's only response was a weak smile.

"Did you also set the dogs on me when I first arrived at the castle?" Lucetta continued.

"That was Ernie," Stanley said. "He'd dashed off while I was going to stop Mr. Macmillan from blasting off the cannon, having come to the belief that Mr. Haverstein hadn't quite realized how much of a threat you and Mrs. Hart posed. Not that you actually turned out to pose a threat, mind you, but with all the other lady shenanigans we'd been experiencing, well . . ." He smiled. "I do believe Ernie has been meaning to apologize about the dog incident, but again, what with all the other shenanigans going on over the past few weeks, I'm afraid he hasn't gotten around to it quite yet."

"Speaking of shenanigans, though," Bram said with a glance Mrs. Macmillan's way. "Why *were* we experiencing so many shenanigans of the lady sort?"

"Mr. and Mrs. Macmillan needed to search the castle more thoroughly, of course," Tilda said before Mrs. Macmillan could answer. "And with you being a writer and all, you were here all the time, so they were trying to drive you away from Ravenwood as well."

Catching Mrs. Macmillan's eye, Bram quirked a brow. "Is that true?"

"Are you still going to let us go if I admit that it is?"

Realizing that he'd been a bit of an idiot, but knowing full well he would not stop bringing in questionable sorts to work at Ravenwood, even if Mr. and Mrs. Macmillan had let him down, Bram rose to his feet. "Of course you're still free to go. And while I'm certainly not in agreement with your actions over the past year or so, do know that I wish you and your husband all the best." With that, Bram left Tilda to get Mr. and Mrs. Macmillan undone, taking Lucetta's arm and walking with her out of the dungeon.

Ruby and Mr. Skukman met him directly outside the door.

"That was a bit anticlimactic," Ruby remarked, taking the arm Mr. Skukman offered her. "We heard everything, and honestly . . . I'm not certain I would have been so forgiving, Bram."

"Life is far too short to hold on to grievances that don't really matter," he said.

Mr. Skukman sent him an approving sort of nod. "Well said, Mr. Haverstein, very well said indeed." With that, he vanished with Ruby up the stairs, leaving Bram alone with Lucetta.

She smiled at him. "I do believe we've just had all of the remaining mysteries solved, although I quite agree with Ruby. It was a little anticlimactic, and not a single gasp-worthy moment was to be had as Mr. and Mrs. Macmillan told their story." Her smile suddenly faded just a touch. "I wonder what the future has in store for the two of them."

Lucetta's mention of the future had Bram pausing for a moment, realizing that with all the insanity of the past week or so, they'd not had much time to talk about anything, let alone what either of *them* wanted for the future.

"Even though I was disappointed with the

explanation behind the supposed ghosts at Ravenwood, you have to admit that some of what Mrs. Macmillan told you would make good fodder for a new book," Lucetta continued, pulling him from his thoughts. "Readers would especially like the part about a hidden treasure, although, in my humble opinion, the hero should get caught trying to find it and . . ."

As Lucetta continued musing about different plot points, it suddenly hit him how absolutely wonderful life would be if he could spend it with the amazing lady standing right next to him. That she was beautiful, there could be no doubt, but her true beauty wasn't physical in nature, it was soul-deep — seen in the way she treated her friends, animals, and even a mother who'd brushed her aside for a man who was less than worthy.

She'd been through so much, and yet, here she was, contemplating his work and what could help him, and . . . he wanted to give her a spectacular gesture, something that would show her exactly how special he found her.

She'd been on her own for far too long, and during that time, she'd decided she didn't need anyone else, or rather, she *wouldn't* need anyone because that could cause her pain — pain she'd experienced when her father had left her, and then when her mother had done the same thing by choosing Nigel.

". . . and I know that you seem to be keen on the whole pirate idea, but really, Bram, if you'd create a hero who is more on the intelligent side, less on the race to the rescue of the damsel in distress side, well, I mean, I'm no author, but . . ."

As she stopped for just a second to gulp in a breath of air, and then immediately launched back into a conversation she didn't seem to realize he wasn't participating in, Bram got the most intriguing and romantic idea he'd ever imagined.

Taking a single step closer to Lucetta, he leaned down and kissed her still-moving lips. When she finally stopped talking and let out the smallest of sighs, he deepened the kiss, reluctantly pulling away from her a moment later.

"I know this is going to seem rather peculiar," he began. "But I need to go to work right this very minute."

"Work?" she repeated faintly.

"Indeed, and I do hope you won't get too annoyed by this, but I need to get started straightaway, which means you might want to go back to the theater so that you don't get bored."

"You want me gone from Ravenwood?" she asked in a voice that had gone from faint to irritated in less than a second.

"I don't know if I'd put it quite like that, but I might be able to work faster without you around." He sent her a smile, kissed her again, but when he started getting too distracted with the softness of her lips, pulled back, kissed the tip of her nose, and then . . . after telling her he'd see her before too long, headed straight back into his dungeon.

27

One week after leaving Ravenwood —
without speaking to Bram since he'd disappeared into his dungeon and had not
come out, much to Lucetta's annoyance —
she leaned closer to the vanity mirror in her
dressing room, smoothing her eyebrow with
a small comb.

"Are you glad to be back?"

Looking up, she found Millie's reflection
in the mirror. "My first reaction is to say
yes, but . . . I'm not sure that's the full
truth. I've been through so much of late,
and now, with all my secrets out, and after
seeing how much Bram has done to help
people from the tenements, I've actually
been considering leaving the theater to do
something else, something . . . meaningful."

"You do something meaningful when you
take to the stage, Lucetta," Harriet said as
she slipped into the dressing room and
moved to stand beside Millie. "You give

people an evening of escape, and that's not something many people can claim."

Lucetta picked up a puff and began to powder her nose. "I don't think I'd leave theater for good, perhaps teach others how to act, but . . . I've been tossing around the idea of helping those in need learn how to make investments — showing them how to take a little money and grow it into something more."

"That's a wonderful idea," Harriet said. "And an idea I imagine Bram would be interested in helping you with, especially since he has so many contacts in the tenements."

"It would be difficult to know at this particular moment what Bram would be interested in since he's made himself so annoyingly scarce."

"And I'm sure he has a perfectly reasonable explanation for that," Harriet said as Lucetta saw her exchange a glance with Millie in the reflection of the mirror, one that clearly said neither one of her friends had any idea what to make of the Bram situation either.

"However," Millie said, lifting her chin, "now is hardly the moment to stew about Bram, especially since you have a full house waiting for you." She smiled weakly. "Apparently society learned that you'll be on stage tonight, not your understudy, so . . . there's not an empty seat or box to be had."

Harriet shook her head. "Society also has learned Oliver and I have returned to town, and they've taken to fawning." She shuddered. "I don't care for fawning in the least, but at least we're sitting in Abigail's box, which does provide a little protection from all but the most zealous of society."

"That's what happens when a real aristocrat comes back to town," Millie said with a wink to Harriet, who simply rolled her eyes. "But speaking of Abigail's box," Millie continued, "we really should go rejoin the others and let you, my dear friend, finish getting ready for your performance." She stepped up and gave Lucetta's cheek a kiss right as someone knocked on her dressing room door, signaling that she had ten minutes until curtain.

Rising to her feet, Lucetta walked Millie and Harriet to the door, kissing Harriet's cheek before she smiled. "Shall we plan on traveling to Delmonico's after the show to enjoy a late dinner?"

"You do remember that I almost burned that place down, don't you?" Harriet asked.

"Which is why I suggested going there, so you can redeem yourself."

Opening the door even as Harriet muttered something about not knowing if they'd let her back in Delmonico's, Lucetta watched her friends walk away as Mr. Skukman stepped forward and followed her back into the dressing room.

"Glad to be back, Miss Plum?" he asked, taking up his usual stance by the door so that he could walk with her to the stage, making sure her admirers didn't have an opportunity to get too close to her.

"I'm not certain about that, Mr. Skukman. I love taking to the stage, but . . . have you ever felt as if you might have moved . . . on from something?"

He smiled an honest-to-goodness smile. "I have, and" — he leaned forward and lowered his voice — "do know that I'll be more than happy to assist you if you decide to move on into work for the poor souls in the tenements. You can help them with investments, I can make sure order is maintained, and Miss Ruby, well, I bet her financial knowledge could be put to good use too, if we'd ask her to join us."

"Ah, so that's going well, is it?"

"She's delightful, and . . . appreciates poems written by Lord Byron."

Lucetta grinned. "She's a keeper — that's for certain."

467

Slipping on the high heels she always saved for last, Lucetta drew in a deep breath and nodded, the nod having Mr. Skukman opening the door for her and then walking with her to the back of the stage. Taking up his position stage right, he sent her a nod as she strode onto the stage just as the curtain began to rise.

Drawing in another breath, she blew it out, straightened her shoulders, and became, much to the delight of the audience now cheering as they caught sight of her, Serena Seamore, the lady in the tower.

Summoning up the lines she hadn't seen or spoken for several weeks, she threw herself into the character she'd been entrusted to play, a character she now knew Bram had created specifically for her. Even though he'd done so to make certain she'd have a steady income, when she'd actually needed nothing of the sort, the knowledge that Bram had sat at his desk, in his slightly disturbing dungeon, and typed out the words she was now saying, humbled her.

Just a few weeks earlier she'd been annoyed by his assumption that she'd needed anyone to take care of her. Why her attitude about that had changed, she couldn't really say, although she was fairly certain it was one of those life-altering epiphanies — an epiphany orchestrated by God, no doubt, and one she knew she'd been blessed to receive. However, since she was currently on stage, and with a full house watching her, she tucked all thoughts of epiphanies aside, to be brought out again at a more leisurely time, and concentrated on her performance.

By the time she reached the third act, she *was* her character, but as she turned to speak lines to one of her fellow actors, she stopped dead in her tracks because that actor was nowhere in sight, replaced with, of all things, a . . . strange-looking contraption being wheeled out on the stage, a contraption that had . . . She blinked and then blinked again.

A man was hanging from what was apparently a ceiling — by his feet, no less — and that man just happened to be . . . Bram.

The theater went completely silent, at least for a second, and then Lucetta heard the distinct sound of ladies sighing, and she couldn't say she blamed them.

Bram Haverstein, even hanging upside down and turning quite red in the face because of the whole hanging business, was a very handsome gentleman.

Blinking out of those ridiculous thoughts because she finally remembered she was standing on a stage with hundreds of people watching her, she summoned up a smile even as she wondered what she was supposed to do.

"You seem to be in a bit of a pickle" was all she could think to say, her words causing Bram to release an honest-to-goodness snort.

"Script," he called.

Before Lucetta could voice a protest, because she'd never, as in ever, had to have someone bring her a script or feed her lines during a performance — the debacle with Miss Dunlap certainly didn't count — Mr. Skukman came strolling across the stage. He thrust a script into her hands a second later, not even bothering to hide a grin as he turned and strolled away.

Glancing at the first page, she brought it closer to her face, the words settled in her mind, and she nodded, just once.

"If you'll just hold tight, sir, I'll get you down," she said even as the thought struck that she had no idea how she'd go about pretending to cut him down when she couldn't reach his feet since they were tied up rather high, and . . . she had nothing at hand to use to cut him down with.

She'd barely finished that thought when Ruby, with Mr. Skukman, trotted across the stage with a ladder and set it up for her. Before they walked away, Mr. Skukman handed her a knife, although she didn't miss the fact that he sent upside-down Bram a wary look, as if to question the saneness of that particular part of the plot.

"You're supposed to climb up here," Bram said, sounding a little winded.

"That direction isn't written in the script," she returned.

"I know, but if you don't climb up here, you won't be able to rescue me."

Taking hold of the ladder, she began to climb, stopping when she got to eye level with him. That, however, turned out to be a mistake, because the moment her eyes met his, she forgot everything — even the lines she'd just committed to memory — because nothing else mattered to her except . . . him.

"You wrote a scene with a strong heroine in it, and one where the hero gets dangled by his feet."

"I did."

"Why?"

"Because I couldn't figure out a better way to let you know I love you, the real you, without dangling from my feet and letting you cut me down."

Lucetta's eyes immediately took to turning a little misty. "You . . . love me?"

471

"I do, but before we continue this, I have to admit that hanging upside down is far less pleasant than I imagined, so if you'd be so kind, I really do need you to get me down from here."

Realizing he was completely serious, but also realizing if she cut him down he'd go plummeting to the hard floor and most likely suffer a horrible injury — which certainly wouldn't have the night turning out well at all — Lucetta looked to the side of the stage and caught Mr. Skukman's eye.

As he, along with a good number of backstage hands, walked across the boards, whispers began circulating around the theater, growing louder after Bram got released and rose to his feet. Smiling ever so charmingly at the audience, he presented them with a small bow right before he took center stage.

"Ladies and gentlemen, I must beg your indulgence for just a few more minutes because you see . . . I am . . . Mr. Grimstone."

The whispers ceased immediately.

Bram smiled. "I'm Mr. Grimstone, alias Mr. Bram Haverstein, and I've come here tonight, with all of you as my witnesses, to proclaim my love for Miss Lucetta Plum, and . . ." He dropped to one knee. "Ask her to do me the very great honor of becoming my wife." He reached out and took hold of Lucetta's hand.

"Miss Lucetta Plum, I am completely and irrevocably in love with you, and just so we're clear, I'm in love with the real you, not the person you turn into when you take to the stage. I love the idea that you're completely oblivious to your unusual beauty, can outrun a goat, and . . . you fascinate me as no one ever has. I'm asking you, in front of all of these people who will probably never buy another one of my books again *if* you turn me down . . ." He stopped talking and turned his head to the audience. "And just to remind everyone, I will have another novel releasing soon, although I haven't decided on a title just yet, something about a strong-willed lady, no doubt, or . . ."

"You're getting distracted," Lucetta interrupted.

Bram immediately returned his gaze to hers. "Quite right, but . . . I've lost my train of thought."

"You were just about to the part where you were going to ask her to marry you," a voice called out, a voice that sounded remarkably like Abigail's.

"Thank you, Grandmother," he called back.

"You're welcome, darling. And just to remind you, I'm not getting any younger, so you might want to hurry this proposal business along."

Grinning, Bram shook his head, brought Lucetta's fingers to his lips, and then sobered as he held her gaze.

"I love you, Lucetta, more than I ever imagined I could, and I would be so incredibly honored if you'd agree to be my wife."

For a second, Lucetta was unable to answer him because her heart had taken to rising in her throat, but after drawing in a deep breath, she managed to nod, ignoring the tears that had filled her eyes and were blurring her vision.

"I would be honored to become your wife, especially since — I'm not sure when this happened, but — I'm in love with you as well."

Bram's hold on her hand tightened for just a second, and then he was sliding a ring on her finger she hadn't even realized he'd been holding. Before she could take even a second to admire what felt like an enormous rock on her hand, he was standing instead of kneeling, looking intently into her eyes, before he pulled her into his arms and kissed her.

The entire theater faded away, as did the whispers, titters, and if she wasn't much mistaken, applause, as Bram continued kissing her before he drew back, cupped her face with his hands, and smiled. It was a wonderful smile, filled with love, hope, and maybe even, a dash of naughtiness and danger.

"That'll keep everyone talking for a while," he said with a wink.

"I'm sure it will, and . . . now that we've gotten ourselves engaged, I, my soon-to-be husband, have a scene to finish."

Bram turned his head and whistled, the whistle resulting in Sweet Pea being led onto the stage, pulling her pony cart.

"That's why I brought a horse."

"Sweet Pea is a mule, but even if she was a horse, there's not a horse in *The Lady of the Tower* — which you know since you penned the play."

"True, but I brought Sweet Pea along because of the scene in my new novel, the scene where you cut me down, then hoist me over your horse's back, and then we go galloping off into the night."

"I'm not sure if a heroine will actually have the strength needed to hoist the hero onto a horse, and . . . again, you brought

Sweet Pea and a pony cart, so . . . I'm not exactly certain how I should proceed."

"I tried to bring Storm, but Ernie pointed out that if Storm doesn't like graveyards he probably wouldn't like the theater, and that's when Ernie offered to loan me Sweet Pea, and . . . maybe I should just climb in the cart and you can join me." With that, Bram took hold of her hand, stepped into the pony cart, pulled her in after him, and pulled her onto his lap as he settled against the seat. Picking up the reins, he gave them a flick, and Sweet Pea was off, prancing as she was wont to do across the stage, down the ramp, and straight out the back door that Mr. Skukman was already holding open for them.

As they rode away into the night, with Bram's arms wrapped tightly around her, Lucetta realized that Abigail had been right all along.

Bram was perfect for her in every way, and it was clear to her now that God, in His infinite wisdom and even with her being less than attentive to Him, had steered her exactly where she needed to be steered, allowing her to reconcile with her past and set aside the hurts from that past, in order to finally accept the love of a fine gentleman, a gentleman who only expected her to play the part she'd been born to play — the part of her true self.

EPILOGUE

December 1882

Reverend Gilmore looked out over his congregation, all of them dressed in their Sunday best, or rather, all of them dressed in a manner befitting a wedding.

The flowers of choice weren't flowers at all, but poinsettias, chosen because the bride adored red but hadn't wanted roses.

Glancing to his right, Reverend Gilmore smiled at Oliver Addleshaw, Everett Mulberry, and Archibald Addleshaw, pulling his attention away from the men a moment later when music rang out and everyone turned their attention to the back of the church.

Rose and Thaddeus Burkhart, followed by their sister Elizabeth, Everett and Millie's children of their hearts, were first to enter, walking down the aisle as they smiled and waved, Everett beaming with pride as they took their places in front of the pulpit.

Harriet was next, looking beautiful in a gown of red with her dark hair pulled on top of her head, and a smile on her face, her smile widening when she caught Oliver's eye and he sent her a wink.

Reverend Gilmore had sorely missed Harriet while she'd been in England. But now she was back, and he was looking forward to enjoying having her around again since she and Oliver had agreed that New York was their home, even though Harriet's family lived in England.

Millie followed, looking quite like a fairy princess in her gown of red, grinning from ear to ear as she practically skipped down the aisle, never one to miss an opportunity to skip. She didn't immediately take her place, but hurried over to her husband, Everett, kissing him smartly on the cheek before she hurried back to join Harriet, grinning broadly as she took hold of Harriet's hand.

Then Lucetta was gliding down the aisle, more beautiful than ever, but with a few wisps of hair slipping out of the knot that had been arranged on her head. The slightly disheveled state of her hair was a direct result of her having to help the bride find something borrowed, the only thing that everyone seemed to have forgotten.

Joining her friends, Lucetta dashed a hand over eyes that had already taken to watering as the music paused for just a second. And then Abigail was standing at the end of the aisle, wearing a gown of ivory that Harriet had designed specifically for her. With one hand she held tightly to the arm of Bram, the grandson she'd finally gotten to know, and the other hand held onto Iris, the daughter finally returned to her. Ruby stood beside Iris — holding a leash, and on the end of that leash was . . . Buford, Harriet and Oliver's motley dog.

"Why does Ruby have Buford?" Oliver asked no one in particular.

"Abigail needed something borrowed, and Buford was what she chose, but I'm not certain that exactly counts since she's not holding the leash," Harriet said in a hushed voice before she put her finger to her lips and nodded back to Abigail.

As Abigail walked down the aisle with Bram, her gaze settling on a smiling Archibald, Reverend Gilmore shot a glance to the stained-glass window that had a simple cross laid into it and bowed his head. His heart was so full from the blessings God had bestowed on the young ladies standing before him — and his dear friend, Abigail, who'd found another chance at love when less than a year before she'd almost given up on living — that he could only summon up two words for the Father who'd been so very, very generous of late.

"Thank you," Reverend Gilmore whispered before he lifted his head, smiled at Abigail and Archibald, who were now holding hands and beaming his way, and then invited his congregation to join him in prayer.

ABOUT THE AUTHOR

Jen Turano the author of seven novels, is a graduate of the University of Akron with a degree in clothing and textiles. She is a member of ACFW and lives in a suburb of Denver, Colorado. Visit her website at www .jenturano.com.